# SOUL WARRIOR

the age of kali

## BY

## FALGUNI KOTHARI

**Published by Falguni Kothari**
Soul Warrior © Falguni Kothari 2015
Cover by Hang Le
ISBN 13 – 978 1-944048-01-3

*For my sister, Santu.*
*You left us too early. You are missed every day.*

*And, to all my sisters, related by blood or chosen by heart.*
*Thank you for being there whenever I need you.*

# ACKNOWLEDGEMENTS

As ever, I am grateful to Lisa Wexler, Sharon Olivier, Usha Desai and Trupti Trilokekar for reading and brainstorming the very first draft/s of Soul Warrior with me. You haven't budged in your support of this book, or me. And for that I am especially grateful.

I have many other people to thank for their unreserved encouragements. Linda Robertson, I bring you Sanskrit with this book. Komal Choksi and Pallavi Shah for keeping me wonky when the world goes sane. The Romance Writers of America, especially the NYC Chapter, and most especially, K.M. Jackson for giving me a place to call home in this big, bad publishing world.

To Jason Sitzes and Karen Dale Harris, for your wonderfully detailed editorial suggestions. I've incorporated most of them, just not all. And I take full responsibility for any errors that occur. Thank you to Julie Cupp and the magical Formatting Fairies. You waved a wand and Soul Warrior turned into a handsome body of work. To Rock Star Lit and Crosshairs Communications, you are my tugboat in this ocean of Indie Publishing.

To my readers, I hope you love this story as much as I do. I promise this is just the beginning of our adventure.

And thank you loads to my family for holding the fort up with me. I can do this without you, but I'd rather not.

# AUTHOR'S NOTE

Twisted myths. Discretion advised.

Dear Reader, this story draws material from the ancient Indian epic, the Mahabharata, and from a lavish selection of South Asian mythology, using much of it for the basis of the novel's reality, but then goes beyond it bringing events to modern times. It is not necessary to be familiar with either the epic or the mythology in order to follow the story as the essential details are woven in, but a familiarity with them provides a greater depth to the events.

I have taken many liberties in this book, beginning with the timeline of the Mahabharata War. I have used a less popular timeline because it suited the purposes of my story better. I have also taken the classic myths and stories and given them my own backstories. I hope that those of you who have your own theories with regard to the myths of India will understand and enjoy my vision of it.

For the timeline: I used the date 5561 BCE from the research article written by P. V. Vartak. (The popular date is 3100 BCE or thereabouts.)

Last, I've always believed Karna and Draupadi deserved a mythic love story, and in this work of fiction, I have given it to them.

*"Once, Gods and demons walked the Earth free as any man. There was a time of great feats and warrior glory. Until that stupid game of dice!"*

**~ The Canons of Kali Yuga**

# PROLOGUE

## SHUNYA: NOTHING AND EVERYTHING

*Kuru Kshetra Battlefield.*
*Day 17 of the Great Kuru War, seven thousand five hundred years ago.*

Death is hot.

That surprises me. I'd imagined death as cold and brutal. Merciless. But in truth, death is hot as blood, and constant like a heartbeat.

*Thrum. Thrum. Thrum.* My lifeblood ebbs to the rhythm. My head ripped from its torso by *Anjalika*, the arrow of death that burns even now with the energy of the sun. Struck from behind like some novice. Felled in battle by that lily-livered usurper the Heavens smile upon— Prince Arjun. *Brother* Arjun.

*What have I done?*

I harness the thought. Cease all reflection and wrench free of my mortal body. I soar up, up into the gloaming, snapping the ties that tether me to life. Dead, I have no use for ties.

"A matter of perspective, Karna, O son of my godsire." The unearthly words strum through the air, and I quiver like a plucked bowstring, overcome as much by the voice as its blasphemous claim. "Bonds of devotion nourish the soul, brother."

There is that word again. *Brother.* Unpleasant laughter wells up in me. Alive, I am abandoned, denied my birthright—Celestial or royal. Death, it seems, changes everything.

A bright, nebulous light brings forth Lord Yama, the God of Death, atop his divine mount. His elephantine thighs ripple beneath a silken *dhoti*, ochre and crimson of color, as he guides the mammoth water buffalo to a halt. An iron medallion sways against the God's powerful cerulean torso, its center stone an ethereal blood orange.

Hypnotic. Pulsing with life. I am drawn to the stone.

"Piteous waste," Lord Yama mutters, surveying the carnage of war far below us.

I trace the trajectory of his gaze and behold the battered remains of my army drenched in the evidence of its mortality. Is it true? Have we died in vain?

Words form inside me and I will them out. "Shall we go, my lord?"

"Ha! Impatient to be judged, are you? Anxious to have your fate revealed?" asks the Judge of the Hell Realm. His red-black eyes burn with intelligence and compassion in a blue-tinged face that is long and lean and hard. "Rest easy, brother-warrior. You are not bound for the Great Courtroom."

*Not bound for Hell? Where then?* Fear has eluded me for so long that I take a moment to recognize it. A hollow-bellied feeling it is, as annoying as a bone stuck in my throat.

"My lord, I have done bad deeds...terrible deeds in my life. I have waged wars, this horrendous bloodshed, and all because my pride could not—would not abide rejection. I have sinned. I must atone for my actions."

Lord Yama smiles in a way I do not like. "You have redeemed yourself admirably, Karna. You forfeited your life for the greater good today. The deed far outweighs any misguided ones. Be at peace, brother, and enjoy the fruits of your karma."

There is but one place to enjoy such fruits—the Higher Worlds.

I'd rather burn in Hell for eternity. I say so. "I won't live amongst the Celestials." Coexisting with the very souls who've spurned me is unthinkable. Watching *her*—for she would surely reside in Heaven soon—will be eternal torture.

Yama shakes his head, the horns on his crown slashing to and fro. "I thought you might say that. Relax. Your destiny lies elsewhere."

"Am I to be reborn then? Am I to begin a new life, and forget the past?" Pain, sharp as a blade, lances through me at the thought. Forget my past? My family? Even her? Was that my punishment? To forget all that made me human?

It must be so. For have I not betrayed them as surely as I've betrayed my prince regent?

"Human rebirth is not your destiny, either. You are chosen, brother. Your war skills are needed for a higher purpose." The God slips off his mount, his garments rustling in agitation. "This unjust war has pushed the Cosmos to the vortex of a cataclysm. Tomorrow, the Kuru War will end. Fearing its outcome, the Celestials rolled the Die of Fate and have unwittingly bestowed on Demon Kali untold powers." Lord Yama bares his fangs in disgust at the foolish gamble. "Imagine the havoc that *asura* and his minions will wreak on the weak if left unchecked. The Human Realm must be safeguarded during Kali's dark reign."

I can imagine the horror only too well as I have battled with evil all my life. But I am done with wars. I am done with defeat. I won't waste another lifetime fighting.

"With due respect, my lord, I am not the man for this task."

"You are not a *man* at all," Yama thunders, fists shaking. "You are the son of Surya, the Sun God. Accept that you are no ordinary soul."

I say nothing. I think nothing. I feel *something* but I squash it down.

Lord Yama's thick black brows draw together. "Demon Kali will try to pervade every particle of good that exists in the Cosmos, beginning with the corruptible Human Realm. Once he obliterates all of humanity, he'll set his sights on the Celestials. Kali will not stop until he's destroyed our way of life. But you can stop him. You are light to his darkness. Do you understand now why you had to betray him? Your beloved humans need you, Karna. I need you. Our father believes in you. Claim your rightful place in the Cosmos."

Impatiently, Lord Yama removes the iron medallion from his neck and holds it out. The vermillion sunstone glows as if its soul is on fire. Nay! It is my soul that is on fire.

Indescribable energy curls through me. I gasp, though not in pain. I shudder and feel myself grow large, grow hot. Was this rebirth?

I am strong, full-bodied and lethal once more. Then I roar as light bursts forth from my very core and I throb with glorious, blinding power. When I come to myself, my world has changed again. Bubbles of color shimmer all around me: cobalt and saffron, azure and rose. By karma! They are souls. Infinite floating souls.

"Behold the spectrum of life: the worthy, the notorious, the righteous and the sinners." The God of Death's soul was a worthy sapphire blue with a tinge of silver. "Your duty, should you choose to accept the office of the Soul Warrior, is to hunt down the red-souled *asuras* and crush them. Whatever you decide, I wish you a long and successful Celestial existence, Karna," Yama booms out and vanishes into the purpling sky.

The parley has stunned me. The world of color holds me in thrall. I was dead. Yet, now I am not. A new path lies before me. *Unwanted, unwelcome*, I insist on principle. I close my eyes. Open them to stare at the medallion cupped in my hand—a golden-hued hand at once familiar and not—and know myself for a fool. I do want this. It's what I am.

Bastard-born. Rebel. Son. Husband. Father. Warlord. And protector. I fist the talisman, buoyed by its concrete warmth. *This is who I am.*

I am the Soul Warrior.

*The Cosmos has no single past or history.*
*Truth is in the eye of the beholder.*

**~ The Canons of Kali Yuga**

# CHAPTER ZERO
## DWANDA-YUDDHA: THE DUEL

*The Himalayan Mountains.*
*Five thousand years ago.*

Absolute darkness shrouded the Human Realm, and had for three days and three nights. Some believed the occurrence was prophetic, like the prolonged *amavasya* or new moon night that had heralded the Great Kuru War two thousand years ago. The war had given birth to the dark Age of Kali, the age of *asura*. In contrast, hope was ripe that this event would trigger the Age of Light. But the Bard wasn't here to succumb to superstition.

The first day without the sun's light had spread confusion and chaos across the realm. The second day had brought desperation in the breasts of humans and fear in the belly of Celestials. The third day—today—was a feast for the *asuras*. Death lay everywhere.

The human world burned without its sun. How soon before the Heavens went up in flames?

The Bard's troubled eyes reread the last line. Then he deliberately scratched it off, lifting his long, pointed talon from the parchment made of dry palm leaf. With a sigh, he rested his aching hand on his trembling thigh. He would spare a moment to ease his body, and his mind from the strain of observation and due recordkeeping. If he didn't, he'd forget his duty as Witness of the Cosmos, and begin to question fate.

Despite the fire that crackled close to his right knee, and the feathered form of his upper body, he was cold. An icy wind had settled around the Pinnacle of Pinnacles, where he sat cross-legged on a seat made of rock and snow. He'd chosen this perch because it gave him an impartial view of the events happening in the world. He was the Bard, entrusted with keeping the Canons of the Age of Kali, just as the Soul Warrior was entrusted with keeping the Human Realm safe from *asuras*. Would they both fail in their duty today?

The Bard shook off the heavy despair the darkness had brought into the world. He mustn't judge. He shouldn't question. He would sharpen the talon on his forefinger, dip it into the vessel of ink kept warm by the fire, and write this tale. That was all he could do. Be the witness to history.

So he raised his feathered hand and began to write again while his eyes, sparked with power, knowledge and magic, saw clearly events unfolding from great distances. A thousand kilometers to his right, Indra, the God of War and Thunder, fought the Dragon. Indra did not fare well. But that didn't concern the Bard as much as the clash between the Soul Warrior and the Stone Demon. Over and over, his eagle eyes were drawn to the duel taking place in the heart of the world, not only because it was a magnificent battle to behold, for it was, but because its outcome would decide mankind's destiny.

The Soul Warrior was more than a great warrior. Karna was a great soul. Fair, honorable, brave and resilient, he was the perfect protector of the Human Realm. Of course, there were other reasons he'd been chosen to fill the office of Soul Warrior—there always were when Gods and demons were involved. But Karna's existence was a testament to righteous action and if anyone could bring back the day, it would be him.

But how did one vanquish stone, the Bard wondered?

Avarice and cruelty, two nefarious desires, had made Vrtra and Vala attack the Human Realm. Three days ago the Dragon had swallowed the Seven Rivers in the north, and the Stone Demon had imprisoned the Sun God, his daughter, and all the cattle of the region in his cave.

The Bard paused his writing as a thin vein of lightning winked across the skies, but without the accompanying roar. Indra's strength waned. His thunderbolt hadn't left Vrtra screaming in pain this time. The Bard spared a moment's attention on the duel, just enough to note that the Maruts, the Celestial Storm-gods, waited in the clouds to rescue their god-king in case of a calamity. Indra would survive even in defeat. Of that, the Bard was sure.

But Karna had no one at his back. His might and god-powers had depleted without the sun's healing warmth and light. His divine *astras*, weapons, had not slowed the Stone Demon down, at all. Only the conviction that he could not fail his godsire, his sister, and the innocents under his protection drove him now. His birth family had once abandoned him to his fate, but he would not abandon them to theirs—such was the greatness of Karna.

The Bard crossed out the last observation. No questions. No judgment. No praise, either. The canons would be free of all emotion. He wasn't here to embellish history or glorify the history-makers, as some bards were wont to do.

It wasn't embellishment to write that the foothills of Cedi were drenched in the Soul Warrior's blood. Or observe the gushing wounds on his body, despite his armor, that would make the hardiest of warriors bellow in agony, but not him. It wasn't embellishment to write that the Heavens were empty for the Celestials had come to Earth to watch the battle, firelight cupped in their palms to light the warrior's way.

The Naga, the Serpent People, also looked on, hissing from the mouth of the portal that led to their underground realm beneath the hills. The Serpent King will not choose a side. Vrtra and Vala were half Naga, after all. All across the Human Realm, demons roamed free, taking advantage of the darkness and preying on human flesh and human souls. It was a terrible moment in history. The *asuras* had the upper hand in the eponymous age of Demon Kali.

Vala did not have arms and half a leg, but still he came at Karna. He had an ace up his sleeve. There were plenty of creatures about, an entire mountain close at hand. He began to chant the spell of soul transference. It was the darkest of all magic, the possession of another's soul. Soon, he would be whole again and stronger than before.

Battered and bleeding, the Soul Warrior veered away from the Stone Demon. He leapt over boulders and charred vegetation. The onlookers called him a coward. Had he forfeit the duel? Has he forsaken mankind?

Karna dove for *Manav-astra*, the spear of mankind, he'd thrown aside yesterday after his bow, *Vijaya*, had shattered under repeated use. In one smooth motion, he rolled, picked up the *astra*, coming up in the spear-thrower's stretch. His tattered lower garment billowed about him as a gust of wind shot through the air. His muscled torso glistened with blood and sweat, tightened as he pulled the arm holding the spear back.

He meant to throw *Manav-astra* at Vala. A futile attempt, to be sure? As long as Vala was made of stone, broken or not, his body was impregnable. Karna should have waited for Vala to transfer his soul to an onlooker. Then Karna should have vanquished the possessed creature.

Taunting laughter reverberated through the foothills of Cedi. Vala had reached the same conclusion. The Celestials looked at each other in angry silence, unable to interfere. A *dwanda-yuddha* duel was fought between two opponents of equal size and strength alone. The humans hadn't stopped screaming in three days, the din simply background noise now.

The Bard scribbled the observations onto the parchment in no particular order. He wished he was a painter, for surely this was a picture worth a thousand words.

The demon hobbled toward the warrior, who stood still as stone with his arm drawn taught behind him. Then finally, with a roaring chant the Soul Warrior shifted his weight from his back leg to his front and let fly *Manav-astra* at the Stone Demon with all his remaining might.

Karna didn't wait to see the ramifications of his action. And there were plenty to come. He ran into the mountain cave to free Vala's hostages. Within moments the rock face rent in half, and bright streams of light speared through the terrible darkness. A new day had dawned on the Human Realm after three days of perpetual night.

The sun's power was too bright, too full of hope. Yet, the Bard looked on pensively, wondering if the Soul Warrior knew this wasn't a victory. It was merely a reprieve.

# PART ONE

ASHT DVEEP, THE HIDDEN ISLE

# CHAPTER ONE
## PRALAYA: THE CATACLYSM

*Asht Dveep, off the coast of Madh Island, North Mumbai.*
*The present.*

"We have visitors, my lord."

Karna paused perusing the *Times of India* on his tablet, and cocked a brow at Lavya. Pale and lean, his friend and housemate loomed just inside the door to the den, hands folded in a neat Namaste. Irritated, but not at the interruption, Karna sighed, wondering why he bothered reading the news at all. Daily bulletins had become standard—or substandard, depending on one's viewpoint. Climate change, economic disasters, terrors and terrorists all held front-page positions, every fugging day.

And what else could one expect in the Age of Kali? It was the age of sin, tsunamis and stock options in this currency-ruled realm. Not that the Gods had ever—not once in his almost eight-thousand-year career as humanity's soul guardian—asked him to interfere with, subvert or reverse any of the realm's natural or man-made calamities. His duty required only that he keep the world free of supernatural evil.

Karna stretched, his spine separating from the fiberglass chair like Velcro ripping. He was shirtless to battle the unrelenting October heat and though he'd queued up his sun-bleached, shoulder-length mane, sweat dampened his forehead, nape, armpits and back.

And therein lay the rub, he thought, coming back to the dos and don'ts of his duties. Being "asked" *not* to meddle in human affairs only made him more determined *to* help the helpless. At times, he managed to contain the disasters, and all was well in the Cosmos. But sometimes, his actions worsened the fate of the mortals, as well as his own. Like when he'd tried to repair the deficient ozone layer with his god-powers a couple of years ago.

Blasting the stratosphere with a load of solar radiation to augment the emissions from his godsire's Celestial abode had been a solid, scientifically vetted idea. The extra UV rays he'd discharged from his fingertips had accelerated ozone production, and for a while he'd believed the crisis slowed, if not solved. But the hyper-paced oxygen cycle had also amplified energy output, creating miscreant solar flares, a couple of which had whipped across the Cosmos and breached the lower regions of the Higher Worlds.

Needless to say, the atmospheric fireworks hadn't amused the Celestials or Heaven's ruling Council. And as punishment for his hubris, Karna had been saddled with an annoying quirk—his body temperature was now directly proportional to his emotions—specifically, high-voltage anger. And stoicism did not come naturally to him.

"Whoever it is, tell them I'm indisposed," he said, turning back to the tablet to scan a news report about a recent grisly murder near Hyderabad. He wondered if *asuras* were involved.

Protecting the Human Realm from the demon race was a fulltime, energy-sucking occupation. He just wasn't in the mood for idle chitchat, heavenly politics or an unasked-for performance report. And from the surging energy levels he sensed wafting out of the living room, one or all three outcomes were assured as his visitors were definitely from the

Higher Worlds. The heightened electromagnetic pulse wasn't the sole indication of uninvited Celestial company—his friend and aide my-lorded him only when heavenly protocol needed to be followed.

"I doubt the excuse will fly with the Patriarchs or the Matriarchs," said Lavya, coming to stand on the other side of the massive black onyx desk dominating the chamber.

Karna went rigid with shock when he heard who his visitors were. The entire Council gracing the Human Realm all at once was highly unusual. Not just unusual—it spelled *cataclysmic.*

Not even a month had passed since the landslides in the Eastern Himalayas. Both Lavya and he had helped the Indo-Tibetan border police salvage the situation, and even then hundreds of lives had been lost. Was that why the Gods were here? Had he saved the wrong human? Had he allowed an asshole *asura* to slip through his grasp while he'd sidebarred his Soul Warrior duties for a week? That couldn't be. Yama would've penalized him if he'd lapsed in any way.

Karna reached for the jug of freshly prepared *soma* juice on the desk and poured a large dose of the saffron-infused liquid into a gold goblet. Today's concoction was milky and sweet. Not to his taste, yet he tossed it back. If he had to tackle the Council, he needed the oomph *soma* provided. It came fast, as soon as the juice washed down his throat. His heartbeat kicked up, his focus sharpened and his lungs expanded.

Pushing back from the desk, he unfolded his six-foot-four frame from his seat and waved a hand in Lavya's direction. "Is this why you're in that monkey suit? You knew the Three Stooges and their Plus Ones were coming?"

"If I'd known, you would've known," Lavya replied. "And I would have dressed more traditionally."

True, on both counts. Lavya was nothing if not intrinsically loyal, and was totally efficient at his job as the Soul Warrior's aide.

Karna plucked his cotton shirt off the chair and shrugged it on, buttoning it as he moved around the desk toward the door. Mumbai's pervasive tropical weather did not encourage the use of clothes at all, much less the linen suit Lavya had on. "So why are you in a suit?"

"Moderated a webinar this morning with a college in South Mumbai. Same old speech. Same old cautionary lecture. Don't know if the kids listen or simply zone out," explained the tech savant, shifting aside to let Karna pass.

Lavya was a spokesman for Three D, an antidope campaign that spread drug awareness in schools and colleges across the Indian Subcontinent. As a recovering hashish addict—Lavya hadn't touched an intoxicating substance in seven hundred years and counting—he shouldered the responsibility very personally.

Karna paused and slapped Lavya on the back. "They listen. People always listen to you."

"In that case, will you listen too and control your tongue today? The Patriarchs don't respond well to being the butt of your humor."

Karna perked up at the thought of annoying the head honchos of the Higher Worlds. The Patriarchs found modern languages a touch vernacular for their elite tastes, and insisted on communicating in formal and flowery classical Sanskrit. For all their age-old commandments about adapting to change, going with the flow, accepting fate and evolving the soul, some of the Celestials still held on to the old ways as staunchly as sins on a sinner.

Pushing the pearl-white fiberglass doors of the den open, Karna strode down the broad marble passageway and into the living room. The rectangular room boasted a wall of windows on the far side. But the east-facing chamber was dark, even at noon, as the bungalow sat in the middle of a thicket of mangroves that all but drowned the ground floor in salt-slick fronds and crisscrossing tree trunks.

Six bright bluish-silver halos bobbed about the room at various heights.

Karna gazed up at astral projections of Lords Brahma, Vishnu and Shiva, whose breathtakingly beautiful faces glimmered with resignation, annoyance and disdain. Which meant they'd heard the Three Stooges comment, he concluded with a jolt of satisfaction. When the Gods didn't immediately dish out reprimands or spout prophesies that predicted the end of civilization, he even allowed himself to relax a bit. Whatever matter had brought them all to his island abode, it wasn't urgent—or, not urgent enough.

Inclining his head, he silently greeted the see-through Gods. The Stooges not only clung to a dated form of communication but also hadn't updated their wardrobe since the alphabet was invented. They were clad in silk *dhotis* and animal skins, and draped with enough bling to sink Asht Dveep to the bottom of the Arabian Sea had they been corporeal.

Karna crossed over to the Matriarchs. No etheric images there. Real flesh and blood females, clad in glamorous designer garments, sat on the concrete settees in his living room. Unlike their soul mates, the Goddesses embraced modernization with open arms.

"Ladies." He bowed with one long leg stretched out and his hand making loops in the air. "Welcome to my humble abode." He straightened with his palm over his heart in a move so fluid the Pasha of Istanbul would've knighted him on the spot a hundred years or so ago.

"Radheya, you look well, if a bit heated," said Goddess Saraswati, Brahma's chief consort. "See? I took your advice. I had my hair styled like you suggested." She shook her head and her silky, sable-brown hair swished to and fro.

Saraswati was a sweetheart. She was the only one who still called him Radheya—Radha's son—a childhood moniker from his previous life. Karna savored the brief, sharp pang in his heart at the thought of his adopted mother. He'd lost her so long ago. He missed her every damn day.

He bent to kiss Saraswati's cheek, and lavished equal attention on the other two Goddesses, bussing their cheeks lightly. Laxmi, the Goddess of Wealth and Vishnu's consort, remained ageless, charming and graceful in a gold lamé sheath straight out of a runway show, while Parvati, Shiva's better half, was in her signature leopard leather garments and red stilettos. Karna saluted her with a wolfish whistle, trying not to react to the color red as he usually did—with aggression. Not all red was bad news.

Above them, Shiva hissed in predictable jealousy, and a sudden inrush of god-power rippled through the living room. The windows rattled, and the four crystal chandeliers hanging from the ceiling tinkled and swayed. In the next instant, all was quiet.

Karna arched an eyebrow at Shiva. "You've mellowed. No earthquakes. No exploding windows. What did you do? Sign up for an anger management seminar? Or is it just age?"

The chandeliers swayed again, and Parvati rolled her big blue eyes even as they gleamed with humor. "Why do you aggravate him, Karna? What pleasure do you get from being chastised over and over again?"

Karna opened his mouth to drawl, "Just a cheap thrill, babe," but shut his trap when he saw Shiva's Third Eye begin to flutter.

The God slapped a hand over the wily orb gracing the center of his ash-smeared forehead. If the Third Eye opened, utter devastation followed.

*Fug-doom-all,* Karna cursed under his breath. Had he lost his mind infuriating the God of Destruction? Was a minute or two of entertainment worth the annihilation of all he knew and had sworn to protect?

"Let's get on with it," Karna said abruptly. "I assume this isn't a social call."

A nasty chill crept down his spine when the Cosmic Triad glanced at each other, confirming his suspicions. The Generator, the Operator, and the Destroyer—a.k.a. G.O.D. Three archaic pains in his coccyx, who seemed to take great pleasure in meddling in his affairs periodically.

Karna shoved his hands inside his cargo shorts, fisting them. "Stop eyeballing each other and just spit out the bad news." The demand volleyed loudly between the walls of the minimalistic living room.

"Not necessarily bad news," Vishnu, the Operator, commenced but promptly broke off to cough into a substantial blue fist, which, oddly enough, resembled a scoop of Berry Blue ice cream atop the bejeweled vambrace on his forearm. "You've been promoted to the office of Celestial Guru. You shall, henceforth, be responsible for the physical and spiritual well-being of six warrior godlings. And they, in turn, shall assist you in your duties in this realm."

It seemed Karna wasn't the only one who'd lost his mind.

"Poor misguided souls," added Brahma, his round, ruddy face woeful. "They sorely need direction and purpose."

"I don't run a babysitting service here," Karna growled. *Fugdoomal!* The last thing he needed was a bunch of Celestial brats underfoot, making him trip over their stupidity.

"They are destined for greatness, Karna. They will make formidable allies." The fish-shaped globs of gold adorning Vishnu's ears twinkled with every word.

"I don't care if they are destined to pitch us out of the Reign of Kali and into the Age of Goodness and Light. Being a guru isn't part of my job description. All I'm duty-bound to do is capture terrorist *asuras* that sneak into this realm without visas, and haul them down to Yama in Hell." And if a red-souled demon or two got roughed up or killed as they resisted deportation, no one blamed him. No harm, no foul and no karmic repercussions.

"We appreciate your every effort in maintaining Cosmic Order during these trying times," said Vishnu, hovering over a bowl of sweets on the coffee table. Suddenly he groaned, and a bunch flew into his waiting hands. "You won't refuse once you know everything," he said, unwrapping and popping a Cadbury Eclair into his mouth.

Karna took his orders from the God of Death and, in Yama's rare absence, from Indra, the God of War and Thunder. Sometimes he did favors for other Celestials. He'd dished out plenty of favors for Vishnu and his various avatars over the millennia. He'd literally laid down his honor and mortal life at the behest of Vishnu's last human incarnation.

"Won't I?" Karna crossed his arms across his chest, making his white shirt stretch thinly over broad shoulders and bulging biceps. The posture was militant, menacing and absolutely appropriate under the circumstances.

"I *can* force you," Vishnu threatened, adopting his own Himalayan pose, though it fell short of intimidating while he chewed chocolate.

It always startled Karna to watch an astral projection eat. Sort of like a ghost taking a bubble bath. It was weird, and creepy.

Parvati positioned herself between Vishnu and him before a brawl broke out. "Can my lords stop posturing and focus on the issue? I left a piece of clay midsculpture to come here. I would like to get back to it in this century, please."

"What sculpture? Never say you're making another baby," Karna teased with a grin. Though he didn't back down from his stance. He would not be bullied.

Once, Parvati had zapped life into a mud figurine and—*presto!*—manifested an offspring. Reproduction amongst the Celestials was atypical and predominantly asexual. Boring, if anyone asked his opinion.

"Actually, it's a life-size statue of my Lord Lover." Parvati smiled prettily at Shiva. "It's for the exhibit on desire at the Celestial Art Gallery. You should've received the opening day evite. Check with your aide.

And if you could 'like' and 'share' our promo pages on the Conscious Web, that would be lovely."

Vishnu and Shiva gave twin sighs of exasperation at the off-topic tech talk. Lord Brahma looked baffled, as always. "What in the Cosmos is this gibberish? What language is Parvati speaking?" His red irises bounced from face to face, coming to rest on his wife.

"I'll explain later," Saraswati promised her pre-dinosaur-age husband.

And that's what happened to a parochial creator God—he lost touch with current reality.

Lord Shiva removed his hand from his forehead and held it up to gain everyone's attention. The Third Eye was shut tight once more.

"Training an apprentice is a veteran's duty, Soul Warrior. Knowledge may not be hoarded. It must be passed down. That is our way. And to show our appreciation for your cooperation, we shall each grant you a boon."

"Yeah…no thanks." Karna didn't trust these Gods in particular, and boons even less so. Boons never came without a curse or caveat attached to them. "Tell me something. Who are these godlings? Are they rogues? They've committed some roguish crime against the Celestials, and have been banished to the realm of the outcasts, is it?"

Vishnu's brilliant blue gaze narrowed. He clearly debated what and how much to reveal or whether to reveal anything at all. Typical.

"Before you fudge the truth, my lord, know that I refuse to swallow any more lies or half-truths. If you can't be honest with me, then I'm not interested in anything you have to say."

"That's enough, Soul Warrior," Laxmi said curtly, rising from her perch on the settee. Her one-shouldered sheath shimmered like liquid gold as she floated toward him. She also shot her husband a warning look. *Let me handle this, I beg you*, it read.

Karna clenched his jaws tight, bowing in deference. He hadn't forgotten his manners. He was just choosy about whom he practiced them on.

"No one has been cast out of Heaven, yet," the Goddess resumed her scolding. "Certainly not you. It was always your decision to dwell in the Human Realm." Stopping in front of him, she raised her hands and set them on his shoulders. "Now, will you promise to listen with an open mind and an open heart?"

That did not sound promising.

Nevertheless, Karna nodded, and the Goddess squeezed his shoulders in approval. "The godlings are your blood kin. Your maternal brothers' offspring," she said, emphasizing "maternal" softly.

Crap. No wonder Vishnu had opted out of this conversation. *Crap* quite aptly described Karna's sentiments regarding the five sons and stepsons of Lady Kunti. They'd been archenemies their entire mortal lives, leading up to the Great Kuru War. But what in heck did he have to do with them or their offspring now?

"I see the whole family remains happily intact?" A familiar bitterness coated Karna's tongue at the unfairness of fate. Warrior souls who died on a battlefield automatically ascended to the Higher Worlds. Other souls ascended after leading honorable lives, or after centuries of penance in the Hell Realm. None of his adoptive family had rebirthed as a Celestial yet. Their human souls weren't even close to the evolved state. His estranged brothers had always been more than fortunate in all things, and it seemed their offspring were just as lucky.

"It was Draupadi who made it so. About three hundred years ago," Shiva began in a gleeful storyteller's drone. "Draupadi and the Divine Mother hiked across the vast rainforests of the Higher Worlds. When resting, they played card games to amuse themselves. Ma Aditi is terrible at cards and lost several games to Draupadi. Thus, she bestowed the appropriate number of boons as payment for losses incurred."

Draupadi. The name triggered a rash of goose bumps all over Karna's body. She'd been the common wife to the five sons of Kunti the last time he'd seen her. He'd wanted her from the first time he'd seen her. She'd wanted him, too. Then, Vishnu in his Krishna Avatar had advised him to forget about it, told him their union was doomed.

Karna had stayed away from Draupadi ever since. She was the main reason he avoided the Higher Worlds like the plague.

"Draupadi was gambling? Unbelievable! Has she forgotten how her own husband gambled her away?"

Shiva dismissed Karna's objection to the vice with, "She won, didn't she?"

"Draupadi was desperate to be a mother again," Saraswati explained. "The sentiment struck a nerve in Ma Aditi's heart. Ma Aditi is, after all, the Mother of All Virtue. And motherhood is the highest of virtues."

"She was lonely, Karna," Laxmi added. "Her lord husbands have other wives and Celestial duties she is not part of. She thought the children would fill the hole in her soul."

Karna knew all about holes in souls and was on intimate terms with loneliness. But he refused to feel sorry for Draupadi. He couldn't afford any sappiness when it came to the only female he loved to hate. Her attractiveness had quickly waned once she'd married his rivals—his hitherto unknown brothers—all five of them simultaneously. How he'd suffered from the insult.

"Draupadi is impulsive rather than prudent. She did not consult anyone before using the boons—not the seers, not the Matriarchs, not even her lord husbands. Thus, a situation has arisen that needs a guiding touch."

"What situation?" Karna asked. What in heck was going on?

"She cloistered her offspring instead of honing their skills. She won't listen to reason even now. The godlings are an unruly, incorrigible bunch," Parvati said in clear disapproval.

"If you cannot rein them in, we will be forced to take harsh steps," Shiva vowed.

Ejecting them from their home, dumping them on a complete stranger, not to mention throwing them in evil's way—these weren't harsh steps? Karna shook his head at the Destroyer's twisted logic. "Why me? Why not some well-stationed Celestial scholar to guide them? Why not their own fathers? Don't tell me the five brothers are too busy wallowing in the splendors of Heaven to fulfill their parental duties?"

"Because none of them possesses your skills or expertise in battling *asuras*. Not even the captain of the Storm-gods," said Shiva.

Arjun was the captain of the Storm-gods and had been for some time. Luck and careful maneuvering in and out of Indra's palace-abode had kept Karna from bumping into his slayer whenever he had a meeting in Devlok.

Karna shot a quick look at Shiva, who smirked like a fox baiting a hapless hare. The vice was as old as time. Try as he might, he couldn't quash the twinge of competition twisting his soul at Shiva's words. It had always been like this between Arjun and him—a fierce, uncontrollable need to one-up the other. Great. Several thousand years of self-contemplation had taught him jack-shit. He wanted to kick something hard.

"Will you be their guru, Karna?" Brahma asked, finally showing impatience.

Karna knew they wouldn't have asked this favor if it weren't crucial. He was the best authority on demon hunting. But he would be savvy about it.

"Fine." Before the Cosmic Overlords broke into a victory dance, he quickly added, "With the proviso that if the brats are not housebroken after a brief trial period, you'll take them back."

"Of course," said a jubilant Vishnu. "Six days is all we ask that you spare."

"That's six human days, not Celestial days," Karna clarified. One Celestial day equaled a full human year. Six days should be enough for a trial period to judge the six's potential.

The number six suddenly struck him as strange. Logically, Draupadi's brood should number five—five husbands, ergo, five kids. "You mention six brats. Were six boons bestowed or did she luck out and beget a set of twins?" Nakul and Sahadev, the youngest of the five brothers, were twins.

The Divine Council froze in tandem. Saraswati took his arm and led him to one of the concrete settees, forcing him to sit next to her. Usually her mustard-hued eyes sparkled with wit and sincerity, but right now they were the lackluster yellow of sympathy with a dash of dread.

"One child—the youngest—is yours," she said, so softly Karna had to lean in to hear.

He recoiled as if stung by a bee and gaped at the Goddess of Knowledge. He had not expected that. Chaos, apocalypse, omens about the end of days, yes. Not this. He swallowed hard, shook his head. It was an error. A mistake. That was all.

"Not mine. You've been misinformed," he choked out.

Saraswati squeezed his hand in both of hers. "It is true, dear warrior. Trust me."

Meaning...*what?* That he'd somehow sired a son on Draupadi in his fugging dreams? That he'd given some sort of telepathic thumbs-up to be a sperm donor? They hadn't crossed paths, not once, since their mortal deaths. He'd been careful, so fugging careful, to stay away from the temptress. Boon or not, it was impossible to create a child without the sire's participation. Wasn't it?

"How could this happen?" he bellowed, making Saraswati flinch. The image of him locked in lusty embrace with the maiden-princess he'd wanted so long ago jumped into his head. His body went instantly hard. His blood froze at his reaction. Within seconds, he'd gone from shock to confusion to straight insanity, and it would not do.

"How is no longer important, Radheya," said Saraswati. "It's done. It can never be undone."

Had she charmed him? Had Draupadi tampered with his memories? "She'll pay for this. That deceitful bi—"

"That's enough, Soul Warrior." Lord Vishnu smacked a fist hard against the palm of his hand. "This world may have changed in fathomless ways, but basic courtesy cannot have changed. You will address the mother of your child with respect in or out of her presence."

Of all the unholy times to take issue over his language, Karna fumed. His body temperature shot up as if a virulent fever raced through his veins.

"You're very angry." Sara snatched her hands back with a wince.

Crap. The Goddess sat within flammable distance. This was not a good scenario. Karna scooted away from her.

"Perhaps *you* should take that anger management course, eh, Karna?" Shiva said smugly.

Karna hadn't yet mastered control of his temper or temperature quirk. Sudden pyrotechnics regularly fired up his abode. Hence the stone and Spartan decorating style. Fireproof, fire-retardant and recyclable materials were all the rage in his abode.

"Remember what I told you would happen should you and Draupadi ever have a child?" Vishnu asked grimly.

Karna took a number of deep breaths before answering, "I remember." But damn it! He wished he didn't. He should've told Draupadi the whole truth then. Fug! Was this his fault?

He stood up and faced the Council. "All right. Here's how this plays out. I'll take these misbegotten godlings under my wing. I will try to mold them into the warriors you claim they can be. And if…if things go wrong…well, we'll see what to do then. But I want you to back off from this business now. No well-meaning advice booming from the skies, no subconscious tweets keeping me up at night. Okay?"

Satisfied, the Gods agreed to let him handle the situation as he saw fit. The Goddesses looked anything but relieved at the exchange. Karna finally got why all six had graced his abode together. The Goddesses had expected him to explode like a bomb—and he'd be totally justified if he did—and blow the island and their husbands' holograms to bits.

"I knew we could count on you, dear Karna." Brahma twirled his waist-length silvery-white beard with a ruddy hand.

Karna decided to wipe the smirk off his face. "Couple of things. Keep Kunti's sons away from me—that means no visiting their offspring. And I'm going to hunt Draupadi down and teach her a lesson if it's the last thing I do."

Warning issued, he turned on his heel and stalked out of the room. Etiquette could go hang. His uninvited guests could see themselves away—as soon as they scraped their jaws off the yellow-gold marble floor.

# CHAPTER TWO
## MURKHA: ALL KINDS OF FOOL

Chest heaving, Karna strode into the den and slammed the doors shut so hard that they bounced right open. He wanted to howl until he lost his voice. He wanted to beat something or someone to a squishy pulp. He settled for kicking shut the fiberglass doors again.

He pressed his thumbs to the juncture between his nose, eyes and forehead. His head throbbed to the beat of the Bollywood hit pounding out of the surround-sound system, which had blasted on in response to the door banging. With a flick of his wrist, he switched the playlist to stress-soothing instrumentals. Then he threw himself on an electric massage chair juxtaposed between two burgeoning bookshelves—the paltry few flammable objects adorning the abode.

Questions sprang up and spread inside his head, painful and incomprehensible like modern-day tumors. How had this happened? She hated him—he'd made sure of that. So why had she chosen to beget his child? Had it been an accident? Some new game she'd thought up on a boring afternoon in Devlok? Was it a belated act of vengeance? Could she be cruel enough to create a child just to make him pay for the sins of his father?

Karna acknowledged the fact that he'd hurt her as viciously and venomously as she'd hurt him. He'd claimed an eye for an eye, traded insult for insult. Only she, he thought, closing his hand into a tight fist... only Draupadi brought out the animal in him.

Did she know that their child was destined to destroy the Cosmos?

The doors opened, and Karna turned his scowl in their direction. Lavya strode in minus the pale blue suit in faded jeans and a tucked-in navy-blue shirt. His broad forehead stood out beneath his slicked-back dark hair. He looked about thirty years old, add or subtract a year or two. Karna himself didn't look a day older than thirty-five, in the prime of his life. But looks deceived, for there were days like today when every one of his life-years weighed on his soul.

"Gone?" Karna indicated the living room with an eye roll.

"Gone," Lavya confirmed with a nod. "Don't you want to change?"

"Into what?" How had that...that *succubus* fooled him into approving the offspring boon?

"There are cigar-sized burn marks all over your shirt. You almost torched the place again, didn't you?"

Karna looked at the ruins of his cotton shirt and the pinkish self-healing skin peeking through. He didn't even feel the burn anymore as the sun's light worked its magic. In another ten minutes his skin would be as supple and tan as ever.

He shot Lavya a nasty look and sprang up from the recliner. "I was provoked!"

"When are you not by the heavenly set?" Lavya pointed out.

"Luckily, I don't see them often. But never mind that. Did you hear everything?" Karna began to pace. The cool marble floor felt good beneath his bare feet.

Lavya nodded again, this time at the computer sitting atop their shared desk. "Heard and recorded the entire conversation. Good call on the time limit to your new duties."

Like Karna, Lavya didn't trust the Stooges and their multiple-meaning metaphors. As previously stipulated, six days in the Higher Worlds were not the same as six days in the Human Realm.

Karna's mouth twitched despite his bad mood. "Caught that, did you?"

"Better to magnify the fine print than be a sorry-assed fool." Lavya shot Karna a curious glance. "What did Vishnu mean about something happening to your and Draupadi's child?"

Karna stopped pacing to rub the nape of his neck. "The usual estranged family stuff. Nothing important," he lied. Then he prayed for mercy for his child. "What if it's all a hoax? The child can't possibly be mine."

"For all their idiosyncrasies and their painful habit of nondisclosure, the Gods do not lie."

"Draupadi could've lied to them." Maybe she'd had an affair with a demon and Karna was the lesser of the two evils to admit to having an affair with?

"They would've double-checked before coming to you bearing the happy news," Lavya reasoned.

That's what Karna feared too. "So now we're stuck changing a bunch of stinking diapers because of that crazy female's whims? *Fugdoomal!*"

"*Shanti*. Relax. At three hundred years old each, your protégés will hardly need diaper changes. They might be termed *young* in Celestial years, but in human terms they'll be old souls." Lavya straddled his ergonomic computer chair, settling in front of the desktop computer along the long side of the L-shaped desk. With a couple of keystrokes, he brought all nine 27-inch flat-screen TVs out of hibernation on the far wall.

"Old souls, my ass," Karna said. "I have a nasty feeling the Peacocks from Paradise will put *asuras* to shame." He knew what young warriors were like. He'd been one, albeit long ago, and trained thousands of warriors and raised nine sons, hadn't he? "What are you doing?" His question became redundant when an assortment of information jumped up on two of the screens. He smacked his forehead with the heel of his hand. "Shit! Forgot to ask when to expect the Peacocks."

"Understandable. Your brain sort of imploded with the mention of her name," said Lavya, enhancing the observation with audio effects of bombs detonating. He nimbly dodged the kick directed at his shin by spinning in his chair.

"I was angry at the Trinity, that's all," said Karna stiffly.

Lavya indicated his disbelief at that bit of myth with an all-knowing smile. "Since my brain always functions at full capacity—no exception—I spoke to Goddess Saraswati before she vanished. She expressed concern about your rising temperature. I assured her you'd have it under control apace. She also said that the godlings were meant to have arrived in Asht Dveep by now. If they don't show up by teatime, we should consider them AWOL."

Karna felt his temperature inch upward again.

"Don't worry, teach. The apple of our eyes will ferret them out." Lavya stroked the keyboard that controlled Baby, their ultra-spiffy genius computer, and an out-and-out lifesaver. Add in her sleek white form, offset by the shiny black of the onyx desk, and Baby was the ultimate combination of beauty and brains.

In truth, god-powers and magic could do only so much. While their usage wasn't prohibited in the Human Realm, powers needed to be used sparingly, and as discreetly as possible due to the Treaty of Quarantine between the various realms of the Cosmos. Each realm had been accorded the power to run autonomously while adhering to Cosmic Law. Still, there were lapses and needless complications arose when mortals came into contact with the supernatural. Most humans freaked in one way or another. Some went into denial over it, while others recorded the events on their smartphones. Which, all things considered, worked out well for all concerned parties. Stories or videos of UFOs, aliens and shape-shifters could easily be dismissed as fantasy, or permanently erased.

Then there were the humans who were born knowing the secrets of the Cosmos and the value of secrecy. Karna liked working with such individuals toward a mutual benefit. The worst were the greedy idiots who expected boons from him in payment for their silence like he was their personal jinni. Karna wasted no time in infecting such specimens with partial retrograde amnesia—a slightly more complicated maneuver than deleting pictures from smartphones, but no less effective or gratifying.

Humans had no reason to feel shortchanged with their lot in life. Their technological advancements over the last few decades were nothing short of magical. What couldn't one do with the press of a few buttons? And when one combined machines and magic, the Cosmos lay at one's fingertips—or vocal cords, with the advent of talking software.

Karna stared at the LCD-heavy wall. One screen ran back-to-back episodes of *Master Masala Chef*—Lavya's pet addiction. Harmless enough, unless one thought that sprinkling nutmeg powder and poppy seeds in gravies was akin to falling off the wagon. A second screen ran NDTV; a third, Nat Geo; a fourth, episodes of *Criminal Investigations*; a fifth, BBC World; and so on.

It forever astounded Karna how the human world had changed and broadened in scope during his lifetime. Once, most souls had clustered on a single continent and the Soul Warrior alone had been sufficient to track and vanquish the *asuras*. Now, without digital aid and a posse of informants—be they alien, hybrid or human—the hunt could be over before it began.

On the ultra-massive center panel, Google Earth spun in slow motion on its axis, paranormal auras highlighted: red-gold for the *asura* souls and silver-blue for the virtuous Celestial souls. Most creatures fell within the rainbow color spectrum, except the über Gods with their unique ultraviolet auras that remained undetectable unless they wanted them otherwise. The average human soul fell smack-dab in the middle of the color spectrum in green, the predominant hue flashing on Google Earth at any given moment. The globe's darkest pockets were usually peppered with some crazy mix of shades. Where there was no sun, there might be *asuras*. Lavya had zoomed in on one sunless area.

"They are in Vegas?" Karna glared in disbelief at the shape of North America. Could one inherit the gambler's disease?

"Not Vegas. That's Lok Vitalas." Lavya let Karna curse a blue streak before extrapolating, "I'm kind of impressed by their daring. Defiant, yet toeing the line. Like you." He squared out a jumble of colorful blurs on the screen, east of Vegas. "Indications of a recent Celestial manifestation right at the crossroads of delinquent and debauched. The EMP readings aren't pure blue. Still, that's a huge blob of a coincidence."

Lok Vitalas was the easiest, and currently the only, authorized portal or gateway in and out of the Human Realm for *asuras*, shape-shifters and the occasional Celestial. Checking in with its leader was mandatory, and creatures skipping immigration were flagged as troublemakers and blacklisted for eternity. If Lavya was right, then it wouldn't be hard to locate the godlings as the leader of Lok Vitalas, Salabha, kept meticulous records.

"I suppose you expect me to check out your theory?" Karna inquired.

Lavya shot him a prosthetic thumbs-up. "And usher them back here in peace."

"Peace?" Karna scoffed. "With her around?"

Lavya rolled his eyes sideways, giving Karna a measured look. "By *her* you mean…?"

"That crazy female! Do you think she's simply going to kiss her sons goodbye? She wanted them badly enough to gamble for their souls. Then somehow managed to keep them all to herself for three hundred years."

There was no way Draupadi would let him waltz off with her offspring without a harrowing fight. Karna relished the thought of confronting her. He imagined his hands wrapped around her beautiful, haughty neck.

Lavya cleared his throat. "Goddess Saraswati has requested that you focus your energies on training the godlings, and leave their mother to her fate. She mentioned that Draupadi has been summoned back to Devlok to face the Council and will be duly chastised. She will, most likely, be forbidden to see her offspring for the foreseeable future, and such punishment should appease even your ire."

Karna's back stiffened. Saraswati had known exactly which button to push. The idea that a mother would be separated from her sons did spark his compassion, whether he liked it or not. He thought it the cruelest of fates for a family—no matter how evil—to be ripped apart. If he had any control over the collective Cosmic Fate, no child would ever be abandoned.

"Find out where her chastisement will take place, and by whom. I wish to listen in on it." He had to know why she'd done it. And how? When? Where? "I'll go change. Then I'll be off to track me some..." Karna stopped in his tracks, stunned. "I can't believe it. For the first time ever, I'm going to stalk blue souls and not red."

"Be careful and don't lose it," Lavya cautioned as Karna headed out of the den to change his clothes and weapon up. "You don't want to set them on fire as soon as you find them."

"Don't lose it," Karna growled, mimicking Lavya. He twisted the gilded tap until it gushed lukewarm water—the coldest H2O ever got in the tropics. He splashed his face and neck repeatedly.

Considering the complicated and violent history he shared with Draupadi and her husbands, the whole fugging Cosmos should pray that the only thing he lost when he confronted their wayward offspring was his temper.

Lavya was right. He couldn't lose it. Karna gripped the thick lip of the marble sink tightly, watching the soapy water spool into the drain. What kind of first impression would he make by scaring his pupils shitless? By scaring his own son?

The idea that he had a grown son astounded him. Memories of his mortal life, of his long-lost family, filled his mind. Tall, strong and full of life, he'd loved all nine of his sons, been so damn proud of them. All but one had died at the hands of his so-called brothers, the enemy faction. Karna had slain some of their sons in turn, exacting his own revenge. They'd been at war and had been warriors all—warriors who held duty, fealty and honor above life itself.

Karna splashed more water on his face, dousing his head under the tap for good measure.

What had the godlings been told about the family history? Had Draupadi raised her sons on a diet of hate and revenge? What had she told them about him? What did his son know about his origins? Did his son even want to know his father? Were his pupils coming to him freely or forcefully? There were too many unanswered questions, and there was only one way to find answers. He needed to talk to Draupadi about his son.

*His son.* By karma, he had another son. Alive. Prospering, by all indications. A young peacock ready to take on the mantle of a warrior.

Long-buried desires shifted inside him. He'd loved being a father. He'd loved every part of his domestic life. Karna exhaled noisily and squashed it all down, locked it up again in the cellar of his heart. He pulled a hand towel from the rail by the vanity. Be it duty, debt or desire, the task of fashioning half a dozen brats—no matter their superior potential—into competent demon hunters didn't bode well for any of them. The Dark Age was harsh on its warriors. There were no rewards at the end of the rainbow. A demon hunter, in essence, was the unwitting martyr in the eternal clash between Gods and *asuras*. A vague sense of foreboding gripped him in light of Vishnu's warning.

No, it wouldn't do to get attached to the boy.

But surely he owed the child something. At the very least, he should fulfill a guru's duty well. He'd assure the boy—boys—nothing was insurmountable, not even death. But evil was unacceptable. He'd teach them how to recognize the different kinds of *asuras* without the aid of the Soul Warrior's unique vision. How to vanquish a *raaksasa* as opposed to vanquishing a *danu* demon. If he'd learned anything from his long career fighting demons, it was that fate wasn't written in stone. But he was getting ahead of himself. He needed to find them first.

Karna scrubbed his face dry with the towel and shook his head to dispel excess water from his hair. He tossed his burnt garments in the trash and strode into the bedchamber to rummage through the wardrobe. Yanking on underwear and jeans, he popped his head through a T-shirt and rough-combed his hair, retying it in a wet ponytail. Then he cupped his hands, and chanted a summoning spell. He never left home without his official badge.

The Soul Catcher materialized on his open palms—from the unreal to the real, from an ideal into a solid shape. Like always, the promise of the talisman in his fist reassured him.

The reddish-orange sunstone had gone through several transformations in its adventure-filled life-span, beginning as a coarse rock embedded in a chunk of iron when Yama had found it at the start of the Age of Truth, eons before the Age of Kali. By the time Karna had inherited it, it was a shiny gem set within a simple medallion, and they'd worked well together until an *asura* used it in a chokehold. After that, the fist-sized cabochon had embellished Karna's various weapons, shields and armor. In its current incarnation, the sunstone sat in the center of an orbicular filigreed belt buckle made of iron and gold. It was cold to the touch, not yet hungry for a soul. Only thrice in Karna's knowledge had an *asura* simply surrendered to the pull of the Soul Catcher, leaving the Soul Warrior dangling without a fight.

Karna cinched the belt around his waist and strode back into the bedchamber to slide on shoes and grab his phone and a fresh white handkerchief from the dressing table. Hunting was sweaty work. Messy too. Next he headed to the armory at the back of the gym room down the hallway. He made quick work of disarming the charmed locks on the solid iron doors, and armed himself with a couple of discreet man-made but magic-enhanced *astras*, in case there was trouble at Lok Vitalas. Then again, from what he'd heard of his pupils so far, he was afraid he'd be bringing them back at gunpoint.

Lamenting the loss of an afternoon fiesta and siesta, he stepped out of the armory and locked it down. Then he forced his mind to empty of everything: memories, taboos, judgments, and most of all, preconceived notions.

With a bittersweet sigh, Karna uttered another offhand chant, and vanished to Lok Vitalas to meet his newly discovered son.

The skull hurtled through space, its destination fated.

Vala's malevolent soul chortled in delight. He was nearly there. The Human Realm looked smaller than a chariot wheel but grew bigger with every passing moment. Soon he would walk on solid earth again.

Soon his true power would be unleashed.

# CHAPTER THREE
## LOK: REALMS OF CONFUSION

The ancient, nomadic cavalcade of Lok Vitalas had staked down for the night in the Mojave Desert. Circus tents of all shapes and sizes, bursting with the kind of temptations the mortals called entertainment, thrived within a thirty-kilometer radius. All were halfway decent establishments run by relatively law-abiding nonhumans who dwelled seamlessly, and with apt mystique, in the Human Realm—as in, different enough to be an attraction, but not sufficiently different to scare away paying customers. As humans were their primary source of income and subsistence, the denizens of Vitalas had little desire, even if they had ample opportunity, to make mischief with them.

Seven *loks* or territories of authorized iniquity had sprung up across the Human Realm in the Dark Age, since the human world was the easiest realm to breach, and stake a claim on, as were the human souls. The *loks* had been created as a harbor to the mixed breeds, the outcasts, souls who didn't completely belong on any one realm. Each *lok* thrived within its own set of rules or anarchy. Lok Vitalas, besides being the least dangerous to humans because its leader ran a tight ship, also had the dubious honor of being the only aboveground one. The other *loks* existed many meters below the Earth's crust or submerged deep in its waters. Gypsy-like in attitude and business tactics, Vitalas relocated to a new location nightly. The transient state of affairs meant the *lok* had limited sanitation facilities and a nonexistent sewage system, and hence smelled terrible.

For nearly two hours, Karna had zigzagged through the bylanes of the encampment, hopping in and out of tents in search of the godlings. Salabha, the leader of Vitalas, had confirmed that some eighteen Celestials had come slumming in the last two days, and he had immediately begun the process of tracking them down. Too restless to sit and wait for results, Karna had set off to do his own reconnaissance. His efforts had reaped zero fruits so far.

He'd run through the list of potentials Salabha had texted to him, the last of whom had turned out to be an old acquaintance of Karna's. Clothal was a Celestial cloth merchant and was in Vitalas on business. Quite obviously, he was not a godling.

What if they were wrong and the godlings weren't in Vitalas at all? What if Draupadi had thwarted her summons and gone into hiding with her brood again? What if the sons of Kunti had created a stink about him being their offspring's guru and stopped their banishment in time? Well, good riddance to the lot of them then. But what about his son?

Karna wound his way back to the heart of the encampment with his thoughts in a jumble. It was just after midnight, and Vitalas pulsed with life and activity. He snaked his way through the throngs of merrymakers queued up around the corner of a massive red-and-yellow pavilion with a flashing neon-green head-sign: The Shrieking Sura—Salabha's bar, and the only karaoke club in the encampment. Shifts had changed sometime during his search. And a fresh face with whom he was well-acquainted was on bouncer duty at the entrance.

"Yo-ho-ho! It's the Boodah Man. How you doin', brother?" said Roy, a former professional wrestler.

Roy knew Karna had personally known the bona fide Buddha. On any other night, Karna would've responded to the witty greeting with a laugh and a joke of his own. But he was too wound up to crack jokes tonight.

Boots planted hip-distance apart, tattooed arms crossed over a barrel chest, Roy looked fit and fierce in a camouflage T-shirt and pants. Roy was good people. His soul was aquamarine, and Karna had no problem being his brother.

"Not bad, Roy. How about yourself?" Karna bumped his right fist and shoulder with the human. They were both sizable, though Karna was two inches taller and a dozen inches leaner.

"Guess who's a married man now?" Roy's fierce expression didn't waver when his lips spread wide in a grin.

"That's fantastic, man. Congratulations." Karna thumped Roy on his back, genuinely happy for the man. "Who's the bride?" he asked.

"Tara," came the prompt and proud answer.

Karna blinked slowly. "Psycho Salabha's Tara? I didn't know you were dating."

"Yeah. I know. It all happened like a Big Bang boom. We eloped. To Vegas," Roy said, tongue-in-cheek.

Karna gave the big man a considering look. "And Salabha didn't go ballistic?"

Roy shrugged. "Didn't really have a choice, did he? Tara thought it best to marry first and announce later."

Which was sound handling on Tara's part. Psycho Salabha was nuts about his daughter, possessive and insanely protective. He was nuts about other things too, like his job as Vitalas's leader, and woe to any soul who brought trouble in Salabha's territory. He wasn't called psycho for nothing. Karna couldn't begin to imagine how Salabha must've reacted to Tara's elopement, but presumably all was well, as Roy still lived and remained in one piece.

Salabha and Tara were shape-shifters. They morphed into giant butterfly-like creatures when needed. Around a century ago, a nasty band of *asuras* had laid waste to Salabha's home realm, destroying or enslaving most of the indigenous beings. Crown Prince Salabha had escaped with his baby daughter and a handful of his kith. He'd sought asylum with Lord Yama, who'd granted it in exchange for their allegiance and services to maintain Cosmic Order.

For the Soul Warrior, the pact was a blessing—not that he'd ever label the extermination of a species a blessing—but in truth, he was damn glad he no longer had to monitor the gateway. Honestly, Salabha was doing a much better job of running Lok Vitalas than Karna ever had.

"Your wife is a wise female. Congrats again," Karna said, and stepped forward to go inside the tent.

"Wait, man. I had a question," said Roy, suddenly serious. "I'll die in another fifty years or so, if not sooner. She won't, yeah?"

Karna nodded. He knew where this was going. Roy had a human life-span. Tara did not. Tara was a shape-shifter, and the only way Roy's body would change shape was by adding copious amounts of fat or losing mountains of muscle mass.

"Take those fifty years and keep her crazy happy," Karna advised. A ghost of a face swam up in front of his eyes—his last lover, Qalanderi. To picture her mischievous, laughing face was an exercise in memory and heartache. They'd had but a moment in time, but he'd never forgotten her.

"Love transcends death, you know," Karna said softly. Against his better judgment, neither had he forgotten Draupadi.

"I'm going to trust you on that." Roy tipped his head in thanks, raised the tarpaulin flap and let Karna into the club.

Karna stepped inside the Shrieking Sura, and with a heartfelt groan banished the two females from his mind. He had better things to worry over than a nonexistent love life. He could use a drink.

The frigid, odorless atmosphere of the club was pure nirvana in contrast to the weather outside. And the fact that no one warbled on stage was something to sing about. Not that he minded singing in general. In fact, listening to music soothed him. Unfortunately, karaoke clubs inspired more amateurs than professionals. Their renditions had his ears ringing off-key for days after the show.

Karna scanned the space packed to overflowing with all kinds of creatures, thankful that he no longer felt overwhelmed by the sheer amount of soul he saw. It was second nature to him now to ignore the bubbles of color and actually see the faces and bodies attached to them.

Humanized *asuras* and demonized humans, both with dirty green souls, socialized together. Yellow-souled shape-shifters and other mortals sat in groups around collapsible wooden tables, conducting a trade or simply having fun. As usual, there weren't many blue souls about—Celestials rarely stepped out of their comfort zone—and no sign of the delinquents.

Neither was Salabha's ochre-colored soul in-house. Karna, however, caught sight of Tara across the tent, where she supervised a table cleanup. Raising a graceful hand high, she showed him the ring finger. He mouthed, "Congratulations." He liked the father-daughter pair a lot and considered them part of his rather small but loyal cluster of friends.

Karna pushed past tables towards the semicircular bar in the middle of the pavilion. "Has he returned?" he asked the bartender, on the off chance Salabha was in the back.

Johnny, a young shape-shifter who'd yet to grow his wings, shook his head, expertly juggling bottles of liquor as he mixed drinks.

Karna claimed a barstool, deciding to wait for Salabha right there, as chasing the delinquents had proved pointless. He didn't even know whom he was looking for. What did they look like? Would his son look like him? Height? Weight? He had no fugging clue.

A humanoid *asura* sitting on the neighboring stool gave him a wary double take, promptly slid off his perch and disappeared into a shadowy corner of the tent.

Karna was used to the reaction. And he hadn't even flashed the Soul Catcher. The creature needn't have worried. He had a mud-brown soul. Karna went after the pure reds. All other soul colors were given the chance to redeem themselves of their own free will.

Just as Karna ordered a *soma* on the rocks from Johnny, his spine began to tingle. He swiveled around to investigate the high-energy source and zeroed in on a glitzy sapphire-blue soul. The apparition jogged across the tent to a makeshift stage, and adjusted the mic to his seven-foot height.

*Could this day get any weirder?* Karna took a careful swig from the tumbler Johnny handed him.

Yama—who should've looked as scary as all get out—was decked out in studded white leather pants, jacket and boots. The God twitched his hips and shoulders in some weird warm-up dance. It seemed Yama had decided to bring Elvis back from the dead.

Karna gave vent to the laughter tickling his throat, chuckling for a good long time. The release of tension was instantaneous. He needed to keep his sense of humor or he'd never get through this task without murdering someone—unintentionally. It sometimes seemed relentless, his peeve with the Celestials.

The club's shadowy ambiance darkened further, and a single oval spotlight illuminated Yama in blue. He began singing "Viva la Vida" by Coldplay, rather melodiously. The crowd fell silent, almost reverent. The voice, the lyrics, the music were as soothing as they were entertaining, and a bit more of Karna's tension oozed out, leaving him a little less insane, feeling a little less trapped by the Gods.

Of course, it didn't last long. His phone buzzed, and Karna read Lavya's reply to his previous text with a sigh. *6 not in Heaven confirmed. Have 2B in Vitalas.*

Karna refused to get bogged down again. He would finish the drink and take another look around, he decided. Burrow deeper into the gambling dens and brothels he'd only skimmed over before. He'd just have to man up and ignore the rampant temptations the venues offered. And he would not think about the fact that he hadn't had sex in twenty bloody years. *Don't! Don't think about Qalli again.*

With a vigorous shake of his head, he paid for the drink with a gram-sized gold disc, adding a few silver ones as a tip. Precious metals and stones, personal IOUs, weapons and charms were the currencies that nonhumans preferred to transact in. Though no one, not even the wealthy Celestials, refused human money if offered. It was just exchanged pronto for something more substantial.

Yama finished his recital, and the crowd went wild. He bowed to the abounding applause interspersed with cheers of "More! More!" He declined modestly, and promised an encore soon. Then he swaggered off the stage, picked up a fur coat from a table in a corner and made his way to the bar, where Karna gave the God his due with whistles and claps while Johnny presented him with a goblet of steaming *soma* to sooth his throat.

The leather-and-fur-clad God plopped down on the recently vacated barstool, obviously enjoying his moment.

Karna's lips twitched in amusement. "You do realize we're in the middle of a desert?"

Yama scratched a furry cheek-long sideburn. "I dwell in the bowels of a burning Hell. This is like standing bare-assed on Pluto for me. Plus,

I blend in." The blue-faced God had a point, as several drunk Elvises had taken the stage and were fighting over who'd sing next.

"I heard about your sudden elevation to the exalted title of Celestial Guru," Yama said.

Karna felt his face flame along with his temper. He hated being the topic of discussion amongst the Celestials. "Did you know about it?"

"They asked me if I'd mind. Why would I? I know you won't compromise your existing duties in favor of the new ones." Yama drained the restorative and flashed his fangs. "I take it you agreed."

Karna gave Yama the short version of the afternoon's events. "So, it seems I can't find my charges. Lavya is positive the Delinquent Six are here, as lots of ungreen souls are out and about tonight, more than usual. He doesn't believe in coincidences of this magnitude. I cannot bloody believe it—Lok Vitalas of all the places! What *is* it with that family and gambling?"

"The Delinquent Six?" Yama slapped his thigh and howled with laughter. "You're truly riled about this, aren't you? Is it because they're Draupadi's daughters?"

"Daughters?" As revelations went, this one struck as awesomely as a thunderbolt. Karna's heart hammered so loud that for a moment he wondered if it would detonate.

Yama stopped cackling when he realized...well, the reality of the situation. "Shit! You didn't know they are females?"

Karna curled his hands into fists one finger at a time. The Stooges had deliberately misled him by omission. Again. He was going to kill them—all of them—the Trinity and Draupadi. He would hogtie them together, leave them in the dead of night in a graveyard and sic a whole bunch of ghouls on them. It would not be a mercy kill. What in hell was he supposed to do with six preening peahens? Six heavenly peacocks had been bad enough. No wonder he hadn't found them. He hadn't been looking for females.

And what in holy hell were the Gods thinking by sending females to battle the Reds? Had they forgotten *asuras* were giant conscienceless monsters that thrived on pain? And his daughter was the harbinger of doom?

His *daughter*. Holy karma! He had a daughter. But how could it be? He'd never sired a daughter in his mortal life, had been so sure he wasn't meant to be that lucky.

His mind recalled the oaths his wives and he had taken. Year after year, the austerities they'd performed, the countless oblations they'd offered to any and all Goddesses to bless them with a daughter. He'd welcomed each of his nine sons with joy, had considered them his strength and pride. But how he'd wished for a daughter in that other life. He'd wanted a sweet little princess to dote on, to spoil, to adore. He had no fugging clue what to do with her in this one.

"It's your own fault, you know," Yama said, yanking Karna out of the past. "Now, now, stop glaring in outrage. When's the last time you stepped foot in the Higher Worlds for anything other than work? As soon as it's done, you leave. You never socialize with the Celestials, so you never hear the gossip. Everyone knew about Draupadi's boons. And most of us guessed she'd use them at some point."

"I hate chitchat," said Karna in disgust. He'd rather burst into flames than gossip like an old hag. And socialize with the Celestials? He'd prefer to cease to exist.

Yama shook his head. "You're too straitlaced for your own good, Karna. Even the sainted Yudhishtir keeps up with gossip. It's good to know stuff."

"That's bullshit. And don't mention your son or his brothers in front of me. I won't be responsible for what happens if you do." Karna ground the words between his teeth. He'd had it up to his eyeballs with the idiot sons of Kunti.

And why was he wasting time on crap? He stood up and was about to beg leave of Yama when Salabha rushed up to the bar. The normally pristine leader of Vitalas looked distraught. Beneath a sharply groomed widow's peak, his paper-white forehead was crinkled.

"What's wrong?" Tara hurried over to him, a smaller, more delicate version of her father.

Salabha shushed her with a look, and with a quick bow to Yama, focused on Karna. "We've been looking for the wrong Celestials."

"Yes, I've just discovered that," Karna said. "I need a new list..." He broke off as his phone vibrated in his back pocket. But he didn't pull it out to read the message, because Salabha had grabbed his arm tightly.

"I've found them. You must get to them, my lord. Quick. They were lured away from the encampment by a group of female demons."

*Fug. Doom All.* Karna almost used the power of vanishment in full view of the club's patrons, a good chunk of them human. Only by the grace of Yama's warning did he stop dematerializing. He spun about and bolted toward the exit.

Opaque fear settled in his gut. His daughter was in danger.

It had begun, just like Vishnu had predicted.

"Stay calm, brother," shouted Yama over the "Yamma, yamma! O, yamma, yamma" being croaked on stage.

Karna didn't slow down. Couldn't slow down. A group of revelers blocked the entrance to the club, dancing their way in. He pushed through them, dashing out of the Shrieking Sura, past a startled Roy, into an unoccupied, unlit alleyway. His pocket vibrated again. He pulled out the buzzing phone and read the message: *Red Alert @ Vishnu Temple peak, Grand Canyon.*

Cursing the vagaries of his existence, past and current, he vanished into the night.

# CHAPTER FOUR
## PUTRIKA: BELOVED DAUGHTER

Yahvi, Draupadi's youngest daughter, decided that the canyons awash in the moon's light inspired a grand story. No wonder the Naga, the Serpent People, had settled in these lands in the aftermath of the great duel between the Soul Warrior and the Stone Demon. It was written in the canons that after shutting down the portal between the Naga and the human world, the Naga king had led his people westward in gilded airborne ships to a land not yet marred by the constant conflict between Gods and demons. She couldn't begin to imagine the size of the snaking exodus. She didn't have to imagine what the Naga had felt when they saw the sprawling canyons for the first time.

The raw power in the rough-hewn mountains spoke of strength, hardship and endurance. The earthy red-black peaks called to her warrior's heart.

Yes! She was a warrior, by blood and by spirit, even if she was powerless and frail now. Her powerlessness was a temporary condition. A very temporary condition if— No! No ifs. *When* she met her goals, she wouldn't be powerless. She straightened her spine and set her shoulders. And she would meet her goals. She would vanquish Vala, for her father's sake as well as her own. Or die trying.

"What are you waiting for, Yahvi? Jump. Or have you turned into a cowardly human on this realm? Friends, did you see how the blue-eyed fair one screamed when I said hello to her?" Giggles and guffaws peppered the last of the demon's abrasive words.

Yahvi ended the vista adoration and turned, joining in with a false chuckle or two of her own. She didn't want Draas and the other *raaksasa* demons to think she was like the little human they'd terrified in Lok Vitalas, even if she was scared.

Draas was three full heads taller than her, weighed two hundred eighty kilos and was butt ugly. That is, ugly according to Yahvi. Apparently Draas was considered quite a beauty in the Demon Realm. It seemed several young *raaksasa* males had parted with a good chunk of their wealth to mate with her. Which didn't surprise Yahvi. Young males of any species did seem to have only one thing on their minds.

"I rejected a second mating with all of them as none proved virile enough to impregnate me on the first go," Draas boasted.

"Except for the baby nonsense, it sounds exactly like it is in our world," Lusha, Yahvi's second-oldest sister, chimed in. "For once, I wish a handsome face would live up to his romantic potential."

Lusha was the family's serial dater and sexpert. She was never without a male on her arm, or with the same one twice.

"Romance?" scoffed the demon next to Draas. "The ability to procreate is of paramount value to a demon. Not romance. Progeny assures glory. Not a mate."

While most social customs eluded her, the nonstop banter fascinated Yahvi as much as the lineup of *raaksasas*. This was her first up-close-and-personal meeting with any kind of *asura*—any kind of creature, in fact. So far, her interactions with demons—with anyone except her family, really—had been restricted to storybooks, storytelling and gleaned information, sometimes unlawfully channeled, on the Conscious Web—which worked a lot like the Internet, she'd found out in Vitalas, but on a cosmic scale.

It had been pure chance that Yahvi and her sisters had been stuck with Draas and her posse in the quarantine tent most of the afternoon, while their IDs and purpose of visit were vetted. The demons had been on their way back to the Demon Realm from Lok Tatalas via the portal of Lok Vitalas, which cut their journey time in half, and had decided on the spur of the moment to stop over in the Human Realm and visit the lands of their ancestors. The last bit was true even for Yahvi and her sisters.

Later, both groups had bumped into each other again in the gaming pavilions, and a "who is mightier" contest had ensued over the slot machines, culminating in this grand adventure during which they'd leapt from the peak of Vishnu Temple to the creek below. Vishnu Creek was too shallow to dive into from such a great height. But the challenge was to stop the fall just shy of the puddle of water, and levitate.

Yahvi had the spell of levitation down pat—the words and the cadence—if she stood on solid ground, that is, and within the confines of her palace-abode. She didn't know how she'd fare while plunging to the earth breathless. If she messed up even half a word, or its rhythm, she'd be in the creek, probably with her skull cracked open. So she hesitated to leap.

"Are you going to jump or not?" Draas stomped forward, setting her giant hands on her hips.

Draas was as naked as the stories told. All six demons were naked. Their nudity was the reason their gang was stuck in the unpopulated areas around Vitalas instead of walking the Las Vegas strip.

*Raaksasa* forms were quite humanlike, except they had hairless midnight-blue hides, tiny frond-like ears, fat black lips, pointy teeth and the typical bloodred demon eyes—all easily camouflaged had they agreed to Ziva's suggestions to blend in with humanity. The demons had flatly refused to blend in any fashion. They hated the feel of clothes on their skin as much as they hated the sun's warmth, and disdained prudish human sensibilities.

Not that cloaking mantras or garments could conceal attitude, Yahvi mused. With their tough, muscular physiques, the *raaksasas* exuded menace as solid and strong as the canyons of their Naga ancestors. They looked entirely capable of tearing a creature—namely her—limb from limb with their bare claws.

Her sister, Lusha, was super-strong too. Lusha could and had decapitated an *asura* limb from limb with her unpolished fingernails. This stupendous feat had happened several Celestial days before Yahvi's birth and was by far one of her favorite family tales.

Yahvi drew her gaze from Draas to her sisters. Satya, Lusha, Ziva, Iksa and Amara looked relaxed, bored even, but Yahvi knew they'd spring into action if she needed them. They were as protective of her and as overbearing as Mama, but they also understood she needed her freedom. She wanted to face her destiny, choose her own path, make her own mistakes and evolve. She didn't want to be a secret anymore, or cause tension in everyone.

Twisting back with determination, Yahvi faced the mighty mountains again. Her present was the open space before her. The past was an illimitable sky above her. The falling distance below her was the future she must grab. She caught her lower lip between her teeth, tasted salt. Sweat had sprung up on her skin, and her cotton clothes chafed. She felt hot, smelled all kinds of stuff. She was out of her confinement and experiencing the world for the first time. And she wasn't put off or scared. Okay. Untrue. She *was* scared about meeting her father, about battling Vala. But she'd *never* admit it out loud. If she did, she'd be locked up again, fast.

"Vee, its okay if you've changed your mind. We can all go home and forget about this."

Satya's words wrapped around Yahvi like a warm blanket. Her sister was using her power of mind manipulation to destress her.

"It's cool, Satya. Just offering a prayer to the Gods in preparation," Yahvi replied, staring at the undulating mass of pitch-black water far below. *Come on. Just do it.*

Besides, they no longer had a home to go back to, did they? Their secret identities had been revealed, their safe harbor barred to them. Mama was in a frenzy trying to create new identities for them and was scoping out potential abodes in lesser-known Celestial realms. Sometime amid that, she had to go to Devlok, the capital of the Higher Worlds, and explain her actions to the family and the Council of Gods and Goddesses.

She wished her mother would just give in to fate. It's not as if Yahvi wanted to die. But if that's what it took to vanquish Vala and save the humans from extinction, she wasn't going to run and hide. Mama wasn't interested in saving the human race at Yahvi's expense. But that was a mother's right.

Truth? She wouldn't mind dying, as there was a good chance her sacrifice would activate her god-powers, whatever they might be. Amara was sure Yahvi would inherit their mother's fiery powers, while Yahvi hoped for her father's fearsome ones. Lusha thought a combo was more likely, but Yahvi secretly feared she'd get neither. The entire situation was a mind-boggling mystery, and was messing with her internal peace and happiness.

Her sisters were all much older than her, and as boon-begotten Celestials, had wielded god-powers since their rebirths. They'd had no issues learning about warcraft and weaponry under Mama's tutelage. They'd memorized most of the ancient texts, the Vedas, and understood and used all practical applications of magic—be it mantras or the art of illusion. They'd spent many a Celestial day enhancing and honing various skills. In human terms, their ages ranged from thirty-six to nearly three hundred, whereas she was only seventeen—nearly eighteen—as wimpy as a human, and as such, not entitled to any divine perks.

That sucked in many varied ways and in all the realms. Why the doldrums had she been birthed in the human way? It wasn't fair even if the tale was utterly romantic.

"That's it. Looks like the demons win," Draas said.

Yahvi stiffened. *Over her dead body!*

"I. Am. A. Warrior," she shrieked, and cannonballed off the cliff.

The instant Karna manifested on Vishnu Temple, a green-souled human jumped off the peak in full view of a gaggle of extraterrestrials. The demons had tampered with a human mind, he instantly concluded. Before he could lift a hand to save the child from certain death, a Celestial maiden in jeans and tank top screamed, "I'll catch her" and vanished after the mind-enslaved human.

*Catch her?* What, like a Frisbee? And were the godlings in this together with the demons?

*Fugdoomal!* His breath seized in his chest painfully like he was having a stroke. He'd suffered too many shocks in one day.

"What the heck is going on here?" he roared. He flung his arms out and ropes of blue light flew from his hands, trapping the demons in an electric net. The gaggle erupted into terrified screams, while the godlings whirled about to gape at him.

"Move!" Ignoring the need to demand which one of them was his daughter, he stalked to the edge of the cliff. First things first. He had to make sure the human was okay. The godlings bowed to him, then parted like the tributaries of the Ganges River, allowing him a clear look-see. He saw one blue and one green dot bobbing safely above the waters, and felt not a whit calmer. He materialized in front of them, amazed to see even the human levitating four feet off the ground. *How deep was her thrall?* He'd erase the child's memory as soon as he sorted out what they'd done to her.

The two females screamed in surprise at his sudden appearance, lost their balance and fell *splat* on their faces into the creek. Gripping each one by an arm, he fished them out of the water, and flashed back on top of the mesa, releasing them. They fell to the ground, coughing and sputtering.

Karna glared at the hysterical females. "Having fun?" he asked, sarcasm dripping from his mouth like water from their hair. The sputtering suffered an abrupt demise. "Collaborating with demons, messing with a human...just how many rules did you break tonight?" No wonder the Stooges had kicked them out of Heaven.

To his utter shock, the cyan-blue-souled maiden sprang up from the ground and leapt into his arms. She hugged him with such enthusiasm that he had no choice but to return the wet hug.

"Uncle K! You found us...so soon," she said, pouting at him. "Whoops! Protocol needed. My bad." She winked, did a funny little bobbing bow, and stood at attention like a cadet on oath day. "I give you my respect and *sometimes* obedience, uncle. I'm Amara."

"Silence," he bellowed, the sound ricocheting across the canyon in ever-fading echoes. He blasted the godlings with a fearsome scowl. By karma! They really were all female. "I'll deal with you in time."

He curled his hands as if holding an invisible basketball and mumbled a mantra, creating a ball of fire. He dropped it on the dusty red ground at his feet. The fire would generate some heat and sweat, but he preferred to unravel the mysteries in something besides the moon's light.

Salabha had materialized sometime in the last couple of minutes and was interrogating the demons already.

"Trespassers?" Karna asked for form's sake. He didn't think so, though. Three of the *raaksasas* had chartreuse souls. They were aberrations, indeed, not to have sinned much. The other three demons were a hotchpotch of oranges. They'd sinned a bit more. The palette of soul colors was a lively complement to the natural backdrop of the moonlit canyon—that is, if one ignored the slight sin-quotient.

"No, my lord," replied Salabha. "I vetted them myself. They are part of *raaksasa* Char Mani's gem trading company. Char Mani travels through Vitalas often. But these six have come for the first time."

There was the number six again. What was that legend about omens and sixes?

*Raaksasas* were the most devolved of all demons, created mainly to serve their highborn masters. They were the bottom feeders, the lackeys of the Demon Realm. Or they used to be. These days, class and caste distinctions weren't as strictly applied in most of the realms in the Cosmos. Char Mani had obviously risen from his lowly roots to become a master trader.

"I am the Soul Warrior," he declared, drawing attention to the Soul Catcher buckle.

At once, the demons dropped to their knees, bowing their hairless heads before him. Which was fortunate, because standing, they'd topped his height by a foot and were twice his breadth. He fixed a beady eye on a relatively sin-free demon, meaning she was still young, anywhere from zero to three hundred years old. *Raaksasas* enjoyed a thousand-year life-span, and didn't erupt into full viciousness until later in life.

"Do you go by a name, demon?" Karna asked. Some didn't. They simply called themselves "Asura." Not that a name mattered when it came to vanquishing them. The subtle differences in the color of their souls were enough to keep them distinct in his mind.

"I am Draas," she said, fangs flashing in a smile.

He didn't smile back but instead crossed his arms across his chest. "Explain yourself." He also kept an eye on the green soul, watching for signs of red bleeding in. She'd been in the company of six demons for Heaven knew how long. There might be contamination.

Draas launched into a fantastical tale about her adventures in Vitalas and the daring leap from the canyon. "You know, my lord, I just realized there are better highs than winning. Friends are such a thing," she finished with another show of curvy incisors.

Karna glanced at Salabha, who seemed to be having trouble containing a smile. Karna sighed. He'd read them right. They'd meant no harm. Not today.

"You may go. Salabha will accompany you back to Vitalas, and you'll be deported immediately." Karna released the demons from the clutches of his god-powers, and suddenly freed, they rose to their feet cheering in relief. The godlings cheered too.

A tall, slim godling with masses of jet-black hair framing her classically beautiful face stepped forward after a brief hesitation. "Thank you, uncle. They're good demons."

It was blasphemy to utter the words *good* and *demon* together. His charges had a lot to learn. "Goodness in the heart of a demon is like a drop of water falling on a red-hot iron ball. Both disappear in a matter of seconds," he warned, not that anyone was listening.

A long, drawn-out hugging and leave-taking session began amongst the females. Draas—the demon seemed entirely too fond of the human girl, and it looked like the feeling was mutual—was the last to disappear down the mountain, followed by Salabha.

Finally, he turned to the godlings and their green-souled pet.

It didn't add up, thought Karna, watching the females narrowly. Five blue to bluish-green souls. Where the hell was the sixth one? He wondered again if there even was a sixth one. Had the Triumvirate amused themselves at his expense by dangling the carrot of kinship under his nose so he'd agree to this madness? It wouldn't be the first time.

And where was their devious mother? How could she leave her maniac offspring unsupervised? Did she know? Had she allowed her daughters to associate with *raaksasas* before? Did she have any clue what aiding and abetting a potential human suicide would cost them?

"Introduce yourselves," he ordered when it became obvious the godlings waited for his permission to speak. He wanted to bypass the intros and get to the bottom of this stunt.

The one who'd stepped forward went first. "I'm Satya, eldest daughter of Draupadi. I give you respect and obedience, uncle," she said, and with inherent grace bent to brush her hands over the tops of his feet.

Though she hadn't named her father, there was no doubt in Karna's mind that she was Yudhishtir's daughter. She had a regal strength, a clear steadfastness in her bearing, just like him. She was named in his honor too. Satya meant *truth*, a virtue Yudhishtir had once claimed to value above all else. Ha! The joke was on him, wasn't it? How was Yudhishtir handling Draupadi's secrets and lies?

Calm now that the demons weren't around, Karna touched Satya's head. "May Hrishikesh protect your senses, and Narayana your life air; may the Master of Shvetadvipa protect your soul, and may Lord Yogeshwara protect your mind," he said, tripping over a word or two of the long-forgotten blessing.

The female who came forward next towered over her sisters. In block-heeled black pumps, she almost matched his height. Her black trousers and grey muscle tee nicely showed off her big bones and lean musculature. She inclined her head—no leg touching for this one—and held out her right hand to shake. Intricate black-and-red symbols twined around both her arms. The flesh tattoos must've been murder to carve into her skin. And to leave that deep an impression, she must've carved her skin over and over again.

With a healthy respect for the female's threshold for pain, Karna took a calculated guess. "You're Bheem's."

"Yes. I'm Lusha. My respect and obedience to you, uncle." She smiled. Actually, to call her brief display of pearly whites a smile was a colossal overstatement. "Don't look so miserable. We're hardly any trouble at all."

Karna refused to be charmed, and repeated the blessing. If they thought being cute would get them off the hook, they were in for a surprise.

Of the remaining three Celestials, one was tiny and delicate, the wraith-like impression compounded by her fluttering lilac sundress. Her eyes were a stunning shade of violet, darker than her dress, and offset by shoulder-length dark hair that curled about a faultless face. Her skin seemed at once petal-soft and iridescent.

She took both his hands in hers, bowed, then went up on tiptoes and kissed both his cheeks. "I'm Ziva, Draupadi and Nakul's daughter. I too give you my respect and obedience."

The ethereal skin tone hinted, and her touch confirmed, that Ziva was an empath or a healer or both. When she touched him, the anger in his belly neutralized, and the headache that had nagged him since the Stooges' visit evaporated.

"I am Iksa. My father is Sahadeva and I am so excited to finally meet you, uncle," said godling number four, giving him a dimpled grin. She wasn't tall but wasn't frail like Ziva either. She reminded him of a Bollywood actress from a movie he'd seen recently in her dark leggings, peach-pink tunic and thick, springy ponytail. He hoped Iksa wasn't inclined to break into giggles at the drop of a hat like the actress.

"And I'm Amara," said the last warrior-female, swaggering forward to touch Karna's feet again. "Don't worry. I won't take Pop's name in front of you. Not on purpose."

A beautiful, brash and ebullient creature was Arjun's daughter. And innately powerful, Karna realized when he pressed a hand on top of her head. She sported an assortment of weapons strapped to her back, waist and thighs. If he was a betting soul—which he wasn't—he'd wager she had a pair of throw-blades stashed in her combat boots.

The apples hadn't fallen far from the trees. Each female mirrored her father in manner and temperament and seemed to have very little of their mother in them. Thank karma for small mercies. He wasn't sure what he would've done if confronted by half a dozen Draupadi doppelgangers. Jumped on the first ship bound for the Demon Realm, most likely.

But all foolishness aside, he'd hoped Amara would be the one—his daughter—the second he'd fished her out of the water. That hope was dashed now. The Gods had duped him. There was no sixth offspring.

"I have an impressive resume, coach. I'm ready for some serious demon hunting." Amara began to wax eloquent about her various triumphs in the training arena.

As she talked, and talked, Karna noticed the other females close in on the human, who'd shrunk into the background through the introductions. She seemed to be having trouble breathing. Ziva and Satya were pacifying her in hushed tones.

"Are you all right, child?" he asked, concerned. She looked exhausted. He should've deleted her memory and seen her safely home first. "Where do you live?"

Satya pushed the child forward with an encouraging smile. The child stepped closer, shivering in her wet T-shirt and jeans. Shy hope radiated out of her soft brown eyes.

Karna's heart began thudding as he stared at the bedraggled female. It couldn't be. *She* couldn't be his. His heart screeched to a stop, then resumed a thunderous tempo. The human pet was his daughter? As the conviction grew, horror filled his soul.

And then fury, the likes of which he'd never felt, stormed through him. Fury at Draupadi. Under false pretenses, she'd borne his child—a human weakling who looked incapable of defending herself, much less her fate, in the age of ungodliness and sin. This was the harbinger of doom? She was the weapon the *asuras* would use to bring the Cosmos to its knees?

It suddenly occurred to him the true reason why the Patriarchs and Matriarchs had come to him. The guru shit had been pretext—or maybe not. Maybe they did want him to train the godlings—the five blue-souled ones, at least. For what purpose, he didn't know, and didn't care to know right now. They'd brought his child to him for a different reason. She'd need protection not only from the *asuras* but also from the Celestials, and the humans too. At last, he understood why Saraswati had looked at him with such remorse. Every creature in the Cosmos would treat her like a pariah once they knew she was the harbinger. His child *was* doomed.

Karna recoiled at the thought of his daughter being shunned by all as he'd been once. Then immediately realized his blunder. She'd been watching him. She'd smiled at him, but deep in his worry, he hadn't reciprocated. Her gaze dropped to the ground, shoulders hunching in dejection. Strong disapproval wafted off the other females for him. How his daughter must suffer. How she must despise her fate. And he wasn't helping, was he?

"Come closer, child." He held out his hand, willing it not to tremble. He'd make it up to her somehow. He'd call her *vatse*—beloved daughter.

She was small even by human standards. She had a nice face. One might even call it sweet, with gleaming brown eyes, a patrician nose, rounded cheeks and wavy light brown hair that fell past her shoulders like his. Her lips were drawn flat in an unsmiling line now. She looked petrified of him. Had he sounded curt?

"Come to me, *vatse*," he said softly this time, and smiled in reassurance.

They were both shaking. He wondered if he should hug her. Kiss her cheeks? Shake her hand? He had to do something besides impersonating a fugging statue. He couldn't recall the last time he'd felt this awkward. Luckily, his daughter took matters into her own hands.

"I'm called Yahvi," she said in a watery voice, bowing low. She touched his feet with her right hand and stayed bent, awaiting his blessing.

He'd frozen like an ice sculpture when he heard her name.

*Yahvi*: of Heaven and Earth, it meant. Like he was, with one foot in Heaven and the other on Earth, but truly belonging to neither. He doubted she'd been named in his honor, though. It was only coincidence that her name held some meaning for him.

He stared at her small, wet head, searching for a connection, that zinging awareness that had coursed through his veins for his sons. *Mine*, his ego had claimed every time he'd laid eyes on them. *They are my flesh, my blood.* But his sons had been conceived in desire and love, not deception.

Bending, Karna resolved to gather his daughter into his arms and put an end to the weirdness. None of this was her fault. She straightened at the same time. In the blink of an eye, her head shot up like a boulder from a trebuchet and clipped him right on the nose.

Flinching, he plastered a hand across his face to block out the pain. It was intense. *Fug!*

"Oh no. I'm sorry. I didn't mean to hurt you...I mean hit you...I mean...are you okay?"

His daughter's anxious words penetrated the orange-red disco lights exploding behind his eyelids. "I'm...fine. I think." He opened his eyes, gingerly tweaking his nose to check for broken cartilage.

A pair of caramel-colored eyes, wide with concern, peered at him. And there it was, he thought dazedly. The connection. Her eyes. The color. They were his eyes. She was really his daughter. A twinkle of laughter flickered within the depths of her eyes, and her lips curved into a timid smile. Their audience wasn't holding back their mirth, though. Amara and Lusha were actually rolling on the floor, guffawing.

"Good job, Vee," Amara said as tears rolled down her cheeks. "Assault by deadly head is a unique way of introducing yourself to your dad. Utterly awesome."

"That's enough, Amu," said Satya, patting Yahvi's head in soothing circles. "Should we remove ourselves to your abode, uncle?"

Karna raised his eyebrows at the impertinent suggestion. "Oh? Now that you've had your fun, that is. I underestimated the trouble the Delinquent Six could…"

"The *Delinquent Six?*" Lusha cut him off midsentence. "Did those tight-assed Celestials call us that?"

Karna forced his lips into a disapproving frown, not wanting to encourage slanderous comments about the heavenly crowd, though privately he couldn't agree more. "*I* dubbed you that. Anyway, let's go home. Settle in. After that, I want answers in graphic detail. And…" He paused to make sure they all looked at him. It was time to show them who was boss. "The next time you do something this foolish, I *will* confiscate whatever powers you possess. Indefinitely."

The groans and moans were expected. One of the things he clearly remembered about commanding troops was that rules needed to be established early, along with the repercussions of disobedience.

"I trust five of you know how to vanish and manifest without mishap?" Affirmative nods answered his question. Vanishment was one of the few god-powers exclusive to the Celestials. It made travelling across the sprawling multilayered Higher Worlds instantaneous and easy. No other beings enjoyed the privilege unless they had procured it illegally.

Karna cleared his throat, and looked at his daughter, whose green soul broadcasted her lack of god-powers. "Do you piggyback on vanishment, *vatse*?"

She nodded, eyes downcast again.

"Side effects?" He suspected she'd have many. She was a puny little thing.

"Mild. I ignore them," she mumbled.

Impressed by her determination, he held out his hand. One piggybacked on vanishment by touch. She started to reach for his hand but stopped when her sister called her name. She neatly caught the backpack Amara threw at her and slung it over a shoulder. Facing him again, she placed her small, cold hand in his big, warm one. To his embarrassed pleasure, she gave him a second wobbly smile.

"That's all you brought?" he asked, frowning at the weapons, strange-hued backpacks and purses held by his charges. He was astonished they travelled so light. They were females, and Celestials to boot—not to mention, their elite parentage. They'd each have a Celestial palace or two to their names.

"We left in a hurry. Our mother will send our trunks directly to your abode once we apprise her of our safe arrival," said Satya.

Karna bit his tongue to stop himself from demanding Devious Draupadi's whereabouts. It wouldn't be fair to have the children rat on their mother. "Come, we have much to sort out."

The Soul Warrior squeezed his daughter's hand, and they vanished to the island of Asht Dveep, along with his motley crew.

# CHAPTER FIVE
## YATRA: JOURNEY

In the megalopolis of Asuralok, the capital of the Demon Realm, Draas dashed through a network of tunnels toward the Dreaded Fringes that crept up and out onto the Forsaken Plains. Preceptor Shukra, the great *asura* mage, had called all demons to congregate in the name of the *asura* king, Dev-Il.

Despite a rocky, bumpy ride through the portal in Lok Vitalas on a public airship, Draas had arrived home exhilarated by her voyage to the Human Realm. Dying to tell the clan about her adventure, she'd been sorely disappointed to find only the servants scrubbing the dwelling from floor to ceiling. She'd set off immediately for the Plains, wondering what sort of precipitous occasion called for all of demon-kind to go above ground.

The ferrous walls of the subtunnel began to shrink as she closed in on the Fringes—the conduits connecting the subterranean cities of the realm to the deadly surface above. The devil stones that lit her path in fluorescent green and yellow also grew scarce as she raced down the tunnel. But Draas didn't slow her pace. Her eyes simply adjusted to the glacial darkness. At the extremity of the tunnel, she dropped into a crouch in front of an opening in the wall. A single devil stone was embedded into the crown of the semi-circular doorway with a warning stamped under it: **Beware. Go forth at your peril.**

Only the desperate, the filthy poor or the hotheads sought the Forsaken Plains.

Draas wondered why the Preceptor had chosen the surface when there were better, safer venues to congregate in within the city burrows. Had he planned some grand demonstration to lure silly *asuras* into the black arts of *asura-maya*? Or had Dev-Il run out of funds already?

Dev-Il's profligacy was a source of unmitigated annoyance to Char Mani—Draas's blood-sire. As owner of the Char Mani Mines, he was often pressed upon to share his bounty of gems and gold with the wastrel king.

Anticipating her blood-sire's foul reaction if asked to contribute to the royal coffers so soon after the last time, Draas began to speed-crawl up the steep conduit. It wouldn't go down well if Char Mani insulted Dev-Il or his chief advisor, Preceptor Shukra. They'd make him pay, one way or another. Her ears picked up the faint drone of a speech as she labored through the juddering canal.

"It is time for *asuras* to take a stand. No sooner than expected, no later than foretold. It is time to seize the future and quit bemoaning the past."

Shukra's words gave Draas pause. That didn't sound like some carefree assemblage of *asuras* being shown a good time, or a bid for funds.

"Five millennia ago, the great Dragon was defeated and the mighty Stone Demon was exiled, and our sovereign was forced to sign the Treaty of Quarantine by Heaven's ruling Council. The sanctions made us weak. Now we stagnate on this realm, cowering in unwanted peace, rejoicing in the small victories allowed us. Dev-Il has become a joke, his snore worse than his bite."

Laughter erupted in the crowd and Draas wondered if the Preceptor was foaming at the mouth at the insult.

"Hear me, O mighty *asuras*! It is time we bring back the mighty Age of Asura. It is time to break free of this prison and reclaim our dominion."

Not again, thought Draas, crawling faster. She was so sick of *asuras* trying to change a perfectly fine way to exist.

She struggled out of the Fringes only to be half smothered by a phalanx of fidgety limbs. She tried to push herself to her feet, but the excitable throngs made it impossible as they stamped their feet in a hard staccato rhythm while Shukra thundered on. To avoid getting trampled, Draas sank her claws into the nearest calf, heard a surprised grunt and sighed in satisfaction when she was yanked up by the armpits and set on her feet.

Instantly, her lungs filled with sulfur-rich air, making her gasp. No acid rain or meteor showers marred the barren horizon for now. It boded well for the congregation, thought Draas, staring at the starless, ebony sky.

The Demon Realm was a dark, cold place. Light never came here. Light wasn't welcome here.

And yet *asuras* had prospered here for over five thousand years. Draas loved her home with every atom of her being, and believed only a mad soul would call it a prison.

"You're late," the helpful *asura* growled in her face.

"I hope not," Draas rumbled in return and began to heave through the throngs of Dev-Il's worshippers in search of her clan members, praying that her glory-seeking brother, Raka, wouldn't succumb to the madness.

Half a day in the company of her father and Yahvi was still afraid to look him in the eye. She didn't want to—she refused to catch another glimpse of disappointment in his face.

It had been disappointment, no matter what her sisters said. She understood his feelings too. There he was, the legendary Soul Warrior. And there were her sisters: gorgeous, powerful, witty and skilled. And here she was—not a Celestial, with zero potential, simply an unmagical green soul with slow reflexes and a bad case of jetlag. She was disappointed in herself, too.

She'd spent the last three hours on the living room sofa, pretty much comatose, until Amara had woken her at sunset for dinner. She was still sleepy. Maybe she was depressed. Who wouldn't be if they knew they'd die on their next birthday? And she missed her mother.

*Spinning satellites!* She had to stop moping. She was sitting beside her father at *his* dining table in *his* abode, and it wasn't a dream. She'd pinched herself to check. She'd fantasized about meeting him for so long that it seemed surreal. She was both excited and scared. Which was odd, because stepping out in the world and meeting Draas and the *raaksasas* should've felt scarier. But coming face-to-face with demons hadn't been nearly as unnerving as facing the legend whose blood ran through her veins.

Of course, the father of her dreams hadn't cringed away from her.

Gah! She was being an idiot. She'd bounced the back of her head against his face. How was he supposed to react? She'd definitely made a smashing first impression.

*An irony of cosmic proportions,* Amu had tittered after the catastrophe. *A tale worth a million retellings,* Iksa had teased, as Yahvi was prone to repeat and reread stories millions of times. Then, to her utter shame, promptly after vanishing home, she'd proved herself not only a weakling but also a liar and fainted at her father's feet. Like some newbie-to-vanishing klutz!

Admission of weakness wasn't the way of the warrior, much less providing proof of the failing.

Truth was, she hadn't expected to *feel* so much. Not just external sensations, but emotions bubbled within her. She wanted. She desired. She needed. She hurt. There was a constant turbulence inside her soul, and she had no idea how to control it—if it was possible to control emotions on this realm in the first place.

The Human Realm was so different from the Higher Worlds, which were suffused with a joyful energy that wouldn't allow a soul to feel any negative emotions—or not for long. Any and all bodily functions were superfluous. There were no toilets in Heaven. Bathing was a purely sensual indulgence, as was eating. She'd never cried once in her almost-eighteen years, but now she was tearing up every other second.

Yahvi set her jaw, determined to redeem herself. She would look at her father sometime during this meal. He'd been nothing but sweet to her since that disastrous first meeting. Satya thought it was likely shock making her act weird, and she might take a day or two to absorb the changes—both mental and physical—before settling down. Maybe so, but Yahvi couldn't afford to waste a single day pampering her weak body. She had just over a week until her birthday. One week until the Stone Demon reappeared and fulfilled Kalika's prophecy. She had so much to accomplish, so much to experience in such a short span of time. Most of all, she wanted to get to know her father.

Yahvi surreptitiously looked at him as he ploughed through his dinner. He was deep in conversation with Satya, who sat on his left, and Iksa, who sat on Satya's left. It seemed a casual and random exchange, more to do with hobbies and passions, a bit of politics—Celestial and earthbound. But an intense grill-session was on the menu. As they'd taken their seats around the dining table, her father had requested—ordered, really—their presence in the den after dinner, adding shivers to Yahvi's already hyperventilating guts.

Why was her stomach churning? Was it simply anticipation anxiety? Would she feel better or worse as the days flew by?

A warm, pinkish-mauve-colored hand settled on her thigh, squeezing it. Yahvi took a bite out of the apple she had no appetite for, munched and swallowed. Then faced her sister. "I'm fine, Ziva. I'm not going to throw up again." She'd vomited thrice in as many hours. This day could safely be chronicled as the most disgraceful day of her life.

Yahvi tried to relax under Ziva's one-handed massage, but her mind was stuffed with thoughts. She'd been wrenched free of her mother and all that was familiar. Naturally her nerves weren't happy, no matter how thrilled she was to meet her father. A sudden vision of her mother's weeping face swam before her eyes. She'd never seen her mother cry before. Never. Mama was strict and funny, even sad or pensive at times, but rarely distraught. Yahvi hated the fact that she was the cause for her mother's current plight.

"Take deep breaths, Vee," murmured Ziva in her ear.

Yahvi did as she was told—Ziva was usually right about all the health stuff—and focused on the sunburst pattern on the wall across from her. Momentarily blinded by the tiny lights beaming out of the gilded mural, she blinked at the dozens of gold and silver creatures—mostly naked and made of metal—chasing each other from light to light. The wall décor was perky, not unlike the decorations in their palace-abode back home. She'd been desperate to break free of the prison her luxurious chambers and private garden had become, but the truth was, she missed her home.

She took another deep breath, drawing her eyes away from the mural. The dining chamber was culled out of the living area in a quirky hexagonal shape. A marble-topped dining table, also hexagonal in shape, dominated the space, surrounded by a dozen concrete chairs with silk pillow seats. Her father's abode was fussy without a lot of fuss, the décor oddly mismatched through the rooms. Quite the contrast from the lush habitat in Alaka she'd been raised in. The palace-abode had been custom designed by Mama and Tvastar, the Celestial Architect, to suit all of their needs—a perfect hideout in plain sight.

She'd prayed for a different life. Wondered what it would be like to be raised by two parents instead of six mothers. To be raised in the open and not in secret. She got why it had to be that way in her head, but in her heart she'd wished for things...and now they'd come true.

Yahvi swallowed the sudden lump that formed in her throat. She missed her mother so much. She'd caused Mama pain by defying her, by coming to the Human Realm to meet her father. But she'd had to do it. Mama would understand that once she calmed down, wouldn't she? They'd left her to face the music alone. It wasn't fair that Mama would be punished for having children. It wasn't fair that everyone was blaming her for this situation—including Father. Mama had sworn she'd find a way to come to them. She'd promised they'd celebrate Yahvi's birthday together.

But what if she failed? What if she didn't get here in time? The thought of never seeing her mother again made Yahvi's stomach hurt in an awful way. *Stop it! You chose this.* She blinked the tears from her eyes. She had chosen her path. But she hated feeling scared. She needed to focus on something else, something concrete, like target practice. She'd be fine once her father knew the score and the training commenced. The mental and physical exercises would demand all of her attention, make her too tired to think, much less feel. Bonus: She'd get to know her father really well. And he'd see she was not a weakling.

Yahvi darted another quick peek at him. He was still engrossed in the *blah blah* with Satya.

"So, what you're saying is that the constitutional organizations on Earth echo the politics of Heaven?" Satya's sparkling blue eyes were a dead giveaway that she was thoroughly enjoying the discussion.

"Of course. Who do you think laid the foundations of human civilization?" her father replied with a raised eyebrow. "Who do you think founded humanity itself?"

"I'm just...surprised. I thought—I expected things to be different. Changed. Especially since...well, clearly the heavenly model has failed." Satya tilted her head and arched an eyebrow in turn. "And is the Soul

Warrior Devlok's ambassador on the Human Realm or mankind's ambas-sador in Heaven?"

The Soul Warrior took a swig of his coffee, golden eyes glowing with amusement above the mug. "What I am is Homeland Security with zero political affiliations."

There began a debate about how that statement couldn't possibly be true, and that any military operation, especially a covert preemptive one, was but an arm of the political system. Did that answer Mama's question about not trusting him? Mama had wanted to run and hide again. She didn't trust Celestial politics and the policy-makers at all.

Yahvi lost interest in the debate. Politics had a tendency to go around in circles. She turned her attention to the happenings on the opposite end of the table—a better distraction for her nerves.

Amara urged Lavya to hold his thumb up for inspection—the springy fake one on his right hand. He refused politely and blithely carried on eating. Yahvi thanked her stars Amara had found another target to poke fun at for the evening.

"Is my being Arjun's daughter a problem for you?" Amara's question was valid, maybe a bit touchy for all involved, but she asked in her usual forthright manner—a stark contrast to Satya's polite euphemisms.

"Of course not," Lavya said, and yelped when Amara ignored his wish and grabbed hold of his appendage anyway. "Are you crazy? Don't fiddle with it like that."

A giggle swapped places with the nausea in Yahvi's throat. Poor Lavya still sported what she and her sisters had dubbed "the goldfish" look. His eyes and mouth had bugged out the second he'd clapped eyes on them that afternoon. The horror-struck expression was the last thing Yahvi remembered before her lights-out swoon. Lavya's overreaction had made sense once they'd learned that neither her father nor he had expected female students, or a human in their midst. For some mysterious reason, the Pat-Mats had omitted sharing those facts.

Yahvi frowned, recalling her father's disappointed face. Had the Gods known that being female and/or a green soul would be an issue for him? Was it an issue? Was that why Mama had never encouraged Yahvi to meet him? *"Next year, darling,"* had been Mama's patent response to Yahvi's appeals. *"When he's less engrossed in fighting demons."*

Or had Mama been worried about something else? Like her own skin? Her father definitely hadn't looked pleased when Satya had mentioned Mama earlier. In fact, his expression had instantly soured. Yahvi let out a long sigh, concluding that it was just as well Mama wasn't here with them.

Abandoning the half-eaten apple on her plate, she peeked in her father's direction again and froze. Shoot. He was looking straight at her. If she looked away now, she'd definitely seem gutless.

It helped that he was smiling and no longer appeared stern. The smile brought out his good looks. He was quite the hunky male with his golden-brown locks and broad-boned features. He'd changed into shorts but wore the same T-shirt she'd met him in. Neither he nor Lavya stood on ceremony, it seemed. No one had dressed up for dinner—which was fine by her, as she and Amara had always found the formality Mama insisted on to be a bother. He still wore the leather belt with the powerful-looking Soul Catcher talisman. But he'd ditched his shoes. His calves were tanned golden and very shapely.

*Sparkling moonbeams!* Why was she gawking at her father's legs? Forcing her eyes up, she fixed them on his face—on the cleft in his chin, to be precise.

"Are you feeling better, *vatse*?" he asked.

Yahvi nodded, feeling monstrously silly. If she could only look him in the eye once and exchange a small conversation, just a couple of words, victory would be hers. The cleft began to stretch wide as she stared, and a large hand swooped upward in a graceful arc. It patted her cheek, squeezed one shoulder and dropped out of sight.

The gentle affection in the gesture caught her by surprise. So did the stinging in her eyes. She grabbed the napkin on her lap and pretended to sneeze into it. She'd make a complete fool of herself if she wailed. Should she make a dash for the bathroom?

"She'll take time to adjust to the energies of this realm, Uncle Karna," said Ziva, yanking Yahvi's napkin-clutching hand to check her pulse. "We overdid things today. Four vanishments in less than twelve hours were too much for her."

"I'm fine, Ziva, really." Yahvi glared at her sister, whose busy fingers danced all around her head, neck and throat, feeling for suspicious lumps. Ziva worried that Yahvi's "greenness," muted for eighteen years in the disease-free Higher Worlds might explode in all its glory in the next few days. Yahvi should expect to make intimate acquaintance with tonsillitis, adenoids, chicken pox, mumps, measles and a whole lot of other rubbish.

Yahvi groaned, begging Ziva to cease and desist from her paranoia. She felt validated when her father chuckled. She'd amused him. Yay! Infinitely better than disappointing him or pissing him off. She sighed in heartfelt relief when Ziva finally stopped hovering and sat down to dinner again.

So silly to worry about tonsils when her whole body was about to be dead soon.

With a few choice words, Preceptor Shukra had roused the sleeping Demon Realm.

This was what he'd been waiting for, thought Raka, electrified by what was happening. This was his ticket out of an unworthy realm and the garden-variety life of a sinless demon.

Heart thundering inside his chest, he cut the massive queues that had formed within moments of Shukra's speech and stomped to the head of the chaos. *Asura* warriors held the throngs in check with arms spread wide, guarding the inner circle where the Preceptor threw oblations and sacrifices into the sacred fire, invoking the blessings of the demon-goddess Danu.

"Power? Age? Tribe?" barked a blank-faced, white-haired giant, a *daitya*, at Raka.

"Vanishment," Raka replied, thrusting his chin and chest out. His mother was a fallen Celestial, banished from the Higher Worlds for practicing forbidden magic. She'd bestowed on him tremendous power. "Five hundred years," he said next, answering the underlying question of experience, watching the *daitya*'s apathy flip over to grudging respect. "And I am heir to the gem trader, Char Mani." Without further ado, the path cleared and Raka was ushered into the inner circle.

Shukra stood on a raised dais by the ceremonial fire, his dark gaze searching the teeming hordes. Raka straightened his spine and held his breath. But Shukra's eyes swept past him, alighting on a *raaksasa* a few demons away from Raka. The *raaksasa* was taller than Raka's eight and a half feet and carried no arms. He marched to the dais as soon as Shukra bade him forward, but didn't climb on. He checked his stance and slowly, oh so slowly, raised his massive arms to the sky, just as lightning rent the night into a dozen pieces. The hordes stilled instantly, staring warily at the sky.

Raka snorted at the preplanned theatrics. He recognized the demon. Mara was one of Preceptor Shukra's minions.

"Behold, the Juggernaut, known to you as the unstoppable Mara," roared Shukra, upending a leather satchel full of *raakh*—bone dust—over

Mara's head, and rubbing it into Mara's skin for luck. The crowd cheered at the spectacle.

Long, white hair flowed down Shukra's back. His body, tattooed all over in magical symbols and smeared with *raakh* as the mark of the mage, shook as he spoke. "You've watched him fight in the burrows, envied his bombardment skills, his absolute focus in hand-to-hand combat that earned him his fearsome nickname. Now, witness his true power." Shukra was a *danu* demon, a direct descendant of the demon-goddess Danu, and human in form and size. He looked powerless next to the four-hundred-and-fifty kilo Juggernaut. As the foremost *asura* guru and mage, the Preceptor was anything but powerless.

Shukra was Dev-Il's chief advisor. More like Dev-Il's boss, Raka sniggered privately. A thousand years ago, Shukra had been an ordinary mage, a charlatan, when Char Mani, Raka's blood-sire, had been the slave-servant of a powerful *asura* lord. Raka didn't know the specifics, but Shukra had come to Char Mani, along with several other demons, with a plan that had been beneficial to all. "*Shukra's conspiracies are magnificent to behold, Raka, like the twists and turns of a tunnel in a thriving mine, all leading up to a colorful mother lode of gems.*"

Char Mani had won himself his first ruby mine in that campaign, while Shukra had usurped the office of Preceptor for himself. This time, Raka would profit from whatever secret coup Shukra had designed.

Planning his own coup, Raka watched the Juggernaut in disdain. Mara was nothing but a thug with a penchant for barroom brawls and an inability to hold jobs. Mara's own family had disowned him from sheer mortification. What power could this nobody from the Plains wield that the Preceptor had hand-selected him for the demonstration? Whatever Mara's power, it couldn't beat vanishment. Raka was sure of that much.

"I shan't tell you what Mara can do," said Shukra, a reptilian smile curving his blood-encrusted lips. "I'll let him show you."

Mara stomped his foot on the ground thrice. The crowd followed suit, save Raka. Red eyes glowing, Mara flexed his paws wide above his head, lethal claws flashing as lightning split the sky again. Raka hissed as the first globules of acid rain struck him, thinking again how perfectly Shukra had timed this. The hordes screamed. Some broke free and ran for the Fringes, or tried to, desperate for shelter. Raka didn't move a muscle, positive that Shukra planned to provide another form of shelter.

Mara brought his paws together in a thunderclap. Power sizzled between his palms and shot down his arms. The demons couldn't decide whether to run to safety or stay and watch the show. Some oohed, others grumbled, more screamed. In the end, most remained because they were trapped.

"Watch him struggle with the weight of a thousand realms as it threatens to tear him asunder. Watch him stand his ground, fight for control, battle for dominance." Shukra hyped his exhibit well. "Watch the fearless Mara, O denizens of Asuralok, and learn from him. Or are you fearless already?"

"Fear is human. We are *asura*," the hordes rumbled.

"Can the Lord Master count on your bravery, on your loyalty?"

"By Dev-Il's honor, he is our Lord Master!"

"Then pledge your souls, brave *asuras*, to his cause. Let us band together and restore a brother to a brother. Let us bring back the glory days of the two Scourges!"

Raka was impressed by how skillfully Shukra slipped that in. So that was the crusade, he mused—the resurrection of the Stone Demon and the Dragon, and control of the Human Realm.

"*Avashyam! Avashyam!* Of course, we will."

Mara snarled with effort through it all. At Shukra's signal, he bunched every muscle in his well-honed body and unfused his hands inch by inch. A small, writhing hole gaped open between his palms. Inside it was blacker than the blackest sky and as deafening as Hell's Well of Souls.

Raka forgot to breathe, staring into the wormhole, a tiny tear in the fabric of space and time. He'd seen such a feat before, used by a mage to travel between realms—a lot faster than the official airships and secret demon routes, a bit slower than vanishment. The mage had come from Naga Lok, the realm of the Serpent People, to buy emeralds from Char Mani. The marvel of a wormhole was that it could be used to transport entire cities, entire civilizations from one realm to another—if the mage was skilled enough.

Wormholes were powerful magic. Merely tearing the metaphysical framework of this realm wasn't enough. Mara had to compress the space between the chosen realms and freeze time, then drill a tunnel, tear out an exit and safely transport the travellers through before the fabric mended itself and all got trapped within. There was no escape from such a void.

Absolute silence descended on the Forsaken Plains. Even the rain dribbled in whispers. Thousands of red eyes, Raka's included, fixed on the wormhole in awe and fear.

"My brave crusaders, do not be afraid," crooned the Preceptor. "I'm here to protect you."

As Raka stepped forward, a hand wrapped about his bicep and pulled. Ready to rip to shreds the fool who'd dared touch him, he whipped around.

"Don't be a fool, Raka," Draas hissed into his face.

His half-emitted snarl transformed into a grin. His baby sister had her dander up. Again.

"Either join me or let me go," he said, already turning back to his purpose.

Draas's claws bit into his arm, forcing him to face her again. "This is madness. Wormholes are tricky business at best and deadly at worst. Come away, Raka. Our sire won't approve."

"He's already given me his blessing. He said I should seize my destiny. He said I should make him proud. Besides, what good is Char Mani's wealth if he can't buy his heir a decent resurrection when things go wrong?" Raka smirked.

Draas looked aghast at the joke, and Raka relented. She was only worried for his welfare. He touched his forehead to hers. "Don't worry. I don't plan on doing anything stupid." He swallowed hard, suddenly realizing the enormity of his decision. "Come with me, Draas. Come whet your powers, which decay and mold on this realm. Come be what you're meant to be."

Draas shook her head as the crowd surged forward, dragging him along. Somehow she remained rooted to her spot. "Raka, you're going to walk into a wormhole. You're already doing something stupid!" Her voice grew faint over the roaring, the pouring acid rain.

"Glory and greatness await us at the other end," the Preceptor shouted. The wormhole had grown large enough to swallow them all.

Raka gazed into the abyss, and dismissed his baby sister from his mind. *Glory…* Yes!

"Follow me, O mighty *asuras*. There's no time to waste," were the last words Raka heard as he left his garden-variety life behind.

Things were just as unsettled in the Soul Warrior's abode after dinner, which had been followed by a round of delicious dessert—orange-mousse-stuffed bonbons and caramel lattes prepared by Lusha, a.k.a. the goddess of puddings.

The feast had ended on a lifestyle lesson: Lord Karna and Eklavya employed no servants, hence all creatures residing under their roof had to pull their own weight, regardless of rank or soul color. For the first time in her conscious existence, Yahvi had helped clear the dinner table, washed dishes, boxed up leftovers—which were somehow delivered to Mumbai's needy—and sweated through a smorgasbord of menial labor.

It had been a humbling lesson, though not the downright traumatic experience Mama claimed the Human Realm was all about. Mama was obsessed with painting the realm in as unfavorable a light as possible—a plan to keep her offspring off the realm, which clearly had backfired. The truth was, Yahvi hadn't experienced anything remotely traumatic on the realm so far. Not even kitchen duty, which wasn't hard to accomplish, just unfamiliar, and made easier by her sisters' proficiency with magic spells. Poofing garbage into nonexistence was better than collecting it for disposal. Her sisters had also, during Yahvi's extended nap on the living room sofa, cleaned out the second floor attic and rolled out the bedding Lavya had provided, readying the chamber for habitation. The attic was the only unoccupied space in her father's abode that was large enough to sleep six. That it didn't have an attached bathroom bothered Yahvi a tad.

Chores done, ablutions complete, it was time for the interrogation.

Yahvi was so nervous she felt a constant need to pee. Lined up alongside her sisters in front of a massive shiny black desk, she fought the urge to fidget as she faced a grim-faced Soul Warrior and his aide. It wasn't their smiley dinner companion or her father who scrutinized them. The warlord the Cosmos called the Death Conqueror inspected them like a jeweler evaluating the potential of a handful of rough diamonds. Like he was deciding whether it would be worth his time and effort to bother with them.

At last, he began to speak. He spoke and spoke and as he spoke, Yahvi's tension multiplied. He wasn't at all complimentary about their situation, their reputations or their cushy backgrounds. Thank Heavens she hadn't brought up the lack of bathroom amenities in the attic, or her father would've thought even less of her. Deeds determined a soul's worth, he said, and so far he'd seen only misdeeds. His words, hot as the sun, burned into her soul. And then he was staring at her, only her. He asked her something, and she had absolutely no clue what. She'd been too busy trying to decipher his expression.

Cheeks flushing red, Yahvi opened her mouth to apologize for zoning out and beg him to repeat the question when a horrific gong went off around the den, accompanied by a series of ear-splitting beeps. A frantic look about pinpointed the sources of the alarms—mobile phones, the computer and other screened gadgets. A bright red dot pulsed like a heartbeat on a map displayed on a large TV screen.

Her father had shot up from his chair on the first alarm, an air of suppressed energy coalescing around him. "I need to change. Keep me updated," he said to Lavya and vanished from the den.

*Flashing moonbeams!* This was so exciting, Yahvi thought.

Lavya was bent over the keyboard, typing furiously. Mercifully, the alarms stopped ringing and Yahvi unplugged her fingers from her ears.

"Coordinates sent. Good luck hunting." Lavya tapped *Enter* with a bit more force than was necessary for the computer to obey his commands.

"Hunting?" Amara whirled about to face the doors, her plait slashing the air in half. "Hunting *asuras*? I am so going with—" She vanished midsentence, leaving the lot of them gaping at the empty spot she'd suddenly left behind.

"The fuck?" Lavya stood up, shouting. His face went red as a beetroot, his eyes comically agog. "Where did she go?"

Before Yahvi could do anything more than look at Satya for an answer, Amara reappeared, screaming blue murder about how she hated the nasty-ass Soul Guru who'd refused to take her on the hunt.

And that's how the dreaded interrogation ended, incomplete in its evaluation, to Yahvi's bladder's immense relief, with Amara in full sulk-mode.

# CHAPTER SIX
## ATMA: SOULS HUNTED AND HAUNTED

Karna stalked down the soulless graveyard, reconfirming the coordinates of the breach on his phone. The Red had been detected at the family cemetery of Tipu Sultan in Kolkata, and that's exactly where he stood.

What mischief had the demon stirred up in the graveyard? Some *asuras* could reanimate a corpse and use the human body as a cover, but Karna couldn't see any sign of a disrupted grave. Nor did he hear any terrorized human screams. Surely, if zombies were about, screeching would have ensued.

How had the *asura* come here? Had he piggybacked on an avaricious or foolish Celestial or shape-shifter by vanishment? He could've mesmerized a human to transport him in an earthly vehicle from Vitalas or one of the other *loks* that were linked via treacherous pathways to Earth. When had he breached the Human Realm? Where had he gone? Why had he come? Did he mean to do harm?

The problem with Lavya's computerized soul detection system was that it couldn't decipher intent. *Asuras* breaching the Human Realm was one thing, breaching it with evil intent quite another. *Asuras* acting on the evil intention was the reason Karna had a job.

Where the heck was it? Karna jogged toward the back entrance of the graveyard, deciding to take the search outside.

Maybe the Red was a harmless ghost or a ghoul with no physical body. Earth's gravity by its very nature was a hindrance to the will of the *asuras*, working against weighty masses and turning large demons into bumbling fools. Then there was the curse of daylight. Five thousand years ago, after two megalomaniac demons, Vrtra and Vala, had trifled with the Sun God, Surya had cursed all *asuras* to suffer blindness in his presence for eternity. Both handicaps afforded Karna a tiny measure of control while hunting them.

That's right, Karna thought, banking down his irritation. He hunted enormous, evil-willed nastiness on a nightly basis. He was the Soul-*freaking*-Warrior, the son of the Sun God. He should be able to handle a few females for a few days without the constant need to combust. There was something going on with them. While outwardly poised, he'd sensed nervousness in them, even tension. Did they know of Yahvi's fate? Did his daughter know? How could the Gods tell her? Karna closed his eyes briefly. How could they not?

But all of that shit would have to wait. He needed to concentrate on the job at hand and pulverize a demon—if he could spot one.

Karna scanned the area outside the back gate, his senses sharp and open to pick up the colorful residual aura that vanishment left in its wake. He hoped he wasn't too late, as the high-energy charge remained visible only for a short time. And there it was—a colorful haze by the pair of rusty wrought iron gates. The jumble of colors spread across a very large area, which meant several demons had materialized, not just one. Better to sneak-attack the bunch.

Chanting the mantra of invisibility, Karna began to track his quarries.

Lit only by the crescent moon, Kolkata's roads were devoid of any animation at this late hour. Homeless souls snored, spread-eagled on the pavements amidst their scant belongings. A quick mantra had packages of food and clothes appearing between the rags. A mongrel dog, curled up next to a legless man, started awake. He sniffed at the packages, then followed Karna's unseen movements with alert eyes, but other than twitching his ears did not raise an alarm. Karna winked at the scruffy black-and-brown mutt whose soul was a striking shade of emerald-yellow. The dog was slotted for a human rebirth soon. He added an order of dog biscuits and an extra-large bone to the bounty and moved on.

Halfway down a shabby shop-lined street, Karna caught sight of the interloper coming out of the Kalighat Kalika temple at the end of the lane. The *daitya* was approximately nine feet tall and, unlike a bald *raaksasa*, had ropes of white hair falling to his waist. His bare chest was drenched in blood. And, he wasn't using anything more than a pair of jeans to conceal his fanged identity. Human blood had the same effect on *asuras* that *soma* juice had on Celestials and a triple shot of espresso had on humans. The *daitya* was punch-drunk on power. It had made him stupid.

The demon was hunting for fresh victims but luckily—or unluckily for him—none were about this late at night. Before he thought to expand the search area, Karna began to sprint toward him. A chant activated the Soul Catcher. Karna opened his palm and another mantra summoned *Asi*, his deadly sharp Celestial dagger. The adamantine blade turned red-hot as soon as he wrapped his fist about the sun-crested hilt.

The demon's obvious brutality toward a human gave Karna permission to slay first and ask questions later. He sprang forward, flying at his target with both arms raised, and buried the blade in the middle of the demon's forehead. The demon went rigid and opened his mouth wide in shock. Before he could scream for help or mercy, his humungous body went slack, dropping to the pavement like a sack of potatoes. Karna quickly recited the death-rite mantra and the moment the *asura*'s red soul detached from its temporal form, the opalescent sunstone of the Soul Catcher swallowed it up.

That was the handicap he had to work around. Unless he killed the *asura* himself and separated the temporal body from the soul, the Soul Catcher was redundant.

*One down. How many more to go?* Karna dragged the dead body inside the temple, shut the doors and armed himself again. A noxious, oppressive energy swirled through the space. The antechamber was unlit and empty, but the carved wooden doors leading to the flame-lit inner shrine stood ajar. The mingled smell of stale flowers, sandalwood incense, blood and pure fear hit him before he came across the two lifeless bodies of the pundits behind Kalika's idol. Chunks of flesh were missing from the corpses, and they'd been completely drained of blood.

Karna hunkered down, squashing the pity and fury that roiled through him. Violence was one thing—he was a violent soul. But some demons thrived on cruelty, and that was unacceptable.

He pressed his hands over the three lines of sandalwood paste marking the bald foreheads of the holy men, then discharged enough radiation to cremate them on the spot. There wasn't another option tonight. He couldn't leave the bodies to be discovered and speculated over. But he could and would make sure the souls reached their rightful destinations. Praise karma the human souls had been left untainted. If they'd been possessed by evil before death, they'd be turning red already.

*"From the Unreal, lead us to the Real,*
*From Darkness, lead us into Light,*
*From Death, lead us to Immortality,*
*Aum, shanti, shanti, shanti!"*

Two pea-green souls split from their flesh and bone abodes and vanished through the ceiling by the end of the incantation.

That's when he heard a low, triumphant laugh followed by the scrape of heavy stone. He followed the sounds to a storage room below the shrine. As he wasn't blessed with night vision like the *asuras*, Karna used his phone's flashlight to take a quick peek inside.

A pair of *daityas* had ransacked the chamber. An antique armoire was split open, its sacred contents flung to the floor. One of the giant demons, gloating with pride, held a black-and-gold pouch.

Shoving his phone into his pocket, Karna raised his arms. Threads of white energy shot out of his fingers, lassoing the hoodlums together. They didn't know what hit them. One roared at the sudden constriction of movement while the other froze, grins and gloats lost to shock.

"Dev-Il take it," said ugly *daitya* bastard number one. "Busted."

"Nope. Dev-Il won't take it," Karna said, coming into view by reversing the invisibility spell.

They glared at him as if he'd popped one of their precious birthday balloons before the party started. Karna grinned and for kicks yanked the sizzling bands of electricity, making the demons grunt in discomfort. Swaggering up to the debilitated duo, he plucked the stolen object from the mean-looking *asura*'s paw.

"What the hell is this?"

Neither *daitya* answered the question. He hadn't expected confessions anyway. Karna jiggled the black-and-gold pouch filled with a substantial amount of powder. He sneezed explosively. Crap! It was *raakh*—most likely the temple deity's funeral ashes.

He tucked the pouch between his belt and back, far away from his sensitive nose—fug, he hated *raakh*—while he stared at the *daityas*, giving them the opportunity to be dumbasses and execute an escape. They didn't oblige. Sad that. He would've loved to get into a nasty, bone-crunching skirmish with them if only to avenge the pundits. Slaking his irritation with the situation back home would be a nice side benefit to the fight.

One of the demons cursed foully when he caught sight of the Soul Catcher and grasped who and what Karna was. He clawed at the air, flailing about.

Karna dodged the frantic attempts to take a swipe at his face, grabbed a chunk of the *daitya*'s thick white hair and neatly sliced the pitch-black throat open. "Adios non-amigos."

"You're making a mistake," said the last *daitya*, his face stoic. No theatrics for this one.

"I have what you stole, and I'm about to help you clean up your act by letting you fry in Hell...so no, it's not a mistake."

"Soul Warrior," the demon growled as his bloodred eyes began to glow. *Asura* eyes had no whites and no pupils; the entire pulpy eyeball gripped within black hairless eyelids was red. "Be warned. Kalika's ashes belong to Lord Master. Stealing them will not stop him. Vala shall rise again."

"Vala?" Karna said, and sneezed on the name. What was this? Shock the crap out of Karna day? There was no way the Vala he knew could rise again. He'd cursed the Stone Demon into oblivion a millions years ago—a curse that would have left the demon weak and insensate. He'd used *Manav-astra*, the spear of mankind, to slice Vala's head off and jettison it and the red soul attached to it into the Cosmos, never to return.

There was simply no way Karna hadn't been informed of any change in circumstance regarding Vala's stony head. The *daitya* was trying to get his goat, distract him with idle threats. That was all. Karna separated the *daitya*'s head from his body, snaring the last evil Red. He hoped last, as he couldn't sense any other evil ripples.

A one-word chant sealed shut the mystical portal of the Soul Catcher. Karna wiped *Asi* clean on his dark jeans, and flashed it back to the Celestial Forge for purification. The dagger was a gift from his godsire, commemorating Karna's first kill as the Soul Warrior. It had simply appeared on his palms one day during morning worship. Such was

Surya's way: silently guiding, quietly protective and, where praise was due, lavishly bestowing it. The Sun God might not have been a hands-on father, but, in his own way, he'd always been there for Karna.

Now that he had a daughter, Karna vowed to do the same. He couldn't help draw parallels between Yahvi and himself. They'd both come into existence through deceit. They'd both been raised in secret. But unlike him, Yahvi hadn't been cast away at birth in a flimsy basket to bob and weave for days across the four sacred rivers to find another family. No, she'd grown up suckling the bosom of that bloody woman without a father. Was he supposed to be grateful for that and ignore the rest? Ignore that Yahvi was cursed, like him?

The harbinger of doom, was she the reason Vala would return?

Cursing foully under his breath, Karna took stock of his messy self—his apparently messy self. Blood soaked his arms up to his biceps, but his T-shirt and jeans didn't look quite so vicious. Thank karma for black. It went superbly with blood. He pulled out his phone and dialed *Home*.

"Need a cleanup crew at the temple," he said.

"Dispatching," replied Lavya.

Karna hefted his revolting burdens and transported the dead *asuras* to the Hell Realm, making a brief pit stop at the temple doors to snatch the third body he'd left there.

Vala will rise again, the *daitya* had warned. He wondered what Yama would make of the grandiose resurrection plan. And what did it have to do with Goddess Kalika's stolen ashes?

Draupadi manifested in front of the Soul Warrior's abode with three large trunks, and her heart racing like a windstorm. She was finally here, mere moments away from reuniting with her babies.

She pressed her thumb to a sleek copper doorbell, buzzed it twice in quick succession. Then she took a deep, calming breath—which turned out to be a mistake as the thick fishy smell typical of coastlines immediately flooded her nose. She exhaled posthaste. The odorous Human Realm remained hideously true to form, she thought, disgusted. She'd never particularly liked coastal lands in her former life, either.

Male-dominated and war-torn, the Human Realm wasn't a happy place for females to dwell. She prayed her daughters had realized it, and had their fill in the two days they'd been here. Fate willing, she'd whisk her babies away to Alaka immediately and never set foot on this realm again. If the Gods and their cohorts thought to use Yahvi as some divine weapon in their never-ending battle for supremacy, they'd have to get through Draupadi first.

She rang the bell again, frowning at Karna's shockingly mundane dwelling of red-and-white stucco peeking out of a forest of mangroves. The abode's only saving grace was a pair of intricately carved doors the brownish-red color of a *rudraksha* bead. Beautifully rendered geometrical starbursts, the symbol of the solar deity, were carved on each panel.

Draupadi was careful not to touch the doors, as they would be charmed shut. The whole bungalow should be secured, so she banked the temptation to manifest inside the abode. She simply dared not. As impatient and excited as she was to see her girls, she wouldn't take a misstep with this—with *him*. The situation was bad enough without adding breaking and entering to her list of transgressions. She would talk to him—calmly—and if he had even an ounce of fatherly compassion in him, he'd understand her motivations for keeping their daughter a secret from him.

*Right! Hold that thought, darling, like a drowning woman clings to straw in a deluge.*

And why wasn't someone answering the door?

That was another thing that remained true to form on the Human Realm and its surrounding *loks*—the red tape involved in running it, and the tardiness with which things were handled. She'd already wasted fifteen hours in Lok Vitalas while the shape-shifter, Salabha, verified her status as a Celestial companion to Draupadi's daughters. This in spite of the glowing character references Goddess Saraswati and the *apsaras*—the helpful nymphs of Devlok, her friends—had given her. It shouldn't have taken Salabha this long to sanction her visit, as the claim wasn't completely false. Qalanderi was one of her legitimate adopted aliases, and one Karna was intimately acquainted with.

Abruptly, the doors flew open, taking Draupadi aback, and a jeans-clad Celestial—or was he a mortal man?—stood before her.

"Hello," he hailed her, watching her through wary eyes. He'd positioned himself across the threshold like a sentry, either barring her entry or protecting whoever was inside. Which made her feel instantly grateful. If the girls were inside, she wanted them protected. One thing was certain, though: He most definitely wasn't Karna. Not unless the son of Surya had downgraded his allure sometime in the last eighteen days—er, eighteen human years.

"Namaste. I was directed here by Salabha, and beg an audience with Lord Karna," she said, her smile stiff. She wiped nervous palms on her beige-colored slacks, and pressed them together in front of her perspiring chest. She didn't bow, as she had no idea whether the man's station was above or below hers, or if he was older or younger than she. Older soul, and not human, but not a true Celestial, either, if she had to guess.

"And you are?" He nodded in greeting instead of bowing. His eyes lit on the trunks piled on the portico behind her, and comprehension dawned before they returned to her face.

Before she could recite the introduction she'd carefully crafted in her head, music burst into existence from somewhere inside the abode. Had she needed proof whether she'd come to the right place, this would be it. With relief, she recognized the mad throbs of Amara's "chillaxing" ballad. That child of hers had the strangest habits and tastes. Evidently she wasn't the only one who thought the music outrageous. The man had winced when it blared on and was now muttering to himself.

"I'm Qalanderi. I've brought the luggage, as you see." A horrible sourness rose in her throat as she shouted over the music. While she wasn't telling an outright lie—she did go by the name sometimes—she was still piling up trouble like boulders on Mount Everest. The subterfuge couldn't be helped. For one, the Council had forbidden her to contact her daughters. For another, Karna had last known her as Qalanderi, and Goddess Saraswati and Apsara Vashi thought she should take advantage of that connection instead of antagonizing him. There was too much at stake and no time to waste on past grievances. *"One catches more flies with honey than vinegar,"* Vashi had counseled. So, here she was at her honeyed best.

"Qalanderi? You're Qalanderi? The *apsara* Karna met in Devlok?" The man's eyes and lips widened into matching Os of surprise.

That's right, darling. I'm the fake *apsara* Karna had his first-ever vacation with eighteen and a half Celestial days ago. It boggled her mind that in human terms that would be nearly two decades. Yahvi's eighteenth birthday was coming up. Her baby was no longer a baby.

Karna had spoken of her to this man? Fabulous! Draupadi's head started pounding for the first time since her Celestial rebirth.

"And you brought the luggage? From Devlok?"

She'd come from Devlok, but the trunks had been sent from Alaka, the golden Celestial city she and her daughters had called home since Satya's Celestial rebirth three hundred years ago. Kubera, the god-king of the shape-shifters and the ruler of Alaka, had been a true friend to her through her trials.

Ignoring the man's incredulous expression, Draupadi pulled out the validation ticket Salabha had given her.

He stared at it for a few gut-twisting seconds, then drew back from the door to allow her in. "Amazing to just show up on our doorstep after all this time. I'm sure Karna will be stunned speechless."

Panic swelled like a tidal wave in Draupadi's belly when she stepped inside the abode. The walls throbbed with Amara's Beats Per Minute music, which only compounded the galloping speed of her heart. When she didn't burst into flames or turn to stone, she forced herself to breathe. Karna hadn't put a hex on her. Maybe he hadn't taken the news of his daughter too badly.

"May I speak with him?" Better to face him first and get it over with before she strangled herself with nerves.

The man continued to stare at her as if she was the final act in one of Lord Indra's notorious revelries.

Draupadi raised her eyebrows and looked him over as carefully as he was looking at her. He was tall, a few inches taller than her, and lanky, with tightly roped muscles like a yogi. He had modest looks: a high forehead and a slightly hooked nose.

His face seemed familiar, but she couldn't recall where she might've met him. It was entirely possible they'd crossed paths somewhere. She'd travelled extensively during the current epoch, for pleasure first, and now her lifestyle consulting work took her all over the Higher Worlds and some of the *loks*.

"I'm Eklavya, Karna's man of affairs," he shouted over the music, and strode out the door, making quick work of dragging the trunks inside.

*Eklavya?* Draupadi didn't know how she managed it, but she forced her expression into neutrality. She surreptitiously eyed Eklavya's right hand with its intact thumb as he paraded in and out of the abode. Arjun's old archery rival? *That* Eklavya? She couldn't believe how quickly things were going from bad to worse. Actually, she could believe it. She'd never been particularly lucky in the Human Realm. Why hadn't her daughters informed her that Karna and Eklavya worked together?

Arjun, her husband number three, had cost Eklavya his thumb. Draupadi hadn't been Arjun's wife at the time, but who remembered such details when vengeance was meted out? She had a crazy vision of him skewering her eye with his new thumb and scrambling her brains about. Sweet shiny Heaven! Was fate giving Eklavya a chance to even scores? Would he try to hurt Amara to get even with her father?

After stacking the luggage against a wall tiled in gold-hued marble slabs, he led her down a hallway. She followed robotically. Overhead, tiny crystal chandeliers lined the ceiling, and shivered with the pounding beats of the music. A plethora of ancient *astras* and shields decorated the marbled walls of the hallway. Among the savagery, arched niches housed sensuous metal figurines flanked by ancient-looking candelabras. The living room was the same, a monochromatic mishmash of stone and metal.

The abode was a man cave. She'd expected no less. Draupadi pursed her lips, eyeing the concrete seating arrangement. Granted, the settee was aesthetically lovely—a solid grey bench inlaid with a mosaic of semiprecious gemstones. And some considerate soul had tried to soften its toughness with pillows and deerskins. But still. What was it with warriors and their fondness for hard places?

Still stunned by Eklavya's presence, she sat down as far away from him as politely possible. She'd truly made the right decision not to trust the Council's ruling.

"Forgive my bluntness, but you're not like any *apsara* I've met. I mean…not that you're not attractive. You are…incredibly beautiful," he said, staring at her again.

"The prerequisites of attraction are more assorted than you deem, Eklavya. Some souls desire angles over curves, a touch of the exotic instead of classic beauty." Draupadi infused her expression with the scent of flirtation. She'd have to play her part to perfection. Yahvi's fate depended on it. And while her own fate didn't concern her much these days, she didn't want to get Saraswati and Vashi in trouble for helping her escape from Devlok and covering for her. She had to pull off the subterfuge until they found a way around Kalika's prophecy. She tilted her head, smiling like a coquette. "What about you? How do you like your women?"

Eklavya refused to take the bait and flirt back. Draupadi's estimation of him went up a notch. "Tea? Coffee? We stock the Celestial elixirs too—if you're weak from travel."

Celestials, especially the Earth-dwellers, needed a glass or two of the sometimes sweet, sometimes tart *soma* juice every day to sustain and energize their physical forms, and the honey-textured *amrita* to heal when the body got injured or ill. *Amrita* could be either applied topically on wounds or imbibed in various forms.

"No, thank you. I had some before I left." Draupadi swished her hand in the air, indicating the Higher Worlds. "And a delicious glass of *soma* strawberry smoothie in Lok Vitalas. I'm fine for now."

An awkward silence yawned between them, and Draupadi lost her patience for pleasantries. She couldn't wait for some ridiculous permission. She had to see her girls now.

"How did our trunks get here, Lavya? Who brought…" A glorious screech drowned out the rest of Yahvi's words. "I knew it, knew it, knew you'd come!"

Draupadi shot up from the settee and whirled about, catching Yahvi in a tight hug as her daughter hurled herself into her arms. All her daughters rushed to her. Oh! She'd missed them.

With a collective "Aw!" her girls surrounded her with their familiar precious bodies, even Amara who was the least mushy of her offspring.

They'd missed her, too. She'd been so afraid they wouldn't. She suppressed a smile when Amara and Yahvi pulled Eklavya into the group hug. He looked as if he'd been attacked by a group of banshees. Appalled, he tried to detach himself and failed.

Her babies! They were safe, together and mischievous as ever. That's all that mattered. She had to make sure it stayed that way.

Draupadi met Eklavya's eyes over Yahvi's head. "I really need to speak to Karna. Now."

# CHAPTER SEVEN

## RTA: COSMIC ORDER

It was just another ordinary day in Hell.

Not that the days and nights had clear demarcations on the realm, what with the star-suns and satellite-moons steering clear of Hell's skyline so as not to get drawn into its fiery vortex. But as was his inclination on most realms, Karna followed human time-keeping there.

He dumped the three carcasses in the middle of a humungous lobby and looked about for Doota, Lord Yama's right hand and Chief Enforcer of Soul Judgments. As ever, it was impossible to spot him in the mayhem. But Doota would know of his arrival. No soul arrived in Hell without alerting Doota.

Hell's lobby resembled the check-in terminal at Mumbai's International Airport with its rows of counters, each one catering to different types and classes of dead beings. The only difference between the two spaces was that this one had a predominantly black décor and was rigged with colorful disco lights. That added to the general feeling of confusion as the vibrant strings of bulbs crisscrossing the ceiling of the great room and the bobbing, boisterous souls, most without bodies, looked exactly alike.

There were several long queues of incoming souls of varied colors who'd died naturally and descended into Hell without fanfare. They were checked in by Yama's minions, sentenced and then taken to their karmic just deserts in the penance zones. A smaller single line of outgoing souls ran along the far side of the hall. Not so long ago, the outgoing and incoming queues had looked the exact opposite. There was no point in reiterating, "It is Kali Yuga" over and over again. It was a nasty age and would remain such until Dev-Il Kali surrendered or was vanquished forever. The Cosmos would just have to suck it up.

Karna fingered the hot Soul Catcher as he waited his turn. Doota had to oversee his bounty personally. The *asuras* Karna captured warranted special attention and treatment. Their actions would be microscopically scrutinized, the cadavers frisked and then incinerated. Karna could have disposed of the bodies at the temple. Immolating them with god-power was a cleaner, less messy way of dealing with *asuras* than stabbing them dead. Not to mention, he'd had to carry them across two realms. But of late, he was taking extra care not to spread inadvertent radiation in the Human Realm. As much as possible, he tried not to add to the damaging greenhouse effects of climate change Earth already suffered from.

"My lord! Ooh, hey, my Lord Karna, long time no see," a voice droned over his head.

Karna stared at the well-camouflaged red soul of the half man, half bat swinging upside down from one of the red ruby chandeliers in the great room. The creature was indigo blue on his top humanlike half and black from waist to bat-feet. He weighed, at a guess, a ton.

"That's a dangerous place to swing, Baital." Karna braced himself to jump out of the way in case the contraption decided to ditch the extra weight. What the hell was the *pisacha*—a blood-drinking, soul-sucking shape-shifter—doing outside his atonement cell?

"Alas, Lord Death forbade me to swing from my favorite spot on top of the Nether Gates. He rudely said I was not an auspicious door garland," said Baital, drawing his fangs over his blue-black lower lip in a weird inverted pout. He plunged a little lower, sniffing at Karna, probably attracted by the scent of demon blood.

"Watch out!" Karna wondered if he should help the *pisacha* or save the damn chandelier that shivered and groaned with every sway. "If that thing gives way, you'll be plastered to the floor. I know how much you'll hate that. Come away."

Baital had a terra firma phobia. He hadn't stepped foot on any ground—charnel or otherwise—as far as Karna knew. Forget feet—he hadn't touched a single part of his body, including his overlong black hair, to the ground. He swung from objects or hovered about or was carried piggyback to his destination. The shape-shifter couldn't use the power of vanishment in the Realm of the Dead—souls could disappear and manifest to and from the main lobby only, and only with proper authorization.

"You're beneath me, my lord," said the *pisacha*. "You would cushion my fall."

Baital was in Hell to atone for some very bad deeds. He'd slurped the life-blood out of countless humans and nonhumans—he wasn't very discriminating—and to add insult to injury, he'd conned his victims out of kingdom, house and fortune.

"I am not beneath you and I'm not responsible for your downfall," said Karna, minding his words. He didn't want to make any statements the unconscionable trickster could twist and misuse for personal gain. Baital might've surrendered his soul and subjugated it to a thousand years of penance, but the time served had hardly put a dent in its bright red color.

Before Baital could engage Karna in a verbal swindle, Doota appeared. The wiry man was clad in a black muslin loincloth, and Karna was tempted to adopt the cooler look suited to Hell's sizzling atmosphere. As it was, his own clothes felt as if they'd been branded into his skin.

"Just in time," said Karna, jerking his chin to the ceiling.

Doota shook his head at Baital. The movements made the shiny black ringlets of his hair bounce merrily against his maroonish face. Doota had dwelled in Hell long enough to have his epidermis permanently scorched. With his help, Karna carried the *asuras* to the sectioned-off loading zone and dumped the bodies on a broad conveyor belt that ran straight to the Everlasting Hell Pyres via a series of X-ray machines. A full-body MRI would catch any nefarious objects imbedded in the bodies. But it wasn't his problem anymore.

Karna unlocked the Soul Catcher and released the red souls onto a lodestone Petri dish. The transgressions of the prisoners were entered into a mantra-controlled supercomputer—technology was a blessing even in Hell—weighed and judged by a program expressly developed for Yama, and condemned appropriately.

The *asuras* got three years each in the second-tier dungeons. It was a light sentence, and Karna wondered if there was any truth to the *asura*'s claim about the legitimacy of the mission. *Shit!* Kalika had been known as a demon-goddess in one or two of her past incarnations. Was she still doling out favors to her *asura* devotees on the sly? Had she doled one out to Vala?

"I need to speak to Yama," said Karna, signing the soul-release forms that Doota pulled up on the minitablet.

Doota tilted his head toward the gates that lead to the palace's inner domain, indicating the God was in residence. Doota was mute by choice. He'd taken a vow of silence when he'd accepted this position so he wouldn't be tempted to engage in fruitless arguments with the atoners. *"Arguments lead to taking sides and having opinions, and what if my opinion differs from the Soul Judgment program? What then?* he'd once expressed to Karna. Doota was the most nonjudgmental soul Karna knew, besides Lord Yama.

"You need to hear this too," said Karna. Doota's hands flew in silent communication that Karna should go ahead and he'd follow in a bit. Karna started toward the palace gates.

"Lorrrd Karrrrnaaaa," Baital sang in an annoying singsong manner above him. "Do you want to hear a strange story about Lord Tvastar?"

"I'm not here to gossip, Baital." Karna increased the length of his strides, trying to outrun the flying *pisacha*.

"Okay, no gossiping. Don't you want to know what Lord Tvastar did?" Baital hovered close, sniffing and snorting alternately.

"No. I don't want to know." Karna navigated the lobby fast but with caution, not wanting to bump and merge with a bodiless soul. Crazy things happened when multiple souls inhabited the same body. Plus, the alien soul never left the possessed without a down and dirty fight.

A loud whoop followed by a bloodcurdling screech made Karna whip about to see what the problem was. The crazy *pisacha* was sucking up souls from his puckered mouth and shitting them out through the folds of his orange-red loincloth.

"What is wrong with you, Baital?" Karna was going to give Yama a piece of his mind. What had possessed the God to let a mischief-maker roam free and in corporeal form?

"I'm on Hell's welcoming committee, my lord," said Baital gleefully. "As mascot, I'm helping the new souls feel at home."

Karna groaned. Yama needed a refresher course on the consequences of bad judgment and lax regulations. "Come along, Baital. Better you come with me than terrorize the newbies."

A long trek through a maze of searing lava stone corridors brought them to Yama's personal wing within the Palace Kalichi. Karna recalled the first time he'd traversed these corridors, forty years after he'd become the Soul Warrior. He'd let a female demon escape because she'd been with child. The fiery temperatures of Hell are insufferable when one is marching toward one's own sentencing. Fifty thousand lashes had been the price he'd paid for dereliction of duty, and ten thousand more for feeling compassion for the undeserving. He hadn't been able to walk out on his own steam that first time. He'd walked these corridors many times since.

Karna hoped the demon and her child had led a worthwhile life.

Chitra, Lord Yama's receptionist, sat behind a sleek U-shaped reception desk, filing her claws.

"I beg an audience with Yama." Karna hunkered down to pet the two black hounds that'd leapt up to greet him. He rubbed below Syama's ears with both hands as Sabala sniffed at his bloody clothes and howled. "I know, I know," he crooned at the hellhounds. "I do smell of *asura*. But I won the fight. Yes, I did. I slashed the Reds to bits and didn't even break a sweat."

"Lord Yama is at home, Lord Karna," said Chitra when he straightened. She flashed him a smile, giving him a tiny glimpse of two sharp but utterly useless fangs.

Chitra was a *daitya* demon with a blue soul. Upon her natural death, she balanced her karma as per Lord Yama's explicit instructions and her soul changed colors. And since Chitra and Yama's wife had struck up a close friendship, Yama offered Chitra a job so she could continue dwelling in Hell even after her soul's evolution.

Karna had a healthy respect for Chitra's strength of character. Plus, her very visible work position advertised the intrinsically fluid nature of a soul—a smart move on Yama's part to broadcast the fact that a soul could indeed be redeemed. And wasn't that what Hell was all about— atonement, redemption and second chances?

He thanked Chitra and waited for the gates to Yama's living quarters to open. The gates to the Great Courtroom were to the left.

"Why is he here?" Chitra stared at the hovering demon. Baital winked at the stupefied female.

"He's with me," said Karna and froze when Baital chuckled in a sinister fashion.

Shit! Twice now he'd intimated that Baital was "with him." Could Baital use that against him? Karna let out a low groan. He'd worry about that later. "Keep an eye on him, Chitra. Behave, *pisacha*. I won't be long."

Yama had swapped the Elvis getup for a soccer jersey in support of his favorite team. He lounged on a cushy couch the shape, color and texture of a water buffalo, watching a sports channel with his chief consort, Goddess Yami, ensconced by his side. She too was rigged out in a team Man-U outfit.

Karna made straight for the couch and bowed. "My lord and my lady, if you can spare a moment." He pulled out the pouch that was tucked into the small of his back, and tossed it to Yama, who caught it one-handed.

"*Raakh*," said Karna unnecessarily as Yama opened the pouch and peered inside. "Goddess Kalika's remains, presumably. Three *daityas*—of the mean, keen, bloodthirsty variety—stole it from the Kalighat temple. Tell me those ashes don't possess special powers."

Lady Yami barely acknowledged Karna and, with a distracted smile, raised the TV volume to deafening levels. She was engrossed in the football game and not the least worried about ash-stealing demons. Yama and Karna moved to a quieter area of the windowless chamber.

"The Kalighat temple is one of Kalika's major shrines. Her Satya Yuga, Age of Truth, incarnation died a bloody, gruesome death. Her ascetic father went ballistic over her affair and then marriage to Bhairav, one of Shiva's incarnations. The foolish man invoked an army of primordial *danu* demons through a ritual fire sacrifice and ordered them to chop up his disobedient daughter into four parts: the head, chest, womb and limbs. Each part was cremated separately in four separate locations. Over time, the humans built temples on the sites. The ashes of her head were buried at Kalighat. About their potency, I would assume they'd hold some minimal god-power. Kalika did not go down easily. She drank the blood from a million *asuras* before Bhairav managed to stop the mindless massacre by killing her."

And now *asuras* were after those ashes. *Fugdoomal.* "Assuming we have the head, Vala will go for the chest, womb and limbs next, if he hasn't already."

"Eh? Who's Vala? Vala, the Stone Demon?" asked Yama, his expression souring at the complication interrupting his enjoyment of the soccer final.

"The Red I captured tonight claimed that Lord Master Vala is about to rise again. And that he can't be stopped, and the *raakh* belongs to him. I don't know if he meant Vala, the Stone Demon. I didn't ask for further clarification. I'm just the demon hunter. It's your and Indra's job to find out what the fug the demons are up to."

Indra, god-king of the Celestials and the God of War and Thunder, was Karna's occasional boss and paternal uncle. Indra was also Arjun's godsire and Amara's grandsire. Oh yeah, cosmic relationships were absurdly convoluted, and incestuous as hell.

"Believe me, I'll get to the bottom of it." Yama cracked his knuckles and bared his teeth in anticipation of an interrogation.

Karna jerked his head from side to side, popping a few tense joints of his own. "Let me know as soon as you find out. Lavya can monitor the other temples just in case the ashes from those sites haven't been lifted yet. If my lord would tell me where they are, it would save precious time..."

Two things happened together that drowned out the rest of Karna's words: Man-U scored a goal, and the gates of Yama's living quarters flew open, admitting pandemonium. The excitable barks of the hellhounds overrode the commotion of the football game. Doota rushed in, grappling to close the massive iron gates behind him. He wasn't quick enough. Baital flew in high and fast and draped his huge blue-black body over the speckled mantel above the fire pit at the head of the chamber. The hounds scampered behind him, thinking it a fun game of catch-me-if-you-can.

"Hey! I dig the eclectic décor, Yams," said Baital, giving Yama and Yami a thumbs-up. "So different from the doom and gloom of the Middle Ages when I last visited."

Karna stabbed a finger in Baital's direction. "I'm having serious doubts about your judgment, my lord, letting him wander about like this."

Yama had the grace to look sheepish. "He tricked me into a Hell hall pass. I couldn't resist solving the riddle to one of his complex stories. I know, I know. I should know better."

Pride comes before the crash and burn. The slippery truth was how Baital tricked his victims into losing bets. You'd think giving the correct answer would be a good thing. With Baital, if you exercised your superior intellect and solved his riddle, you lost.

"It was an outstanding tale about Lord Tvastar," said Baital. "You ought to hear it, Lord Karna."

Ignoring Baital and the returning twitch in his nose, Karna held the pouch out to Doota. "Guard this with your life."

"Don't leave that here," Yama gasped. "It's the Hell Realm. There are a couple of billion souls residing underground. A good chunk of them are red, some with access to any and all corners of the realm. The *raakh* will be safer with you."

Karna looked up at the ebony stone ceiling and through the circular central skylight to the fiery red-black sky peeking through. Would this day ever end? His job description had expanded beyond recognition in the last twenty-four hours. He shoved the pouch into his back pocket with some difficulty.

"Ooh! What is that?" Baital began his creepy sniffling again. He floated away as Doota tried to grab him. "Wait! Wait, my lords. I know what that is. It's Goddess Kalika's head."

Every soul in the room froze. Even the hounds played dead.

"What do you know about this affair, *pisacha*?" Yama boomed.

Karna stared at Baital, replaying his time in Hell. It wasn't coincidence that had put Baital in the right place at the right time, sniffing the right things. Summoning *Asi*, Karna grabbed the airborne demon's hair, yanked hard and pressed the tip of the divine blade to his blue throat. "Start yakking. Now." To press home the threat he nicked the *pisacha*, drawing a drop of gooey blood.

Baital yelped. "Careful with the pointy thing. I'll bleed. And if I bleed, I'll need blood."

Karna eased up a tad but didn't release his hold. "Are you in cahoots with Dev-Il, Baital?"

Demon Kali had started calling himself Dev-Il a thousand years ago. If anyone had pulled strings for Vala's return, it was Dev-Il.

Baital looked scandalized at the accusation. "I am not stupid, my Lord Karna. No one cozies up with D' Evil One and comes out with all faculties intact."

That was news. Even *pisachas* didn't want to deal with Dev-Il anymore.

"What do you know, Baital?" asked Karna.

Baital emulated a yogi in a mountain pose. Awkward, as his hair was still wrapped around Karna's fist. He deepened his already low-pitched voice and droned austerely, "He, O Kalika, who in the necropolis, naked and with disheveled hair, intently meditates upon Thee and recites Thy mantra, and with each recitation makes an offering to Thee of a thousand-seeded Akanda flower, will become the Lord of Earth."

"What does that mean?" It sounded like a divine prophecy of some sort.

"Nothing comes for free, my lords," said Baital with the sly grin of a veteran extortionist. "I will answer your questions if you agree to compensate me."

"Go to Hell." Karna pushed the *pisacha* away.

"Already here," said Baital. "Tick-tock, tick-tock. Time's a-wasting, my lords. My cooperation has an expiration date. Oh! Soccer finals. What is the score, Lady Yami?" He flew off to the sofas.

Giving his victims privacy to discuss how many pounds of flesh and whose, thought Karna sourly. He stared at Yama for a few charged moments. "I'm not involved in any boon gifting business. It's up to you. Do you really believe we can trust the word of a *pisacha*?"

Yama shrugged. "I'll find out what I can from the *daityas* you captured first. I'll have Doota contact Kalika's current incarnation, though I doubt she'll answer. No one has seen or spoken to her in a while. If all fails, then we negotiate terms with Baital."

With three hundred thirty million deities and ten times as many Celestials sharing the Higher Worlds, keeping track of everyone was difficult. Figure in the rebirths or reincarnations and the temporary avatars the souls adopted for specific purposes, and confusion was a given. Goddess Kalika was known for her nomadic ways, forever appearing in new avatars and searching for newer realms to rule, so it was hardly surprising that no one had seen her of late.

"Sounds good." A small sneeze made it out of Karna's nose before he could pinch it closed. "So, the whole deal with the Triumvirate is starting to make sense. The *asuras* are cooking something again. Is that why they've sent the females to me? Damage control?"

"No clue. I'm usually the last one to be informed about what goes on up there. I didn't even know you had a daughter with Draupadi until yesterday." Lord Yama poked an elbow into Karna's ribs. "You sly dog, doing the down and dirty with my favorite daughter-in-law. And here the Cosmos writes ballads about how much you hate her."

Karna snorted. "I didn't do anything with her, dirty or otherwise." Not even back then, when he could've taken advantage of her innocence and ruined her. Crap! Don't dwell on that.

"Really? That's not how a human soul…" Yama clamped his mouth shut and squinted thoughtfully. "What do *you* think happened? How came you to sire her offspring?"

"The crazy female bamboozled Ma Aditi into bestowing the children on her." He clucked his tongue. "Haven't I always said divine boons are more curse than gift?" That gave him pause. Were all the godlings cursed, not just his daughter? "Am I a wimp for getting heart palpitations at the thought of another cataclysm?"

Yama let out a less-than-happy growl. Earth-shattering change affected Hell as well.

"You know what's scarier, my lord?" Karna said, jadedly. "That the Gods think a bunch of green—pun intended—godlings will save the day."

"And you, brother. And you," rumbled the God of Death.

Karna stashed the pouch of Kalika's *raakh* in the IMS super-platinum safe inside the iron-walled armory of his abode, and on a horrific sneeze, shut its door. Screwing in the five-point handle, he placed his right palm flat on the safe and began invoking a complicated binding mantra. Bands of electricity seeped from his palm, weaving a fine net around the metal chamber. The web glittered brilliantly before it poofed at the end of the incantation. The safe was now airtight and sealed, and only his fresh blood could counter the spell.

Groaning, Karna stretched his tense back and shoulders, but the movement was arrested when his nose exploded again. He'd sneezed so many times since confiscating the *raakh* that his respiratory passages felt as raw and bruised as a warrior's in the aftermath of war. Probably looked as nasty as a battleground too. It amazed him that not one soul in all this time had come up with a spell to get rid of ash allergy. The Celestial Healer Lord Dhanvantari's brilliant advice to Karna's peculiar work hazard was, "If you know you're allergic, stay away from it."

He would, and gladly, if the Cosmos let him. Karna stepped out of the armory and into the gym, both of which were attached to his own private chambers. He closed the iron door and keyed in the locks. Then, foregoing a bath or even a change of clothes, he vanished into the den to speak to Lavya.

The den was as soulless and silent as the cemetery in Kolkatta.

Karna frowned at his aide's unoccupied ergonomic chair. Where was Lavya? He looked past the open doors of the den. The abode was quiet, a little too quiet. Seemed the lot was out, including his daughter. Irritated by the instant fear that had snaked into his belly at the thought of her, he pulled out his phone to text Lavya and caught sight of the text Lavya had sent an hour ago. They were out for a stroll along the beach. Damn it. Why had Lavya defied his instructions to keep the Delinquent Six—especially Yahvi—within the walls of the abode?

Karna eyed Baby humming on the desk, faithfully undertaking whatever tasks Lavya had programmed her to do. The list needed to be updated to include a search for Vala's nasty red soul zinging through the Cosmos in a skull-shaped rock, details of Kalika's incarnations and her ashes, Baital's life story and a zillion other things. Karna debated whether to fiddle with the computer himself or wait for Lavya, whose relationship with the cyber realm was stronger and considerably more fruitful than his own.

Giving Baby a grimace of pure disgust, he poured himself a much-needed goblet of *soma*, guzzling it down in two gulps. Hmm. The vitality drink had been prepared with tomato juice today. Tasted good. He poured himself a second glass. He was tired and filthy; his clothes were bloody, sooty and snotty. He smelled foul. He needed a shower and copious amounts of food. He was famished. He hadn't eaten anything since dinner last night. Well, dehydration down and the rest to go. The battle with Baby could wait ten minutes. He was tempted to lock the females up in the armory until he figured out what in heck was going on. He should up the security around the island, especially along the beach and boathouse.

Karna walked out of the den. The sneezes had stopped. Or would eventually stop, he corrected himself, feeling a tickle run up his nose. He pinched it into oblivion. It was late in the day and wisps of twilight streamed in from the open windows, giving him a small boost of power. He paused to absorb some more of the sun's light, insta-healing the minor scratches on his skin and bruised knuckles. Once he had a plan of action for the Six, maybe he'd have some time to crash for a couple of hours, reenergize before heading out for his nightly patrol. He intended to hit every *asura* hotspot in the seven *loks*, find out what plans were being hatched and by whom, and quash them in infancy.

Karna strode past the kitchen and stopped dead. He sniffed and got a whiff of the scent of jasmine and cinnamon lingering in the air. Even as he thought it couldn't be, he was sure it was Qalli's scent. He'd never forget it. And that's twice in as many days he'd felt her presence close by. Hunger was making him hallucinate.

He walked into the living room. Colorful scarves lay over the backs of the concrete settees. Shoes and feminine paraphernalia lay helter-skelter. The abode looked lived in, he thought with satisfaction. That's it. Being near the females had unhinged him. Was he actually glad he'd come home to this?

Karna frowned at the new jewel-toned cushions lining the concrete settees. His senses picked up traces of the females, and Lavya and... Holy crap! There was Qalli's scent again.

Vala's metallic black soul appraised Earth like a lord would his mistress just before he took possession of her. She waited like a lover to be claimed. Waited for him to finish what he'd started so long ago.

The Gods had abandoned her. The *asuras* neglected her. But he would not.

This time, he would be her master.

# CHAPTER EIGHT
## ASATYA: UNTRUE AND UNLAWFUL

A longish boardwalk ran from Karna's modest abode all the way down to the docks on the west bank of Asht Dveep. The path cut through thickets of mangroves in a zigzag pattern, marked every few feet by sturdy, old-fashioned lampposts. The lamps ran on sensors, magically lighting when Amara and Lusha rushed past. It wasn't night yet, though the sun was only half visible over the horizon. Gauging by the soft pink and blue sky smudged with grey-blue clouds, Draupadi estimated that darkness would fall within the hour.

And Karna wasn't back from Hell.

"He leaves you unprotected at night? This is unacceptable," said Draupadi. "Some guardian he's turning out to be."

Satya gave her a one-armed hug and pointed to the male walking ahead flanked by Yahvi and Ziva. "He's not left us unprotected. There's Lavya, and his electronic and magical security systems are top of the line. Plus, we're not exactly helpless, are we?"

"I wish you'd listen and come away with me." Draupadi looked at her eldest daughter, her most sensible child, who hadn't been very sensible of late. "There's nothing any of you need to prove." But her words fell on deaf ears. Satya's attention was on her sisters.

The heat on the island was unbearable, the salty air unbreathable, and the worry she felt was untenable. The only saving grace in this terrible situation was the girls. She'd never tire of watching their antics and hearing them bicker and laugh with each other and with her.

Up ahead, Amara leaped into the air and swatted an overhanging branch that swayed in the breeze, causing a rankled owl to hoot out of the trees. She landed in a crouch and looked over her shoulder, eyes gleaming with mischief. Lusha grinned, ran and leapfrogged over Amara, landing in a squat ahead of her sister. They did that until the next bend of the boardwalk. Those two needed to let off steam on an hourly basis. If they didn't, people around them paid for it with headaches—they got that grouchy.

Karna had ordered the girls not to venture beyond the walls of the abode alone—a rule Draupadi was in full favor of. But keeping six excitable young females cooped up in a small space had proved too much for Eklavya. He'd allowed the girls to roam the island, if chaperoned by him, but ignored their demands to experience Mumbai City in all its overpopulated glory. They'd spent the past hour at the beach, the girls cavorting in the water, and were now making their way back to the abode. Yahvi had just asked Lavya how he'd come to be Karna's aide.

Draupadi was a bit curious about it too. As far as she'd understood, the Soul Warrior worked alone and dwelled alone. Karna had never once mentioned an aide during their brief affair in Devlok. Of course, talking hadn't been exactly a priority for either one of them.

Eklavya waved at the trees. "We met right here. Around seven centuries ago."

"In the trees?" asked Ziva, clearly delighted.

Ziva was a nature lover. True to her spirit, she sparkled like a water sprite in the aqua summer dress she'd slipped over her swimsuit. Unlike her sisters, Ziva was completely dry from the swim, because like her father, Nakula, she was able to control the element of water to affect her or not affect her as she wished.

Amara and Lusha had stopped horsing around, and milled around Eklavya as if drawn by the story, too.

"Let me guess. You smashed into each other while trying to smoke out the *asuras* hiding in the forest," said Amara, banging her fists together in demonstration. She'd changed into a tank top and shorts after dinner. The Joysticks—a pair of matching swords Arjun had gifted Amara on her sixteenth birthday—hung from their sheaths on her hips. Angry little welts covered her midriff and bare limbs. Typically, Amara had ignored all motherly and sisterly advice with regard to using insect-repelling charms and salves.

Every realm had its pests. Heaven's forests were inundated with wood sprites and water nymphs that cast bothersome spells on travelers, while earthly mangroves swarmed with mosquitos that bit and drew blood.

"Not quite. The hunt brought Karna to the brothel where the *asura* had taken refuge."

Draupadi's jaw dropped open. It was obvious Lavya had meant the revelation to have impact. Shock reverberated through the foliage as the girls inundated him with questions.

"Holy crap, Lavya. Do you mean the abode was a brothel? And one you frequented?" Lusha snorted with glee.

Draupadi wondered if Karna had frequented it too. She wouldn't be surprised. She'd met Karna inside the heavenly version of a brothel, after all.

"Apparently, brothels are a great place to strike up friendships," Amara said, reading Draupadi's mind. It was an obvious a dig, but meant for whom—Karna, Lavya or Draupadi?

What was it about warriors and brothels? wondered Draupadi, trying hard not to judge Karna for his life choices. She hardly had a moral platform to stand on, did she?

It didn't matter that she'd been in the Pleasure Palace on business. She'd been hired by the *apsaras* to modernize their antiquated rose-quartz abode with the latest trends in technology and an art deco theme. As a special thank you for a job done fast and superbly, the *apsaras* had immersed Draupadi in an evening of frills and frolic in their private outdoor spa—the type of decadence only nymphs enjoyed.

She'd been so happy and relaxed that evening. Her five daughters had grown into beautiful, cultured young Celestials. Her own career flourished. Celestials from all corners of Heaven begged for her services as a personal lifestyle expert and coach, consulting with her on everything from designing homes and gardens to existential issues. Life could not be sweeter, she'd thought, swinging from a swing made of blue lotus shoots and bougainvillea vines.

But it had become sweeter when a dashing warrior-soul had walked into the woodlands, and into her life. His steps had fallen in perfect rhythm with the music strumming through the air. That he strode purposefully, as opposed to gliding or floating as the populace of the Celestial realms tended to do, had impressed her. She'd thought it odd that he violated the feminine sanctum. All souls were welcome inside the Pleasure Palace, but no male, to her knowledge, had ever been allowed into the private glade behind.

Tall and brawny, his shoulders had stretched the cotton jacket he wore over a starched white shirt and a lopsided tie. The large iron-and-gold buckle on his belt, twinkling in the star-sunlight, had drawn her gaze to his taut stomach and lean hips. He was barefoot. She'd wondered why he obeyed the "no shoes in Paradise" rule while clearly snubbing the others. He carried a plastic bag in his hand. As he came closer, Draupadi had caught her first clear glimpse of his face.

A wholly unexpected physical reaction overcame her. She'd felt short of breath, somewhat lightheaded, and she recalled squashing down a ridiculous urge to giggle. She'd frozen on the swing, barely moving, just a slight rocking motion of momentum.

He wasn't just fine-looking. He'd dazzled her, all golden-haired and sun-kissed skin, just like the *apsaras*.

"Hello, sweethearts," he greeted the trio of *apsaras* while staring straight at her.

Draupadi's heart began to skip down the hillside.

The deep timbre of his voice sent shivers up and down her spine. His eyes left hers for a moment as he hugged and kissed her friends. Then his liquid-gold gaze snared her eyes again, and Draupadi thought she'd float straightaway into space.

Instead, her bubbly fantasies popped like champagne gone flat when Tilo squealed, "Karna! I was wondering if you'd come."

*Karna?* He was *the* Karna? The babe Mother Kunti had abandoned because she'd birthed him out of wedlock? The man the Cosmos thought she'd insulted? Oh! He couldn't be. Had he looked this good when they'd known each other before?

Draupadi stared at the noble face, the broad laughing mouth and the cleft winking beneath it. She honestly hadn't recognized him. Besides, that Karna had died in the Great War and his corpse cremated, she'd reasoned. Clearly, this was the son of Surya's Celestial avatar.

The physical form a soul took depended on how, where and by whom the soul was incarnated. Draupadi herself had emerged from a ritual fire and had neither a birth mother nor a father to emulate, and as such had no fixed form. Or rather, she had an assortment of forms she'd learned to manifest under the tutelage of the Goddess of Illusion.

Draupadi made good use of her knowledge in her business, often altering her looks to show a client that a bit of variety was good for the soul. She liked matching her looks to her whims, making small changes to body shape, number of limbs, hairstyles, features, skin color. She experimented with every part of her body except her eyes. She never changed her eyes—the one feature all five of her husbands, and assorted admirers, had unanimously adored. She was renowned for her lotus-petal-shaped eyes.

She'd studied the gorgeous new Karna and tried to recall the old one. Her memories of him, her feelings for him, had always been a study in contradiction. She'd insulted him, then done her utmost to flirt with him. She'd angered him by ignoring him, but begged him to meet her in secret. She'd loved him. And hated him. He'd been arrogant and stiff and anal in his mortal life. And an absolute monster to her, once she'd inadvertently bruised his ego.

He'd been her family's blood enemy during the turbulent times of the Kuru War. She wondered if her husbands had ever realized that he was her one regret.

Karna gave the plastic bag to the *apsaras*. "Here you go. Videocassettes, as requested, of the latest Bollywood blockbusters: *Khalnayak, Darr, Baazigar*. I've added *Jurassic Park*, a Hollywood flick. And my personal favorite: *Mrs. Doubtfire*. It's a film about a man who won't let stupid laws or fate destroy his family."

Vashi oohed and bunny-hopped in place. "You're a darling for bringing these on such short notice. Want to watch one with us? Can you stay awhile? Qalanderi loves watching films too. You'll stay, won't you?"

Draupadi wanted to kiss Vashi for calling her Qalanderi and not Draupadi, as the divine woodland was no place for a blood bath. Her heart in her throat, she slid off the swing and onto her feet. She should excuse herself from his presence. Leave. Now. Before he realized who she was and left the Pleasure Palace himself. He'd walked away from her once before. It was her turn to walk away from him, exact revenge. But her feet hadn't moved.

"Hello." Karna inclined his head formally. Two rows of neat white buds gleamed at her when he smiled. Beautiful. He was just too beautiful.

The urge to giggle came back with twice the force.

"Hi." Draupadi clasped her hands behind her back and dug her nails into her skin. Her deprived libido hadn't cared that he was the enemy.

After several moments of checking her out with gooey, caramel-colored eyes, he blinked as if waking from a dream. "I can spare a few hours."

Great Heavens! Did he think she was an…*apsara*? Draupadi gulped. He looked as if he wished to…be entertained in a number of ways.

A small bit of sanity had prevailed, and she'd yanked Vashi aside. "What are you up to? Why didn't you tell him my name? You know he'll go crazy when he finds out."

"Why should he find out? None of us will ever tell him. And no one else will be around until the palace's reopening two days hence. Besides, Qalanderi *is* your name."

The *apsaras* had started calling her Qalanderi after they'd read a bunch of Persian parchments for their reading club. Her friends thought that the contents of the poems were an apt description of her old life. Gambling, games and intoxication were the gist of Qalanderi poems.

Draupadi frowned. "But why?"

"I know you're not stupid or blind. Look how he's watching you. His eyes are devouring you. And I can hear your heart pounding from here," Vashi whispered.

"I can't just have some fling with him. We hate each other." Draupadi was aghast that she was tempted to throw caution, and the gruesome past, several leagues away.

"That's history. You can't base the rest of your existence on what happened in your past incarnation."

It was an ingenious argument, and one Draupadi had drilled into her daughters. "What about my lord husbands? They wouldn't like it, I don't think." She bit her lip. That she was even discussing this was worth a scandal and a half.

Vashi pooh-poohed her statement. "What rubbish. They won't twitch an eyelid."

It was true. Her five husbands were her "husbands" in name only. She didn't dwell with any of them, and the choice was entirely mutual.

"Okay, okay, you are so right," she said, getting all fired up, a common reaction when she thought of her husbands. Oh, they'd been so critical about her resurrecting their offspring instead of just being happy. "I don't care what they think anymore. And anyway, it's not Draupadi who is going to...um...entertain Karna, is it? It's Qalanderi."

Vashi giggled in delight. "That's right, darling."

"Am I going to regret this? Tell me I'm not going to regret this, Vashi."

The *apsara* had smiled kindly. "Believe me, my friend, he's entirely worth the regret."

Vashi had been right. Draupadi didn't regret the affair. How could she when she'd gotten Yahvi out of it?

The thought of Yahvi snapped Draupadi back to the present, and to the realization that she'd missed most of Eklavya's story. The sun's light was fading fast, and their outing neared its end. The bungalow lay but a dozen feet away.

"Back then, Asht Dveep was one of the eight trading and fishing island-ports under the patronage of King Pratapbimba—Bombay Island being the largest. When Karna moved here permanently, Asht Dveep had to disappear from existence. The Soul Warrior's abode has to be hidden from the human world. So it's also known as the Hidden Isle for two reasons: one, for the secret passageway the wealthy patrons of the brothel had used to get on and off it incognito, and two, because it's literally invisible. It's not on any map, in anyone's memory or part of history. The rest of the archipelago was consolidated into the city of Mumbai at some point. By the way, Mumbai was known as Bombay for a time, which is an Anglicized version of the Portuguese *Bombain*..."

"Holy-moly farts, Lavya. I don't care about the history lesson. Why were you in a brothel? Isn't that a sin that can taint your soul?" cried Amara.

"Good question," Draupadi murmured. It was a worrisome situation. The realm reeked of sin, and the only way to be safe from bad karma was not to engage with it. Which wasn't what her daughters had planned.

"Depends. Some sins are worse than others." Eklavya gave a lopsided smile and climbed the porch just as the front door flew open. "Ah. You're back," Lavya said, sounding relieved.

"Where the fug have you been?"

The raspy growl prompted a quake in Draupadi's spine from neck to tailbone. She wanted to turn and flee, but steeled herself to look at Karna and begin another lie.

Some sins were unavoidable when the heart was at stake.

"Ew!" was the collective consensus from his charges as they gathered around him in the foyer, their pert noses scrunched up in disgust.

"You smell yuck," Amara added, in case he'd mistaken their exclamations for praise.

The outburst was understandable. The gym had a mirrored wall, and he'd happened to catch his reflection in it. His ponytail was a joke, for half his hair flopped about his head. His face was dirty and sported a dense growth of stubble. His weary eyes were bloodshot. Had he been a nubile female, his own appearance would've scared him.

But he had no attention to spare for the jabbering females.

"Qalli?" He gawked at the shimmering blue soul that had walked into the abode, unable to digest what his eyes beheld. She really was here. Looking gorgeous in a sleeveless silk shirt, and pants, peach-painted toenails peeking out of mile-high heels. He hadn't hallucinated her scent. "Qalanderi?"

"You...recognize me," she whispered. Her big, smoky, lotus-petal eyes watered with emotion.

"Of course..." He broke off, shook his head to clear it. Of course he recognized her soul. What was she doing here? "What are you doing here?" *Holy shit.* She looked amazing. He couldn't stop gawking at her. He took a step forward, but stopped when the giggling around him escalated.

Dazed, he watched the Six disperse and climb the stairs, chattering about showers, and dinner...and pizza. His stomach rumbled at the thought of pizza. He'd kill for a chili corn *paneer* pizza right now. Lavya began to explain what was going on. It took a while, but his words finally sank in.

Qalli, the *apsara* who'd disappeared from his life as abruptly as she'd entered it, was handmaiden to the godlings?

"I'm a bit more than that," she said stiffly. "I'm their godmother."

"What?" he asked, swallowing a glob of spit and more confusion.

He couldn't get past how incredible she looked. The differences were not at all subtle but very attractive nonetheless. Her clothes were au courant to the realm and time. Her hair curled about her torso in a glorious multicolored mane, vastly different from what he remembered. It had nearly touched the soles of her feet and had been jet-black back then. An image of her flashed through his mind: red-tipped hands clutching the vines of a bougainvillea, hair rippling in the breeze as she kicked her sari-clad legs to make the swing go faster, higher. Her hair had teased his face when he'd pushed the swing, filled his hands when he'd loved her.

She was taller too, even without the four-inch heels she wore. If he stepped two feet closer, he'd be able to kiss her forehead without stooping much. She was also skinnier than he recalled.

He wanted to crush her into his arms. He was overwhelmed by the revival of feelings he'd long suppressed. Her scent—the heady scent of the divine lakes and the blue-petaled *pushkara* that grew there—was driving him mad. And that touch of cinnamon. He closed his eyes, breathed her in and felt his soul laugh again after eighteen god-awful years.

He wanted to shake her until her teeth rattled. "I came back for you. I left for two days for work and when I came back, you were gone. Vashi said that you'd left Devlok for good. She wouldn't give me any sense of your whereabouts, no explanation." He squeezed his fists until his nails bit into the flesh of his palms. The craziness he'd felt when she'd left him, when he hadn't been able to find her, resurfaced. "I feared you'd been reborn."

For years he'd searched for her, reeling from helplessness to determination, anger to devastation. He'd mourned her loss as deeply as he'd mourned his mortal family.

And all along she'd been Draupadi's handmaiden?

He stepped back from her. His whole body protested his movements, but he got ahold of himself. He couldn't afford to touch her, to feel that kind of crazy again. He glanced up the steps where the females had disappeared. His duties took precedence over everything now.

Qalli pressed her hands to her face briefly. When she drew them away, her eyes were dry, her face composed. She was so beautiful. "I had to leave. I had…have reasons. Good ones. I'm sorry, Karna. But I couldn't stay…I had…have an obligation to my girls."

"Your girls? You mean Draupadi's daughters?" What about her obligation to her lover? What about the simple courtesy of saying goodbye to him? A note. Anything!

"Yes, Draupadi's daughters. They are my responsibility. I mean...I've shared their responsibility with Draupadi since their births. I am their godmother. Oh *deva*! How can I make you understand? Everything is so complicated," she cried as if tortured.

Karna went rigid. Complicated? That was an understatement. He couldn't think straight. He couldn't form a single coherent thought in his head right now. Godmother? Handmaiden? *Apsara?* Who the hell was she?

A stranger. He swallowed the bitter truth. She was a stranger. A stranger whose fathomless black eyes reflected the same yearning he saw in the mirror every day. He wanted to drag her into his arms and never let go. He wanted to breach her mouth with his tongue and see if she tasted the same—of cinnamon.

His stomach chose that moment to growl loudly—a warning against sheer stupidity.

He dragged his eyes away from Qalli and noticed that Lavya had given them some privacy. "Lavya," he shouted. His aide would be in the kitchen. It was dinnertime. "I'm going to shower and change. Ten minutes. And there'd better be pizza." He turned and began to climb the stairs two at a time.

Her scent followed him. Between the sneezing and the stink of Hell, it was a wonder he could smell her. It was a wonder he hadn't exploded. He might have, he reasoned, had he a smidgen more energy in him. As it was, he felt drained by his latest hunt and preoccupied by some insane revelations—not the least of which were hers.

"I need to talk to you," she said, dogging his heels.

That was a surprise. He remembered her aversion to talking in Paradise. Correction: She'd talked. Just not about anything personal. Not that he'd been overly interested in exchanging life stories. He'd come off a long hunt Indra had sent him on—mission successful—and had needed to chill. It was why he'd accepted Vashi's invitation to a movie marathon at the Pleasure Palace in the first place. Then he'd met Qalli and he'd stayed longer than intended. Fearing that he'd get tagged about a new hunt any second, he'd made every moment of the affair count. A week could last a lifetime, he'd realized.

And a lifetime could shrink into the second it took to remember.

Karna paused at the threshold of his bedchamber, hand poised to push the door open, when he caught a glimpse of his blood-encrusted arm. Memories of Qalli surfed his consciousness like a hangover after a night of bingeing. He remembered her OCD with cleanliness. He narrowed his eyes. She must be screaming inside about his ghastly appearance. She must want something from him quite badly to overlook it without comment. What did she want? And what did it have to do with Devious Draupadi?

"I know all about your needs and how to fulfill them," he said, slashing his gaze to her face. Inappropriate amusement kicked up the corners of his lips when she goggled at him, though he didn't let it manifest into laughter. "I wish to bathe, then eat and sleep. You may speak to me while I accomplish the former two, and massage my aching feet as I undertake the last."

He slipped into his chamber, trying not to think about the other achy bits of him the "handmaiden" might consider massaging too.

He'd officially lost his mind. There'd be no massages until he got to the bottom of the charade he suspected Qalli and Draupadi—even Vashi—had played, and why.

History should never be repeated. What kind of fool makes the same mistake twice?

Sputtering in outrage, Draupadi rushed behind Karna. She'd suffer the buffoon's wicked sense of humor for Yahvi's sake. Massage his feet, indeed. Like some...handmaiden!

Oh, right. That was what she was pretending to be. She took a deep breath and let it out. She'd endure it, she vowed with queenly fortitude, for her daughters. He had to let her stay.

She marched into the buffoon's chambers with her chin in the air, and screamed when she slammed straight into him. The scream came out muffled against his rock-like chest. Her wedges wobbled. She would've dropped on her butt had Karna's arms not shot out, steadying her. So much for queenly dignity, she thought, cheeks burning.

Then followed a ridiculous two-step between them, each trying to move one way and ending up blocking the other, until Karna grabbed her shoulders and very firmly set her inside the room. He shut the door, and locked it with a decisive click.

Draupadi took another long breath and let it out. She'd survive this. She was honey to his fly; she simply had to remember that.

She looked about the chamber—anywhere but at him—trying to settle her nerves before she launched into her prepared speech, and stiffened when the stark reality of where she was hit her. She was in Karna's bedchamber. With him standing not two feet away. And he'd locked them both in. Not that locking a Celestial in a room was a real threat—merely an implied one. Now, if he'd locked her in an iron-walled chamber. That would've been telling.

Cosmic custard! She was face-to-face with Karna again, within touching distance. Heavens! This was complicated. No, she decided firmly. It needn't be complicated if she stuck to the plan. She was here for her girls, and Yahvi deserved all of her focus.

"Look, I'm here on Draupadi's behalf. She can't be with the girls yet. She's dealing with stuff in Devlok, and..." She broke off when Karna snorted.

"Right. *She's* dealing with stuff." He sauntered off toward the wardrobes lining two adjacent walls, where he proceeded to strip off his belt, watch and boots. Nothing else, thankfully. Stick to the plan. Er, what was the plan? she wondered, distracted by the way his shorts had slipped from his waist, floating precariously on his bladed hipbones. A hip twist and they'd fall. And she knew just what they'd reveal.

She tore her gaze away from his hips. "I know you don't think much of her...you never have. But believe me, she has the best interests of the girls at heart. She'd do anything for them." It was no more than the truth. She had gambled for her daughters. Lied for them. She would rip her own heart out and let Karna trample it if it meant Yahvi would be safe.

Would Karna do the same? Could he set aside his duty as guardian of this realm and do what was best for his daughter?

Draupadi walked forward. A handmaiden would help her lord or lady disrobe. She sank to her knees before him and was gratified to hear a sharp intake of breath above her head. He was as affected by her presence as she was by his, she thought with satisfaction. And, he was upset—he had to be. No matter his stoic stance.

She made quick work of untying the laces on his filthy boots. But before she could help him remove them, he wrapped hard hands around her arms and lifted her up in the air. She shrieked.

"What game are you playing, woman?" He stalked across the room with her dangling from his hands.

Her arms burned where he touched her. He was hot. Literally hot to touch.

"Ow!" she exclaimed when he dropped her on the concrete slab he called a bed. She shot to her feet immediately, rubbing her backside. Then she quickly felt his forehead. "What is this? Why are you feverish? Are you hurt?"

"It's nothing." He glowered, looking as if he was about to set her on fire with his caramel-colored eyes alone. He looked as if her wanted to kill her. She'd much rather he projected warrior-like stoicism at least with her. She was used to dealing with the type.

"Must you be contrary just for the sake of arguing? You're burning up." She wasn't going to back down. She needed to know what to do about Yahvi if he was sick.

"It's not a fever, Qalli," he said in clear exasperation, and went on to explain his problem—his fluctuating body temperature curse and unintentional pyromania—in short, clipped sentences. "So don't piss me off," he warned.

She stared at him, aghast. "You poor thing. The Gods really mean for you to suffer, don't they? Do they know how easily you get angry?" She took his warning to heart, though. Not that she was afraid of a bit of fire. It was her element, and she controlled it well. But there was Yahvi to consider. "Is that why your abode is decorated caveman-style?"

"Concrete and marble are popular building materials on this realm. Not everything needs to glitter like Heaven," he mocked. He turned, and walked toward the bath chamber, leaving her frowning at his broad, muscled back.

He'd mistaken her meaning. She wasn't making fun of his lifestyle. It was his ideals that confounded her, and his disdain for his own kind. It was that very disdain she would use to sway him to her way of thinking.

For herself, she didn't mind being lumped with the Celestial snobs. So she liked a bit of luxury and opulence. What was so wrong in that? She'd experienced all that fate had to offer, from a fiery birth to a cold death; intense pleasure and debilitating sorrow; embarrassing riches and shame-filled poverty; love beyond imagining, and a hatred so pure that it had left a nation of burning pyres in its wake. She'd learned to take her pleasures as and when they were offered, for just as quickly they might be snatched away.

No one would accuse Karna of the sin of snobbery or decadence, though. His bedchamber was large, made airy by an adequate number of windows and an adorable balcony that overlooked the island. But there any abundance ended. The wardrobes and a prayer alcove graced the right side of the chamber, and to the left, facing east, was his bed—a raised concrete platform stacked thick with animal skins. Not one pillow graced its breath. The chamber wasn't equipped with a desk, and the nightstands and TV console displayed only the bare necessities.

Did he still prefer comedy to drama? Family sagas to horror? She'd assumed he needed the laughter and love shown in such movies to combat the stress of his high-octane professional life. They'd watched *Mrs. Doubtfire* with the *apsaras* that first evening, and by the time the credits had rolled, they'd been left alone. They'd sat close together on the same sofa and had reached for the video control together. Their hands had touched, and it had been instant electricity. He'd pulled her onto his lap—or had she climbed there herself? They'd kissed for so long, she'd become breathless. He'd laughed. Wickedly. So wickedly. Then he'd laid her back on the sofa and made her forget her own name—both her names, all her names. The world had simply fallen away when she'd looked into his honey-warm eyes.

The warrior was dangerous. Volatile and gentle, aloof and loving, he'd been everything to her since the first time they'd met. And yet he'd been nothing. How was she to deal with him? What could she possibly offer him to ensure his compliance with regard to Yahvi? Draupadi glanced at the bed, then at Karna.

It seemed he'd been waiting for her to look at him. Arms crossed over his chest, he leaned against the door of the bath chamber. His eyes blazed golden. They were the exact shade of the setting sun beyond the window.

Her heart began to perform feats known only to winged shape-shifters.

She recognized the look. He'd looked at her like this in the glade at the Pleasure Palace. He'd looked at her like this the very first time they'd met as mortals in her father's palace at the commencement ceremony of her *swayamvara*—marriage contest.

He wanted her now. He'd wanted her then. He might tease her and taunt her, mock her, even loathe her for what she'd done, past and present. But beneath it all, he desired her. Why wasn't she gloating? She had him right where she wanted him, a slave to his passions. He'd do anything for her if she offered to wash his back.

And if she did—if she touched him—would she lose her mind again?

"Wash my back?" he asked in a horrifying parody of her own desire.

Draupadi shook her head. She couldn't risk being a slave to her passions. But oh, how she wished things were different between them. "I'll wait here, thanks."

His eyebrow quirked—or, she thought it did. She couldn't tell for sure beneath the violence and brimstone coating his face. But his sigh, long and loud, was unmistakable.

"Qalli, you came to me. To my abode, without an invitation, without my knowledge, I'm guessing for a reason. Perhaps to spy on me for Draupadi?"

Draupadi opened her mouth to protest but closed it when Karna raised a hand.

"If you wish to remain here in any capacity, you will tell me the truth. And you *will* obey me in all things, be it as a handmaiden or an *apsara*. I leave it to you to define your duties in my household. But understand this: I am master here. Not Draupadi."

She stared at him, stunned. Had she thought manipulating him would be easy? And had he just given her permission to stay without her asking for it? Eklavya had it wrong. It wasn't she who'd rendered Karna speechless. It was the other way around.

*Deva!* Would she ever crawl out of the hole she'd made of her life with any kind of self-possession?

Rejuvenated by a cold shower, Karna strode out of the bathroom ready to kick ass. Didn't matter whose ass—the demons', his students' or Qalli's. He stripped of his towel and donned his demon-hunting attire of black jeans and black T-shirt. He pulled his wet locks into a no-fuss ponytail and looped the Soul Catcher belt and buckle around his waist.

Qalli wasn't in his chambers anymore. She'd decided to retreat into the handmaiden persona, though, as she'd laid out his garments on the bed before leaving. He wasn't sure whether he was relieved or disappointed by the decision.

He sighed. He'd come so close to taking her. Touching her had been a mistake, especially in a state of anger. He'd thrown her on the bed, and only he knew how he'd controlled himself and not followed her down on it. He'd wanted to so badly. He'd wanted to cover her body with his and make her beg for mercy. Make her pay for walking away, for hurting him. Thank karma he'd found the strength to put a sizable distance between them.

The scent of melting cheese drew Karna and his hollow stomach to the kitchen, where Lavya and Lusha worked in tandem to make the best pizza this side of Italy. The rest of the crew were helping, or not, but everyone seemed to be adding to the chaos in the kitchen—save Qalli.

Karna felt a brief flare of panic, wondering if she'd left him again without word. Then, disgusted with his reaction, he leaned a hip against the granite countertop of the kitchen island and scarfed down four slices of pizza. He wasn't going to care what she did anymore. He wasn't going to think of her, period.

"Lavya, if you're done pizza-making and eating, we should brain-storm." Karna guzzled every last drop of his Sprite, which he'd spiked with ten drops of *soma* concentrate, and set the goblet in the sink. Did he smell cinnamon? He quickly turned to his *shishyas*. "Once you're done eating and cleaning up, get ready. I want you in the den in, say...half an hour? We'll go over some *guru-shishya* rules and regulations, and then I test you. Okay?" The instructions were met by very enthusiastic reactions.

Satisfied that he actually had a plan forming in his head, Karna walked into the den. Lavya shut the door, made for his ergonomic chair, and started playing with Baby. But Karna was too wired to sit. So he paced while the LCD screens came alive.

"No Reds?" he asked, getting down to business.

"None yet. But, Lord Yama texted the names of three cities while you were showering." Lavya nodded at the screens. "Puri, Behrampur and Guwahati." He raised his eyebrows. "What's up in those places? Are we expecting trouble there?"

As usual, Yama had texted a fill-in-the-blanks sort of message.

"I didn't get a chance to update you. Major trouble seems to be brewing. The *asuras* I captured the other night at the Kalighat Temple stole Goddess Kalika's *raakh*. I confiscated it." Karna stabbed a thumb in the direction of the ceiling and the vault beyond. "The pouch is now safe within our safe." He gave Lavya a detailed account of the events thereafter, including repeating verbatim the prophecy Baital had recited.

"Keep monitoring the temples, assuming the relics haven't been stolen already," he said, staring at the TV screens showing aerial views of the three sprawling temples. Only green-souled pilgrims and pundits moved about. If the ashes were stolen already, well, he'd just have to re-steal them. "We need to find out everything about Kalika's ashes. Why do the demons want them?" He felt antsy. Good antsy or bad antsy, he couldn't tell yet. "I'll need help tonight. Stakeouts are no fun alone. And worse case, if there's trouble in all three places at the same time, I obviously can't be everywhere at once. And I want to speak to our informants. And visit the *loks*." He was going to have a busy night. Excellent!

Lavya and he worked with a bunch of associates, all Earth-dwellers but not all human, who helped out from time to time in various capacities. But for tonight's missions, he thought the females might do. But first he needed to know what skills they possessed and which god-powers.

"Summon my students. Let's get this show on the road," Karna said, feeling a lot more in control now that his plans were in action.

# CHAPTER NINE

## SAMADHI: TOMB OF SECRETS

The cave was deceptive.

From the Earth's crust, its flat mouth was barely big enough to accommodate a crouching demon cub, but once you wormed your way inside, it yawned into an enormous cavity capable of housing thousands of *asuras* comfortably. Hidden in the scattered hills that rose like sand dunes on the barren plains of Cedi, or what used to be the Kingdom of Cedi but was now part of an area called Bundelkund in the center of India, the place was devoid of humans and their meddlesome natures.

It was the perfect spot to bury an ancient secret.

Without hesitation, Raka marched toward the Juggernaut. *"You hesitate, you die,"* Raka's blood-sire and guru, Char Mani, had once snarled at Raka after punching him in the mouth. He'd been teaching Raka hand-to-hand combat, but Raka found the advice worked in numerous situations.

Mara stood on a high ledge as still as the tombstone being excavated in front of him, keeping a vigil around the subterranean cavern and the progress of the minions under his command. Raka was one of the minions, but not for long. He stopped beside Mara, taking delight in the frenzy below too. The groans and grunts filling the space thrilled Raka; the sound of rock scraping against rock was ecstasy. They'd worked nonstop since their arrival on the realm between realms, preparing the terrain for habitation. Stairs had been cut into the walls, linking the cave to the realms it had once connected: The Human Realm lay above, the Realm of the Naga below.

At Mara's gesture, Raka ambled forward and bowed.

"*Agrata.*" Raka abhorred addressing a *raaksasa* inferior to him as a leader, but he would, until he didn't have to. "I may be of use to you."

Mara's thick lips peeled apart in a sharp-toothed smirk. "By leaving your post and the task you were assigned? I think not."

Raka inhaled the insult and waited. Raka had the patience to win this pissing contest.

Volcanic vapor rose from the abyss at the bottom of the cave in heavy, pungent clouds. Once the portal to the Realm of the Naga, the Serpent People and ancestors to the Lord Master, the abyss was no more than a vast, bottomless hole in the ground now. Raka wondered if anyone would notice if he threw the Juggernaut in.

"Speak. What can you do for our Lord Master that they cannot?" asked Mara, staring at the countless *asuras* of various shapes, sizes and evilness working their asses off. The minions excavated—no, they had exhumed—the stone remnants of Lord Vala's limbs and were diligently moving rocks and boulders off the hallowed stumps. The next moonrise would see the remains completely unearthed.

Raka had many doubts about the condition of Vala's corpse. Being buried for five millennia could not bode well even for stone. And he wasn't the only one doubting. To the right, master sculptors were hard at work on a massive slab of consecrated demon stone they'd brought from the Demon Realm, crafting a new headless form for Vala, mixing the new with the hallowed.

Preceptor Shukra was expected back tomorrow with more *asuras* for their army. All was ready for Lord Master's arrival five moonrises hence. The only loose end was the package they'd lost in Kolkata.

And that's where Raka came in. "If you lend me some *asuras*, I will retrieve the lost *raakh* for our Lord Master."

Mara might be the Juggernaut, but it would be Raka who'd find the Soul Warrior's weakness and smash through it. It would be Raka who'd present the head of Kalika to Lord Master Vala.

"Glorious gizmos!" Draupadi exclaimed in absolute delight, following the girls into Karna's den. She spun about, taking in the floor-to-ceiling bookshelves, the leather armchairs, the huge ficus tree that dominated one corner of the room and the wall of TV screens blipping out information. While Karna's office was undoubtedly a masculine domain, it wasn't like the rest of the abode. It was stylish, cozy and completely high-tech. She loved it.

"Is this room safe? I mean, won't you blow all this up if you get upset?" She looked at Karna expectantly. He didn't answer her. He didn't even look her way. He simply began to chat with the girls.

"He does. That's why we keep fire extinguishers in every room," Lavya answered on his behalf. He sat behind a busy-looking desk, doing something fancy on a sleek keyboard. "And the walls of the abode, both inside and out, are fireproof. You might want to brush up on fire-repelling spells, just in case."

Draupadi noted several handheld red cylinders within easy reach in different corners of the chamber. Karna and Lavya did seem to have things under control here.

Ooh! These modern times and human gadgets quite fascinated her. When one had lived as long as she had, and in every conceivable realm, one would think nothing could astonish her. Not so, as the jet age on Earth proved. While one couldn't even begin to compare heavenly magic and technology, she was still amazed by the ideas the modern humans had managed to discover, invent and revolutionize. The age for which the Gods had held no hope had actually become the age of industry and progress. Celestial society regularly got whiplash trying to keep up with the rapidly evolving Human Realm.

"*Too fast,*" the Celestials had begun to complain of late. "*The humans are moving too fast. They rush thoughtlessly onward, unwisely celebrating their victories. Do they know the price they will pay for such greed?*"

But mistakes were wisdom's price. The Heaven-dwellers conveniently overlooked the fact that they too had learned such lessons the hard way.

"Don't you love this chamber?" Yahvi whispered in Draupadi's ear.

"Yes, baby. I can see you love it too." She smiled at her youngest, who lived and breathed through the Conscious Web.

"Gotta go. Father's talking rules and regulations and Amara's groaning already." Yahvi gave her a quick peck on the cheek and scooted off.

Draupadi poured herself a goblet of *soma* juice from a tray on the desk. She looked up and was accosted by Lavya eyeing her in a mixture of disbelief and suspicion. What had Karna told him? She took her drink and sat down on the divan in a corner, determined to be on her best handmaiden-cum-*apsara* behavior. She wouldn't give them a chance to doubt her story.

"Let's go into the armory, *shishyas,*" Karna said, walking backward toward the doors. "I want you to pick a weapon. We'll do a brief test run. If I'm satisfied with your choice and skill in using it, we go on a stakeout. Then I get to test your mettle in real-life."

"What?" Draupadi yelped and jumped up from her seat, forgetting to be docile and handmaidenish. "Test their mettle in real-life? Are you crazy?"

"I beg your pardon." Karna had stopped in his tracks by her outburst.

She inserted herself between him and her girls, who began groaning in unison. "What is wrong with you? You can't just take them on some demon hunt because you're short-staffed. I knew it. I know how you love playing with fire. I just knew it!"

"What in fug are you blathering about, woman?" Karna asked, red-faced.

"I warned the girls about this." She wagged her finger at him. She wanted to poke his chest with a pointy fingernail. "I told them hanging out with you would be a dangerous mistake. Just being around you is dangerous...and a mistake. But to take them along on a demon hunt on the first day? What is the matter with you?"

"Hanging out?" said Karna incredulously. "They're not here on some holiday. They've bloody been dumped on me like a bad case of hives."

Lavya cleared his throat loudly. "He doesn't mean it like that. Its his anger talking."

Karna sucked in a deep breath and looked at his aide, at his affronted *shishyas*, and finally at his daughter, whose face was leached of color.

"He's right. I don't mean it." Karna's head threatened to split open, and he could feel a rise in his body temperature.

"You warriors are all alike," Qalli yelled, gesturing madly with her hands. "You're never satisfied until every single soul near you is sucked into your blood wars. But I won't let it happen. Hear me? I will not let you sacrifice my girls in your ego-boosting power plays."

Scorpion stings had been easier to bear than Qalli's allegations.

"Clearly you've not been apprised of what's going on, as it's indubitably not your concern, but the females are in training with me," he said, cutting straight through the crap. She thought him so prideful, so stupid, that he'd put his students in danger, even his own daughter? "I am their guru by decree of the Gods. Their welfare, their very souls are in my care. Not yours."

"Some guru you're turning out to be, taking your brand new *shishyas* on death missions," Qalli retorted nastily.

"How long before Uncle Fireball burns the place down?" Amara mock-whispered behind him. "I say another ten minutes. Anyone want to take a bet?"

The joke fell flat. Karna couldn't find anything remotely funny in the situation. Was this what Qalli thought of him? He felt numb. Cold. Deserted all over again. And why wouldn't she? He'd never claimed to be anything other than a warrior, ruthless in his execution of duty, single-minded when it came to ambition. He'd never hidden his true self from her. Was it any wonder she'd run from him?

They should all run from him, most especially Yahvi. They should run while they still could.

"Look, Karna, I don't know what game the Celestials are playing, but the girls are hardly warrior material..."

"Hey! That's insulting," half a dozen females protested.

Qalli went on as if she hadn't been interrupted. "I am their godmother. I've helped raise them. I fed them, burped them, bathed them and played with them since they were babies. I am practically their mother. So believe me when I tell you I know exactly what they're capable of and what they're not." She took a step closer and touched his arm. "Please. Think about what you're doing. Think about why the Gods have dumped them on you. There's more going on than we've been told. Draupadi is sure of it and is trying to figure it out."

His forearm went rigid under her touch. The protests from the Six grew louder. "What are you implying?"

"You're angry. Fine. You have the right to be pissed off. I'm pissed off. But taking the girls on a demon hunt is not going to solve the issue."

Karna was completely confused. On the one hand, he wanted to throttle Qalli for thinking so little of him. On the other, he wanted to kiss her fears away. She seemed genuinely freaked.

"I have no clue what you're talking about. You need to calm down. We both do," he said. "And the rest of you shut up." He was about to ask Qalli what she'd meant by Draupadi trying to find a solution when Amara butted in again. Someone needed to teach Arjun's offspring some manners.

"Is the fight settled? Wonderful. Where are we going?" she demanded. "Finally! I get to kick some major *asura* ass!"

"Am I the only one who sees how utterly idiotic this whole thing is?" Qalli's dark eyes glittered dangerously as she glared at him. She flung her arm out to the females. "Look at them. They think this is a video game." She abruptly ceased talking, her chest heaving with agitation. "You know what? I should leave. I'm leaving right now, because I refuse to stay here and worry over the color of your souls. And I absolutely refuse to sit around stitching shrouds for your dead bodies, wondering when and how you'll get yourselves killed. One lifetime of such horrors was enough. I will not put myself through that again."

"Then leave," Karna snapped, at the end of his tether. He glanced pointedly at the open den doors. "Go on, leave. Go back to Devlok or wherever the hell you've crawled out of after eighteen years. I didn't ask you to come, nor did I ask you to stay. But if you want to stay, you will shut up and stay out of my business."

Absolute silence choked the den for a minute. Qalli glared at him the whole time, and when he didn't relent, she vanished from the room in a flounce. Good. Karna swallowed the bad word stuck in his throat. She was gone. She'd listened. Great.

He forced his mind to focus on his *shishyas*, truly seeing them for the first time tonight. What he actually wanted to do was claw his heart out with his bare hands to stop its painful throbbing. *Why did she affect him this way?*

"Ziva," he said, cramming a preternatural calm down his throat. "No dresses. And Amara, you need to tone down the action figure costume."

She was decked out in full combat mode, complete with mantra-treated body armor and a dozen different weapons.

"But this is my demon-hunting outfit—think *Lara Croft: Tomb Raider*. Get it? *Tomb Raider?*" Amara chuckled. He simply glared at her until she obeyed.

"And I don't own anything but dresses," Ziva said.

"Borrow from your sisters. Boots too," Karna added, noticing her high heels for the first time. "Learn to adjust, Ziva. That's what you're here for: to learn, to train and to obey."

Iksa, Satya and Lusha were in jeans, leggings and track pants paired with shirt, T-shirt and vests, sneakers or boots on their feet. They were good. Yahvi had a longbow slung over her right shoulder and a full quiver across her back. She wore an all-black Kevlar jumpsuit, and a mean pair of biker boots protected her feet.

"But ..."

He held up a hand. "Karna's Demon Hunting Academy rule number one: Dress appropriately for the occasion. We might need to run, roll, cartwheel, levitate or leap into the air in pursuit of the trespasser, so no dresses."

"I can do all that in a dress," Ziva insisted, then added an after-thought. "Although, I wish to make it clear from the beginning that pursuing *asuras* is fine. So is catching them. But I am uncomfortable with taking a life. I am a healer, Uncle K."

Karna raised both brows high. "Rule number two—actually, this should be rule number one: The guru is always right. No arguments."

He swept a hard gaze over the females, coming to rest on the one he anticipated would give him the most trouble.

"Shi-shi, Master Shifu's never wong," Amara said, bowing sassily. She'd obeyed him, though, and now looked more like a Goth initiate than Cat Woman. It was still overkill.

Karna pressed the heels of his hands over his eyes. What the hell was he doing? Qalli was right. The females were novices in spite of their enthusiasm and innate god-powers—which he only suspected they possessed. He didn't know what kind of powers they actually wielded, or if they even knew how to use them to any effect. What if they didn't? Yahvi didn't even have god-powers yet. Or did she? Nothing about this situation was normal. And now that it had been pointed out, their lack of practical experience was glaringly obvious. If he took them along on the stakeout and, karma forbid, something nasty came their way—even something a million times less nasty than Vala—the sextet would be roadkill. He didn't even want to imagine what would happen to Yahvi, or the measures he'd have to take to save her green soul.

"Look, change of plans. Let's start off slow. You guys go with Lavya... for ice cream. Drive down the Queen's Necklace in South Mumbai. Take in some city sights." That should be a safe enough public activity until they regrouped at Club Suristan, where he and Lavya would meet one of the snitches later in the night. Karna would do a thorough reconnaissance at the three Kalika temples, ideally catching the demons red-handed with the ashes like last time, and join his crew after.

Amara and Lusha squawked—yes, squawked—in protest.

"You cannot just dismiss us like this!"

"Oh, *now* you send us sightseeing?"

"Whatever happened to the academy rule: No soul left behind?"

Fugdoomal! He couldn't deal with this—with them—right now. He worked best alone.

Lavya—bless his soul, he always came through—calmly herded the females together. "Move along, *shishyas*. You heard your guru."

Satya clasped Yahvi's hand, preparing to vanish. His daughter hadn't looked at him since he'd said she'd been dumped on him. He'd have to be more careful around her. She hurt easily, it seemed, both inside and out. Should he take her with him? Fug! What was he thinking? Luckily, the lot vanished before he did something foolish.

Annoyed and alone, the Soul Warrior got down to business as usual.

"Quit moping, Vee. Lavya said Shifu didn't mean it." Amara pulled Yahvi up from the seated niche carved into a treetrunk she'd been sitting in since their abrupt advent into the Seven Hells. The club was going for a naturalistic atmosphere with its overuse of wood, especially tree trunks for benches, stools and tables. There were actual trees growing inside the large area in a corner or two, and their table was under the shade of one. It seemed to be a prime spot.

They'd had to depart the swanky coffee shop across the road a little earlier than anticipated because Lusha had tried to get herself a date for the night. She'd had a dry spell in the mating department of late, what with the prison-like setup in her father's household. It occurred to Yahvi that she—and because of her, also her sisters—had simply exchanged one jail sentence for another.

"I'm not moping, exactly," Yahvi grumbled, but allowed her sister to drag her away.

"Then get moving." Amara plastered the front of her body to Yahvi's back and tried to make her move like a puppet. The music in the Seven Hells was exactly to Amu's taste—strong base, repetitive notes and deafening.

Yahvi felt the music snake into her bones. She began undulating.

"That's it. Twerk it, sister. Move your ass!"

They joined their sisters on the super-crowded dance floor of Club Suristan, a popular nightclub in South Mumbai, also known in nonhuman circles as the Seven Hells because of its unique architectural formation of seven floors. The top floor was at sea level while the rest of the floors descended downward into Lok Talatalas, a realm where magic had no restrictions and sorcerers thrived. The club was on the top floor, the only floor within the boundaries of the Human Realm. The only floor humans and females were allowed and *asuras* were not, Yahvi and her sisters had soon realized. Probably why her father had thought it safe enough for them. The club was wedged between the iconic Taj Hotel and the Gateway of India, a famous tourist attraction in Mumbai.

Dancing quickly improved Yahvi's mood. Amara was right. Her father had simply said what was on his mind. And wasn't it true? They had been dumped on him without warning.

*Pa…pa…pa! Da…da…da…da…da…da!* Yahvi sprang up and down on the dance floor, pumping a fist in the air.

"What's *she* doing here?" Amara frowned over several bobbing heads toward the bar. "Did you ask her to join us, Satya?"

Over at the bar, Mama sat talking to a male, sipping a drink.

"I did not." Satya shook her head emphatically. "She was here before us."

"She won't stay out of our business, will she?" Amara groaned, stating the obvious.

Suddenly, Lavya stood right in front of Mama. Yahvi quit pumping her fist, but continued bouncing. Annoyance flashed across Mama's face before she schooled it into serenity. Lavya was probably asking her how she'd found them too. After a brief discussion with him and a shrug, she walked away with her companion to the other end of the bar.

Then Lavya looked in the direction of the dance floor, nodded and slipped out of sight again. He'd been doing that every ten minutes—popping in to check up on them while her father conducted his business, first at the club, then down in the Seven Hells. Father and Lavya were talking to sundry creatures about the possibility of thwarting Kalika's prophecy.

Her sisters and her had had a sisterly discussion about it in the club's woodland-style bathroom. Iksa thought it a good idea. She'd had another one of her "dreams" and said something was different in them. She'd sounded happier.

Yahvi grinned and bounced, her dejection falling away like feathers from a bird in flight. Maybe...just maybe, she wouldn't have to die.

Karna rode a shape-shifter in griffon bird form, in lieu of an elevator, from the seventh floor landing of the Seven Hells to the top, stopping at each floor to allow passengers to get on or off. He got off on the first floor, walked across two largely empty chambers and into a jam-packed Club Suristan, none the wiser than he'd been three hours ago at Asht Dveep.

His boots had stirred up nothing but dust scouting Kalika's temples. Not a whiff of any incoming or exiting *asuras*. No red souls anywhere at all on the Human Realm right this minute, period. It was an absolute anomaly.

Karna strode to the bar, hankering for a drink. He kept an eye out for the Delinquent Six—all accounted for on the dance floor. Lavya sat alone at the table they'd accrued. He had his laptop open in front of him, but at the moment his eyes scanned the club like a bouncer on duty. Amused, Karna ordered his drink and did a double take when he spotted Qalli's blue soul at the end of the bar. A yellow-souled shape-shifter in human form stood way too close to her.

He looked away fast. It wasn't his business if she wished to flirt with someone or form an attachment. Had it ever been?

Irritated with himself for his inane thoughts, he paid for his vodka on the rocks and stalked to the table to enjoy it in manly peace.

"What did you find out?" Lavya asked as soon as he sat down.

"No one knows anything about Vala. No more than we do. Less, in fact." Karna took a swig of vodka. "Or they've decided that silence would benefit them more. For now."

Lavya glanced at Baby. "No hits on the Conscious Web either."

No surprise there. Demons weren't fond of technology, and weren't the type to keep up with current events or update them. They were in-the-moment creatures, very insular to their own needs and agendas.

Karna frowned. "Something to consider. The leader of Tatalas told me to beware of aliases and imposters. Vala could be an alias for Dev-Il." Even as he said it, the theory didn't sit well with him.

"Dev-Il wouldn't risk leaving his demon-dom masterless for a moment, even if someone offered him every single soul on the Human Realm as his personal pet. You know that. Plus, he'd never take an alias. He's too arrogant not to take full credit for his evildoings."

Karna agreed with Lavya's assessment of his ex-best friend. Duryodhan had been the last human incarnation of the *asura* Kali, a.k.a. Dev-Il.

"The mages had nothing concrete to add to the *raakh* mystery either. One used bone dust to invoke the blessings of ancestors by smearing it on the body. One can use it to make an idol to worship. One can imbibe it through food and drink for power…though that can cause several undesirable effects, from soul possession to death."

It seemed the more questions he asked, the more unanswered mysteries he had. He resumed the conversation he'd been having with Lavya before his aide had ascended to the first floor to check on the

Six while Karna had descended into Tatalas to talk to its leader. "As I said, the head pundit at the Puri temple had no idea if there are relics missing, or if any 'robbers' or 'shady characters' have been about. And as thousands of people come to the temple everyday, there's no telling what might have gone on. I couldn't sense any evil at the temples."

"Trail long lost. They must've gotten the *raakh* from all four temples on the same night," Lavya said through a huge yawn. He cracked his neck, first left, then right, and returned to being vigilant. "We should go. We've tapped out all our sources here. I need to document the info while it's fresh in my mind. We should go before something else goes wrong."

The safe clubs weren't safe from the Delinquent Six. Lavya had already told him what had happened at a coffee shop across the club, but apparently it bore repetition.

"I took my eyes off them for a minute to pee and the next thing I know, there's a brawl right in the middle of the café. Men were scrambling over each other for the privilege to buy the females a cup of coffee...or I hope that was all they were doing. It was nuts. I froze them all with a spell for the second it took me to push the Six out and march them here."

Karna grimaced, recalling Qalli's words about brashness and naiveté. He couldn't help looking at her again. She'd changed her clothes. She wore a strapless knee-length dress, the fuchsia-colored fabric glowing bright, then dark, in the flashing disco lights. Her hair fell straight over one creamy shoulder.

Qalli. Qalanderi. She was the cause for his mental state tonight. What the hell was he to make of her? What the hell was he supposed to believe? Had she really expected him to make nice just because her beautiful *pushkara*-petal eyes watered up?

"By the way, she's been talking to a lot of creatures tonight," Lavya said, glancing at Qalli with a frown. "I'm guessing the Six told her where we were."

Karna downed half his vodka on the rocks. He couldn't get over the fact that Qalli knew Devious Draupadi—had always known her, in fact. There should be a cap on the number of times a soul got stabbed in the back.

Qalli and Draupadi. He swore viciously at the thought of the co-conspirators. Whatever the two had cooked up regarding the Six, he wanted no part of it. Qalli's divine descent obviously had something to do with his guardianship of the females. Draupadi must be livid about it and had sent Qalli to monitor the situation in her stead. But if the Gods had confidence in his abilities to nurture and protect the godlings, then who in hell was she to question them? *Their mother*—pointed out an insidious, unwelcome voice in his head.

Lavya was right. It was time to go home.

Karna downed the rest of his drink. "You get the Six. I'll get the handmaiden," he said. Disregarding Lavya's smart-aleck comparison between him and the pathetic swains who'd fought over the females at the café, he stalked to Qalli.

Clouds of perfumes and auras swirled inside the club, yet Qalli's stood out for him. He'd find her by her scent alone. He came up behind her as her overly handsome companion leaned in as if to kiss her. Heat exploded in his body. Without thought, he snaked his arm about her waist and pulled her back. She gasped, spun about. Her eyes went round in surprise, then immediately narrowed on his face.

"What are you doing?" she said through gritted teeth.

"Is there a problem?" the shifter asked, glancing from Karna to Qalli. He took a step closer, his hand stretched out to touch her arm. He dropped it immediately when Karna flashed the Soul Catcher. "My lord, I should've realized she was a demon when she asked me about Dev-Il," he said apologetically. He inclined his head, turned on his heel and left.

Qalli gasped again, her stomach trembling beneath his hand. "Demon? You made him think I was a demon?" She twisted in his hold. He didn't let her go. She shoved at his chest. He didn't budge.

"Not that it would've stopped him from doing whatever he was planning to do to you," Karna drawled. He swept his eyes around the club, where all sorts of wretchedness was on display. Drunks and whores and human thralls had been lured into shady corners as sport. Most had gone willingly. It could've been worse, though. One floor down it was worse. And while what was going on around him disgusted him on a certain level, it wasn't evil. Or even illegal by human standards. Okay, maybe some of it was, he thought, spying a drug dealer making a deal with an addict. He'd set Lavya on him as soon as he took care of Qalli.

"Why do you care what he was going to do to me?" she asked haughtily.

Karna drew his eyes back to her shiny, pink lips. "I shouldn't," he said softly.

Her lips parted. A tongue darted out, swiped at her bottom lip. "Karna..."

"Why were you asking about Dev-Il?" He pressed her to the bar as she stiffened against him. Their bodies were flush against each other. He leaned in, brought his lips close enough to hers that he could taste her breath. Cinnamon. *Shit! Focus, man.* "Just get your mistress to talk to me. Face-to-face. I have to know about Yahvi...and Dev-Il," he coaxed.

"Get my mistress to talk...to you?" She blinked. Swallowed. Blinked again.

A scream cut through the club music like a bad horror movie. Karna spun around as the club erupted into chaos.

"What's happening?" Qalli shouted, clutching at his shoulder.

Karna flicked her a glance. Damn it. He'd had her. She'd have spilled her guts in another second. "I don't know." But he could guess.

He spied the six delinquents in an all out brawl in the middle of the dance floor. He ran to them, elbowing creatures aside. Within seconds, the whole club was tussling with each other.

He reached Yahvi and wrapped a hand around the scruff of her neck. He looked around for a split second, deciding whether the disco lights would cover vanishment. But that split second was enough for a fist to land in his face. After that, there was no doubt in anyone's mind why the club was fondly called the Seven Hells.

# CHAPTER TEN
## THA: SIGNS OF DANGER

Deep into the night, Karna stood on the haphazard rock formation where, five thousand years ago, he'd fought the Stone Demon for three days and three nights. Then, this region had burst with vegetation and forests, settlements and cattle. He and Vala had burned them down to a crisp in their frenzy to win. The land had since turned barren. Unlucky. Silent. He saw no colors here—no living colors of souls. No animals roamed this region. No flora flourished in this land anymore. It had become a desert. The rivers and lakes had dried from drought.

The Vindhya Mountains, so named for that ancient battle. *Vaindh* meant obstruction. Vala had used these mountains to hold the Sun God hostage, to obstruct the path of the sun in the sky. And *vindhya*, the hunter, had freed him.

He should've fought harder. He should've captured Vala and taken him to Hell.

Karna half jogged and half jumped down the mountain of rubble, trying to sense out evil. But there was nothing here, only the remnants of an ancient energy. And it was making him sick to his stomach. Probably why there weren't any villages close by. Even benign human instinct could sense danger. The problem was that most creatures ignored their instincts to their detriment.

Like he'd done when he'd flung Vala into space.

He materialized in his bedchamber, carrying the weight of his mistake in his soul. Qalli's flowery scent lingered strong even now. He couldn't bear it. He vanished into the den before he started behaving like some love-starved puppy again.

Lavya was at the desk, furiously fingering the keyboard. How the man could sweet-talk Baby into obedience was pure science fiction. If only living, breathing females were so obliging.

"Anything?" Lavya asked.

"Apart from some vomit-worthy vibes around the last known location of our mystery *asura*, nothing. He's definitely not on this realm." He didn't like the way Lavya was looking at him. He didn't want analyzing or advice. He poured and guzzled a chilled goblet of *soma*, then plopped into the massage chair and switched it on to *Knead*.

Lavya traced an imaginary goatee around his mouth with his prosthetic thumb and forefinger. "Here's what I think," he began.

Karna groaned when the mechanisms of the chair began to push into his back muscles.

"Just hear me out. We have this situation with the *asuras*...and another with the females. And they've both landed on Earth in more or less perfect synchronicity."

"And you think Dev-Il has something to do with it." His words vibrated along with his body. Mercifully, his face no longer throbbed from the sucker-punch at the club. Though, another part of him did because of the sexy temptress he'd almost kissed tonight.

Karna was positive he'd never told Duryodhan about Vishnu's ghastly prediction should he ever join with Draupadi. But he'd often sat drinking late into the night with Duryodhan, neither one recalling a thing the next morning of their actions or conversations.

"Dev-Il." Lavya paused for effect. "And Devious Draupadi."

Lavya had never had a problem connecting the dots. "That's crazy." Karna switched off the massage chair and sat up.

"Just think for a minute. How did she manage to elongate the life-span of her green-souled daughter to three hundred years? That kind of dark magic taints a soul." Lavya rubbed a fleck of lint off his precious keyboard, neatly avoiding Karna's eyes.

Yes, Lavya would know all about dark magic. But they weren't cataloguing Lavya's sins here.

"Did you contact Draupadi?" Only she could answer the question of Yahvi's soul. Green signified human or nascent. So which one was Yahvi? Not that it mattered with regard to fate.

Lavya shook his head. "I made Satya and Qalanderi leave her messages. And I've left a message with Goddess Saraswati. No reply yet."

Karna snorted. Of course she wasn't going to reply. But he'd track her down. Once he didn't have Vala looming over his head. "Something's not right. While the females have been nothing but forthcoming about their past and what brought them to me, I can't help feeling they're covering something up." Something to do with Yahvi. But what could be worse than her being the harbinger of doom?

"Clearly why the Gods want them down here, cleaning up the mess they've made of their karma," Lavya said.

Karna was shocked at his friend's unsympathetic tone. "I've been a bad influence on you. My prejudice toward my maternal family has rubbed off on you."

"Nah! Never liked Kunti's sons to begin with. Didn't much care for Draupadi either." Lavya rubbed the corner of his mouth with his prosthetic thumb.

Karna barked out a fake laugh. Couldn't claim the same, could he? "And look where we are now. Surrounded by half a dozen of their progeny." What Lavya had said about cleaning up karma made sense. Still. "I can't get over the idea that Draupadi used boons to beget the Six."

"Don't tell me you admire her actions?" Lavya asked, appalled.

Did he? Karna shook his head. "I'm merely pointing out that she did the unthinkable. She grabbed fate by its neck and shook it." By karma, that's what she'd done.

Draupadi had balls. He'd known that from the moment she'd dragged him into her father's garden maze to apologize for insulting him. She was a law unto herself. It was that strength of character he'd fallen for. But it had been her irreverent sense of humor—like his—that had him going back to the garden again and again every night after the tournaments held in honor of her *swayamvara*. They'd laughed together for five long nights before Vishnu had put a stop to the affair.

"Don't you find it odd that she sent a friend—one she must know you're deeply interested in—to act on her behalf?"

Karna had thought about it and hated Qalli's role in this mess. Resented the fact that Draupadi could still play him like the flute she'd played for him during their furtive trysts. If this was her idea of payback, it was working.

"You're right," he agreed, calling himself a fool for the umpteenth time. "This whole situation is beyond bizarre. For one thing, why me? She loathes me since the time of the Kuru War, so why suddenly beget Yahvi and tether our fates together?"

"That's what I'm talking about," Lavya said and slapped his thigh in excitement. "What kind of dope was she on at the time?"

Karna frowned. "How did she explain her absence from Devlok to her husbands? Didn't they question her whereabouts? Didn't they look for her and their offspring?" Did they know about Yahvi? Did they know he was Yahvi's father?

"You should find out," Lavya said. "Talk to your brothers, if she won't talk to you."

Talk to his brothers? And then what? Beg them for help? Karna felt the usual resentment swell inside him. "I'd rather talk to Dev-Il. See if you can set that up." He walked to the door, more than ready for some shut-eye. "Um, did Qalli come back from the Seven Hells safely?" He'd been too busy trying to get the Six out of there to check whether she had followed or not.

Lavya looked disgusted, by the question or him was anyone's guess. "She's in the attic with the Six. She's smart enough to steer clear of the hair-trigger inferno. That would be you."

Karna nodded, embarrassed by the relief he felt.

"I suggest you keep her close, very close, until we have all the answers. And please, do yourself a favor and get her out of your system, one way or another."

Karna gave up on sleep as soon as the first blushing rays of dawn seeped into his bedchamber. His mind had wandered and whirred all night, conjuring stone-faced demons, naked nymphs and unruly little hellions vying for his attention, allowing not a moment's respite. What he needed was a muscle-pounding workout to calm the fevers in his brain. After his morning ablutions, he changed into sweatpants and a grey muscle tee, grabbed a towel from the bathroom and headed up the stairs to the gym on the second floor.

First thing, he threw open the windows to let in the dappled and dewy morning light for a much-needed energy boost. Then, facing east, he warmed up with yoga, chanting hymns with each salutation. Movement to movement, stance to stance he flowed, reconnecting to the elusive, finding balance within and without. In and out he breathed. Strong and steady beat his heart. Until slowly, very slowly, all movement stopped, all thought ceased and everything in the Cosmos became one pulse, one motion, one sigh within him.

His next inhalation started it all up again. Whirling. Colliding. Dancing. Being.

The natural course of things cannot be altered. That was fact. But it was also true that unless one pushed oneself into a headstand, it couldn't happen.

Halfway through his cardio, the chaos-magnets trickled in. He was surprised they were up so early after their exciting night. They came in ones and twos, carrying mats and towels, dressed as he was in workout gear. They went about their business noisily. They sighed, they grunted, they moaned and groaned and giggled. *Giggled?* What the hell did they find amusing about push-ups?

"How's your lip?" asked Amara, matching him push-up for push-up. They faced each other nose to nose on the floor.

He heard the laughter in her tone, understood too the exhilaration of a victorious fight, but she needed to understand how much more wrong it could've gone at the club. The riot had started because some puny human had stepped on Amara's toes and she'd accidently flattened him on the dance floor with a backhand and laughed. The boy had taken offence and called his testosterone-filled friends to "talk" to Amara. And she'd talked, with her fist.

"Healed. Unlike your nose," he said. "Unlike that boy's broken foot."

"It was reflex, coach. I swear!" Amara's face glowed with health and humor instead of contrition.

Back in the day, if he'd ever ever misbehaved in such a fashion, his guru would've taught him some manners via the vicious end of his stick.

"Hmm. What about the arm-wrestling match?" He raised a brow at Lusha who was lifting two-fifty in a series of steady reps. She'd been responsible for the café incident.

Lusha's cheeks puffed out, and her muscles bulged with effort. "The guys challenged me. I told them to settle it with coffee. They decided to arm wrestle. I could hardly refuse."

Lusha had won. The thugs got pissed. And Lavya had whisked the jinxed Six to the Seven Hells.

"Okay, enough foolishness." Karna pushed off the floor and sat up, cross-legged. Sweat trickled down his neck, soaking his T-shirt. "Come, sit before me." He placed his hands on his knees, palms to the ceiling, and joined his index fingers and thumbs in the Wheel of Law *mudra*. His *shishyas* mirrored him on their yoga mats, backs ramrod straight.

He waxed out a sermon on rules, regulations and expectations, much like his own guru had done every morning. The Six, besides a bit of eye rolling and groaning, were real troopers about it. Even so, Karna wondered who amongst them would break first.

"*Asuras* are the antithesis of Gods. Both species were spawned from the same seed, almost simultaneously, but from different wombs. Both are the descendants of the primordial Spirits."

Amara groaned. "Really? A Celestial anthropology lesson?"

Ignoring her, Karna went on, "They are further classified into several races, of which the three main are *danu, daitya* and *raaksasa. Danus* are primordial demons, created alongside the first Celestials. They are very powerful, intrinsically evil and very rare. Not a single one has been spotted on Earth in the last five thousand years."

"Heard you booted their asses off this realm all by your lonesome," Amara butt in again.

"Shut up, Amara. Before I punish you for insouciance, disobedience and the crick in my neck. You want me to teach you how to hunt demons, you will first understand what makes them demons."

Amara clapped her hand over her mouth and tried to look tragically apologetic.

Karna swallowed a laugh. "*Daityas* are mostly dark-skinned giants and a bit dim-witted. When *daityas* began breeding with other species, mostly the shape-shifters, their bloodline devolved into *raaksasas*. *Raaksasas* are all brute force and no logic."

"That's not true, Father. Draas is a *raaksasa* and we can vouch for her intelligence and innate sweetness," said Yahvi. Actually, she mumbled.

The child barely spoke to him, so he didn't reprimand her. She barely looked at him and he had no idea how to ease her shyness. The brutal truth was that his daughter had been more at ease with a demon than she was with him.

"I'm sure there are exceptions to every rule, *vatse*, but any race as a whole has more in common than not." He held up his hand. "I'm not getting into an argument about the vice of generalization or bigotry. Notice, I said vice. You six have eyes, ears and a brain. I expect you to use all three before making a judgment on the character of a creature."

Amara let out an exaggerated yawn. "We know all this, Sensei. We know every make, model and color of demon that exists and how to change their shapes too. Believe me, we've had years of training."

That had become as clear as the powder blue sky outside the second he'd sensed their god-powers. He'd seen their weapons. He knew who their fathers were.

"You might have had years of theoretical training, but you've not trained specifically as demon hunters. You believe that not all demons are bad. How do you tell the difference? I'm blessed with the power to see all souls. I can tell the difference between vermillion and saffron and what it might mean for the fate of the demon. How will you tell? Can you swear that Draas or the other *raaksasas* had no intention of doing evil to you or anyone else?"

He was glad to see his *shishyas* consider his words. Even Yahvi stared directly at him, her eyes bright, slight giddy with the heady feeling knowledge brings.

Pleased that he was finally doing something right, Karna stood up and motioned for his *shishyas* to follow him. "I'm surprised your gurus or your fathers haven't taught you this," he commented, after disarming the door of the armory and swinging it open. While he stayed outside the iron door so as not to crowd up the chamber, he motioned for the Six to go in. Awestruck, they took in the floor to ceiling racks and hooks holding a shitload of Celestial *astras* and manmade weapons.

"We only had one guru, uncle," said Satya, her bright-blue eyes falling on an impeller rod. "We got to know our fathers much later in life. Though we do train with them off and on."

"Go on. Pick it up," he encouraged when he saw her hesitate to touch the staff. "Do you know what it is?"

"The rod of Dharma. It's a simple club, unless invoked by the right mantra. Then if you strike someone with it, he or she will be compelled to follow the laws of Lord Yama."

"Very good," he said, thankful he wouldn't have to start from scratch with the Six.

Once he'd given the go-ahead, the Six quickly picked up different *astras*. It was common for a certain weapon to attract a certain type of warrior, or vice versa. A bow and arrow called to an archer, a blade to a swordsman, a hammer to a wrestler, etcetera. It was less common for one warrior to call a huge number of different weapons. As Karna's personal arsenal was huge and ridiculously varied, he never really fixated on any one weapon. Though he did call on *Asi* more than he called any other weapon to assist him.

He observed the Six. Ziva had gone for the benign *Varshana*, a dart that when invoked caused a torrential downpour that made even walking in a garden, much less warring on a battlefield, impossible. Amara went straight for *Punisher*—figured, as Indra had awarded the broadsword to Karna. Iksa picked up the Noose of Time, *Kaal Paasha*, that had the power to either accelerate or decelerate time when invoked.

Like Ziva and Iksa, Lusha had gone for a defensive rather than an offensive *astra* called *Saila*. It invoked calm when launched against the indomitable gales of *Vayu-astra*.

Yahvi couldn't seem to make up her mind what weapon to choose. She touched, weighed and scrutinized all of them.

"I see you know your defensive weapons from your offensive ones. Here's a scenario...say an enemy is covered in an armor that is power-enhanced by Shiva's protection mantra. How will you defeat him?" Karna asked, grinning. He couldn't believe he was actually enjoying being a guru.

Following a brief huddled consultation, Satya answered for the Six. "We'd neutralize the charmed armor with the spear of Rudra, weakening his defence. Then we'd attack with whatever means we have at our disposal."

"Who in heck was your guru?" Karna asked, impressed that they'd gotten it right, even if theoretically. Then suddenly wondered if his own guru, Parashuram, had taught the Six. He'd never bothered to keep in touch with his teacher, as they hadn't exactly parted on friendly terms.

"Guru Parashuram has retired to a small mountain-realm within the Higher Worlds," Iksa replied to a question he hadn't asked aloud. His eyebrows shot up at her. She smiled, dimples twinkling. "I'm not using mind-reading spells. Sometimes, I can sense thoughts. Yours were pretty easy to guess. You asked who our guru was and then looked thoughtful. Naturally, you'd be thinking of your own guru," she explained.

He was fascinated by Iksa's reasoning skills, and how she'd avoided one answer by deflecting it with another. "You didn't answer my question, though. Who was your guru?"

"She's a highly skilled warrior princess from Alaka," Satya said, evasively.

"Does she have a name?" It baffled him that they'd tell him the truth up to a point but no more.

"She goes by many names. All we can tell you is she's the daughter of Lord Agni, the God of Fire. We don't want her getting in trouble for secretly helping us."

Last score, Agni had close to three thousand progeny.

"Hmm." Karna let it go for the moment, knowing the females would clam up if he pushed. He'd have Lavya make inquiries about the lady-guru through Kubera, the god-king of the shape-shifters and ruler of Alaka. Yahvi had been raised in the small, prosperous city-realm, floating on the outskirts of the Higher Worlds. Alaka was a liberal place where not just shape-shifters but all soul colors alike were welcome, so long as everyone got along peacefully. If he had to stash a green soul anywhere besides the Human Realm, he would've chosen Alaka too. Damn it! Draupadi had made all the right moves with Yahvi so far. How was he supposed to remain angry with her?

Further disclosures and discourses were put on hold when Qalli entered the gym with a tray of beverages, like an Air India flight attendant—she even had the requisite top bun hairdo—and went around distributing smoothies, juices and water. As Karna watched her odd behavior, a muscle began ticking in his jaw. The harder it was to maintain his anger at Draupadi, the easier it flared up at Qalli.

She was driving him mad with her constantly seesawing attitudes and attires. His gaze strayed to the slender sway of her hips covered in a red sari, then changed direction and roved over the gossamer-red blouse when she twisted past him to go into the armory. Kohl-lined eyes skewered him as she offered him a glass of fresh pomegranate juice. She was hopping mad at him for the stunt he'd pulled at Club Suristan. He wasn't going to apologize until she confessed her cloak-and-dagger agenda.

Karna finished the juice in three strong gulps and set the glass on the bench of the weights machine. He cleared his throat to resume the lesson when Qalli bent forward, delicately whisking the glass away. He lost his train of thought the second she flashed her cleavage. Crap.

"If you've finished the morning lessons, my lord, breakfast is ready."

"I'll be down in a minute," he said, wisely not looking at her. "The six of you will skip breakfast as punishment for starting two fights, destroying a club even if you set it to rights after, and putting humans in danger of my wrath. Luckily, I have tremendous self-control, and that's what you need to learn. Leave the weapons for now, sit back down on your mats and meditate on your actions."

"Is it wise to starve them?" Qalli challenged his authority again.

"Woman, do you ever shut up?" He closed the armory and stalked across the gym.

"You know what's coming in six days. And I know you're going to involve the girls whether it's a good idea or not. They need all the sustenance they can get. Especially Yahvi. She can't afford to miss a meal," Qalli said to his back.

The Six protested against their handmaiden's protest.

"We can handle it."

"Stop ruining our lives."

"We just had a humungous smoothie."

"Missing a meal won't kill me!"

"Silence!" he roared, turning about at the door of the gym. Would he never have peace and quiet in his abode again? "I will have silence for an hour. Pick up every fallen leaf on the boardwalk, and collect them in bags for mulching. Then you will pack up food boxes in the kitchen—a hundred for each of you. Then, you will accompany me to Mumbai, feed the poor with your own hands...and then, only then, you may break your fast."

By karma! Females were trouble.

She'd definitely gotten off on the wrong foot with Karna even as Qalanderi.

Draupadi indulged in a second cup of afternoon masala tea, and cursed her luck for losing her temper the previous night, and again, this morning. It was funny how her mortal habits—like tea, toast and temper—had manifested with a vengeance as soon as she'd stepped foot on Earth.

If she didn't start behaving like a dutiful handmaiden, he was sure to kick her out. And that wouldn't serve her purpose at all. She needed to be here to manipulate the situation in her favor, without alerting him or her daughters. Tiny slivers of doubt, that's all she needed to plant in his head about this mission, and the dominoes would topple.

Draupadi set her teacup on its saucer and began to nibble on a slice of toast. Her hula-hooping emotions weren't allowing her to imbibe anything more palatable. Ziva had given her the same restorative she'd given Yahvi, but it hadn't settled Draupadi's stomach. Nor would it, as her problems weren't physical issues, but stress-related.

She had five days to convince her daughters that nothing in the Cosmos was worth dying for—not honor, not duty, not even love. Life was the only victory. Five days to convince Karna to go against the Gods.

A burst of laughter across the table drew Draupadi's attention. If she disregarded the fact that this was the Human Realm, and that their souls were in constant imminent danger, the lunch tableau seemed as normal as it had been in Alaka. She noticed, with no small amount of envy, her daughters' easy acceptance in Karna's household. Ease she'd never felt anywhere.

Twisted, knotty relationships were her curse. She didn't have a single relationship that was smooth and uncomplicated. Even her bonds with her daughters were fraught with tension and sometimes tears because, though she tried very hard not to have a tug-of-war with them regarding their life choices, most often she had no control over them.

And here she was again, stuck in another tricky situation and relationship. Not just tricky, but dangerous as well.

She'd be a fool to think of Karna as anything but dangerous. He even looked it. His lion's mane was loose about his shoulders, darkly wet at the temples from sweat. As was his habit, he'd tucked the sides behind his ears. Dared she trust him with her babies? *Deva!* What was she thinking? Trust a war-mongering warrior with her daughters' welfare? Never.

As if he felt her stare, Karna raised his head and locked eyes with her. Afternoon shadow darkened the rakish slant of his jaw. For an impractical second, she wondered what would have happened if he'd kissed her last night. She shuddered in relief when he looked away. He pushed his empty plate back and whistled sharply, surprising the room into silence.

"Let's clear up some things up." He addressed the room at large, not her specifically. "The last two days have been chaotic. I don't know what the future will bring, but I'm guessing more chaos." He picked up his goblet and took a sip of coffee. "Since we've been forced into this together...what is it, Amara?" His golden eyes flashed, and Amara froze with her mouth comically open. "Can you wait for me to finish what I have to say before giving us your invaluable input?"

Amara pressed her lips together and mimed zipping her mouth shut.

"This is not a game," he said, putting an end to the low laughter brought on by Amara's antics. He took another gulp of coffee. "*Asuras* are real. Evil is a fact. I face it every day. I struggle to overcome it every day. It is not easy to do. But it is not impossible either. The Gods asked me to train you as demon hunters. Now I'm asking you. Do you want this for yourselves? Free of force, free of punishment, free of everything but your own will and desire? If you don't, then I'll do everything in my power to make the Council reassess your duties. But, if you do…?"

Draupadi willed her babies to grab the out Karna had offered them and run, but they were already nodding and saying, "We so do!"

He nodded once. "Then I want you to understand it's an absolute commitment of mind, body and soul."

He went on to give a fine, bolstering speech, but it had the opposite effect on Draupadi. With gruff bluntness, he outlined plans, considered goals and asked for opinions—everyone's but hers. His honesty frightened her. He didn't sugarcoat the situation. He didn't offer them glory on a platter. He didn't offer any false promises at all. Draupadi wished he would, only so she could hold him accountable when it all went awry.

Why had her daughters agreed to this task? And Yahvi. Dear Heaven, what would happen to Yahvi if she was captured by an *asura*? Any *asura*—forget Vala. Dread tore through her soul, threatening to choke her. She could not lose her children again. She couldn't let her world go dark again.

"I think this is a big mistake," she said. "Draupadi hasn't sanctioned any of this. Believe me, she won't take kindly to her daughters coming to harm. She…" She suddenly found her mouth pressed against Iksa's shoulder.

"Stop! Mama, please stop," Iksa whispered in her ear, hugging her tight. "This is how it has to be. I've seen the future."

An ominous chill swept through Draupadi. Iksa was quiet and introspective by nature and necessity. She guarded her words carefully for she always worried that her "sight" was more prophetic than an option. When she did speak though, it behooved them all to listen.

"If Draupadi has an issue, she's free to take it up with the Gods." Karna pushed back his chair and stood up. "We officially commence your training today. Bring your weapons to the prayer room once we're done with lunch. I want them anointed as per the Cosmic Codes. I want everything done right, no stone unturned. The *asuras* are not going to get away because we forgot to consecrate a nail file. Lavya, you'll see to the sacred fire?"

"If I have to climb Mount Meru and get kindling from the Holy Tree personally, my lord." Lavya's deadpan tone diffused some of the tension around the table.

Everyone's but Draupadi's—*what had Iksa seen?*

"Phew, Yoda, that was one long speech," Amara said. "Seriously, I thought only I could yap for that long and without a water break. And could you have sounded any more disgruntled that we're in this together? FYI, the Gods didn't force us into this. We chose our destinies. And we chose you."

"Why, I'm honored by your faith," Karna said, looking pleasantly surprised.

More than surprised herself, Draupadi leaned in to whisper in Satya's ear, "The Patriarchs offered you a choice? Why didn't you refuse this task?"

"It's complicated," said Satya.

Draupadi's nerves jangled. "How much more complicated can it be?"

"Very," Satya answered sheepishly.

Draupadi wanted to pull her hair out by the roots at the one-word answer. Her daughters were keeping secrets from her. She was not going to like what they had to say, was she? She had caused this. How often had they seen her tell a white lie and manipulate and hide things to get her way? Cosmic custard! Too often.

Eklavya's cell phone rang, jarring the room into sudden silence.

"Hey! Uh-huh. Yup. What? Uh-huh. No shit. Let me call you back, boss." Lavya stared at Karna all through that cryptic exchange, then clicked the phone off. "That was Ved Prajwal. Missing person reports have suddenly escalated within two days at his police station. Bodies are turning up, and body parts by the dozens. It's not restricted to one area. He said it's happening all over the country."

"Who is Ved Prajwal and what does he mean, bodies are turning up?" Satya asked. "Shouldn't the computer have alerted us if *asuras* were running about kidnapping and murdering humans?" As always, her eye was focused on the ball while Draupadi's was stuck on the horrors.

"Hmm? Ved is an assistant subinspector of the Mumbai Special Branch. He's one of us. Well, he's human, but he keeps his ears to the ground for us in Mumbai's jailhouses. Evil sooner or later ends up behind bars," said Karna. He didn't even look shocked.

By this time Eklavya, who never seemed to be without a gizmo or two, had flipped open a tablet, tapped on the screen and set it up on a pedestal. A staid-looking newswoman reported into a mike, discussing the mysterious and gruesome happenings with due horror. The police had no idea what to make of it and swayed between calling it an act of horrific evil by a cult of serial killers, and extreme terrorism by enemies of the nation. They cautioned the public not to venture out alone even during daylight hours.

"Shit," said Karna, then cursed more strongly when the screen switched to a gruesome picture of body parts. He looked at the girls.

Was he checking whether they cringed from the picture? Would they fail some test if they did? None of her daughters looked away. Neither did she. She'd seen much worse. She'd seen the slaughtered remains of her five young sons.

"Baby is set up to alert us only if the Reds are within the boundaries of the Human Realm or within the Global Satellite Spectroscopes' reach." Lavya went on to speculate that the *asuras* had most probably lured their victims to the other *loks*. But the Soul Warrior had no jurisdiction in the *loks*—such was the nature of treaties—and had no way of stopping the atrocities there. "Assuming the humans are being forced and not going with the *asuras* of their own volition, because a lot of idiots are lured by the promise of immortality or endless wealth. Sometimes, not even for that much." Lavya shot Karna a grey look.

"Tell Ved we'll help look into the disappearances," Karna said.

"He knows we will. But that's not all. He hit the two clubs we asked him to. And at Mumbai Magic, he overheard some punk kid tell the bartender that a huge reward waited for the dude who knew the way to the Hidden Isle."

"A kid?" Ziva asked, frowning. "Human or *asura*?"

"Hardly matters. They'll be after the *raakh*," Karna said, nodding as if he'd expected it. "The *asuras* will want it back. It belongs to their Lord Master, after all."

"Can they find us?" Yahvi asked, horrified. Finally, thought Draupadi, a child who was sensibly scared.

"They shouldn't," Karna replied, not very convincingly. "Nothing is impossible, *vatse*. Don't be scared." He patted Yahvi's hand in reassurance, and Draupadi's heart squeezed painfully watching the tenderness of the gesture. Surely, he'd want her safe now?

"I vote we lay a trap and get it over with," said Amara, stabbing a Joystick in the air.

"Behave," said Draupadi and Satya at the same time.

"There's no need to panic. We have our protection perimeters set up well." Karna drained the coffee from the goblet and set it back down, narrowing his eyes on Yahvi. An icy calm settled over his features. The warrior had made a decision, and Draupadi prayed it was something she wanted to hear. It was. "Let's err on the side of caution. All of you will move to a safer location."

"I'm not that scared." Yahvi flushed pink in outrage as the rest of her daughters sprang to their feet. Draupadi was certain most of the Human Realm could hear their objections.

"Shall I take the girls back to the Higher Worlds?" she asked. Once there, she'd force them into hiding again. Two birds. One stone.

"No! The land of the Kurus," Iksa announced and stood up on her chair for good measure. "I've had visions of mountains and forests and a place that is full of suffering. I thought it was the Human Realm. But I was wrong. Well, not totally, but it's the land of the Kurus I dream of. I am sure of that now."

Draupadi gasped in dismay. "No, darling, Kuru Kshetra is a most inauspicious place. It was even before the Great War, and it certainly is now. It's overrun by mortals and…"

"She's not talking about Kuru Kshetra," Karna cut her off. He looked stunned too, then a bit resigned, and a lot irritated. And it didn't make Draupadi feel any better.

"The Valley of the Gods. The dominion of the Kurus. Iksa means Har-ki-doon."

# PART TWO

HAR-KI-DOON, THE VALLEY OF THE GODS

# CHAPTER ELEVEN
## ABHAYARANYA: SANCTUARY

Har-ki-doon was situated on the northeast end of the Tons River Valley in Uttaranchal, India. A stunning piece of highland at the confluence of a trio of glaciers, it displayed in every direction the magnificence of the Himalayan Mountains—the once legendary abode of the Gods.

Yahvi took in the rolling Valley of the Gods and wondered why her father had ditched his principal seat and bunked with Lavya seven hundred years ago. Her father wasn't one to shirk his responsibilities, so whatever had happened had been cataclysmic.

She didn't know that story. The canons, of course, described Har-ki-doon in vivid detail—and they were right. Har-ki-doon was like a garden in paradise.

History rang of tales of her father's wholesome generosity. Time and again, the Celestials had put him through the harshest of tests to catch the tiniest sliver of selfishness in him. Time and again, they'd been struck by his unstinting willingness to help others no matter the cost to himself. Her father had earned the honorific of *Daan Veer* at a very young age, an epithet used for the bravest, most altruistic of souls.

In the past three days, Yahvi had seen his altruism toward the needy humans with her own eyes. So it was no marvel that Har-ki-doon was in part sanctuary for the less fortunate, and in part hospice for the wounded.

As prisons went, Har-ki-doon wasn't too shabby.

"This is so bloody unfair! And chauvinistic and demeaning."

Yahvi rolled her eyes as Amara angrily ran down a gently sloping hill. Amara's temper was like a lightning bolt. Good thing lightning never struck the same place twice. Not much of a comfort, though, if the first jolt killed you.

They were on a minitrek-tour around the property, getting acquainted with the new surroundings. Her father and Lavya had brought them to Har-ki-doon that afternoon, introduced them to Ash, the abode's overseer and resident healer, and the *pahadi* or highlander staff who worked in various capacities in and around the citadel, then vanished right after to meet up with Ved Prajwal. That was the reason Amara was upset. Father had left them behind. Again.

Of course, he'd explained that a couple of lessons did not a demon hunter make. He couldn't just thrust the lot of them into Soul Warrior business without proper training and mock trials—no matter what the Gods would have him do.

"He hates us." Amara stormed through an oak grove. "He's never going to take us."

"Don't exaggerate," chided Mama with perfect aplomb. But her patience was wearing thin because Amara had been spoiling for a fight since morning—since Mama had once again tried to spirit them away. "He's protecting you, which is only right."

"You may think it valiant to cower in fear, but I don't."

"Be thankful it's only North India and not Devlok or some other peace-loving realm," Lusha pointed out, deftly deflecting the twig Amara threw in her direction.

"I hate that he keeps referring to us as *females*. When will he take us seriously? And for that matter, when are you going to stop playing games,

*Qalli*?" Amara tended to use sarcasm as a weapon too. She abruptly came to a stop in front of Mama.

"What do you mean, darling?" Mama sounded cool. But Yahvi noticed her flinch. Ziva had sidled up next to both, trying to calm mother and daughter down.

But Amara was not to be consoled. "We aren't here to sit on our butts or have joyrides about town, *Qalli*." Even Yahvi winced at that.

Mama's mouth firmed with disapproval. "I understand that."

"Do you?" Amara slapped her hands on her hips, right on top of the sheaths housing her swords. "Or are you too busy making cootchie-coo eyes at Yahvi's father?"

Their mother sent Amara a withering glance. "No one understands better than I the urgency of our situation. You won't let me help. You won't allow me to protect you. Do you expect me simply to stand aside while you walk into mortal danger?"

"Yes!" Amara yelled. "You have kept us imprisoned by your bloody cowardice and whims all of our lives and I am sick of it."

Yahvi was sick of it too. This was all her fault. They were sworn to protect her green soul. But she'd make it right. Once she had powers, they'd all be free. Tuning out the familiar argument between Amara and Mama, and Lusha as well, Yahvi jogged out of the woodland, toward the ancient citadel of Har-ki-doon.

Black umbrella-like cupolas jutted up from the highest rooftop of the multilayered building, while charming little balconies and *jharokhas* fringed the exterior. It was an imposing structure, made from large chunks of petrified wood. Logs that had long ago—long before they'd been unearthed and chiseled into uniform bricks—been compressed to stone. The curvilinear style of architecture brought out the many variations in color, texture and grain within the rock. There were parts where the original tree stump, with its typical light and dark striations, could clearly be seen. Then there were corners that lit up like stardust, and arches that seemed to have rainbows superimposed on them.

The fort's façade was rough and pitted now. Weather and time had eroded the floral and geometric carvings into indistinguishable lumps, just as they'd once choreographed the creation of the building blocks.

Just like life, in which each moment lived stacked up, one by one, like petrified bricks until they formed some shape, some form. A shape then polished or pitted by the results of one's actions.

Yahvi snapped a picture on her phone, wondering again why her father had left this beautiful place.

"You okay?" asked Iksa, slipping her arm through Yahvi's.

Sighing, Yahvi shut her phone, wondering if she should contact Draas and ask her if she knew anything or could find out what was going on in the Demon Realm.

"Don't ask Draas. Uncle is right. We can't trust anyone but ourselves in this, Vee."

"I've caused this, Iksa, all this tension and unsettlement in our family...and in Heaven. Everyone is so angry at each other, and I'm afraid it'll only get worse until I...until I'm gone." Her stomach hurt at the thought of dying, but she immediately straightened her back. She'd chosen this. There was no room for softness.

"We're lying to him, Iksa, and to Lavya. They're not going to appreciate it. My father thinks I'm a weakling, and in a couple of days, I'm going to lose his trust too when he finds out who Mama is." She kept seesawing between embarrassment and dread with him. She felt awful for putting her sisters and mother in this soup, for they were all here only for her. "Is there no other way, Iksa? Can't you tell me what to do? How I can stop this agony sooner? I can't bear five more days of this."

"You know I can't do that. I can guide you to a point, but your actions have to be free of influence." Iksa gave her a quick hug.

But how free of influence could any action be? Weren't all actions hostages of an individual's understanding and circumstance? What did she understand about life, anyway?

Suddenly Ziva slipped between them. "Stop worrying, little sister. Enjoy this moment. This place. See its beauty. Feel its magic. Breathe, Yahvi, and let the mountain air heal you." She grabbed Yavhi's hands and they both began to spin in circles.

Har-ki-doon was truly enchanting. It was enchanted too. Like the Hidden Isle, it was veiled from human eyes. The valley radiated out from the main abode in every direction until it merged with the natural fortification of the surrounding mountains. Several waterfalls gushed or trickled down from various rocky edifices, gathering sporadically into wide, frothy basins. A stream spilled from one such lagoon, flowing merrily across the valley floor before disappearing into the folds of the southern mountain range. The evening sun had painted everything in shades of fire and gold.

When they stopped spinning, Ziva looped her arm through Yahvi's and winked. Somehow, Yahvi's nerves had vanished, and utter joy suffused her senses. Giggling, the two set off on a stroll along the gurgling stream. They didn't bother to check whether the rest followed. Yahvi hoped they didn't until they'd calmed down.

A million wildflowers dotted the carpet of luscious green grass beneath their feet. Yellow, orange, red and pink nasturtiums blossomed across the meadow, white chrysanthemums swayed merrily in the cool breeze and wild thornless rose bushes bordered the pebbled path they skipped on. Giant trees grew in thickets here and there. Pine, cedar, oak and chestnut were in full growth and bloom, providing shelter to the birds and beasts alike.

A sudden gust of wind had Yahvi gasping and huddling into Ziva, who remained unaffected by the chill. At nearly twelve thousand feet above sea level, the valley had a temperature much lower than Mumbai's. They'd been duly warned of the difference and had changed into appropriate clothing before journeying here.

They climbed up the steps of a gazebo close to the west entrance of the fortress to catch their breaths and wait for the rest of their group. Unfortunately, the argument still raged on when the rest caught up. Yahvi had had enough.

*"You are what your deep driving desire is;*
*As your desire is, so is your will;*
*As your will is, so is your deed;*
*And as your deed is, so is your destiny."*

She recited the proverb in flawless Vedic Sanskrit, rendering everyone, especially her mother, speechless. "You taught us that, Mama. Are you now saying we shouldn't listen to our hearts?"

"Trapped by my own words, am I?" Mama murmured ruefully. Then she didn't speak for a long time, just stared at all of them pensively. "I don't believe it. I don't believe that you want to die. I did not raise cowards. I raised warriors, and I want you to fight. I want you to fight to live."

Yahvi would fight to live too. But if it came to a choice between her life and her father's, Yahvi wouldn't hesitate to sacrifice hers. Mama didn't need to know that.

"And if you won't fight for your life, I will," Mama declared with finality.

"Long ago, when the Cosmos was but an infant, Gods and *asuras* worked as one to churn the Ocean of Milk, using Vasuki, the god-king of the Serpents, as rope and the Mandara Mountain as the whisk. Both sought the Elixir of Everlasting Health—some call it the Drug of Immortality but they're mistaken, for it's not—that would emerge from the churning. I rewarded them for their collective labor by rising from the ocean with a pot full of the precious nectar, *amrita*, cupped within my hands. But the unscrupulous *asuras* stole it away instead of sharing it, and that spelled their doom."

Lord Dhanvantari, physician to the Celestials, took a breather in his storytelling to puff on a hookah. For the next several minutes, he sucked on the pipe with a hypnotic *gut-gut* sound, periodically blowing *shisha*—tobacco smoke—out of his mouth. The vaporized *shisha* undulated in the air like a genie escaping from a bottle. Yahvi sniffed at it, deciding that the mingled scents of tobacco and pine were not unpleasant at all.

"What happened then?" she asked when her patience evaporated with the *shisha*. She loved listening to stories and found that most souls, with very little encouragement, were willing to spill their tales of woe and spice to an avid listener.

"I cursed the *asuras* for displaying such abominable manners," said Doc D cheerfully. "Since then, *amrita* cannot heal them even if they consume barrelfuls of the medicine."

Which was not necessarily a good thing, as the *asuras* had found other ways to boost their health—human blood being one of them.

"My dear Yahvi, as much as I'd like to regale you with tales of my persnickety youth, alas, duty calls." After a final quick inhalation, Doc D restored the pipe to the hookah hook, unfolded his legs and stood up from the swing they'd shared for the past half an hour. Smiling grandly, he adjusted his green upper garment over one shoulder, tucking the front end into the waistband of an elaborately embroidered *dhoti*.

Yahvi stood up, touched his feet respectfully and got a health blessing out of it. She sat back on the swing, watching him stroll off in search of Ash. His hair was completely white under his crown, shimmering thickly down his broad blue back to his calves. She wondered how old he was. Would he remember? Did it even matter? They could hardly put the correct number of candles on his birthday cake even if he did.

A few times a year, Doc D came to Har-ki-doon to replenish Ash's stock of *amrita*, which was used to heal the patients. The Soul Warrior and his aide had come back to Har-ki-doon that evening with a truckload of human victims, and Doc had been called in especially to replenish the vats. Ziva and Ash had been in the infirmary ever since.

Only *amrita* could cure the supernatural ailments caused by a curse, or a Celestial or demonic weapon, or an *asura* bite. *Amrita* and copious amounts of luck, that is.

Yahvi prayed that her luck and Ash's supply of the healing balm never ran out.

"Come on. Let's go. I thought he'd never stop yapping." Amara strode past her suddenly, not even stopping to look whether Yahvi followed. She had a red juicy apple in her hand.

Yahvi jumped off the massive antique swing she'd been sitting on and ran after her sister. Although to call the contraption an antique would be to insult antiques. "You told me to distract him, so I did. Are we going?"

"Quit grinning at the moon, especially when there isn't one in the sky. You look demented," Amara said, flashing a wicked smile over her shoulder.

Yippee! They were going. Yahvi fairly danced across the courtyard, into a smallish copse in one corner. The Soul Warrior's official seal of the Earth surrounded by the rays of the sun was carved on a stone bench and inlaid with silver. The motif was all over the fort, embedded into lintels, fresco-painted on the walls, woven into the tapestries, paved into the floors of the courtyard. The opulence of the abode did not jibe with what she knew about her father. Was it why he'd left here? It hadn't felt like home?

"Can't help it. I feel euphoric thanks to Ziva, and you," said Yahvi, coming to a stop next to Amara. She looked about. They were alone. But they had a clear view of the courtyard, where the elders of their party still lounged. "I think something is rekindling between Mama and my father. What do you think?"

Amara sliced a piece of the apple with her wicked sharp pearl-hilted boot knife and held it out. Yahvi declined the offering. She'd eaten way too much at dinner, including a huge helping of Lusha's seven-layer choc-attack cake.

"Don't know, don't care." Amara shrugged and popped the slice into her mouth. A couple of peacocks cooed from the woods.

It wasn't that Amara didn't care about Mama's happiness. Amara's philosophy was simple: Do the deed and forget about the outcome. Amara was a doer, not a thinker. If she was forced to think about things, she thought about war and weapons.

Yahvi couldn't shrug off her parents' relationship quite so nonchalantly, especially when it was obvious they couldn't keep their eyes off each other. She had no clue how things might work out, with Mama still pretending to be Qalanderi, and her father's indiscreet aversion to Draupadi. Although he had stopped making disparaging comments about Devious Draupadi, at least in front of them. That gave her hope. She was filled with hope tonight.

"Hellhounds and Himalayan Yak! Danger, twelve o'clock," Amara exclaimed out of the corner of her mouth. "What's he doing away from his patients?"

Yahvi stood up and watched, transfixed, as Ash strode into the courtyard and made his way straight to Mama, and—*spinning satellites*—began chatting with her. Mama and Ash had to be kept apart for as long as possible. The minute either one of them realized who the other was, it would be the end of the world—before Vala even got here.

"How long before she realizes he's Freddy Krueger inside and out?" Amara wondered.

Freddy Krueger indeed. Ash looked downright scary even in broad daylight. The entire length of his seven-foot frame was covered in robes the color of pewter. His head was wrapped in a matching turban and had a long, flowing end that cut across his face from cheek to collarbone. Only his eyes, black fathomless orbs, and the surrounding stretch of pasty skin could be seen. No other sliver of skin was exposed anywhere on his body. He wore black leather gloves on his hands and black boots under the robes. A long gold chain hung from his neck, ending in a filigree pendant the shape and size of a tennis ball in the center of his chest. Incense glowed inside it. At regular intervals, sandalwood smoke wafted out, lending atmosphere to his ghostly appearance.

"Please, not yet," Yahvi prayed fervently, as a couple of monkeys started whooping from the trees sheltering them. She had an adventure to enjoy.

"*Shh!* Be quiet," Amara shooed them away, but the monkeys were persistent. They began slapping at the apple in her hand. She threw it deeper into the woods, and the monkeys hopped off behind it.

Within minutes, Ash broke away from Mama without incident and took a seat by Lavya and her father, a reasonable distance away from Mama. Amara and Yahvi let out a duet of relieved sighs.

"Midnight," Amara muttered, wiping her blade clean with the corner of her flannel shirt.

Yahvi glanced at her sister. "Are you sure?"

"The only way Yoda will be convinced of my Jedi powers is if he sees me in action."

"Amu," Yahvi began only to be interrupted.

"They're setting a trap at Asht Dveep and won't take us. They haven't even told us. It was my idea!" Amara's jaw tightened stubbornly. "Come if you dare. Sha-sha is coming."

Amara was right. Lusha would go.

"Where is she? I told her to be quick with her food prep. She's going to spike the sentries' drinks with a sleeping draft."

Yahvi's stomach fluttered half in fear, half in excitement. "He won't like it," she said. "All we've done is piss him off since we got here."

"Make up your mind, Vee. Do you want to be remembered as the girl who never did anything, or do you want to finish what started at your birth? It's the only way they'll let you live as you wish. Besides, Yoda's pissed at Qalli, not us."

Amu knew her too well. Yahvi desperately wanted her Jedi powers to get activated. She wanted her father to be proud of her. She wanted her mother to laugh again.

In any case, Lusha brought their sisters to the hideout for a final conference. There was safety in numbers, after all. Satya asked Iksa what she'd seen again.

"I see only celebrations in the near future," Iksa replied. "I see us happy."

Satya nodded. "We stay together. And you do as I say."

Whew! Amara's game plan would not be booted.

After that, the only thing left to do was draw straws, and the short stick winner would have to distract their mother in time—or be left behind.

Later that night, Karna, Lavya and Ved Prajwal scoped out Madh Fort, which had been chosen as the site of the trap. Through the snitches, they'd spread the word that a map of the Soul Warrior's abode was for sale.

The ruins of the old fort were drenched in darkness, as were the beach it stood on and the road leading up to it. By the time Karna was done sweeping the place for any extra colored dots zipping about the place, besides the souls of his friends, Ved Prajwal had his nausea under control and was actually helping out.

"See anything suspicious?" asked Lavya, coming at them from the direction of the beach, where he'd gone to place the iron traps and recheck the protection spells. Karna wanted the contamination contained in a very small area.

"Nope," Karna replied. "Not even a residual trace of evil."

Since Ved's phone call that afternoon, they'd been integrating the information trickling in. Too slow to count, but it was better than nothing. Someone had bought the map an hour ago. No confirmation on whether the buyer was Vala or not. Didn't matter. Whoever had bought it wasn't planning on using it as wall décor.

"The fort is monitored by the air force, being so close to the naval base. We can tag them if needed. No one can come here without permission anyway, so no casualties."

It was Karna who'd commissioned the construction of the fort in the 1700s to cover the tunnel running beneath it. He'd also insisted that the surrounding land be made off-limits to civilians. The Soul Warrior and the Indian Defense Ministry had an understanding.

"Unless, of course, you're an *asura*." Ved's gravelly voice betrayed his jumpiness.

Now here was a sensible man who knew the score, as opposed to his foolhardy *shishyas*.

Karna was glad the females had been moved two thousand kilometers away to a remote, hard-to-breach location. He'd posted a dozen sentries he'd borrowed from Salabha there and instructed them to be on high alert until further notice.

"Yes." Karna's own anxiety manifested into a grin. He'd known Ved Prajwal for the better part of five years. Ved had gone out of his way to help Karna more times than he could count, yet Karna hadn't trusted him with full disclosure for his own good. This wasn't the time for secrets, though. He glanced at Lavya, giving him the go-ahead.

"There's a tunnel under the ruins connecting the mainland to Asht Dveep." Lavya gave Ved a quick rundown of the area's history. Shocked, Ved asked how it was possible to link Madh Island to Asht Dveep if Asht Dveep wasn't even part of the Human Realm. "The island abode is part of the Human Realm. It's just not part of its reality," Lavya clarified.

"But there's nothing there." Ved pointed at the blackness beyond the beach. "And I know you don't live underwater. Bloody hell! You've taken me to your house."

"It's an illusion. Think Bermuda Triangle in reverse. Things get drawn to the Triangle and disappear...or so humans think. Well, Asht Dveep repels ships, planes, animals, humans et al. And unless you know its exact location, you won't find it."

But an *asura* would find it tonight because of the rigged map. There really was no time to chitchat. The *asuras* would come tonight. Of that Karna had no doubt.

"Meet you at the abode," he said, and, touching Ved's shoulder, he vanished to the gym room. Ved fell to his knees gagging and swearing as Lavya materialized. And as if on cue, Ash appeared right behind him.

"Ha! Got here in time. Patients are asleep. Dhanvantari couldn't stay, but Ziva and Qalanderi have promised to keep watch. I'm at your disposal, my friend," Ash said, grinning fiercely. His voice was muffled, covered as his mouth was in gunmetal-grey cloth. "Whoo! The heat and humidity on this island are horrific. How do you live here all year round?"

"With a lot of sweat and a scanty cotton wardrobe," replied Ved with a laugh, plucking at the red T-shirt he wore over jeans. "Mumbai's not so bad once you get used to it, and of course, air conditioning helps—most of the time. Take off your robes, boss, if you're uncomfortable."

Ash wrestled visibly with the tempting suggestion, but Karna knew even before his friend shrugged that he wouldn't. Not in front of Ved, who, in spite of Karna and Lavya's high praises about his discretion and trustworthiness, was still a stranger to Ash. And Ved was human. Humans weren't known for their steely stomachs or nonjudgmental natures.

Ash, Ashwathama, was his oldest friend in the Cosmos. Their friendship hadn't faltered even after death. Cursed to suffer all manner of diseases ceaselessly, Ash was banned from the Higher Worlds during the Dark Age so he wouldn't find reprieve anywhere. His whole body was covered in open sores and pustules. His muslin robes padded the wounds as well as hid them from sight. A just retribution, the Gods had declared, for the heinous, unrighteous act of murdering five unarmed boys in their sleep—Draupadi's five young sons.

*Fugdoomal!* It crossed his mind that Draupadi might not like her daughters associating with her sons' assassin. Karna stiffened at the thought. And why was he worrying over the woman's likes and dislikes? Ash was his best friend, and what souls in the entire bloody Cosmos hadn't done something they were ashamed of?

And wasn't Ash paying for his mistake every single day with excruciating forbearance? Between caring for the sick, his cursed sickness and Har-ki-doon, Ash rarely got a day off, much less the chance to play cops and robbers. No wonder he'd seized the moment with both gloved hands when Karna had asked him to join their *asura*-trapping party tonight.

Karna snapped back into focus, sprinting across the gym when alarms went off around the house. He disarmed the gun room with key codes and a mantra. They had maybe a half hour until full attack.

The *asuras* would have their own *vyuhas*—battle formations. Their moles would be up front, smashing through the root-infested sand flats and traps blocking the tunnel, leading the contagion to the island.

The floor began to tremble under Karna's booted feet, making his gut clench.

"What. Is. That?" asked Ved as the quaking increased.

The abode began to quiver like the leaves on the grey mangroves that surrounded it, knocking dumbbells, barbells and other thingamujigs off the gym equipment.

"Here they come." Lavya slapped a hand on his thigh and rubbed to get his blood flowing. He checked his phone for enemy position and ETA. "What the fuck? They're not in the tunnels."

"They came straight to the island?" Karna pushed open the iron door of the armory. How was that possible unless the *asuras* were working with more than a map?

"They're popping up all over the place. They're using vanishment… some powerful-looking demons out there…and shit! A humungous black cloud just poofed into existence and it's growing. Fuck! It's opening a portal…that's a bloody wormhole," Lavya shouted, peeping alternatively at the phone screen and through the slats of a window.

"It's about time I had some fun," said Ash, and popped the joints of his shoulder and neck with several rapid jerks.

Assistant Subinspector Prajwal was nothing if not quick to grasp the situation. As Ash stretched lazily, Ved strapped on a bulletproof vest and weapon holster, clipping on his standard police-issue 9-mm Smith & Wesson and the handheld fire blaster Lavya passed to him. He picked up the 38-mm riot gun and placed it over his shoulder like a badass awaiting trouble.

"That's overkill," said a stupefied Ash, his hands grazing the light fixture hanging from the ceiling.

"Hey! You forget I'm human. I don't have gamma rays leaking out of my fingertips or divine nuclear-type *astras* at my disposal."

But Ved's enthusiasm was catching. Karna allowed his bloodlust to well up and rush through his veins. He slapped Ved on the back. And since their ambush strategy had been shot to hell, he quickly thought up plan B.

"Stay inside the abode at all times, Ved. That's über-protected. I guarantee no *asura* or their nasty *asura-maya* will get to you here. Remember, if the *asuras* grab you, they'll gobble you up. They won't even spit out your bones."

"How environment-friendly, to be consumed whole without wastage." Ved's tone was light, but his face had gone dead white. "I've seen what they do to humans. I won't be stupid."

"You'll be fine," Karna said with complete confidence. Confident that he, Lavya and Ash would not let the demons get anywhere near the human and confident that Ved, in spite of being human, was capable of defending himself. He was ex-army and a policeman. Ved knew the drill.

"One more thing. Try not to kill them. Just disable them." The Soul Warrior's handicap: Karna had to kill the *asura* personally for the Soul Catcher to seize the soul.

"Fifty and counting. They're big and fast on their feet. They're circling the abode now, testing the structure for weakness," said Lavya.

There wasn't any.

Karna ambled out of the strong room armed with sword, knives, serrated boomerangs and minibombs. He tied a black bandana over his head to keep his hair off his face and blend in with the dark-skulled foe. Activating the Soul Catcher, he grinned fiercely at his three amigos.

"*Mauja, Mauja,*" he growled. "It's time to tango."

Yahvi materialized inside the island abode, clutching Satya's hand. It took her a second to find her land legs, another to realize the battle had begun.

*Breathe through the vertigo. Do not faint.*

Satya released her hand and ran for the windows, yelling orders as she took stock. Her voice sounded faint in the electrically charged atmosphere. The house moaned as if in objection to the mayhem going on outside. With her longbow gripped solidly in her right hand, Yahvi took off after her sisters down the hall and into the foyer, where they all abruptly stopped running. Iksa let out a huge gasp like she was having a vision. She stared at the man standing in front of the open doors. Or was she staring at the sea of demons beyond him?

"Who the hell is that?" shouted Amara as six pairs of eyes zoomed in on the stocky man in a crew cut shooting at the waves of *asuras* clamoring to ram into the house. His red T-shirt had the same effect on the *asuras* that a red muleta cape would have on an enraged bull. He aimed and shot. They bled and multiplied.

*Oh shit, shit, shit,* thought Yahvi in tandem with the man's "Fuck! Fuck! What the fuck?"

It was too much. The vanishment, the negative energies swirling outside and her own excitement made Yahvi's head swim. She staggered to the steps and sat down hard.

Lusha, Amara and Satya reached the man together. After Lusha had safely yanked the gun and fire blaster from his hands, Amara pitched him back from the door, put her nose in his face and screamed, "Who the hell are you, dumbwit?" Then she shoved him out of her way, looking in Yahvi's opinion like a very angry dragon.

"Who the hell are you?" he croaked without falling on his butt. That was impressive.

"Reinforcements," said Satya and took his spot at the main doors. "Stay back!" she ordered as if to the *asuras*, but Yahvi knew the order was for the only two humans in the house—on the island, in fact.

Ziva smiled up at the man. "Who are you, sir?"

"Ved...Prajwal," he sputtered, chest heaving as if he'd run a marathon. He was staring at Satya in terror. She looked formidable in head-to-toe *mantra*-treated black spandex—they all were dressed the same. Her long black hair was coiled in a chignon on top of her head. She didn't move a muscle as she concentrated on infiltrating the minds of the *asuras* in front of her.

"Ah, the policeman with the connections," said Ziva in a tone one used while having guests over for tea. "I'm Ziva. That's Satya, Amara and Lusha, and this is Iksa and Yahvi."

Ved Prajwal tore his eyes away from Satya and glanced down at Ziva. Excitement and nerves made her colorful skin sparkle like sunlit crystals. He then gawked up at Lusha as she swaggered past him—up because she topped him by at least six inches.

Yahvi couldn't help but laugh at Ved's horror-and-lust-struck expression. Her sisters had that effect on males, and it was super-amusing to watch every time. Lusha cracked her knuckles, and the carvings on her forearm seemed to come alive when she flexed her arms. It was a scary sight. She was raring to have a go at the *asuras*.

"What are they doing?" Ved jerked his chin in the general direction of Satya and Lusha.

"Satya is mentally influencing the *asuras*. She wants them to believe they are docile dogs and she is their master. Lusha is waiting for her signal to go bash them up. By the way, those are *raktabeejas* you were shooting at. You don't know what they are, do you?" Ziva patted his arm in sympathy.

Ved shook his head, clearly bedazzled by the goings-on. He really couldn't seem to decide which of her sisters to focus on.

Yahvi had the same issue. Iksa came and sat next to her. She looked peaked. As if she'd seen a ghost. "Vision?" Yahvi whispered. But her sister simply shook her head. She was looking at Ved very curiously. Yahvi hoped whatever she'd seen for him wasn't dire.

"Fabulous," growled Amara, baring her teeth. "Yoda-man recruits this moron who can't tell *asuras* apart and forbids us to help?"

"Yoda-man?" Ved's mouth formed the letters without sound, not even a squeak. The poor man was tongue-tied—a common occurrence in males around her sisters.

"Lord Master Karna," Amara spat out sarcastically. "You have to kill a *raktabeeja* without making him bleed because from each drop of blood spilled, a fully formed clone emerges."

"Fuck! No wonder the bastards kept multiplying. Karna said to wound the demons and not kill them. Only he can kill them to suck up their souls or some shit."

Yahvi was quite impressed that the human had gotten over his speechlessness so fast, even if Ziva was helping him along.

Ziva petted Ved one last time before dropping her arm. "Sometimes you improvise."

"Got it. So, how do we kill them without making them bleed?" he asked.

"Watch and learn," said Lusha and Amara in unison and strode past Satya to dive into the fray.

Yahvi watched her sisters closely, recognizing their moves, admiring their skill, filing it all away for when she'd be one of them. Satya had managed to mind-grip the *raktabeejas* closest to her—there seemed to be at least two hundred more behind that lot. She got a good chunk of *asuras* to drop their weapons and go down on their knees while Lusha and Amara methodically snapped their necks. No blood spilled, but a lot of dead demons were piling up.

"That's it?" asked Ved. But it wasn't as easy as her sisters made it seem.

"For that type of demon, yes."

Ved narrowed his eyes. "Huh. I thought all demons were the same."

"Are all humans the same?" Ziva went puce in color. She hated generalizations.

Outside, Lusha and Amara brought out the big guns. They'd reached the end of the mind-stoned line. Lusha used her arms, legs, elbows and head, anything, to get the undulating hordes off her back. Amara and her eighteen-inch blades were slashing their way through the enemy ranks with both hands, without spilling any blood. Her Joysticks pierced the skin of the foe and messed up his insides, then while exiting the body the hot blades, enhanced by a spell, would seal the wound up. That took more than skill. That was warcraft.

Her sisters moved beyond vision range, and it grated on Yahvi's nerves. She was desperate to witness it all, frantic to be a part of it. But she'd wait for Satya's signal.

"I'm going to take position by the windows," she yelled, running up the stairs and into the first bedroom on the left. An archer needed to find elevation and distance from the battlefield. She yanked the blinds apart and gasped at the sight outside the window.

She'd always envied the god-like grace her mother and sisters possessed: the fluidity and ethereal beauty of their movements. They turned a mundane thing like applying eyeliner into a ballet. But her father...

Yahvi pressed her hands to the windowpane and stared at the breathtaking display of strength and prowess. Bright as the sun, he spun in the midst of a hurricane of *asuras*. He shouldered a bunch aside, jabbed one with a dagger and pivoted on his heels, slashing a circle of them across their necks in one move.

Jab…jab…sidekick…zap…zap…whirl…kick…flip…crouch…uppercut…

"Okay, now why is he drawing blood?" asked Ved.

"Because *he* can tell a *raktabeeja* from a *daitya*," replied Ziva, launching into Demonology 101 for Ved's benefit.

Ash was on the far right of the melee, a blur of pewter robes and flashing steel. Yahvi could barely see the broadsword clutched between his hands, his movements were that fast. Most of the *asuras* fought with swords too. The clash and clang of the kissing metals created a cacophony of sound and light. And, it seemed, Lavya was up on the terrace-roof, because blazing arrows rained down on the demons without pause, burning them on the spot.

Yahvi yearned to be part of it. She should be up on the roof with her bow and quiver too. She felt impotent standing and just watching. But Satya hadn't given her the go-ahead yet.

"Apparently it takes more than two to tango." Awe fizzed through Ved's words as he too watched the Soul Warrior at work.

"What do you mean?" asked Ziva.

"Karna compared a battle to the tango."

So true, Yahvi thought, her gaze riveted on the show outside. It *was* a dance. The macabre Tango of Death.

# CHAPTER TWELVE
## VIRUDDHA: HOSTILE LIASONS

Karna thrust *Asi* through the *asura's* throat, then pressed his hand to the creature's chest and zapped him with white-hot power. And to be thorough, he yanked out the blade and stabbed him in the groin even as the *asura* disintegrated into *raakh*. He'd held his breath to prevent a sneeze attack and when he whirled to exhale, his peripheral vision caught a blur of bright blue ribboning through the blanket of red.

That was not Ash. *Oh, hell, no they didn't!* Karna leaped into the air, somersaulted twice and landed in front of a delinquent.

"Yo!" Amara greeted him, lopping off the heads of two demons—one on each side—with remarkable ambidexterity. She shot past him to jab her blade through a third.

The urge besieged him to twist her ear and vanish back to Har-ki-doon and lock her up in the dungeons beneath the fort for the rest of eternity.

"You disobeyed a direct order," he roared, and whirled into a back-to-back defense position with her as waves of *asuras* converged upon them from all directions. If she got hurt, he'd never forgive himself.

"You can thank me now for my brilliant foresight and be a god amongst gurus..." She ceased yelling, slashed through the hordes for a bit, then resumed the conversation as if she'd never paused. "Or you can pout and punish me and I'll never, ever think of you as my Yoda-poo again!"

Karna closed his eyes for a split second and prayed to the God of War for deliverance. *O! Indra, give me strength and fortitude to deal with this maniac.* For the next several minutes, he got busy vacuuming up as many Reds with the Soul Catcher as he could, all the while worrying about the menace behind him.

True, he'd seen her fight last night, and she was good. But that had been with her fists and against humans. Didn't matter if they'd been nasty little thugs.

"You're scarily good!" he praised her when he spied a nice slashy X move she made with flair. It calmed him just a tad.

"Duh!" shot back the daughter of bow-wielder, Arjun, and granddaughter of Indra, the wielder of thunderbolts. The fact that Amara was the direct descendent of the God of War eased him more.

Karna might have laughed but for the giant choking the life out of him. "You on your own?" he asked after dispatching the bastard into oblivion.

"No. Sha-sha's fifty feet to the left." Amara spun her blades like the propellers on a helicopter and beheaded the Reds as if swatting flies. "And Satya is guarding the front door. Your policeman pal goofed. He shot a *raktabeeja* and within minutes a couple of hundred of them were at our doorstep."

Karna cursed under his breath. He'd miscalculated a number of things, it seemed.

"I am formally lodging a complaint against you, my lord guru, for displaying such pathetic judgment." She stomped over to him, then slapped her hands on her hips, blades and all, right in the middle of a freaking warzone and scolded him. "And for being so blind and biased! Ved Prajwal's dick doesn't automatically make him a candidate for warriorhood."

Amara had not only shocked him but also managed to flabbergast the clump of *asuras* within hearing distance.

"I like her!" roared a midnight-hued asshole, gazing at Amara with admiration and possibly the beginnings of love.

Flicking Amara a sardonic glance, Karna stabbed lover boy and his entourage to death. But he miscalculated again. As Guru Parashuram always said—"*Keep your head in the game or be fool enough to lose it!*"

An *asura* got close enough behind Karna that he literally felt nasty hot breath on his neck a split second before a bomb of pain exploded through his body. His back felt as if acid had been poured over it. Even breathing hurt. Karna twisted around and smashed his fist into the demon's face and kept smashing until he'd pulverized him. He blinked though a haze of pain, sweat and blood, primed to take on the next Red, and his heart plummeted down to land at his feet.

Yahvi stood framed against a window amidst the chaos that surrounded him. She looked small and vulnerable, so easily breakable. Then a wall of black hurtled toward her, obscuring his view completely.

Fear can paralyze a soul. It can also mobilize one into a demented frenzy.

Karna raced forward, bellowing at her to get away, take cover, hide. He flung *Asi* at the evil cloud. He raised both hands and fired up the demons in his path.

He knew, rationally, she was safe inside. That no *asura* could breach the protection mantra he'd cast over his abode. But was any emotion rational? His fear gave way to anger, and the anger to a cold focus. He would destroy them all, every single one of them, before their evil so much as glanced in her direction. His mind emptied of everything but his need to exterminate.

He didn't know how long he fought. He became blind and deaf to everything but intent. Thus, it was a knee-jerk reaction to head-butt the creature whose arms came around him in a viselike grip.

"Holy mother of *pain*. That bloody hurt more than the *asura* bite," Ash shouted into his ear. "Slow down, my friend. Karna, stop! They sounded their retreat. Look, they're fleeing back into the hole."

Karna gulped in huge mouthfuls of air as his vision cleared.

Satya, Lusha and Amara stood before him. As one, they sank to the ground as his soldiers would've at the end of any battle—won or lost—with one knee touching the ground, forearms resting on the slightly elevated thigh, their backs straight and their heads bowed, their weapons on the ground. He ought to be charmed by their age-old actions. He should've blessed them with long life and endless valor. He should have praised them and told them they'd fought like the godlings they were.

"You disobeyed my orders." His voice cracked through the air like thunder and extinguished the smiles on their faces.

"I apologize, my lord guru," said Satya. At his signal, she rose to her feet, her midnight-blue eyes without remorse. "I take full responsibility for this."

Ash's and Lavya's eyes bored holes into Karna's now badly throbbing back. They silently urged him to let it go, he knew. But the Six had willfully disregarded his rules for the third time. They had put everyone in danger. They had put Yahvi in danger. That could not be tolerated.

"You are all responsible," he said, striding toward the abode. He needed a drink.

The minute he crossed the threshold, Yahvi threw herself into his arms. "You were awesome, Father. Simply awesome! You have to teach me that tumbling-through-the-air move."

He gripped her shoulders and set her aside. It was the first time she'd touched him of her own volition, spoken to him without mumbling, and yet he pushed her away. He had to.

"You shouldn't have come, *vatse*. It was a foolish risk. You cannot be around these creatures. Your will is weak, your green soul feeble. You are powerless against the *asuras*. You are the harbinger of doom, don't you understand?" His heart wouldn't stop pounding.

She flinched as if he'd slapped her. Karna raised a hand in apology or regret—he didn't know which—but Yahvi stepped back from him, allowing him to do neither. He dropped his hand and curled it into a fist.

"I stayed inside. I'm not stupid," she mumbled at the floor.

She'd argue. Even now? "No, not stupid. I can forgive stupidity. What I won't forgive is willful selfishness."

Yahvi's head shot up, her cheeks and nose burning red in shame.

"How dare you put us all in danger because you have an itch to have fun? Do you know? Have you any idea what saving your ass is going to cost us? Wherever you go, destruction will follow. That is your fate. And because of your selfishness, it is our fate too. And you have the gall… the sheer gall to think of this as a game." Fury made his back hurt like a son of a bitch.

"Oh my. Uncle K, your hand is on fire again," exclaimed Ziva, breaking the pall that had descended over the group. "And your back is bleeding." She tried to touch him. "Stay still. Let me help you."

"Leave it," he rasped, moving beyond her reach, beyond everyone's reach. His skin would heal. But his heart—by *karma*—would his heart ever stop aching?

"It wasn't her idea, teach," Amara inserted her two-penny bit.

"Shut up," Karna snarled at her. "You shut up. All of you! I want you to go back to Har-ki-doon this second. If you argue, if any one of you argues with me, I will send you back perforce. And you will not like where you end up."

For the first time since he'd known them, they obeyed him. The Six vanished from his sight without another peep. The last thing he saw was his daughter's tear-streaked face.

"Dude! Catcher gone awry," Ved joked, trying to lighten the death mood.

"You should go home too," Karna said. "You shouldn't be here." He shouldn't have involved a human—even if he was a veteran—in this situation.

Ved frowned. "I didn't screw up that badly. True, for a time there, I didn't know demon up from demon down. But it seems pretty simple once you know how and where to aim."

Karna tasted the metallic tang of blood in his mouth where an *asura* had punched him. He ran his tongue over the swollen cut inside his lip. He flicked a glance between Lavya and Ash. "Take him home, one of you. I'll clean up the mess outside before I go to Hell."

"What the fuck is wrong with you? A severe case of adrenaline withdrawal or what?" Ved sounded genuinely confused. But he didn't know. No one knew of the danger Yahvi was in.

"One mistake, one lapse and they would've gotten her. If they catch her, if they know..." Karna broke off, shuddering. It was a matter of when, not if, he thought with a sick laugh. When Vala found out about his daughter, Hell would seem like paradise.

"Listen, man, I saw those babes in action. You don't have to worry about them. They're like the Shaktikis, the ancient female spear-bearers. The ones I told you about. My ancestors, remember? But I thought that chick's name was Yahvi, not Vatse. And she's human? I didn't realize she was human. So is Iksa human too? Ziva can't be. She's too...vibrant."

Lavya made a slashing motion with his hand at his neck, quelling Ved's twenty questions. "Come on, Prajwal. Help me clean up outside before I take you home."

"Why don't you go deliver your evil burdens?" Ash suggested a bit severely after the other two exited the abode. "Maybe that will clear the funk out of your head."

Duly chastised, Karna went straight to Hell.

The minute Draupadi got the news that Karna was back from delivering demon souls to Yama, she headed straight for his bedchamber. She walked in without knocking and locked the doors behind her before she lost her nerve.

Dear Heaven, she was still reeling from the stunt her daughters had pulled tonight.

The bath chamber was closed, and a shower ran inside. She sank down on the four-poster bed in the center of the chamber to take a breath, gather her thoughts. Just for a minute, though. Then she'd knock on the door. Karna was hurt and needed healing. But she wasn't ready to face him yet. She had to be very sure about how she was going to handle him.

She'd done it, hadn't she? Her daughters had told her what had happened at Asht Dveep. And what Karna had said. He was trying to save Yahvi's ass. He wasn't going to roll over for the Gods and allow his daughter to succumb to fate. He wanted to find a way around the prophecy.

Hope blossomed like a *pushkara* in her belly. Dared she trust him with her plan? Karna would definitely have more success with it than she. She'd tried a hundred different ways to contact Dev-Il and make a deal with him, but he was unreachable. He wouldn't be for the Soul

Warrior—his nemesis, once his best mate. Dev-Il wouldn't say no to a deal with Karna, if only to regain the upper hand this time.

*Deva!* If such a deal came through, would it automatically dissolve the Treaty of Quarantine? Would it open all the portals between all the realms again? Would the Cosmos regress back to the age when all creatures lived everywhere and strife was rampant?

Draupadi stood up to pace the room, one eye on the shut bath chamber door.

Strife was rampant even now in the Cosmos. So, no big change there. Only she knew the paths she'd taken to shield her offspring from life's hardships, horrors and hurts. What was one more path? But would Karna see it like that?

Restless with indecision, Draupadi cut across the large, airy chamber. Besides the en suite bath, Karna's chambers included a walk-in dressing room and a prayer room. The bedrooms allocated to her daughters and her just down the hallway had similar layouts, though Karna's suite was by far the largest and the most opulent.

Stepping out onto the terrace, she noted the view was the same as hers too. There wasn't much to see tonight but an unbroken blue-black panorama. The air was tinged with pine and frost, and a chill she was coming to love. She wouldn't mind if she never saw Asht Dveep again. Yes, she loved her comforts. She wanted her daughters pampered and not roughing it out on some island, or battling *asuras* to prove their worth to the Celestials. She wanted them safe and happy. She wanted a mundane, tension-free existence for all of them. Was that too much to ask?

She didn't think so. But she had to find the right words to put forth to Karna. He angered easily. And he reacted contrary to his nature when angry. Draupadi had tried to explain that to Yahvi, who'd been distraught by her father's biting words.

Warriors and their tempers, thought Draupadi, shaking her head.

It was *amavasya* night. The moon was invisible, the sky a glimmering cradle for the stars. Had she been the superstitious sort, she'd have pinned tonight's misadventure on the sometimes auspicious and often ominous *amavasya*. In the old days, one wouldn't travel on a night devoid of the moon's light, let alone embark on a new journey.

"*A sure way to lose one's way on perilous roads,*" Mother Kunti had often warned.

"*Ridiculous! Why can't we light a torch and proceed?*" Draupadi had argued to no avail.

Her husbands had always minded their beloved mother's words. Always, no matter how vile and abhorrent her dictates.

To this day, Draupadi detested the hold Mother Kunti had over her sons and how she'd manipulated their fates. Was it hypocritical of her to want the same kind of influence over her daughters?

She went back inside to see if Karna was done with his ablutions. He wasn't. A fire danced high and wild inside a massive mosaic-tiled hearth opposite the bed. She stood in front of the flames, letting the heat slowly begin to warm her cold flesh.

She wasn't that kind of mother. She wasn't. She wanted only to protect her daughters.

Eventually, the shower stopped gushing and total silence reigned for exactly two heartbeats before it was shattered by a bellow of pain, followed by a series of profanities.

Karna seemed to be in a seriously foul mood. Probably caused by the wound. He'd been clawed by an *asura* in the back. Both Ziva and Ash had explained to her how to treat the wound. And she was to call them, no matter the hour, if Karna wouldn't allow her to heal him.

Draupadi wondered if it was the right time to propose her plan. Karna was obviously in the middle of a major tantrum. She stared at the door, debating whether to interrupt or not. Well, why not? She'd taken far too many liberties with him already, so what was one more? Plus, he wasn't beyond playing games with her. And if she must justify the invasion of his privacy, then there was his injury that needed mending, wasn't there? She straightened her spine and barged into the bathing chamber.

She quickly shut the door to prevent the lovely hot steam from escaping. That Karna was wet, naked and mouth-dryingly gorgeous became inconsequential at the sight of his ruthlessly lacerated back. The vanity mirror remained fog-free and displayed his reflection clearly. His eyes were scrunched shut, his face clammy and drawn tight in agony. The muscles on his powerful arms jumped and twitched as he leaned on the jade-stone countertop.

She felt his pain as her own, hating that he suffered so, bewildered that he chose to suffer so by dwelling on Earth instead of enjoying the comforts and climes of the Higher Worlds. There, he wouldn't feel any pain. She groped for the jar of medicine in her pajama pocket. The movement caused her shawl to slip off her shoulders and fall to the floor with a whoosh. The stirred air triggered a ghastly odor, making her shudder with revulsion.

Hell had a unique scent; a blend of burning flesh, rotten eggs and onions. It clung to a body until one washed it off with strong soap combined with a mantra to dispel nasty odors. Right now, the stink wafted from Karna's discarded garments lying on the floor at her feet. She conjured a single fragrant blue flame on her palm and poured it over the bilious pile. She didn't care to be reminded of her time in the Netherworld via her olfactory sense. Her hellish sojourn was branded on her conscience for all eternity and was the reason she wanted her offspring far away from such a fate.

Another blasphemy rumbled through the space. This time, though, it was aimed at her. Feverish golden eyes fixed on hers in the mirror. A fraught few seconds passed. Then Karna casually reached for a towel and wrapped it about his hips. Just as casually, he turned to face her, raising one dark, wet brow.

"I brought salve," she said, holding up the etched glass jar. "Ash wants you to put it on the wound as soon as possible, before the infection sets in. Once it does, you will need more than these basic remedies to purify you. But you know all that."

He continued to glower, arms crossed over his broad chest in a classic hands-off posture. She glared back, unperturbed, even though his biceps looked impossibly thick and unforgiving in that pose.

"Turn around," she ordered. "Actually, sit down on the edge of the tub."

After a brief hesitation, he did as she asked. His quiet, though smoldering, acquiescence shocked her and confirmed that he was in considerable pain. So much pain he'd allow her to nurse him. She screwed open the jar, dipped three fingers in and scooped out a glob of buttery yellow goo. The salve was made of freshly ground turmeric, aloe vera extract and a large dose of *amrita*. Turmeric was a natural antiseptic and anti-inflammatory, the aloe a skin soother, and both enhanced the healing properties of the divine nectar.

She began to chant the specific healing spell Ziva had made her memorize and repeat twenty times until she had the meter, the tone and inflections right.

Karna hissed, trembling beneath her hand while she chanted and applied the ointment over a particularly deep cut. Draupadi winced in sympathy but said briskly, "Oh! Don't be such a baby. It's hardly a scratch."

She knew he wouldn't appreciate mollycoddling. A warrior does not get hurt and does not bleed. He does not feel pain and does not cry. A warrior shows no emotion and no weakness—especially not to a foe.

Or was she misjudging him? The warrior before her shuddered and swayed as if he was about to faint. He swore breathlessly at her ministrations. His skin turned the color of a blood orange before her eyes. Draupadi gasped. Was the salve helping or making things worse?

The fog of pain eased, slowly but surely.

In fact, the burning and stabbing sensations across his back had mellowed enough that Karna could now focus his attention elsewhere—on someone else. He watched Qalli wash her hands in one of the vessel-sinks, and as had become his hobby since yesterday, he lazily ran his gaze over her body. He took in her thin silk pajamas and the ochre-and-gold strappy stilettos.

The female was certifiable. Who the hell wore silk and heels in the highlands?

She wiped her hands on a towel and came to stand directly in front of him. "Are you very mad at the girls? Are you still very, very mad at me for..." She paused, flapped her hand and ended with, "...the past?"

When he didn't immediately oblige her with an answer, she placed her hands on her hips, encased in the flimsiest pair of pants he'd ever had the fortune to see, and tapped her right foot. She had pretty feet, he observed with growing interest, and slender toes painted a pale pink. His eyes traced a meandering path back up to her face. The harshness of the vanity lights behind her, made doubly powerful by the silver-framed mirror, had him squinting his eyes into slits. She'd changed her hairstyle again—third time since yesterday. This style was short and perky, wispy bangs tipped with golden highlights. They made her face seem sharp and angular as a blade, like a flirty little water sprite's.

He remembered her voluptuous and naked beneath the waterfall in the glade behind the Pleasure Palace, her arms and face raised up to the three star-suns lighting up Devlok's skies.

Karna inhaled strongly, breathing in her unique natural cologne—fresh, pretty, spicy. He exhaled through his mouth and the last of his hurt faded away.

"Will you please talk to me? You haven't uttered a single word to me since our fight last night. I know I shouldn't have yelled at you in front of an audience. I know I shouldn't have accused you of not caring about the girls. But their welfare is my responsibility. Karna, please, you must understand how scared I am for them." She cupped his cheek with one hand and rubbed, the bristles of his stubble rasping against her soft palm.

Her touch made him shudder, so he closed his eyes. He'd never been mad at her, though he'd tried very hard to be. He was mad at himself for his mistakes.

"What's wrong? If it still hurts then it needs more than that ointment. I'll go get Ziva. Or Ash, if you prefer his healing touch," she said and half turned to go.

He caught her wrist, tightly circling it with thumb and two fingers. He did nothing else. He simply held her and watched her and waited. Her eyes widened. Then slowly she kneeled before him on the cold, wet floor. Like a subject in front of her lord, a supplicant to her God.

A maelstrom brewed inside his belly. The last few hours had been manic—no, the last few days had been manic. His whole life was suddenly off-kilter. Starting with his newfound vocation, the threat of a daughter he never knew existed, an ash-stealing *asura* who might be Vala and might not, Qalli's connection to Devious Draupadi, and finally what had happened tonight. He needed his *apsara* to soothe him as she'd soothed the pain in his back.

She shouldn't be on her knees before him like a handmaiden.

With a jerk of his hand, he drew her up and onto his lap, then pressed her flush against his chest. An array of expressions danced across her pixie face, from surprise to understanding to wicked calculation. They distracted him. They delighted him.

He brought his hands to her hips and slid them up her sides, over her breasts, to the first button on her blouse. He made quick work of opening them and in one shove pushed the silk off her completely. Before he could bend his head and taste her *pushkara*-sweet skin, she rose to her feet and, eyes glued to his, wriggled her pants off. He pulled her down to straddle his lap.

Placing her hands on his shoulders, she rose to her knees and took a peek at his back. "It's less red but still very raw. Are you sure you want to do this?"

He threaded his fingers through her hair and brought her lips a hairsbreadth away from his. He rotated his hips against hers in case she was in any doubt as to the veracity of his desire. She blinked once. Then her diamond-black eyes began twinkling with mirth.

"Shut up," he advised her gruffly when it looked as if she would speak again. Then he made damn sure she followed the advice for the next hour. Mostly.

They made love on a stone bench in the bath chamber. Luckily, it was wide enough to hold him.

"Are you sure you're comfortable?" he asked, watching her narrowly.

"Yes," she replied and promptly proved to be a liar when she wiggled under him like a worm and winced.

"I knew it. You're not." He sat up and shoved his hands through his damp hair, pushing it off his face. "Let's go into the bed chamber. If the mattress catches fire, I'll deal with it."

He didn't know how he'd react to having sex, as he'd been celibate since the last time he'd been with her.

"And be distracted by mantras and magic and dousing fires instead of focusing all your attention on me?" Qalli's mouth formed a prim little pout.

Laughing, he straddled her thighs and hoped for the best. "The sacrifices one makes for the sake of vanity."

"You talk too much. I should be telling you to shut up." The docile handmaiden had disappeared completely now. "Don't worry. I can control your fire," she said suggestively. "It's my element to control."

"That's fortunate," he said and grunted when she raked her nails down his chest. Then her hands changed direction and tactics, caressing him with exquisite featherlight stokes that left him no less shaking with lust.

The God of Love and the Goddess of Beauty had been more than generous with his *apsara*. Qalli was the embodiment of love and desire, beauty and grace. Her eyes, shaped like the petals of a lotus, were fringed with thick, curly lashes. Her pupils glittered like fresh dewdrops within irises so dark that he couldn't tell them apart. They drifted shut as he watched her, as though embarrassed to show him her desire. He kissed her eyelids, her forehead, her nose. She sighed, her breath warm on his face. He shifted lower to the pale pink blossoms of her lips, glossy and swollen from his kisses. Pleasure erupted in his soul and spread across his being as he took her mouth again.

He'd missed her. Just how much, he realized then.

Before he'd met her, isolation had been an integral part of his nature, part of his soul. He'd chosen a solitary existence, had accepted his seclusion as the Soul Warrior. It was duty he lived for, duty he'd die for. But after Qalli, he'd understood just how lonely he'd been. How hungry his soul was for a mate. She'd shown him a glimpse of paradise. He wanted that again.

With hands and lips and tongue and teeth, he worshipped her body. She had a dark beauty. Earthy. Enthralling. It hit you with the power of a mace, straight in the gut. It had struck him hard, unbalanced him, two decades ago in Devlok. He'd been insane for her then. And she'd yielded utterly to his madness, and yet claimed him—body, mind and soul.

He'd been lost in a desert and had stumbled upon an oasis. How could he resist sipping from it? Why shouldn't he quench his thirst?

Because she'd left him without word or warning, and she'd returned only because of Draupadi and her offspring. His breath turned harsh and his thoughts chaotic.

Qalli placed her hand over his heart. "What is it? I can control fire, I promise."

Karna pressed his forehead to hers. Had he thought he could control her by demanding that she obey him? Had he contrived to punish her? Test her loyalty? And now that she'd yielded to him, what now? He didn't know if she'd given in because she desired him or he was a simple means to an end. In truth, he didn't want to know. He didn't want to think about the past, or about tomorrow.

"You are so damn gorgeous. You take my breath away," he whispered hoarsely.

"Take my breath away. Take my breath away, Karna." She ran her hands over his shoulders, down his back, and gripped his buttocks.

His skin broke out in gooseflesh, but he ignored her suggestion to hurry up the proceedings. He wanted to gorge on her and the feelings only she invoked. *Liar.* His unruly mind brought up another face, blurred through time, that of a bold young princess. She'd made him feel too much too. Was he nothing but a game to these two women? A conquest?

They weren't going to win it, if it was. He turned to the task at hand, touching Qalli with slow, gliding movements.

"Can you still breathe?" he inquired after some time.

"Kar-na!" she gasped, her body thrumming in response.

"Ah. Pity. What about when I kiss you here?" He touched the tip of his tongue to ocean-fresh skin.

"*Deva*, yes!" Her breath hitched and her body arched toward him. It made his pulse leap.

"What about here?" He pressed his hand firmly and sucked hard. He wanted to believe in her. He knew he'd be a fool if he did.

"Karna, Karna, Karna," she chanted his name in frantic whispers.

He rocked against her, again and again and again. Her eyelids fluttered closed and her mouth opened in wordless wonder when, at last, he robbed her of breath.

Five thousand years was a long time.

Five thousand years was soul-wrenching when spent alone on a rock subject to the whims and cravings of fate. He'd travelled across the Cosmos, circled innumerable worlds. He'd ignored most invitations to stop. He'd not even been tempted. His exile had begun on Earth and there would it end.

The Human Realm must have changed. Five thousand years was a long time, after all. No matter. He would adapt. So would Earth. So would the humans—weak, pathetic creatures that they were. Cattle-like in thought, blind to the treasures of life. They constantly sought Heaven, foolishly praying to the Divine. Had they realized in these five thousand years that praying would not save their souls?

He doubted it.

Earth had once been his playground, the mortals his instruments of power. His dominion assured, until that careless moment, that single thoughtless instant when he'd made himself vulnerable to the Soul Warrior.

The black soul screamed at the thought of his defeat.

The Soul Warrior had made a terrible mistake five thousand years ago. Vala would make sure he paid for it for all eternity.

# CHAPTER THIRTEEN
## SMARNA: RAW RECOLLECTIONS

Draupadi lay in bed facing Karna. A white waterfall of mosquito nets surrounded them, secluding them from the rest of the world. The curtains rippled with every breath of breeze blowing in through the open terrace, bringing the crisp, fresh scent of the mountains with it. The chamber glowed from the light cast by the hearth-fire, while a cluster of thick white candles on the nightstands flickered light onto the bed.

It was a beautiful space, to be sure. The decorator had used cedar wood, silver and peacock blue silk in eye-catching abandon in the decor.

"Why did you leave here?" she asked softly. "It's so picturesque and peaceful here. So much closer to Heaven than that smelly island."

She still didn't know how to ask him to speak to Dev-Il, and whether to trust him or not. She didn't have much faith in warriors and demigods. But Karna made her want to believe. He always had.

"Spoken like a spoilt little *apsara*," Karna murmured as he reposed on his stomach with his head pillowed on his arms. He looked indolent, like a well-satisfied lion ready for a siesta.

His back was nearly healed. The salve, the Ayurvedic charm and his inherent vitality had worked their magic well. He never scarred.

Back in Devlok, when she'd first noticed that his body carried no visible marks of his battle-scarred existence, she'd teased him about his vanity. She'd assumed he used magic to keep his skin in a state of golden flawlessness—like she did. He'd been outraged by her accusation, telling her stiffly he was no preening peacock and he'd leave such affectations to the Celestial crowd who were obsessed with looking good. He came by his beauty honestly. His skin had the ability to heal without scarring, especially when he exposed it to the sun.

Heavens! To be so blessed and never suffer sunspots, stretch marks, scarring or acne. Draupadi knew all her daughters and possibly two of her husbands would kill for such naturally perfect skin.

"Yes, I am," she said, smiling at him. "Though I'm not the only spoilt one here. Har-ki-doon was your abode for…?" She raised an eyebrow questioningly.

Karna ran his finger over her arched eyebrow, down her cheek and across her lips. He sighed when she bit him. "Since the beginning," he answered gruffly.

Draupadi waited for him to say more. He didn't, not immediately. He seemed preoccupied by some weighty thoughts.

"Have you heard about the Great Kuru War?" he asked abruptly.

And just like that, her amusement faded. She pulled the blanket up to her chin to hide her face from him. Heard? She was the primary cause of said war. As infamous in human history as Helen of Troy—Draupadi of Indraprastha was the queen who'd launched a thousand armies. And all because a bunch of mad warriors had coveted the lands she'd inherit from her father, King Drupad of the Five Kingdoms of Panchala.

"I have," she said, though she could've spewed so much more vitriol about the war. So far, Karna hadn't singed the bed—a proper bed with a deep cotton mattress, a thick silken quilt and a mound of fluffy pillows—and she would keep it that way. He'd believed in the war.

"Every kingdom, every princely state, every province within the vast lands of Aryavarta, the northern half of Ancient India, was called to arms in that war. Every soul was compelled to choose a side. I was Prince Duryodhan's wingman, his chief recruiter. I travelled to every corner of the nation to amass an army, persuading and sometimes forcibly coercing the kings, the fief-lords or their vassals to side with the Kurus. I convinced the rulers of the Mountain Kingdoms to fight under the Kuru banner. They believed my tales of grandeur and glory. They believed in me and I got them butchered." His face was wiped clean of all expression in the stoic warrior mask.

"That's ancient history, Karna. What does it have to do with your choice of abode?"

"Do you know who Duryodhan is? You must know who my best friend, my brother in all ways but blood, is." An ugly grimace twisted Karna's lips, shattering the mask. "He is Dev-Il. Demon Kali. Evil incarnate."

Draupadi's breath wheezed out and dug into the mattress. Had it really been that easy to steer the conversation to Dev-Il?

"Of course, I know that. The entire Cosmos realized who Duryodhan was the second Bheem slew him," she said.

Karna frowned. "You knew Bheem?"

Oops. She'd have to be more careful dropping names. "No. I've heard the popular story. But go on with yours."

"When I became the Soul Warrior, I decided to live in these mountains. I'd always loved the highlands. I didn't want to dwell in Devlok, though I could have. Part of it was pride. After my failure in the Kuru War, I couldn't bear the thought of facing my foes and my follies for an eternity." Karna sat up in bed and ran his hands through his hair, fluffing it out in its habitual lion's mane. "It is one thing to be best friends with an arrogant young prince...but it is quite another to realize you've put your faith in evil."

"You couldn't have known, Karna. No one knew Duryodhan was Demon Kali's incarnation until it was too late." Kali's agenda was to invoke the eponymous Age of Kali and enslave the Human Realm. The *asura*-king had accomplished the former. He hadn't accounted for the Soul Warrior in the latter.

But Karna wasn't appeased. "I didn't believe it at first. I couldn't believe it. To admit that Duryodhan was the personification of evil would mean I'd been completely wrong in my beliefs—a complete fool. So I, in my infinite wisdom and injured pride, gave him chances to redeem himself. Right at the beginning of the Dark Age, when humans were scarce and *asuras* plenty, he used to dwell on Earth too. We came face-to-face a dozen times and I let him go every time. I kept convincing myself that this time his soul would change color, that this time he would honor our friendship and surrender. He never did. It finally got through my thick skull he never would. I got serious about vanquishing him then. He caught on quickly, realizing I would no longer spare him. So he made a deal with the Gods and asked them for a piece of the Cosmos to establish his Demon Realm. By then, the Celestials had been ready to commit to any terms if he only departed the Human Realm with his nasty minions and never returned."

Cosmic custard! This conversation was practically steering itself in the right direction.

"What are you thinking? Would Dev-Il be receptive to a deal?" Draupadi puzzled aloud, drawing Karna's stormy caramel eyes to hers. She sat up and scooted close to him. "Would he dare dissolve the Treaty of Quarantine and help us stop Vala from fulfilling Kalika's prophecy?"

"At one time, I would've staked my soul that Duryodhan wouldn't do half the things Dev-Il has. Power does weird things to souls, Qalli. Dev-Il cannot be happy that Vala is about to get a thousand times more powerful than him." He clenched and unclenched his fist. It was a nervous habit she found endearing—worrying, but endearing. "He'd help. Vala threatens his authority too. He would beg, borrow and steal powers and shower them on Yahvi so she can vanquish Vala as per her destiny. And Dev-Il won't have to go against one of his own. Very neat, isn't it?"

Yes! That was why she wanted to meet with Dev-Il. "Well? Are you going to ask him?"

"You said the other night that Draupadi was working on a way to save Yahvi." His face flushed in a mixture of embarrassment and annoyance the second he took Draupadi's name.

"She is." Draupadi dropped her gaze to hide the myriad conflicting feelings this conversation was wringing out of her. *Deva!* The hole she'd dug had just gotten larger.

"By making a deal with Dev-Il?"

She plucked at a blue silk thread that had come loose from a peacock feather patch-worked into the quilt. She counted the stitches sewn into the patch. "Maybe."

"Qalli, look at me." Karna gripped her chin and raised it to his still-flushed face. "Has she ever told you about what happened between us—her and me—a long time ago?"

Drauapdi nodded, going slack-jawed at his expression, his tone. He couldn't have feelings for her? He'd walked away! He couldn't still want her?

"She said you met secretly every night during her *swayamvara*. You fell in love. And on the fifth night, she waited and waited and you didn't appear." She'd waited. Sweet Heaven! She'd waited all night, every night for the next ten days for Karna to come to her and explain what she'd done wrong. Whether she'd said something to offend him again. Anger him. But he hadn't come. And he hadn't looked her in the eye ever again. Not even when he'd come to congratulate Arjun and her for their nuptials. Coward. Oh, how she'd hated him after that.

"Why, Karna? Why did you not go to her? Did you fall out of love? Did you not want her? Was it only revenge that you sought because she'd insulted you?"

"No. No!" Karna ran his fingers through his mane. "No, none of that. I was afraid of what she made me feel. It was so much…it was so intense that I…" He laughed self-deprecatingly. "I was scared of love. Scared that I wouldn't be able to stay away if we remained friends. I had to make her hate me, you see?"

"What?" Draupadi frowned. He wasn't making any sense. "No, I don't see. Why did she have to hate you?"

"Vishnu foresaw our union. He said our firstborn would be cursed. That he or she would bring about cosmic destruction. Some seven thousand five hundred years ago, Vishnu had predicted that I'd sire the harbinger of doom with Draupadi."

Raka had failed.

*Thwack!* He stiffened as the *chabuk* whipped across his torso.

Hundreds of *asuras* had been slaughtered under his command, and the rest had turned tail and run from the Soul Warrior's wrath like rodents on a sinking ship.

*Thwack.* His demotion was just.

He fixed his eyes on the stone statue in front of him. *Thwack!* The Soul Warrior hadn't been alone. Who was that band of impossibly gifted Celestials helping him? Even the *raktabeejas* had proved no match for them. *Thwack.*

Raka flinched as the spiked leather pierced the skin of his arm, releasing blood and flesh. Mara's arm didn't halt or fumble. *Thwack!* Raka deserved the flogging. He deserved to suffer, to be humiliated in front of all demons. The gashes on his back would help keep his folly fresh until he whitewashed his shame.

*Thwack!* The rope curled about his calf and retreated, almost making him lose his footing. He would've fallen to the ground were his limbs not tied to the fang-like pillars that grew in the Cave of the Tomb.

Five hundred lashes. *Thwack!* One for each *asura* lost. It would be over soon. And when it was... *Thwack!* He would go to his sister. Ask her about the name the Soul Warrior had bellowed. A name Raka had heard on his baby sister's lips recently.

It had to be the same female mortal. *Thwack!* Raka could not ignore this omen. He needed to speak to Draas. No, Raka grunted, ignoring the sting of the *chabuk* across his back, not Draas. That sister was a human-lover. She had strange notions about friendship between nonequals.

*Thwack!* He would talk to the other one. After all, it was the bitch, Lobha, who'd brought him the information about the Hidden Island. Lobha would tell him what he wished to know, for a price. The price would be steep, but Raka would pay the sadistic half-human whatever she demanded if it got him what he wanted. The second he bore out his shame, he would go to her.

*Thwack!*

It would've been simpler had he a mobile phone or laptop. But the cave was a machine-free zone. Preceptor Shukra was old-school. He thought advancement in technology was the work of the Goddesses of Knowledge and Fortune and thus to be spat on. Shukra relied on pure and simple *asura-maya* to get things done.

*Thwack!* Soon, thought Raka. Three hundred sixteen more and he'd have his answer.

"Do you see why I had to stay away from Draupadi? Why I continued to stay away even as a Celestial?" Karna asked. But it seemed that he'd only put off the inevitable.

He'd thought telling Qalli the truth would lighten his burden. It hadn't. He realized that it wouldn't until he apologized to the one he'd wronged. He should have told Draupadi everything, long ago.

"Why did you keep this from her?" Qalli cried, her lotus-shaped eyes distraught. "You should have told her. She deserved to know the truth. If she'd known…she'd never have…" Qalli pressed her face into her hands and moaned. "Oh, *deva!*"

"If she'd known, she'd never have had Yahvi," Karna finished with a heavy heart. He couldn't bear the idea of his daughter not existing anymore. He took a deep breath and blew it out. "I need to speak with Draupadi as soon as can be arranged."

Qalli drew her hands down from her face and stared at him. Her mouth was trembling. "No," she said aloud, shaking her head. "She would have had Yahvi. No matter the cost. And no, she won't speak with you. You made sure of that when you walked away."

Heat rose in his cheeks at the thought of groveling. "She can't go around making deals with Dev-Il, okay? You can't go around making deals on her behalf, either. Forget for a minute that such an act will risk the treaty that keeps the demons in check. Or what the Gods will do to the two of you if they even get a whiff of your intentions. Think what Dev-Il will do. He's been waiting for an opportunity to get even with her. The enmity I share with Draupadi and her husbands is nothing compared to the loathing Dev-Il feels for them. They stole his kingdom, striped him naked of pride and honor. He'll take nothing less than her soul in exchange for sparing Yahvi her fate…all of the Six their fates. And even that won't appease him."

"Then you must send them away from all this. You have to let me take them away."

"Surrounded by the *asuras* tonight, Yahvi looked so small, so delicate, as if a zephyr would blow her away. Like you." Karna bent his head and took Qalli's mouth, swallowing her cry of pain and pleasure. He touched her tongue and drew back when she said stop. "Whether Vala works to his own purposes or Dev-Il's, do you understand that he will come after her? They both will."

"Of course I do," Qalli cried. "That's why I must…take them to their mother. We can take them to Alaka. Draupadi has an arrangement with Kubera…"

Karna kissed the rest of her words away. "Doesn't matter where she hides, Qalli. Once Dev-Il knows of her, he will rip apart the Cosmos to find her. She's Draupadi's and mine. Even if she wasn't the harbinger, Dev-Il would still go after her."

"Don't say that. You don't know that. People forget the past. They move on." Tears pooled in her tortured eyes and slipped one by one down ashen cheeks.

"Yesterday you made me ask myself why the Triad had dumped the girls on me. This is why. My actions, my secrets, my cowardice have led to this. It has to be I who puts an end to this." He hadn't vanquished Dev-Il or Vala, and now his child was in danger.

"No. Please, Karna. Let me take them away."

He wiped the tears from her cheeks and kissed her again, slowly and thoroughly. He'd never get enough of kissing her. "I've made a great many mistakes in my life. Some forgivable, some not, and I've paid for every one of them dearly. Yahvi will not be one of them," he vowed with grim determination. He whipped the netted curtains aside and got out of bed. Stood there, looking down at her.

She rose to her knees. "If that's meant to reassure me, it's not working. What do you want me to do? To say?" Her pink-tinged nails dug into his forearms as she gripped him tightly. "And where are you going?" she asked, looking alarmed.

He had to kiss her again. "I need to check on things. Go back to sleep."

"Karna! What do you mean to do?"

"I'm asking you to trust me. Work with me and not against me. Trust that I can protect my daughter and my *shishyas* and you. I'll even protect Draupadi, if it comes to that." He took her hand and held it over his steadily beating heart. He knew he was asking a lot. He was asking her to split her loyalties between him and Draupadi. But the thing was, all three of them had one common goal.

"Trust me, *manmohini*. Please."

She woke alone. And for the first time in an age, Draupadi didn't mind it so much.

She had a great deal to think about and wanted to do it in peace. It helped that her daughters were close and safe—at least for today. Karna had promised to keep them safe forever.

Was it possible to thwart Kalika's prophecy, keep Vala weak and senseless enough that Yahvi could slay him? And it was Yahvi who had to slay him. Goddess Kalika had made that very clear the day Yahvi was born.

Draupadi opened her eyes. Pale streams of twilight played peekaboo with the curtains, shining watery light into the room. Birds twittered on the terrace, announcing the birth of a new day—unaware and uncaring that death was only days away. Karna was off on his morning run and prayers with his *shishyas*. She recalled, vaguely, he'd whispered something to that effect and left their bed while it was still dark. He'd only just come back from his nightly hunts.

Well, good luck to him if he thought his *shishyas* would even speak to him after his hurtful words last night.

She rolled across the bed to his side and hugged his pillow to her heart. She inhaled his scent, burying her face in the fluffy softness. She should get up. She had things to do, decisions to make. Perhaps even a confession?

Mired in indecision, she got ready for the day. To beat the cold, she buttoned on a pashmina vest over the butter-yellow silk shirt she wore with an emerald-green pantsuit. She'd purposely dressed in a business-like fashion as she'd agreed to act as a communications liaison between Karna and the girls and Draupadi.

She sat down on the chair in the dressing room, abruptly lightheaded. Sweet Heaven! *She was Draupadi.* How could she hold a liaison with herself? When had she started thinking of herself as Qalanderi?

It *would* make things easier if she actually split into two people. Child's play for her, considering she'd spent the better part of two lifetimes being five different women—a by-product of her polyandrous fate. Each husband had wanted or needed different things from her. Satya's father had wanted a selfless queen by his side; Lusha's father had needed an obsessed love addict. For her two youngest husbands, she'd been part playmate, part confidante and advisor. They'd hardly needed a wife. And Amara's father...

Draupadi stood up. What was she doing? She had no time to sit around and introspect over a past that was long done. Maybe a brisk walk before breakfast would set her head straight.

Outside, the valley was painted in a grey-blue mist like a still-wet watercolor. The cold rolled around Draupadi as she squelched her way across the lawn, moving eastward toward a rugged, rumbly section of the property. As morning prayers generally were offered to the Goddess of Dawn and the Sun God, she had a feeling Karna would've taken this direction for the run. He was, by and large, a creature of habit.

He'd spoken of trust last night. He'd spoken of open communication. He'd even asked her to assure Draupadi that she had no reason to fear him. Draupadi grimaced. They'd see about that when she told him the whole truth. And she had to tell him. Not telling wasn't an option anymore. Clearly, not telling her about Vishnu's premonition had landed them in this pickle. She didn't blame him for not telling her. And she would never wish Yahvi away.

Sighing, she waded through the dense fog lying thick on the ground. The sun hadn't risen yet, and even with the predawn pastels streaking across the sky, the woodlands remained dark and heavy. But not quiet. They echoed with life. Crickets called out to their mates in a monotonous drone—obviously the mates were fast asleep, for they were not responding to the urgent calls at all, judiciously. The *crik-crik* sounds were interrupted sporadically by the snapping of twigs that found their unfortunate way beneath her feet. Small furry animals scurried about to find breakfast for their young, or to find their beds if they were nocturnal. Birds chirped and tweeted, flapped and cooed, spraying fat raindrop dew across their nests.

And she'd been right. The creature of habit jogged toward her from the east, herding his *shishyas* along. Their breaths lisped out of their mouths and noses in puffs of white smoke. He wore full-length sweatpants. Sensible attire to run through closely packed, sharp-needled trees, unlike her daughters who were garbed in skimpy shorts and colorful tanks.

Karna stopped before her, not even breathing hard. His faded grey tank was damp across his chest, and he smelled faintly of the forest. She wanted to slip into his arms and kiss him. But she couldn't, not before she spoke to her daughters and they came to a decision. She should involve Goddess Saraswati and Vashi in it too. After all, they were a part of the subterfuge.

"Good morning, darlings," she wished them, accepting a chorus of greetings in return.

A brief glance told her that Yahvi was past her upset, possibly the result of her crying jag, a good night's sleep, some exercise and an apology from her father. He'd managed to make amends so quickly? Draupadi was impressed.

"Good morning, *manmohini*." Karna drew her close and kissed her, his nose icy against her skin. "Slept well?" he rumbled against her ear.

Her heart started jogging on the spot. He'd called her *manmohini*—enchanter of his soul—like he used to in Devlok. *Deva!* Karna had just kissed her in front of her children and called her an enchantress. Their relationship had gone beyond complicated. She had to tell him the truth.

The timing and reason had to be perfect. She wouldn't have him blame the girls for her lies. She would not drive a wedge between Yahvi and Karna—not anymore. She'd kept them apart for a reason and that reason no longer existed.

Lusha kissed her on the cheek, grinning mischievously at her and Karna. "We're heading back, coach. I'm so hungry I could eat a horse."

"No horses, Lusha. You promised." Ziva came forward and kissed Draupadi's cheek. She'd charmed her skin tone to appear more human-like. They weren't to draw attention to themselves here. "Good morning, Qalli," she said quickly, then continued to scold Lusha about leaving the cattle and their meat alone. Ziva and Iksa were her horse-mad offspring, and Lusha was the biggest tease in the Cosmos.

One by one her daughters pecked her cheek until Draupadi thought she'd be permanently branded by embarrassment. They left after the greetings, chattering and horsing around as usual.

"I don't understand why they giggle."

Draupadi smiled at Karna's perplexed expression while he watched his *shishyas* disappear into the mist. "They're girls. Girls giggle."

He raised one eyebrow. "You're a girl. You don't giggle."

"I can if you want me to," she offered.

He shuddered and pulled her into his arms again, kissing her as she yearned to be kissed, slow and thoroughly. Oh *deva*! The pleasure of his touch, of his very presence left her wanting more than she had any right to expect. They stayed that way for a while, hearts touching, lips teasing, in perfect rhythm with each other and the Cosmos.

"Want to walk a bit?" he asked after a long, long while. At her nod, he took her hand, and they set their path through the brightening forest.

*"I don't want to be alone, Qalli. I'm tired of being alone,"* he'd professed last night. She was tired of being alone too. And she was very tired of fighting her natural instincts with regard to him. What if they had only these two or three more days? Though he hadn't told her, she understood that the only way he could twist Yahvi's fate in a different direction was by forfeiting his own. She had to tell him before it was too late. He had to know that she was in love with him. Had she ever not been in love with him?

"Qalli!" Karna's growl shattered the noisy solitude of the woods.

Oh, but she didn't want to exchange words, not yet. Words led to talking, talking to discussions, and discussions would precipitate confessions. Nope, no words. She was quite content with huddling into his armpit and breathing in his masculine, woodsy scent.

"What's this?" He frowned at their feet—his covered in Nike Zooms and hers in lemon-yellow wedges.

"Footwear?"

"That," he said, pointing to the neat little path that stretched out in front of them, leading out of the woods. It was the path she'd taken in search of him.

"It's a path," she said unnecessarily.

"You conjured up this trail, didn't you?" he accused, eyes narrowing.

The path was the width of a chariot, fenced on either side with decorative logs about a foot high and carpeted with an extra-thick layer of red, yellow and green leaves.

"What if I did? I didn't want to risk breaking my leg," she admitted.

"Woman, must everything be convenient and easy for you?"

"Warrior, does everything in the Cosmos need to be an Olympic hurdle always?"

Hot, golden eyes raked over her body from head to toe. "Your constant unnecessary beautification of every-*freaking*-thing is a frivolous waste of magic on this realm—on any realm—but especially here," he said, his tone aggrieved.

She couldn't believe what she was hearing. "A waste? A waste!"

"Magic uses up vast amounts of energy." He waved his hand, encompassing her whole body and then the entire forest. "Energy better spent on…"

"On what? Wars and *asuras*? On doing oh-so-important tasks for Celestials who don't even acknowledge what you do most of the time? Well, that's your prerogative. If you want to make life as hellish for yourself as possible, be my guest. But I won't." She pivoted on her heels and sailed out of the forest in anger. How dare he? How dare he think her frivolous and silly?

"Don't be pissed, *manmohini*."

She marched on.

"You're adorable when you're angry."

That did it. Draupadi swung around and shoved him back using—no, *wasting* her not-so-trifling powers. Caught unawares, Karna flew back twenty paces and yet landed on his feet like a big, lithe jungle cat. He loped back, holding his arms up in front in symbolic surrender.

"*Shanti, shanti,*" he said. "No more teasing, I promise." He touched her hand with extreme caution, as one would a burning cinder. "It's just that your multiple personality disorder is baffling."

Draupadi froze, taken aback. "My what?"

"How many times in the last two days have you changed your looks, your mannerisms, your hairstyles and clothes?" he asked, waggling both his eyebrows.

Six times, as he'd so astutely noticed.

"But that's not the point I was trying to make." He heaved a sigh.

"Heaven save me from warriors and their pointy things," she said dryly.

Karna snorted and tugged on a lock of her hair. "My point, woman, is that you don't need magical enhancements. You are beautiful as you are."

Oh! That definitely was a boost to her ego. But would he still think her beautiful when she told him the truth? Would he still offer her sweet compliments and sweeter kisses?

Her secret was like a malignancy inside her. She had to cut it out. Should she just blurt it out? *Hi! I'm Draupadi.* With any luck, he'd faint from the shock and wake up with amnesia. That would be perfect. The humans didn't know how lucky they were to have memories as short as their life-spans.

"About Draupadi," she began, quaking under the pressure of her lies.

He stiffened as expected. "What about her?"

Why did he blow hot and cold where Draupadi was concerned? Should she tell him or not?

"Um, I spoke to her. Told her everything. She was upset, of course. But I reassured her. I said I trusted you. The children trusted you. And she would be wise to do so too. She agreed." The lies poured forth in a giant rush of assurances.

"I see. How...trusting of her." Karna cleared his throat. "Are you hungry, *manmohini*? Because I'm famished." He changed the subject neatly. Taking her arm again, he began to walk back to the citadel.

Draupadi followed his lead meekly. She was so, so screwed.

# CHAPTER FOURTEEN
## VARADANA: BOONS AND BLESSINGS

Baital's red soul glowed as he finished a bout of sex, in his dreams. Back from his escapade around Palace Kalichi, he lounged in his karmic prison cell thinking lascivious thoughts about Meenakshi, his one and only love.

He wished he hadn't surrendered his temporal body to the Body-Guard Unit to be preserved until his next release—so much better to have sex in a body, and with a body, than in imagination. But he'd had to give his body back as per the rules of Hell. He was still in shock at how much the storage facility's rates had skyrocketed since the last time he'd wrangled their services.

Everything in Hell was a rip-off these days. He'd been in Hell for seven hundred years already. The first two hundred had been spent bleaching his considerable sins in a variety of soul-scrubbing ways. After that, his penances had been more tedious than painful. Talking for centuries with Hell's soul therapist was no joke, though being a garrulous creature, he hadn't minded spilling his guts all that much. The bonus to any thought-provoking monologue was that he got to relive his past actions—the nastier the better, in his opinion. And as recently proven, the sexier the better too.

A sudden benevolent miasma whirled through the cell, converging into Goddess Kalika, also known as the Dark One. She was in true hideous form, more demonic than divine, with her black skin agleam, her lolling tongue and plumped lips the color of blood. She had four fangs and four arms, and her long bluish hair was loose and touched the heels of her feet. Her celestial ornaments—she wore no garments—were but garlands of skulls and bones and sliced-off fingers all strategically positioned for decency's sake. She was the Goddess of Destruction and absolutely looked the part, even naked.

"You're a prude, Baital. No matter the content of your dreams. That's why you fell for your human like a ton of cows. Your priggish heart couldn't resist Meenakshi's vestal virgin scent," said Goddess Kalika. She'd minimized her superimposing self to fit into his microscopic cell, which could hold only three-fourths of an ounce of soul.

"Do you mind leaving my private thoughts alone?" Baital said in affront. He tried to blank out his mind. If he had no thoughts, she couldn't read them, could she?

"I can't. You submitted your soul to me. No part of you can be hidden from me so long as I own your soul." The skulls around her person shook obscenely as the Goddess laughed.

Baital's mood dimmed.

"How is she?" Only the Goddess where Meenakshi was and how she fared.

"She's fine. Alive, as I promised."

Baital was frustrated with the meager update, but he let it go. "I did as you asked and made sure the Soul Warrior knew the prophecy. Have I earned my release?"

Hell was the price he'd paid for Meenakshi's immortality.

The Goddess's lips curved into a taunting smile. "Do you think a thousand years of penance too high a price for your beloved's long life?"

"As you won't refrain from reading or voicing aloud my intimate thoughts, you know my answer." It wasn't too high a price. He would spend twice that length of time in Hell to be with his Meenakshi for the rest of eternity.

"There's a truism the humans are fond of quoting: 'Be careful what you wish for.' For your sake, Baital, I hope when you find your Meenakshi, you will be happy with your choices."

Baital's soul stilled. "What do you mean, 'find?' Don't you know where she is?"

"She moved." The Goddess shrugged. "Now then, other matters press upon us. It seems I've misread a number of souls. Yahvi is in two minds about her death. The Soul Warrior is behaving oddly paternally. And Draupadi, as usual, is up to her old tricks. I cannot rely on them anymore. I have spoken to Lord Yama, and he's agreed to release you after I promised him an arm and a leg—your arm and leg. You shall go to the Human Realm. Do not sneak off to see your Meenakshi until you have fulfilled your obligations to me. Go off course, Baital, and the consequences won't be pretty. Remember, I own your soul."

"I have sworn you an oath that I will do as you bid, and even though I'm a dastardly *pisacha*, my word is my honor," Baital growled.

"I know. It's why I tolerate you. Strange are the ways of the Cosmos." The Goddess smiled in a show of tiny white fangs. She stretched out one of her four arms and cupped Baital's soul. Without words, she told him the plan. His first task was to befriend Yahvi.

Baital wouldn't mind befriending poor Lord Karna too. He froze, clipped the deviant thought, and killed it dead. He'd become way too comfortable in Hell, it seemed. *Pisachas* drank blood and conned souls for kicks. He shouldn't be feeling sorry for his future prey.

"Do not fail, Baital. It's not just your soul you risk in this but hers as well," Kalika warned and disappeared in a tumultuous puff of black smoke, leaving Baital to ruminate in private once more.

He knew the risks. Execute the mission well and be free of Hell. Fail and remain here for another thousand years. He also knew he'd never get another chance like this one. The Soul Warrior would not make it easy for him to carry out the Goddess's plan. But like a cobra in the grass, Baital would lie in wait and strike at the right moment.

One way or another, Karna's daughter had to die.

The difficulty of being good turned out to be less boring than Yahvi had anticipated because of the festive atmosphere at Har-ki-doon.

Twice a year, Ash held a harvest festival for the *pahadi* or mountain folk who dwelled in the remotest regions of the surrounding mountains. The festival was the only time they came down from their village-dwellings to barter goods, make money and have a drink with friends they rarely saw otherwise. Hence, Ash and her father had decided to keep it on. To cancel it at the last minute would've raised suspicion and incited a riot in the villages.

To Yahvi's surprise, her father didn't ground them for their disobedience. Though he did restrict their movements to within his line of vision until further notice. Yahvi was still a little upset with him, in truth, but not enough not to play matchmaker between her parents. When one had only a few days to live, hanging out with one's favorite people took precedence over everything—*hanging out* in the literal sense of the term.

High above her, Lavya hung one-handed from a windmill. Ash and her father were perched on equally wobbly footholds to his right and left, offering him advice on how best to screw in the bolt.

It started a half hour ago when all of a sudden, right in the middle of their training run across the property, they heard a squeak that shouldn't have been heard from the windmill. Lavya, Ash and her father had at once decided to wrestle the machinery into obedience.

"When on Earth, do as an Earth-dweller," her father remarked, grinning down at Mama, who obviously was not hanging from anything. This was in response to Mama's "What on Earth do you think you're doing on the windmill?"

Yahvi wondered if that logic applied to the Demon Realm as well—as in, when in Asuralok do as an *asura*? Amara did ask it aloud and was quickly silenced for her cheekiness. She was hanging from the weathered mill too, just for kicks. Yahvi was in charge of handing out tools and the occasional bottle of water to the erstwhile laborers. Ziva was sprawled out in the grass with a tome of Ayurveda beneath her nose. Lusha was setting up a picnic lunch some distance away, and Satya and Iksa were holed up in Satya's bedroom trying to decipher Iksa's latest vision.

All in all, Yahvi was pleased everyone was getting along and no one was fighting. Yet.

Like a giant golden spider, her father crawled up the grey stone tower. He slipped and nearly fell twice, making Mama wince.

"Why won't they use magic? I'm all for the whole do-it-yourself revolution, but this is ridiculous," Mama said, staring at trio of Celestials on the mill. "Pigheaded buffoons! If they break their necks who's going to protect you?"

Yahvi gave her mother a peck on her cheek as Ash launched into an explanation of what they were up to and why.

Har-ki-doon, being completely energy-independent, ran on a combination of solar and wind energy. Three windmills had been rigged as wind turbines, and countless ultramassive solar panels had been erected on a large expanse of a south-facing mountain on the northeast end of the property. Somehow, one of the blades on one of the towers had come loose. More specifically, one of the bolts that attached the blade to the hub was wobbling.

"The smallest infraction can severely affect energy output. Can't afford that today, not with the number of people coming over to partake in the harvest festival," said Ash.

"And Baby needs to be online to work her magic," Lavya added.

Which made sense to all but Mama, who kept muttering, "Mad men!" at regular intervals.

"Doesn't Father look hunky shirtless?" Yahvi upped the matchmaking.

"I'm glad you're not upset with your father anymore, darling," Mama replied primly.

Yahvi rolled her eyes. "Would you please chill?" She shot a significant glance at Ziva, hoping her sister would take the hint and guide Mama's attention back on target. "What do you think, sis?"

Ziva looked up from her reading. "Yup, Uncle K is definitely that. But while being hunky helps, I'd much rather be with someone who's generous and sweet and capable, of course, and smart...witty smart...I can't abide dull creatures. Quite simply, he must be extraordinary."

Yahvi crowed secretly because her mother seemed unable to tear her eyes off her father. Then her jaw dropped in awe as he leaped forty feet to the ground to land in a crouch before rising smoothly to his feet. The sun's light bounced off his skin like a Celestial halo as he stood, his hands on hips exposed by his low-riding jeans, and contemplated the power tools spread out on the bright green grass.

"Oh, Father, you look so sweaty and dehydrated," said Yahvi slyly. But she needn't have bothered.

Mama was already sashaying toward him with a bottle of water. She slid her metal-rimmed Ray-Bans on top of her head and murmured something too low for Yahvi to hear, but which the nonhumans heard clearly. Masculine laughter wafted down the windmill, while Ziva giggled and Amara looked ready to gag. She despised flirting.

Amara jumped down from the windmill and with the jerk of a hand signaled Yahvi to follow. Yahvi scrambled to her feet.

"Where do you think you're going?" Lavya shouted down at them.

"To throw up," Amara yelled over her shoulder as she brisk-walked toward her. "Don't worry, we'll stay within sight. Come on, Vee. I need to run." She took off.

A clear uphill path led to a settlement of some twenty-odd dwellings, flat-terraced and bright blue in color, all clustered together.

Yahvi caught up with Amara some ways up and only because her sister had deigned to wait for her. "Slow down, Amu. What's your hurry?"

"You've been fidgeting all day. Wanna tell me what's wrong?" Amara wasn't even breathing hard.

Yahvi shook her head, bending to rest her hands on her knees and catch her breath. "What did Mama whisper in Father's ear?" she asked once her galloping heart slowed to a trot.

Amara sneered while stretching her hamstrings, then sashayed up to Yahvi. "'I have a suggestion, darling.'" Amara imitated their mother's voice perfectly. She ran her forefinger from Yahvi's shoulder to bicep to forearm, just as Mama's red-tipped finger had run down her father's sweaty and muscled torso. "'Why don't you just rig yourself up to the cable lines? You generate more than enough wattage to illuminate Asia for eternity,'" Amara finished in a throaty whisper.

Yahvi laughed. "Yay! My matchmaking worked." No wonder Father had smacked Mama's bottom, making her yelp and rub it.

"Ugh! How can they flirt like that? It's disgusting."

"I think it's cute. They're falling in love."

"In lust, Vee. Moo-moo's like that with all our fathers. She flirts to get her way. That's all."

Yahvi didn't think so. "No, this is different. You're just cynical about love."

Amara snorted and began jogging up the path. "Don't get your hopes up. She's probably trying to change his mind about your big fight or running away…or whatever."

Suddenly Yahvi's phone began to quack like a duck. "The windmill's up and running. We're back on the web. Ha! Both of them."

The Conscious Web and the Internet functioned independently of each other, a rule from the updated version of the Treaty of Quarantine. But if you were smart, and had figured out a spell to connect them…

"Amara," Yahvi said, reading the latest email from Draas. "I might have done something stupid. I've accidently sent a picture of Asht Dveep to Draas."

No, it was never easy being good.

Relief poured over Raka as Lobha confirmed his suspicions about Yahvi. Not only confirmed but took it a step further and garnished the revelation with whipped blood and a bone on top.

Yahvi was the Soul Warrior's human daughter. Raka was amazed the Soul Warrior even had a daughter.

"Draas met a human called Yahvi in Lok Vitalas. I followed the trail of information once I knew where to look. It was easy," Lobha boasted.

She lied. It couldn't have been easy. If it had been easy, he'd have the same information. He didn't ask Lobha who her source was. He didn't care as long as he reaped the rewards. But she told him anyway.

"It's the machines—the human machines. Get someone to decipher them for you. I believe you can manipulate them too. Get them to do what you want."

Shukra wasn't interested in human machines. But Lobha had never given him false information, so Raka listened.

"And you must whip the arrogance out of Draas. Char Mani didn't. He's amused by her friendship with the human."

Lobha envied Draas, who was Char Mani's final hatchling and the apple of his eye. And, Draas was smarter and sexier than Lobha. Lobha was too humanlike to be attractive to an *asura* male or female. So loathsome was her resemblance to humans that no one had offered to breed with her. Lobha was doomed to be nothing more than the occasional blood donor, an *asura's* quick fix in tough times.

"Don't be foolish," Raka said. "And don't speak of this to anyone. Do not spoil my kill by your petty jealousies. And for Dev-Il's sake, do not sneer at Draas about any of this. I mean it, Lobha. Do not screw this up." He gripped her puny arms and shook her hard, giving her his most menacing glare. Then he turned her, pushing her face into the rough, ferrous wall of her cell. The wall was studded with rubies like every wall in Char Mani's lavish dwelling. Raka bent Lobha in half, braced a hand to the wall and thrust himself in her. He pandered to her greed and her ambition as he'd done many times before. The barter was done within moments. He hoped there would be a child this time. He wished to be free of her. She didn't utter a sound the whole time she used him and told him to get out as soon as he grunted in completion.

Raka vanished to the Cave of the Tomb, wasting no time in clambering to the top of the ladder. He went directly to Shukra with the priceless information. The Juggernaut was history.

*"Act in haste, repent at leisure"* was a mantra for losers, not Raka.

Damn right he was pigheaded!

Karna had been accused of being pigheaded all his life. Frankly, he considered it a compliment and not a character flaw. His attitude naturally pissed females off, and now six madder than wet peahens sulked in the building because he'd refused to let them leave the four cardinal corners of Har-ki-doon, even with airtight supervision. If they wanted to spa-hop or shop or whatever, they'd just have to wait until the crisis was over. By karma, didn't they understand there were demons after them?

His authority hadn't worked quite that well on Qalli. She'd gone shopping.

"I need time away from all the testosterone," she'd claimed. "I'm quite capable of taking care of myself and have been doing so for many millennia. I don't need you to spare bodyguards for me. I'm not the target."

He'd sent a couple sentries with her regardless.

Approving of raging amounts of testosterone himself, Karna made his way into Ash's office and was accosted by the familiar sight of Lavya huddled on a chair behind a desk stacked high with tomes and books, frowning in consternation at the laptop in front of him.

"Again, no one is offering any information about Vala's return date," Lavya reported. "Whether he's landed or in flight or smashed to smithereens against an asteroid. Like Baby, Salabha confirms that no nuance of red has crossed Lok Vitalas in two days. The *loks* are as they always are—full of half-breeds and lowborn demons. It's not bloody possible."

"What's not possible?" Ash strode into the den, his robes aflutter. "I assure you whatever you've found on my hard drive is extremely possible, my friend."

"I wouldn't touch your hard drive with a ten-foot pole, Lord Lothario," said Lavya. "Do you have any idea how many viruses you expose it to by downloading pirated ebooks? And you don't even have virus scans.

A two-year-old would be able to hack your machine with one finger." Ash showed Lavya a gloved middle finger, which Lavya ignored. He blithely went on, "No *asuras*. No red blips on the dark side of the realm. No demonic footprints on Earth at all."

Ash blinked, surprised. "And that upsets you, why?"

"Because its not normal," answered Karna. "One, evil doesn't take days off. Two, what? All of a sudden they don't want the *raakh*? Three, human bodies are piling up every day, so someone or something criminal is definitely on. Four, even if the *asuras* aren't the criminals, there should be red blips, period. I can go on, but I'm sure you get the gist."

"Exactly! Why is the Wi-Fi so damn slow? Ash, your equipment is pathetically out-of-date. I strongly suggest you upgrade it," said Lavya.

"My equipment is fine for what I do with it."

No one missed the double entendre. Karna grinned and high-fived Ash, even if Ash was all bluster and no show. Ash had self-sworn celibacy after he'd been cursed. So pretending to be the Casanova of the Lower Himalayas was just his way of letting off steam.

When their laughter wound down, Ash, in deliberate slow motion, reached up and unveiled his face, exposing the raw, oozing sores. He waited, eyes averted, giving Karna and Lavya time to adjust to the sight. He needn't have bothered. They'd never show how his face repulsed them. The accursed sores oozed not only pus but also a rank stench, hence the sandalwood incense that Ash used by the truckload.

"Maybe we should all take a day off," Karna suggested, making his friends stare at him. He felt like a mental patient being appraised by psychiatrists. "What's wrong with taking a day off?"

He dropped onto a dark blue chintz couch and closed his eyes and mouth before he asked his best buds if they too smelled the sweet tendrils of romance in the air. They'd lock him in the dungeons below the fort with the rats and melt its one and only key for sure then.

"Not a thing...except for plot points one through four you just enumerated," Lavya said.

Karna felt a small spark of guilt for even thinking of stinting on his duties during this unusual time. "You're right. I should comb through the *asura* hotspots again. Go down to the *loks*. I've already convinced all seven leaders to either side with us or stay neutral in this fight. But I can speak to them again. Make sure they stay on track. Something has to click somewhere. Some of them have to know more than they're letting on."

One quick nap and he'd go. He'd hardly slept last night. And ideally, when he came back, Qalli would be back too, and might be in a frisky mood from her retail therapy. He grinned, settling his head against the spongy backrest of the sofa. He couldn't stop thinking about her. He couldn't stop touching her.

"You've got it bad, haven't you?"

Karna's eyes snapped open. He couldn't refute Ash's observation, so he said nothing in his defense.

"What will you do when she betrays you?" Lavya's question electrified him.

Karna stood up fast, hands curling into fists by his thighs. "She will not betray me," he said, gut twisting.

"Shit! Karna, shit! Have you lost your mind? You know she's lying through her pretty little teeth. You know something's off about her, about all of them."

Karna uncurled his hands and slid them flat into his jeans pockets. "She will not betray me," he repeated more strongly. "And exactly how do you think she'll betray me? Sell my soul to Dev-Il? You already tried that, remember?"

Lavya went rigid at the reminder of his less-than-stellar past. "You were meant to get her out of your system, not dive into a relationship blindfolded."

"Is there any other way? And I'm not blind, Lavya. I don't trust her completely, not yet. But I do trust what I feel for her. That can't be a mistake." He'd never felt anything like it before. Not once in his ceaseless existence. "I'm sick and tired of being suspicious all the time. My whole life I've suspected people's motives. Was the man genuinely nice to me or did he want a huge favor in return? Did the woman offer me food and drink from the goodness of her heart or are her eyes on my gold medallion? I've suspected my friends, my wives, my soldiers…there was even a shameful instance when I suspected my father of adopting me for personal gain."

Asshole that he was, he'd voiced the accusation out loud. Adiratha had been thunderstruck and Mother Radha had cried herself to sleep that night. He'd bruised their hearts with his callous words.

The memory left a bitter taste in his mouth. "Most of the time, I am absolutely right in my mistrust. You know I'm not naïve. Most souls are opportunistic in one way or another. Does that make them bad?"

"Are you so besotted that you'd make excuses for her?" Lavya asked incredulously.

"Not excuses. We spoke for a good long time last night. She's not the enemy. My heart trusts her already. There's nothing I can do about that. We fit, Qalli and I. We fit perfectly, Lavya. And I know I'm not the only one who feels that way."

She cared for him. He saw it in her eyes, felt it in her touch. He heard it in her words. So no, he wouldn't ruin it by suspecting her motives.

"Are you going to stand there in stoic silence or are you going to preach some sense into him?" Lavya asked Ash.

Ash shrugged. "He's a big boy. And I'm not sure he'll listen at this point."

"Thanks, both of you, for your amazing confidence in me," Karna said, lips twisting in irritation.

"Damn it, Karna. It's not that I begrudge you the affair. It's not that I dislike Qalanderi either. I think she's funny and engaging and completely devoted to the Six. Those are huge points in her favor. But her stories don't add up. And until they do, you should be careful."

"Their stories never add up, friend." Ash shook his head at Lavya. "It's in a woman's nature to conceal facts and reveal them at the most inopportune moments."

"Romance novels hardly make you a connoisseur on women," Lavya shot back.

"Actually, that's exactly why I'm an expert. And celibacy gives me an impartial bird's-eye view on matters apropos the female persuasion. Besides, if he"—Ash jerked a gloved thumb in Karna's direction—"could salvage your drunken and sorry soul, then I'm sure Qalli's lying one is guaranteed a safe landing."

"Drunken? Yes. Sorry? Absolutely. But I never lied!"

Ash laughed at Lavya, the pustules around his mouth stretching obscenely. "Only because you thought Karna could read your mind."

Karna sighed, watching his bickering buddies with gratitude. Whatever past shit had brought them together, the three of them had become a solid trifecta. Not as magnificent as the Three Stooges, but damn close.

He stopped the escalating argument with a whistle. "Now who's wasting time with nonsense? Lavya, find out what Yama has gleaned from Baital about the prophecy. Meanwhile, I'll go speak to the leader of the Naga." Naga Lok was the largest of the underground *loks* and ruled by a reasonably levelheaded seven-headed serpent.

"You better be back in time for the final festivities tonight," Ash said.

Karna smirked at his friend's slightly skewed priorities. "Lavya's right. Those romance novels have addled your brain."

# CHAPTER FIFTEEN
## BHOOTBHAVYA: PAST IMPERFECT;
## FUTURE UNDECIDED

That evening, Ash proved that romance novels had indeed turned him into the pasha of party hosting.

A million clay *diyas* lit up the fort's façade and fires roared within beaten copper pots across the gardens, taking on the duties of the absent sun. Humans, mountain goats and sheep milled about the entire west lawn, basking in the glory of a good harvest.

Half the revelers were on the improvised dance floor, bouncing to the beats of *pahadi* folk songs the DJ was remixing with pop music. The other half enjoyed the refreshments spread across the mile-long buffet lining the festival zone.

Every single edible foodstuff known to man—from the simple wheat-and-barley-based fares of Vedic Aryavarta to modern India's obsession with world-class fusion grub—was available for consumption. Karna could even smell the tantalizing scent of peacock roast swirling in the air. It was a delicacy not often offered on the Human Realm anymore, a sure feast for the chicken lover. Not for him, though. He'd given up meat for good when he'd become the Soul Warrior. Witnessing on a daily basis what an *asura* fed on had totally put him off meat.

Nevertheless, the rich and delicious aromas wafting around him had tempted him enough that he devoured his third ice-*gola* in as many minutes as he waited for Qalli to make her appearance. He hadn't had an ice-*gola* in years, and never this combination of chocolate and *kalakhatta* syrup.

He ambled around the grounds, slurping sweet and tangy juice from the purple ice stick, nodding and smiling at the people he passed, pausing now and then to strike up a conversation. He recognized none of the faces, not even the elderly ones. Why would he? He hadn't come to Har-ki-doon since the Indo-Sino conflict in 1962. Once he would've known each and every soul here personally. He'd stepped away to protect the mountains from his cursed existence, to shield its residents from the evil his presence attracted. But now he questioned what he'd achieved by barricading himself from his home, from denying himself a full life. This valley, the humans, this realm were no more or less in danger because of his cop-out.

Karna stopped to watch a group of overzealous dancers on the dance floor. They seemed drunk, certainly high on life. Ash dipped up and down in the middle of the throng, swaying to and fro like a snake charmer. He shook a *damua*, a small drum, in his fist vigorously.

Karna caught sight of more blue souls on the dance floor. Not all males, then. Amara and Lusha shook and gyrated in time to the music. Yahvi too, though her moves would be classified as more martial arts than dance. She was a trooper, his daughter, he thought with a smile.

In black jeans, a black tank and her ubiquitous army boots, Amara had made only one concession to dressing up: She'd combed out her hair and left it loose. Lusha was in jeans too, paired with a multicolored muscle tee, with her waist-long hair spilling out of a ponytail high on her head. Yahvi wore a pair of dressy white pants, a frilly black blouse and three-inch silver heels. But for all her heels and frills, she was as much of a tomboy as the other two. All three were flushed from their calisthenics, and if they'd bothered to put on makeup, it was a washout by now. Smiling at the merry picture they made, Karna waltzed toward them.

When firecrackers lit up the night sky—Ash had seriously gone off the deep end with this shindig—Karna caught sight of the rest of his *shishyas*. They stood just off the dance floor, enjoyment sparkling on their faces.

Qalli's shopping trip had paid off. Satya looked beautiful in a brocade *sherwani* jacket worn over silken slacks. Next to her, Ziva, her skin normal and humanlike, still shimmered like a rainbow in a one-shoulder blouse and a skirt that swept the ground. Iksa was in a velvet skirt and a sleeveless velvet vest, her upper arms adorned with gold and amethyst armbands.

The Barbie dolls and the tomboys, he thought in amusement—though Satya would fit either label. His chest swelled with pride as he watched them. He felt humbled, grateful for the chance to know them. His first impressions of the Six—of Satya's iron will, Lusha's physical strength, Amara's unshakeable grit, Ziva's natural nurturing, Iksa's quiet battles to do right by all and Yahvi's simple sweetness—still held, but were expanding in waves with every passing moment. The Stooges were right. The Six had so much untapped potential in them, and he couldn't wait to help them reach it.

They'd changed him too, reminding him of the man he'd once been—a man who was more than a warrior, more than just a sword of duty.

His cell phone buzzed, a stark reminder that some things never changed. His face tightened as he read the message: *Leave*. He'd been receiving the messages since that morning, anything from *"Untrustworthy coward"* to *"You've outstayed your welcome, Abhayasinha."* Fearless lion. Seven centuries ago, Bhadra had honored him with the title and his descendants mocked Karna by using it now. Soon they wouldn't be satisfied with just warnings. If he didn't bow to their demands and leave

Har-ki-doon, they'd rouse the rabble in the surrounding valleys against him. He couldn't let that happen again.

Karna blew out a breath. Priests had begun ritually purifying Asht Dveep only this morning. They estimated a full cleansing would take five days. Karna hoped Bhadra's clan-folk would hold their patience for four more days.

"What's wrong? Why the frown?"

A whisper of a smile tugged at Karna's lips. Lavya was outfitted in a royal-blue *pathani*—Karna likewise in black. Garments purchased by Qalli during her shopping trip, which she'd insisted they wear tonight.

"You look dashing," Karna said, not in the mood to discuss his inglorious past.

"That I do." Lavya grinned, puffing out his chest. "What did the Naga King say?"

Karna wasn't in the mood to discuss the mystifying present either. Not that there was much to discuss. Vala was certainly holding his cards close to his chest. And Dev-Il had flatly refused to meet him.

The Serpent had no news except *"The darkness spreads, Soul Warrior."* All of a sudden their formerly reliable information channels had become as unpredictable as the weather.

*"A kindling beacon is enough to shun the darkness,"* Karna had volleyed in kind, thinking of Yahvi.

*"Provided the beacon is not extinguished,"* the Serpent had cautioned.

As warnings went, that one had been a whopper.

Then his personal beacon stepped into his line of vision and brightened up his dark world. Yes, he thought as his heart began to pound. He was changed forever.

"Lavya," he murmured without taking his eyes off his beacon. "Go find a woman and live a little. The darkness is freaking spreading." He desired no morbid discussions tonight.

A round of firecrackers shot across the sky as Qalli made her way to the Barbie dolls. Her hair was pulled off her face in a complex hairdo pinned into place with dozens of glittering pins and spiraling down her back in a profusion of ringlets. She wore a sari, a yellow net concoction embellished with gold lace and pearls. Thick strands of pearls hung from her neck and ears, braceleted both her wrists and looped around her tiny waist.

*Chal chaiya chaiya chaiya chaiya*, the music throbbed around him.

"Karna." Lavya grasped his shoulder. "I'm sorry for what I said earlier. But have a care, my friend."

Karna nodded and swallowed the last chunk of ice from the *gola*. A quick area scan found a garbage bin, and he flicked the stick into it. Then he sauntered toward the *apsara* who made him want to celebrate life in all its pulse-pounding glory.

"I'm not blending in, am I?" Draupadi asked as a fresh crowd of people stopped in front of her and stared. Not mean stares or anything, but the fascinated stares reserved for movie stars and celebrities.

The highlanders were simple folk with simple values and tastes and simple joys. Not at all like the Celestials, or the citified swarms of New Delhi, where she'd shopped that afternoon for Yahvi's birthday presents and had ended up buying some extra things.

"Not even a little, Ma….aaah! I mean, Qalli." Iksa corrected her mistake quickly and looked about guiltily to check if anyone important had heard the lapse.

"Be a bit careful, darling," Draupadi said. "I'm going to confess soon, I think. He's beginning to like me again…er, both the me's." The ruse had become as convoluted as the labyrinthine battle formation of the Chakra Vyuha. No one escaped from it unscathed.

Draupadi searched through the merriment for Karna, spotting him at once. His bare head gleamed golden within a sea of colorful goat's wool turbans. He was making his way to her.

Praise the Goddesses, but he was gorgeous. In black *pahadi* pants and a knee-length silk tunic, he looked downright dangerous. She'd known that, hadn't she, while selecting the outfit for him? But knowing and seeing were two very different things.

Four ruby buttons held his tunic together, and he'd rolled the sleeves to his elbows. Black thong sandals covered his feet. In stark contrast, his shoulder-length hair and what skin could be seen was set to gleaming in the firelight.

*Karna. Karna. Karna.* His name had become the rhythm of her heart.

His eyes were riveted on her face. She loved that he couldn't take his eyes off her. But at the same time she didn't want him to look at her possessively. Oh *deva*! Stick to flirting. Keep it frivolous. Nothing good could come of this. Vishnu had said so.

"Hello." She felt fearful of him—for him. He meant to trade his fate for Yahvi's.

"I was looking for you." He smiled widely and winked at her daughters, who stood by her. His lips and tongue were stained purple, like he'd eaten *jamun* fruits. Then, as he was about to take the first stair up the garden steps to join her at the top, a glass shattered on the ground close to his foot and the strong scent of Madeira infused the air.

"Abhayasinha!" The name uttered with contempt shot waves of disquiet through the gaiety.

For a moment, only a moment, Draupadi was grateful she didn't have to answer the question in Karna's eyes.

Karna spun about to face his attacker. His shoulders went rigid. The people standing closest hushed up, but the music raged on.

A middle-aged man separated himself from the crowd and began speaking roughly and loudly enough to draw attention. He looked out of place in a suit and tie, with his air of urbanization. He wasn't a local hill farmer or goatherd, for sure. He began accusing Karna of hideous things—of wild orgies, evil hunts and dishonorable deeds. The man was beyond nasty and within minutes, the circle around them thickened with people.

Draupadi couldn't understand why Karna allowed the man speak to him in that fashion. Why didn't he defend himself? Compel the man to shut up or leave? Why did he let a mere mortal denigrate him like that?

A wave of déjà vu swept through her then. She'd expected her legs to cave under her in New Delhi, the city once known as Indraprastha—the city-capital she'd ruled as queen long ago. It hit her now instead and took her back to another time and place, when she'd met Karna for the very first time.

Dressed in bridal finery, she stood on a large festooned podium with her family and female companions. Noblemen from all over Aryavarta had come for the event, some to participate in the contest to win her hand, some to support their allies and some just to watch the tournament. Her father had designed an impossible test for the occasion, and she was to choose her husband from the winners. At the end of the day, she would be married to a stranger—granted, he would be the world's most prolific bow-wielder, but she didn't care about that. Stress over leaving her home and everything that was familiar had driven all joy from the occasion.

Then a dazzling man with fair hair broke free of the throngs of black-haired, wheat-skinned noblemen. He'd loped up to her like a lion advancing on his prey. She'd giggled at his daring. The sudden burst of fascination at the leonine man with a thick upturned moustache replaced the sadness in her belly.

The whole assembly, noisy with gay music and humming aristocracy, faded into the background when he climbed the five steps toward her.

He'd done so deliberately. There was no need for a contestant to meet the princess bride before the contest. It was as if he thumbed his nose at her father's rules.

He stopped halfway up the red-carpeted steps, holding her gaze for an eternity. At some point along that eternity, he'd held his hand out to her. Nervous and dismayed, she hadn't known what to do. So she'd asked the warrior lord who he was and where he hailed from, who his father was and what clan he belonged to.

His radiant face had hardened then. His mischievous, arrogant eyes went cold with contempt. The look had stilled her, scared her to the bones. He'd dropped his hand and walked away, one deliberate step at a time, with his head held high even though most of the assembly laughed at him. Her brothers had laughed the hardest.

*"He's an imposter, beloved sister. He's the son of a lowborn chariot driver. He's not of royal blood and is fief-lord only because of the misplaced munificence of Prince Duryodhan."*

Seven thousand five hundred years ago, Karna had borne those insults with a dignity and bravery she hadn't appreciated at the tender age of sixteen. But she did now.

"Will you stand beside a coward, O fools of Har-ki-doon? He slaughters young innocents in the name of duty. He cares not about protecting you. He seeks only glory and your fawning worship. Oppose him, defy him and he'll throw you in Hell. Isn't that so, Abhayasinha?"

Except for his caramel eyes going flat, the Soul Warrior did not react. Draupadi pitied the stupid man who thought that was the face of cowardice.

"You are drunk, brother Bhadranath," said an old *pahadi*, coming up to pat the suited man on his shoulders. "Go home and be at peace."

*Bhadranath.* Was he a local after all?

"What an ass," Lusha muttered. "I wish Uncle K would thrown him in Hell."

"We are loyal to Har-ki-doon's master, you fool. He is our savior."

The comments and murmurs grew amongst the *pahadis* until Ash and Lavya intervened and escorted Bhadranath off the property for his own safety—not that he deserved the courtesy. Karna thanked the highland-folk for their loyalty and trust, graciously accepting their outrage on his behalf. He asked them not to let the episode ruin the evening. Then, with the slightest of hesitations, he turned to her, his warrior mask firmly in place.

He expected her to ask him about the man. He waited for her to demand an explanation, she could see. But she didn't want to know about what he'd done or not done in his past. She only cared about what he'd do tomorrow. Dared she trust him?

His gaze curious, Karna stopped halfway up the steps. He reached his arm out, offered his hand to her. He wore rings on his thumb and middle and ring fingers. Rubies and diamonds winked at her from the thick gold circlets. In these past few days, or in Devlok for that matter, she hadn't noticed any jewelry on him except a watch and the Soul Catcher.

The old Karna, the King of Anga, had worn ornaments. The old Karna whose hand she'd rejected before the whole of Aryavarta. The man she'd loved in secret.

Draupadi took the three steps to meet him halfway and took his hand in both of hers. She felt with deep satisfaction the relief that quaked through him. She would never again hesitate to take his hand in public, she vowed silently. She would never again make him feel unwanted or unworthy. She would never again deny what she felt for him.

For a fleeting moment, Mother Kunti's displeased face swam before her eyes. Then a hand caressed her lower back, pressing her forward, and Karna bent his head to the cheers of her offspring.

Not even the Gods could stop them now, Draupadi thought, and sealed her fate with a kiss.

# CHAPTER SIXTEEN
## SHIKSHA: TOUGH LESSONS

Following a hearty breakfast the morning after the harvest festival, Karna and his *shishyas* decided to sweat it out in a gym only to discover Har-ki-doon didn't boast a machine-packed gym room. Ash had never felt the need to install one.

Improvisation had Karna herding the Six into the courtyard to do freestyle training, which somehow morphed into a demonstration of Kalari by Ash and him as a warm-up exercise.

Kalari was the mother of all martial arts and once upon three ages ago been developed and taught to the highborn warriors by none other than Karna's own guru, Parashuram.

Naturally, the Six wanted in on the fighting technique, and Ash organized thick rubber mattresses to be laid out as protection before they began flinging each other to the ground.

Amara and Lusha preferred the hand-to-hand aspect of the discipline and were soon grappling with each other on and off a mattress. Ash took Iksa and Satya through a specific series of exercises called *vaytari* that increased flexibility in their legs. And Karna showed Ziva and Yahvi how to wield a shoulder-length spear effectively.

For an hour and a half, everything rolled smooth as butter.

"I can handle more," Yahvi insisted, totally disregarding the fact that she vibrated like a discordant tuning fork from fatigue.

Ziva lay flat on her back on the floor doing *pranayam* to get her breath back. He'd put them through a vigorous workout, but Yahvi refused to take a break.

"I'm sure you can. Even so, rest a bit." Karna bit back the retort: No need to kill yourself until you actually have to. But he couldn't help reiterating like Guru Parashuram, "A *shishya* must carry out her guru's orders—harsh or not—for they are given with the intention of enlightening and guiding the *shishya*'s fate."

He'd been remembering his guru a lot of late. Not surprising, considering the role he was playing.

"You think I'm a stupid, silly, powerless soul." Yahvi's eyes flashed fire. The child had a temper exactly like his own.

"You are a powerless green soul, and if you keep arguing with me, you'll prove the other two adjectives as well." He would not fight with his daughter today.

The child sucked in an offended breath. "I embarrass you. Admit it! You think I'm worthless, a gigantic liability who can't even call on divine *astras*. A stain on your legendary status."

"That's not what I said." It amused him that Yahvi forgot to feel shy when she was angry.

"You are thinking it. I know it!"

"You don't know what I'm thinking," he muttered under his breath. Karma save him from moody females who believed they'd mastered the power of telepathy. He narrowly looked at his offspring. "Why is that, anyway? Even if you are green-souled, after three hundred years of education, you should be more seasoned. You should be able to call *astras* in a jiffy."

Frankly, her lack of skills troubled him more than her green soul. There was no way she could fight Vala even if she magically evolved into a blue soul overnight with stunning god-powers.

"Why don't you ask Mama?" She stared back belligerently.

"Save the taunts, child. Your mother and I don't speak."

"Yes, well, isn't that the whole problem?" She jabbed the floor with the neoprene-tipped spear. "I feel fine. See? I'm not even sweating."

Karna threw up his hands. "Fine. Join Ash's group."

Instead of being pacified, she growled like a bristly little lion cub. "I don't want to do some namby-pamby tai chi moves. Why are you treating me like a wheelless chariot, Father? You of all people...I never dreamed you'd be this way. You, who refused to be confined to the limits set by caste, circumstance or fate—how can you push me down like that?"

Everyone had stopped their activities to gape at them.

"You don't know me. You haven't even bothered to get to know me. How dare you make assumptions about me and write me off? How dare you be disappointed in me? Well, you know what? I am totally disappointed in you, too." She threw the fake spear to the ground and stalked off. The spear bounced twice and rolled, coming to rest by his feet.

Karna rubbed the back of his neck, watching his daughter's retreat. Could she be right? Was he treating her like a liability? Had he written her off just as her fate had?

"She knows her limitations, Uncle K," Satya said. "She doesn't need you to remind her of them every minute. She needs your support, not your skepticism."

"Uncle, I vote you go and give your daughter a hug." For once, Amara had addressed him as Uncle and not by some pop culture appellation. His gaffe was that serious.

What a strange and unpredictable twist his life had taken. He'd started the week as the guru and by midweek he'd become the *shishya*.

"Okay! Okay! I'm going...I'm gone."

The making of amends didn't happen immediately. Duty and the search for an evil nemesis did hold precedence over minor matters such as family spats. But that afternoon, when the opportunity came up again, Karna wondered how he'd ever thought of his daughter as unskilled. Yahvi was right. He hadn't been paying attention to her.

Karna leaned against a scarred *devadaru* cedar and watched his daughter methodically empty a quiver full of arrows into a variety of targets. Her posture was perfect, her focus absolute as she drew length and released arrow after arrow with fluid grace and timing. She made an impressive picture in a black Kevlar vest, skinny jeans and fur-trimmed Uggs. Her hair had been combed off her face in a tight ponytail, and despite the cool autumn breeze swirling around them, her skin glowed with perspiration.

Next to Yahvi, tough-cookie Amara looked equally worked-out. Black leather vambraces banded her upper arms and wrists; the one around her left bicep had a slot for her phone. Bose noise-cancelling headphones—his, he deduced with surprise—clung to her neck.

The Siamese Twins—the label seemed apt as the two moved as a pair when they separated from their larger group—had found his archery range, one of the many training zones he'd set up around Har-ki-doon when he'd called it home. Karna exhaled noisily. It was still his home whether he dwelled here or not, and whether his neighbors liked it or not.

The targets had been set up at random heights and distances. There were several bull's-eye boards intermingled with gunny-bag mannequins. The dummies vaguely resembled *asuras* and had four small wooden disks tacked on the heads, hearts, groins and thighs—the four deadliest spots on a body. All of them were neatly littered with holes and arrows.

That the Siamese Twins had the energy for this after the morning workout spoke volumes about their mindset. He'd been just the same at their age—possibly worse. He'd been too desperate, too cocky, too determined to prove his worth as a warrior par excellence. He'd not let anything or anyone come between him and his ambition. In that, too, Yahvi had been right.

The warrior's arena had been his drug of choice—an addiction he'd never overcome. Watching the young Kuru and Pandu princes train in the various fields of warcraft had given rise to an alien desire within his own teenage breast—to become Aryavarta's premier bow-wielder. The aspiration had grown and magnified until it had become impossible to contain. He'd become impossible to live with after that.

Adiratha had never understood that need or the compulsion that drove Karna. He'd looked at his son's disquiet with bafflement and not a little sympathy.

*"Learn to be satisfied with your lot in life, son. Ours is a noble profession. We are the bulwarks of our kings and princes. We grip their lives in our hands, as surely as we hold the reins on their chariots. We drive the warriors into battle, and it is our skill that helps them vanquish their enemies and stay alive on the battlefield. Chariot drivers witness a king's glory and tell the world his story. There is no higher calling."*

But Karna hadn't been satisfied in telling a story. He'd wanted to be the story.

*"Half a loaf at home is better than a whole one abroad. Contentment is the only way to true happiness, Radheya,"* Adiratha would plead to his son's deaf ears.

Can a lion find contentment in the meat thrown to him? No, a lion needs to hunt. He needs to stalk his prey. He must enjoy the kill to justify his place within his pride.

Mother Radha had understood that, had understood Karna well. It was she who'd finally forced him to cut himself free of guilt and never look back. It was she who'd told him to listen to his heart and seek his true calling.

His mother had been his staunchest ally. She'd been the cornerstone of his life. She'd be ashamed of the way he'd been neglecting his daughter.

"Yo! Obi-Wan." Amara waggled her fingers at him. "What do you recommend? Split-finger aiming or three fingers under?"

Karna shoved off the tree and jogged down the lazy knoll toward the flatter range. "If you want my unparalleled bow-wielding advice, Padawan, you may prostrate yourself at my feet and I will reveal the secret of my success to you."

One half of the Siamese consortium snorted, while the other half didn't bat an eyelid. Both stared at his white snakeskin cowboy boots, then at each other, and burst into chuckles. Ash had smirked at his boots too. Karna failed to comprehend the humor. They were just boots.

"It's not so much one method over the other. Although three fingers under the arrow does focus the eye better. By the way, I like what you've done here," he said, pointing at the dummies.

Amara's skill with weapons he'd witnessed firsthand the other day, so what she'd done to the targets wasn't such a shocker. But Yahvi's prowess pleased him greatly.

"I'm impressed, *vatse*," he said, breaking into a smile. His mother would've loved Yahvi.

"Thank you," she mumbled to the grass. "It's my turn to collect the arrows." And then she was gone.

Karna blew out a breath, debating whether to run after her and apologize—again—or let her steam it out. Sons were so much easier to handle; whack them over the head regardless of who'd stepped out of line and that was the end of the matter.

Truth was, they were all feeling the effects of nonaction. Once, it started, once Vala made himself and his purpose known, there wouldn't be any doubts.

"Agreed, Ms. Skywalker is not yet initiated into the Force, but it doesn't mean she can't handle a lightsaber."

Karna wondered if he should be worried about his mental health because, freakish as it sounded, he actually understood Amara. He spared her a brief glance. "She's a novice, Padawan."

"Don't underestimate her."

"Don't overestimate her skill," he said sharply.

"Don't be such a fusspot, Obi-Wan."

"Amara, promise me you'll protect her. Whatever happens, you will keep her safe." He didn't add, *When I can't.* He was glad Yahvi had chosen archery over other types of war skills. It would keep her in the action while out of immediate danger.

Amara slung her arm around his shoulder and gave him a sloppy kiss on the cheek. "We won't. Mama already made us swear blood oaths, or something to that effect, the day Vee was born."

Draupadi was a good mother. His surprise at that was waning rapidly.

Karna watched his daughter begin the drill again. "How do I make it up to her?"

"She's not mad at you...or not only you. She's mad at herself too." Amara cocked her head to one side and assessed him. "If I break sisterly confidence and tell you something, will you swear not to blow up?

"Amara..."

"She sent two pictures to Draas. You know *asuras* haven't seen the sun in a while. In Lok Vitalas, Draas had lamented not having seen a sunrise and a sunset. She'd begged us to send pics. Yahvi took the photos on our first day at Asht Dveep. She thinks it's her fault it was attacked."

"Whoa." Karna ran his hands through his hair and linked them at the back of his head. "You tell me such a story and expect me not to get pissed?"

"You swore, Yoda." Amara clucked her tongue. "Draas swears she hasn't shown them to anyone. But she normally doesn't lock her room. Anyone could've waltzed in and fiddled with her gadgets. And now Vee doesn't know whether to believe Draas or not. But it doesn't matter as she's made up her mind never to ever contact Draas again—so calm down. She didn't sleep all night because of that, and we ended up having a *Star Wars* movie marathon. She gets grouchy without sleep."

Yahvi had run through her quiver. Karna stiffened abruptly as his mind fully registered what Amara had just accounted. "You're still in touch with Draas when I explicitly asked you not to befriend *asuras*?"

"Oops?" Amara had the gall to flutter her eyelashes at him before her expression turned devious. "Let's have a knife-throwing contest. If I win, no punishment, but if you win, I'll obey you for...a week."

He knew better than to encourage a born gambler, but this was too good an opportunity to waste. "You're on."

Yahvi settled down under the shade of an old Himalayan oak and systematically checked her arrows for damage, slipping the undamaged ones back into her quiver and the damaged ones into her backpack. She was finally pooped. Done for the day. Drawing a bottle of water out of the pack, she drank deeply.

Her two blade-mad relatives weren't done, though. They were busy taking turns throwing their knives at the huge cedar rising in the distance. The tree's trunk was peppered with ancient nicks and cuts and would be marked by more by the time those two were done showing off. She'd declined her father's invitation to join them. She didn't want to disappoint him again as she wasn't at all good at turning knives into projectiles. And probably never would be, what with the whole imminent death situation.

Yahvi hugged her knees, rounding her back in a spine and neck stretch. The air was marked by the fresh, tangy scents of wet earth, green grass and cedar wood and the light, cool breeze began to refresh her heated skin. She sighed, wondering if he'd mourn her. They hadn't known each other long, and he clearly didn't think much of her, so why would he? She looked up after a side stretch to find him standing over her.

"May I?" He gestured to the spot next to her. When she shrugged, he sat down, mimicking her pose.

"Hey," she said, stomach fluttering. Nervous and upset were the only two emotions she felt in his presence. Which was just stupid, because the whole idea behind her journey was to get to know him.

"Hey!" He smiled.

She felt horribly self-conscious. She *had* been showing off earlier. She wanted to impress him. And maybe he'd been right to stop her before she hurt herself. She had to be careful until her birthday. She had to stay whole and unhurt.

"You're good with that." He nodded at her peacock-hued longbow lying on the grass between them.

Almost as long as her, the bow was fashioned out of a single piece of dyed heavenly yew with a leather-bound center, for a firm grip, and horn-shaped silver nocks at its ends. A strand of tensile hair, plucked from the tail of a *kimpurusha* when he took the form of a horse, was strung through the nocks and pulled taut in a D.

He picked up the bow to examine it, plucking the string. "It sings well. Good curves. And the length is perfect for you. Tvastar's work?"

Lord Tvastar was the Celestial Architect and the god-king of artisans. He and his team had built everything in the Higher Worlds, from the cities to the abodes to the transports to the weapons.

"No, no his. I don't know the bowyer's name. Uncle Arjun gave it to me just before we came here as an early birthday present."

"Did he? So he knows about you?" her father asked carefully.

"Of course." Yahvi looked sideways in surprise.

"Do they all know about you?"

She frowned, not getting what he meant by that at all. "Yes, Father."

"Did they…" He broke off and cleared his throat. "Were they good to you?"

"They sent me presents, so yeah."

"That's good. But…did they ill-treat you in any way, ever?"

It dawned on her what her father was circling around. He *was* worried about her. He did care. Maybe he would mourn her. She shook her head, her chest suddenly feeling very tight.

"What about the others?" He'd gone stiff, as if braced for bad news.

Yahvi wondered if she said yes, if she showed a smidgeon of hurt, would he go wreak havoc there? "No, Daddy," she said softly, lying just a little bit. "No one was mean to me. I wasn't allowed to meet anyone. My sisters were my only windows into the outside world. Anyway, I'm sure Mama wouldn't have stood for it had I been mingling with the Celestials, nor would my sisters and my uncles."

He'd gone quiet during her speech. After a bit, he tugged her ponytail and kissed her forehead. *Spinning satellites!* Yahvi was positive her face had gone pink with pleasure.

"I read a great deal about you and my uncles. They are such fun stories."

"*Fun* stories? I don't think my dealings with your uncles can be called *fun* from any angle, *vatse*," he said, his lips kicking up in a half smile.

"Some of them were fun." She grinned, feeling impish. "Uncle Bheem warned Lusha never to get on your bad side. He said you make Dev-Il look like a joker when you're angry."

"Rubbish! He should talk. Bheem was the biggest bully that ever existed. Do you know he used to fling his cousins into the air and laugh as they crashed to the ground and broke various bones?"

"I know!" She'd never understood why Uncle Bheem would do that.

"I bet Yudhishtir still walks around with a stick up his backside." Her father did a marvelous imitation of Uncle Yudhishtir at his pompous best. She'd only ever met Uncle Arjun, but she knew stuff about all her uncles.

Yahvi burst into gales of laughter. "What about Uncle Nakul and Uncle Sahadeva?"

"Too smitten by their reflections to ever be of any use to anyone," he said and affected a pose that Yahvi had seen Ziva strike on several occasions.

"Daddy, you're awful. And what do you think about Uncle Arjun?"

Karna's guard went up at his daughter's sly-toned question. He looked over his shoulder and sure enough, Amara stood right behind him, swinging a Joystick in each hand. She was quick enough and well-equipped to do some major damage to his body, yet he threw caution into the wind.

"Arjun has a false pride in his accomplishments." The words gave him pause, told him how much resentment he still harbored for his slayer.

Amara stared daggers at him for a couple of heartbeats, before plopping down across from Yahvi. "That's true, Coach Touchy-touchy. Pops knows the Gods had a hand in his victories. In fact, he thinks you're pretty much unbeatable in most types of war games."

"Is that so?" he asked, startled.

"Ye-es. Why so psyched? Your brothers hold you in high esteem, you know." Amara took off her headphones and headband and shook out her hair. Yahvi dug out a hairbrush from her backpack and handed it to her sister without being asked. The bond the Siamese Twins shared was unmistakable.

It occurred to him that Arjun and he might have shared such a bond had they grown up as brothers instead of rivals. And because the thought freaked the hell out of him, he pointed at a twelve-hundred-year-old *devadaru* cedar, which quite oddly seemed to be flashing steel.

"Did you see that?" He stared at the foliage. "There's something hanging from that branch."

A loaded silence met his exclamation. Amara was making goggle eyes at Yahvi, and Yahvi's eyes had narrowed to slits in answer. He could practically see the argument zinging between them.

"Is it a target?" Stupid question. What else could it be?

Yahvi nodded. "We're trying to teach ourselves how to take it down but haven't managed it yet."

"Maybe you could show us?" Amara asked.

The Siamese Twins looked far too innocent not to be guilty of something. He stared at the *devadaru,* trying to see between its shivering leaves. Shooting targets from trees was basic training for an archer. Maybe they simply weren't focusing right. He stood up to take a closer look at the object.

"All it takes is focus," he instructed them. "The smaller the focus of your dominant eye, the more accurate your aim. Don't look at the whole target. Look at one tiny part of it. And use instinct to shoot it down. Trust your gut."

"Wait!" Yahvi ran to him and thrust her longbow and quiver into his hands.

"Go ahead, Legolas. Let's see who wins the bet," said Amara.

"Another bet?" He shook his head. "I will disabuse you from this propensity to gamble at the drop of a hat," he vowed as they walked the thirty paces to the tree. He squinted at the flailing leaves and white flashes of steel, gauging the distance of the target.

"Not up, Daddy. Look down!"

His gaze dropped automatically, and Karna felt as if Lord Indra's thunderbolt had been let loose on his spinal cord.

A large, circular mirror was embedded between the roots of the age-thickened trunk. In its reflection, a metallic discus rotated on a nylon string from a high branch. A silver-blue fish was attached to the serrated edge of the disc with its head angled downward. It spun around dizzyingly. The fish's unblinking, beady eye mocked him through the mirror.

Every single hair on his body stood on end at the impossibly clever and chillingly familiar target. It was the same target from Draupadi's *swayamvara*. The target he would have shot down in front of the whole of Aryavarta to win her hand in marriage had he not been disqualified.

The target he had shot down in the middle of the night as she alone watched with love and pride shining in her lotus-petal eyes.

He whipped around to glare at Yahvi and Amara. "What the fugdoom-all is this?" he asked, right before he burst into flames.

# CHAPTER SEVENTEEN

## AHVANA: DO OR DARE

Draupadi took her first sip of her perfectly brewed Darjeeling tea when the sounds of murder and mayhem set her bones rattling. She set down her cup on the nightstand and bolted out of bed. Were they being attacked? She garbed herself in a silk dressing gown and vanished from Karna's bedchamber into the courtyard. She shuddered in relief when she found all her chicks in one piece—hyperventilating like crazy, but still in one piece.

The commotion had brought Eklavya into the courtyard too, with a dozen or more sentries and *pahadis* running behind him, carrying guns and swords at the ready.

"Holy Mother of All Virtue, what have you done now?" Draupadi rounded on her daughters. She'd seen a variety of expressions on their faces in the past, but never such a combination of horror, alarm and excitement.

"He went whoosh!" Amara flung her arms up in demonstration and brought them down in a circular motion. "Never ever seen anything like it," she said, awestruck.

"And then…and then…" Yahvi couldn't even finish the sentence. She bent in half, pressing her hands to her stomach and wheezed.

Draupadi rubbed her back and raised her brows at Amara. What had they done to make him that angry?

"Take a deep breath and explain, one lucid word at a time," advised Satya.

"Obi-Wan is on fire," Amara said.

"Daddy blew up like a volcano," Yahvi said in tandem.

"Was he upset when he did that?" asked Draupadi, more startled by Yahvi's use of "Daddy" than the blew-up-like-a-volcano bit.

Amara and Yahvi exchanged guilty glances. "Kind of."

"That's normal," Lavya assured them. Like her, he'd come to the conclusion that it wasn't an *asura* invasion. He jerked his head, signaling the sentries to go back to their posts.

Draupadi patted Yahvi's back one last time. "See? Not to worry, darlings. It's normal."

"No, no. This was baaad. Really bad," said Yahvi. "You have to go to him, Lavya."

Draupadi narrowed her eyes at her daughters. "What did you do?"

"Never mind that! Just go, please?" begged Amara.

"You're wasting time asking questions. He'll set the whole valley on fire while we stand here and argue." Yahvi was clearly very upset.

"Why don't you go?" said Lavya.

It took Draupadi a second to figure out he meant her. "Me?" she squeaked in surprise. But she'd just woken up. She wanted her tea and a long bath. Actually, she wanted to go back to bed. Karna hadn't let her sleep a wink last night. He'd been in a funny mood since the Bhadranath episode.

"Who better than an *apsara* to soothe a troubled soul?" Lavya asked.

Why did this feel like a test and not teasing? "All right. Where is he?" she said, not at all sure how she was supposed to hose fiery Karna down.

"We don't know. He just poofed!" Yahvi said unhelpfully.

"Then where am I supposed to find him?" she asked, beginning to feel irritated. Why was she nominated to go on a wild goose chase?

"He's probably at the lagoon. It's on the extreme northeast end of Har-ki-doon, near the Jaundhar Glacier," Lavya replied helpfully.

With a long-suffering sigh, Draupadi vanished to perform her *apsara* duties.

Fresh, blue-green water bubbled within the rocky jaws of a jagged mountain massif, right above a lush skirt of evergreens. Because of its proximity to the snowcaps, it was colder up there than in the Valley of the Gods, which was all but invisible from this vantage point.

Draupadi hugged herself tight, yearning for a hearth-fire, a warm bed and a few blankets, and rued the days her youngest two had come into existence. Wisdom and temperance hadn't made themselves known to Amara yet, and Draupadi wasn't holding much hope for Yahvi either.

Behind her, the rock face yawned open in a spacious grotto, echoing with the whoosh of a waterfall that seemed to be the source of the pool. Dusk-light had turned the water's surface into a gleaming mirror. Her gaze lit on a pile of charred clothes discarded on an overhanging ledge, but no inflamed warrior thrashed about in the lagoon.

She made her way to the mouth of the grotto and peeked inside, not bothering to call out, as Karna wouldn't be able to hear her over the deafening waterfall.

She turned to check the pool again but got distracted by the imposing panorama before her. A golden-orange sun dipped low between the frosty peaks like a giant ball of melting lava. Before it, a majestic Himalayan griffon, pale as a grey pearl, soared and circled, then disappeared behind a thin clump of denuded conifers in the distance. The altitude, with its lack of oxygen and moisture, was an inhospitable environment even for the evergreens. Inhospitable maybe, she thought, but the view was absolutely breathtaking.

Wild and beautiful Nature: It appeared unruly but it strictly followed the natural laws of the Cosmos.

Perhaps this was a healthier wake-me-up ritual.

"Boo." The deep gurgle travelled eerily over the lagoon a split second before a spray of ice-cold water hit her face.

Her shriek petrified a nest of snow pigeons, a Himalayan warbler, a thrush, a woodpecker and some pink-browed rose finches out of their roosts in the nearby bushes. They chattered shrilly close to her head, then flapped away in indignation.

"You're such a buffoon!" She put a hand over her pounding heart and wiped her face with the other. He was the reason Yahvi was a brat.

Karna threw his head back and hooted in hilarity. She could barely see him what with all the steam rising up around him in ghostly ambience.

"It's not funny." She chanted a quick mantra that dried her directly.

"It is from my perspective." He chortled. "Enjoying the view, *manmohini*?"

"Oh, yes." And now that she had him in her viewfinder, her enjoyment hit new levels. Forget the mountain views or the kick of Darjeeling tea; nothing suffused her senses as completely as Karna.

He bobbed up and down in the water, giving her tantalizing peeks of his taut shoulders and perfect pectorals, all deliciously wet. She had to remind herself she'd come here to cool him down, not flame the bonfire. But what if they had only another day or two?

She kneeled on the outcropping and leaned forward in clear invitation. He half rose out of the water to kiss her, oh so thoroughly. Too soon, he sank back down, leaving her mouth inflamed and wet and aching for more.

"Come join me." His voice was gruff with arousal.

"The water..." she began, but was interrupted by a cacophony of flutters, chirps and rustling branches as the birds flew back and settled into their avian abodes.

"Come in, *manohara.*" He watched her through hooded eyes fringed with wet eyelashes. The look was so utterly beguiling that she was tempted to strip down at once and dive into the frigid water.

She shook her head. "It's freezing. You come out."

"I can't. I'm still on fire."

"Really?" She stared at him closely. What she'd thought was his natural radiance was actually a low glowing flame. "Well, huh. How long do you think you'll take to stop smoldering?"

"With you sprawled like that with your cleavage artfully on display and your robe open to your navel, maybe never," he said in all seriousness.

Draupadi burst out laughing. "Pervert, you make my head spin." She gasped when he grabbed her wrists. "What are you doing?" She shrieked when he pulled her with single-minded intent and the top half of her hovered over the water. The birds flew off again.

"Stop that inhuman screeching, woman. You'll attract some unwanted animals."

"The only animal I'm attracting is you. Karna, stop that! I've not even had tea yet."

Karna ignored the protests, in no mood for coyness. He couldn't get the fish target out of his mind, or Draupadi.

With hands hot enough to sear flesh, he arranged her until she sat at the edge of the pool with her legs splayed in front of him. He slid his hands up silky skin and bobbed up to flick his tongue across her navel.

They said that the navel of the Supreme Goddess was the source of all life and creativity. Was that why the sight of a woman's navel aroused a man to fever pitch? Or was it her eyes?

"Hypothermia isn't my idea of a pleasurable interlude," she cried when her feet hit the water.

Karna sighed, resting his head on her thigh. She was not getting with the program. He flicked his tongue out and licked her.

"I'm not going in the water, Karna. I mean it."

She wasn't saying no for sex. Which was good. Besides, she didn't need to be in the water for what he had in mind anyway. He pressed his mouth to a small patch of skin and sucked. She squirmed but didn't draw back. Diving headfirst into the frigid water hadn't helped him much. But there was another way for him to cool off. Granted, he'd have to turn up the burner before it shut down.

He bit her gently on the other thigh. She whimpered. The sound aroused him to fever pitch as well, so he bit her again. She whimpered again and tunneled her fingers through his dripping hair and pulled him close.

*The dart and the bull's-eye...*

"I'm getting wet, after all," she whispered, making him smile against her sweet-smelling skin.

*The shaft and the discus...*

"Karna, please. Don't tease me so."

He pushed her robe off, and the homing pigeon landed in the coop.

Yahvi had homework. *Bleah!*

She was expected to commit all the *asura* repelling spells in the Atharva Veda—the Veda that contained any and all spells known in the Cosmos—to memory in less than twenty-four hours. She'd memorized the simpler ones over the years and knew them well. But learning spells by rote was the easy part. Chanting them was hard. The mantras worked only if vocalized in the right tenor, for the right situation and embellished by the right emotion. It took years of practice to get it all right, a fact her sisters were totally disregarding.

That morning, Daddy had decided that Ash would handle the academic lessons while they were at Har-ki-doon—Ash being a warrior-scholar with the patience of a priest and all. Yahvi suspected it was more because her father found such lessons tedious himself, but that was beside the point.

"There are stages to learning. First you conquer the books, then the training ground, and only then can you whet your inner *shaktis* or god-powers. I've drawn up lesson plans for each of you. See that they're done by afternoon," the incense-scented taskmaster had said at breakfast.

Which was all well and good if she had three hundred years to learn it all. It'd taken her sisters exactly three minutes to brush up on the charms he'd handed out, while Yahvi had been struggling for hours. Okay, that was an exaggeration. She'd struggled for maybe an hour, as Daddy's weird outburst couldn't have happened much before that. She'd memorized exactly two and a half spells before boredom had set in—permanently, she was very much afraid.

Yahvi sighed. So not fair! Amu wasn't being subjected to such torture. That she must've been at some point in her formative years was only slightly appeasing. Luckily, Sergeant Satya was no longer supervising, and when the cat's away…

Yahvi discreetly switched to her gaming screen.

"What is it?" asked Lavya, startling Yahvi to switch the screen back to her lesson page. He'd been installed as supervisor in Satya's stead. *Bleah.*

"Naaathing." Yahvi thrust her lower lip out. This really wasn't how she wanted to spend her last days. Someone should take her clubbing. Who cared if an *asura* got her today as opposed to tomorrow? Well, Iksa did. Iksa was big on events happening at the right time and place.

A huge white forehead popped up over the computer across the desk, a deep furrow forming between two bushy eyebrows. Lavya was such a nerd. His whole inward and outward demeanor shouted *NERD* in capital letters. No matter what he wore, fashionable or not, he looked nerdish. Today he was dressed in a black sweater-vest over a blue shirt and jeans. He'd rolled the sleeves of the shirt up to his elbows, displaying nice, solid forearms lightly dusted with hair—maybe the only unnerdish parts of him.

All the while he frowned at her, his hands typed furiously. Blink. Twenty words. Blink. Twenty-five. Blink. Twenty-two words. Mother of Mars! He was fast. Faster than her, and she was pretty awesome on the QWERTY herself. When she came into her god-powers, she too would type with the speed of light.

That's if she was allowed to fulfill her destiny. With Iksa's latest vision, which her sister refused to discuss with them beyond saying, "Something has changed," it didn't look too likely. What could've changed? Yahvi heaved another sigh.

"What?" Lavya asked, impatience sparking his inky eyes this time.

"Why do you keep asking me that?" Yahvi demanded. If hair could be called nerdy, Lavya's was it. It was slicked back off his shiny forehead with no parting. Gross.

"Because you keep sighing."

Yahvi drew in a huge, noisy breath and let it out in a gargantuan sigh.

Lavya dropped his gaze to his laptop, punched a few keys and looked up again. "It bothers me."

"My sighing bothers you?" Yahvi decided that anything, even a stupid conversation with a nerd, was less boring than homework.

"Not yours, per se. Anyone's sighing bothers me. It's such a weird sound. Not quite a groan, not quite a breath. Like it's trying to be something but falling way short of its goal."

*Seriously?* Yahvi stared at Lavya. "The philosophy of a sigh. You are such a nerd."

"Thank you." His lips tweaked up in a smile.

"It wasn't a compliment!"

Lavya laughed out loud. "You are so much like him, it's frightening."

Yahvi sat up straight. "Him? You mean my father." Oh! She hoped so. She desperately wished to be like her father.

"You have the same whacko humor."

"You have the same sense of humor, Groucho Marx," she pointed out.

He shrugged. "I didn't before. But it rubs off on a person after seven hundred years of listening to it day in and day out." He rolled his shoulders, emitting a loud groan. No sighing for the resident nerd. "But it's more than that. You're like him in every way but physically. In every way that counts, Princess," he said, and abruptly went red in the face.

"Princess. I like it." She hopped off the ergonomic chair, sashayed around the desk and parked her ass by his chair.

Lavya cleared his throat. "You're done with your work?"

Yahvi rolled her eyes. "I hate spells. I'd rather just develop my god-powers."

"And until you do, the spells will help. Magic has to be learned, memorized vigorously. Though I get your frustrations," he sympathized, standing up to stretch his back. "I still have a bloody hard time remembering the proper spells for the precise actions at the moment when I need them."

"Exactly! I'd much rather rely on my bow and arrow."

Lavya brought his right hand up to her face and curled his fingers closed. He suddenly opened them and dozens of bubbles showered over them.

"Show off," she grumbled, popping the biggest one with a finger.

"Impatience will not win you any treasures," he rebuked her.

Of course she was impatient. She'd been patient for eighteen years and enough was enough.

Up close, Lavya towered over her. His hand danced inches from her face, creating more bubbles. He grinned when she slapped his hand away. When he didn't stop, she wrapped a fist around his fake thumb and squeezed. Its rubbery smoothness surprised her. She'd expected it to feel as real as it looked.

"How does it work?" she asked, fascinated that it bent in any direction when she applied pressure.

"Like a real thumb mostly. It's made of a resilient elastomer and can withstand most chemicals and extreme temperatures without melting or breaking."

"How's it staying on? I can't see any straps or ties holding it to your palm. Can it just pop off accidently?" She stared at him, appalled.

Lavya laughed. "No, silly human. The base of the prosthetic is vacuum-sealed to my hand, and I've wrapped it in enough magic that it won't just pop off. See why you should memorize all magical formulae?"

Yahvi made a face. She tilted her head to one side, puzzled by something. "Why not grow a real one? I'm sure the Goddess of Illusion can help you."

Lavya shrugged. "I'm not allowed in the Higher Worlds."

"Really? Punished, are you?" Yahvi grinned. Clearly there was a story here, and she knew just how to squeeze it out of him. "It was very brave of you to do what you did. To cut off your thumb knowing exactly what it was going to cost you. Foolish, but very heroic."

He was staring at his hand, cupped snugly between her palms. He began to rub the back of her hand with his thumb.

"It wasn't heroism. It was anger," he said, brusquely.

"I'm sure," she agreed. "I would've been angry too. At society, and the custom that forbade a talented young man to learn from his choice of guru because he hadn't been born in the right social class. Angry with the guru who hadn't lifted a finger to hone the bowman but demanded a fee—a *gurudakshina*—regardless. But mostly, I'd be angry with myself for choosing a nasty-ass guru as my idol in the first place. I sooo get your chopping off your thumb and throwing it in his face. You did it so you wouldn't be tempted to punch the old fart."

Lavya burst out laughing. "Old fart? Shit, little one, that's exactly what I'd thought then."

"Insulting me when I'm upgrading you from a nerd to a hero?" Yahvi *tsk-tsk*ed, shaking her head. "I hate being called 'little one.' Stick with 'Princess.'"

"And calling me a nerd to my face is not insulting?"

"Not if it's the absolute truth, Prince," she said and winked. Lavya had been the prince of the Nishada forest tribe in his mortal life.

He boomed out another laugh—the sound distinctly nonnerdy. "Your eyes are like his too. Molten chocolate sparkling with flecks of gold."

Pleased by the poetic comment, Yahvi fluttered her lashes outrageously.

"Though Karna's are almond-shaped and yours are…not," Lavya concluded abruptly.

"Not what?" she asked, feeling bothered by his close scrutiny.

"Lotus-shaped," he mumbled as if to himself. Then suddenly his own inky pair went razor-sharp. "Holy shit!"

"What's wrong?" Yahvi's pulse began to throb below her ears. He couldn't have guessed, could he, simply by the shape of her eyes?

"Your eyes…your sisters' eyes, they're all shaped alike. Big, shapely lotus-eyes."

Yahvi nodded feebly but her heart thundered like crazy.

"Gift of the gene from your mother, yes?"

*Shoot. Shoot. Shoot.* Yahvi nodded again. She could hardly deny what was so obvious. Her sisters and she were actually surprised her father hadn't guessed yet. They'd laid bets regarding the timeline of when he'd figure it out. They weren't making it easy by constantly changing eye color and eye makeup.

"Why, Yahvi? Why the lies?" His voice was stark, ringing with betrayal.

"We didn't lie. We just didn't say the whole truth." She wrapped her arms about her stomach and bent her head, hating the disappointment on his face. How would her father react?

"This is bad, Yahvi. After everything that's going on with you and Vala...this is the worst. He deserves to know the truth, damn it. Your father doesn't deserve to have his feelings molested like this."

"Please don't tell him. Please, Lavya, give them a chance to fall in love," she begged.

"Are you kidding me? He's never going to forgive her. He'll never forgive any of you for playing him for a fool."

"We didn't mean any harm," she protested—a pathetic excuse.

"Bullshit! It's what he'll believe."

"No, he won't." If he loved them he'd forgive them.

"Oh, yes he will. I suggest you have a heart-to-heart with your mother and convince her to come clean. One hour. That's all the grace I'll give her before I tell him myself. Got it?"

Yahvi nodded. Cosmic custard! Was this the change Iksa had seen? Were they all about to be banished from her father's abode? Mama would surely kidnap them back to Alaka if that happened. Then her father would face Vala alone and die because it was not his destiny to vanquish Vala. It was hers.

# CHAPTER EIGHTEEN
## SATYA: BITTER TRUTH

The grotto could have been an exhibit for the Celestial Art Gallery.

Carved into a massive section of its rock wall was Karna's personal insignia—the Earth surrounded by a blazing sun. Emblazoned above it was an old warrior credo: **Yudh kale asi-jeevi, shanti kale masi-jeevi**—*to live by the sword during war and by ink during peace.* The carefully applied gold leaf on the motif and the letterings shone in the dappled rays of the drowning sun.

To ward off the chill, Karna had started a fire. He seemed moody as he went about gathering firewood to build it up, which left Draupadi free to explore the grotto.

Every last inch of it—the floors and the ceiling, even the areas hollowed out by the waterfall and the shallow indoor pool—was covered in bas-relief and high-relief murals depicting Karna's life, so far as she could tell. She hummed in deep appreciation, more to herself, but the hollow cavern absorbed the sound and multiplied it through the space.

"The warrior and the artist," she said in wonderment and pleasure.

"It gets boring between tasks. And I don't know about 'artist.'" His words echoed back. "Saraswati finessed some of the trickier ones. See there, and there in the back?" He pointed a thick log at a scene out of the distant past, where a herd of war-horses raced against the flow of a river. He chucked the wood into the hissing, crackling blaze, making it soar.

"They're stunning." Draupadi moved in for a closer look even though it took her away from the toasty bonfire. She conjured a woolen shawl and wrapped it about herself.

Karna came up behind her, rubbing her arms and shoulders vigorously to get her blood pumping. She pressed into his embrace. "Hmm... you're like a live furnace."

"I'm sorry," he said, kissing her, his lips hot on her icy ear. Her ears and lips were probably as blue as her fingernails. "I didn't mean to drown you, but I lost all control at the end."

She shook in his arms, trembling with cold and laughter. She kissed his jaw, and before he got ideas for a repeat performance, she pointed to the wall. "Tell me about this one." She scraped a sliver of ice out of the mouth of an *asura* whose last ghastly moments alive had been immortalized by his slayer.

He obliged her with the story as he took her on a private tour along the autobiographical walls of art. It was clear he disliked talking about his feats because while he described some scenes in humorous detail, he simply answered her questions or watched her reactions in most.

The murals were sculpted so masterfully that every fold of garment; every curve and body contour; every muscle, flexed or relaxed; every expression on the projected faces; every tear and twinkle in the eye could be seen. More than seen—emotions leaped out of the figures and washed over her senses.

Her awestruck feeling for the artwork was soon replaced by an unspeakable sadness. *"It gets boring between tasks,"* he'd said. She knew exactly what these walls symbolized—hours, years, centuries, an entire lifetime of loneliness. Not boredom, as he claimed. She could imagine Karna's extreme isolation. Imagine it extremely well.

Overflowing with tenderness, she traced her fingers over his achingly familiar half smile—Yahvi's smile. The mural emphasized just how much their daughter favored him. He was young, depicted as a teenager, and was laughing at a petite woman carrying a large earthen water pitcher tucked in the crook of her arm and hip. Her features were soft and ordinary but so full of love that Draupadi's heart hurt to think that she no longer lived.

It was Karna's mother, Radha. It could be no one else.

Draupadi moved to another section where the change from boy to man—from a simple village-dweller to a proud king—was complete. His innocent, open smile had disappeared. No, not disappeared. It had changed: less open, less bright, but no less potent. In the scenes where he stood with his wives, he looked arrogant, possessive, more than a bit lustful. And yes, Draupadi noticed the twinkle in his eyes and theirs, the twinkle that hinted of satisfaction and a blessed marriage. That twinkle had been the envy of many a nobleman and woman of Aryavarta, because once again, the lowborn King of Anga had thwarted courtly custom and chosen his brides not for their correct social status, but for love.

How she'd envied him and his wives and did to this day. Which was completely stupid because she was with him now. But was she with him? Could she truly be with him?

"Do you have something to tell me, Qalanderi?" Karna nuzzled her ear.

Ice froze in her veins when he called her that. And wasn't that the crux of the matter? Qalanderi might hold a place in Karna's life. Draupadi did not. Could not. Could she?

Draupadi closed her eyes, cursing fate. What kind of a mother was she, thinking about her own happiness when her daughter's life was in danger?

"Tell you what?" She couldn't face him. She knew, deep in her soul, that he knew. He'd guessed who she was.

Making love in front of a fire was meant to be conducive to romance—for a normal couple. For Draupadi and him, romance had always come at a high price.

Their first clandestine liaison had cost him his honor. The fate of the Cosmos stood in balance because of their second affair in Devlok. He couldn't begin to imagine what they'd set in motion now.

Karna heaved a sigh of regret, wondering why the heart always wanted the things it could never have. "When were you going to tell me?"

He'd stunned her. One moment she was soft and quivery in his arms, the next like the block of wood he'd thrown into the fire. She lurched away, spinning around. Her throat convulsed on a cry. Emotions spilled from her eyes—horror, regret, abject humiliation. He wanted her to feel it all. He was not a forgiving soul.

"Before Vala attacked? After? Never?" He reached out with a finger and brushed a lock of her hair off her cheek. Then traced the long, wet straggle down her naked shoulder. He loved every inch of it. He loved every inch of her.

He dropped his hand, pride stinging as she flinched. He'd been a fool to let this game go on this long. If she still denied it, he'd walk away.

"I was going to tell you. I began to tell you a million times…but it was never the right moment." She pressed a hand to her forehead as if plagued by a sudden headache. "How did you guess?"

"I think I suspected it from the moment you came to Asht Dveep," he told her truthfully. He was a fool, but not that big a fool. "You kept saying 'my girls' with a mother's conviction. Draupadi was always unavailable. From the mother you described to me, she would not have sent the handmaiden to mind her daughters under any circumstances, especially not such dire ones. I let it be, as it wasn't affecting anything. In fact, keeping you in line worked to my benefit." He smiled ruefully. "Then this afternoon brought it all back with a bang."

"What happened this afternoon? What did those menaces do to upset you?" Her eyes sharpened and he saw the wheels turning behind them.

Yes, last night had been a test to confirm his doubts. He'd offered her his hand like in her *swayamvara,* and this time she'd taken it. Albeit hesitantly.

"They set up the fish target from your *swayamvara* and practically goaded me to shoot it down. Everything just came rushing back when I saw it." He rubbed the nape of his neck, embarrassed that a harmless prank had rattled him so. He'd remembered the humiliations he'd suffered. The constant rage he'd lived with. The pain he'd felt walking away from Draupadi. Even worse was the heartbreak he'd felt when Qalli had disappeared from his life. Most of all, he remembered defeat.

He was not dragging his family down with him this time.

"I think Yahvi wants us to be together," he said.

"I know. She's been matchmaking in earnest."

"Tell her it's not possible."

For a second she looked bemused. Then she dissolved into a puddle of laughs.

"It's not funny," he said stiffly.

"Our entire relationship is funny," she sputtered, giggles fizzing out of her. "It's bordering on ridiculous—a divine comedy."

Anger sparked his gut. He'd never liked being laughed at. He stalked to the other end of the fire to cool off.

"So you're not going to propose?"

"You know why I can't." Karna stared broodily into the fire.

"It seems I've waited a lifetime for you to propose to me, Karna," she said, coming closer but keeping the fire between them. "Now it looks as if you'll make me wait another lifetime."

Gods, she was beautiful. Pearls of wet grief ran down her blood-less cheeks. He curled his hands into fists. He wouldn't touch her anymore. He didn't have the right to touch her anymore. The game was over.

Sharp shards of agony pierced his soul at the thought of losing her again. A sudden bitter wind howled through the grotto, slapping at him from all directions. Gooseflesh erupted all over his body and he realized he was still naked. He snapped his fingers and clothed himself in jeans, shirt and boots. He repeated the action when he noticed her shivering. Her robe was beyond use and lay in a sopping heap exactly where he'd taken it off.

"Really?" she sniffed, gave another short laugh. She spread her shawl wide, then used one end to wipe her face. "Baggy, shapeless jeans and a shirt so large it would pass for a tent?"

"Can you stop complaining for once, woman? At least it's decent," he said.

"You think I dress indecently?" she asked, suddenly outraged. "Why, you bloody hypocrite. You love the way I dress. You can't take your eyes or hands off me."

"That's because you beguiled me," he shot back, nastily. Nasty was good. Rage was better. Supernova rage was a welcome emotion. It obliter-ated every other worthless one. "You made me think you were an *apsara*. You lied to me, Qalli." Shit—Draupadi.

"Beguiled you? Lied to you?" Her arms shot out in front of her, as if fully prepared to strangle him or push him into the bonfire. "I did not lie. Think back to our meeting. You assumed I was one. I wasn't introduced as an *apsara*, was I?"

"You and your convenient loopholes," he scoffed. "You let me think you were an *apsara*. That's as bad as lying."

Her eyes narrowed. "What about at my *swayamvara*? I was hardly pretending to be an *apsara* then."

"No, then you were simply amusing yourself by pretending to enjoy the attentions of a lowborn chariot driver's son," he said unthinkingly. An awkward silence followed his outburst.

"If painting me as a villainess keeps your conscience clear, so be it," she said curtly. "We would be better off hating each. But I wasn't pretending then. And I'm not lying now. I wanted you. I still want you. Is that so wrong?"

No, it wasn't wrong. But it wasn't meant to be.

Wolves howled out of the mountains, making him want to throw back his head and join them. He wondered if they could be persuaded to eat his wretched heart.

"Ask my five husbands if you don't believe me." Draupadi lifted her chin, held his eyes hostage with feral, fiery eyes. "And if you have the sense to let go of your warlord ego—unlike my lord husbands, who chose to sacrifice their sons rather than deviate from a righteous path—you will ask them to come save your ass. Or is your pride worth more than our souls, warrior?"

They made a bulky circle around the abyss.

Innermost were the *daityas*, behind them danced the unruly shape-shifters in their animal forms and bringing up the rear were the *raaksasas*. All eyes were on Preceptor Shukra as he threw oblations into the burning ritual fire, the *yagam*.

Shukra and his chief disciples, Dund and Mhat, were coated in ceremonial *raakh* from the tops of their ash-white dreadlocks down to their naked feet. Shukra sat cross-legged in front of the *yagam*. His eyes and torso circled in a trance-like rhythm while he chanted hymns to the drumbeat of the *dholak* Mhat played, invoking the spirits of the dead to come bless their travails. Dund danced around them all, around the *yagam*, around the chasm, around and around, clanging a pair of iron cymbals together, driving the tempo faster and faster into a crescendo before all three, with a roar and a clang and a thunderous thrum, brought the chorus to an end.

A cow, a goat and a crow had already been offered as sacrifice. Two hot pokers lay across the *yagam*, ready and waiting to be pressed into the human sacrifice. In sullen silence, Raka watched as Dves, with his strawberry-shaped nose in the air, herded the mortal to the center, Mara bringing up the rear of the puny procession.

Raka was disgusted. His disgust was aimed not at the human but at himself. He'd been stupid. Distracted by the mystery of Yahvi, he'd forgotten the obvious. There had been another human, a male warrior in a red shirt, at the Soul Warrior's abode.

But Dves hadn't forgotten the warrior. Dves had lured the mortal into the Cave of the Tomb while Raka had wasted time, energy and his seed for nothing. Dves was now second-in-command to Mara instead of Raka.

Dves shoved the human to his knees in front of Shukra. The human was trussed up hand and foot, bloody and swollen from a hard beating.

"The new whereabouts of the Soul Warrior, if you please," demanded Shukra in clear, unhesitant Hindi. The Preceptor had come prepared to blend in with humanity, if need be.

The human swayed like a drunkard. "What...the...hell...is a... ssssoul warrior?"

The effort earned him a nice backhand across his face from Dves. The *thwack* resulted in screams as the mortal's cheekbone shattered and blood spurted like a geyser from his mouth and nose. In spite of his demotion, in spite of being at the back of the throngs, Raka felt excitement boil inside him. He licked his lips, anticipating the kill even if it wasn't his.

"Where is he?" Shukra drew the poker aloft and stabbed the mortal in his belly.

Spine-tingling screams and profanities reverberated through the cave. The mortal knew some interesting words. True, some of them were impossible to carry out in reality, but an *asura* could dream, no?

"I...don't...know...what...you...mean," the man gasped.

Raka shook his head. The foolish mortal was making things needlessly difficult for himself. Warrior or not, he should be petrified of them. He was surrounded by thousands of *asuras*. The mortal's walnuts should have shriveled into peanuts by now. Why hadn't they?

Lord Shukra poked him harder. "Tell us."

The mortal's eyes rolled back inside his head and he collapsed on the floor, corpse-like. Only he wasn't a corpse yet. Raka could see his chest rise and fall.

"All right, the hard way it is." Shukra gestured Mhat to come forward. "Possess his soul and take what we need from him."

Raka craned his neck for a better view. The process of possessions enthralled him, especially when the possessee resisted. Mhat squatted on the floor and placed an ash-grey hand upon the mortal's forehead, the other over the mortal's heart. Mhat bent and pressed his mouth to the human's slack one, then slowly pushed his long, black tongue in.

The human started awake. "Stop!" He thrashed about, groaning. "What are you doing? Stop!" He tried to wriggle away.

"Talk and he'll stop," said Shukra, sounding as amused as Raka felt. Mhat raised his head to allow the human to speak.

"I don't...know anything. Please...just let me...go. I'm not...I swear I'm...not one of them. I'm only human."

Only human. Raka snorted. The *asura* race's survival hinged only on the humans now. Barrenness and infertility afflicted demon blood, and not a single hatchling had been birthed in two centuries. They needed human females to birth their young. They needed human blood to heal their forms. Most of all, a demon could feast on human souls and live forever.

"Continue, Mhat. And don't stop," ordered Shukra.

Raka climbed on a boulder. He didn't want to miss a single moment of the possession.

Pushing an extra soul into living flesh wasn't difficult. But it was temporary and unreliable. Once the mortal was possessed, they would need to move fast. They had to find the *raakh* before Mhat's soul got ejected.

The human moaned in earnest now. He flailed about like a fish out of water. His moans turned to sobs and the sobs to screams as his body and then his mind were possessed. Suddenly, Mhat rolled over in a lifeless heap. Next to him a pair of human eyes snapped open. The human stared up at Shukra, blood seeping into the sclera, changing the whites in his eyes to red.

"*Agrata,*" he growled as he got on his bloody knees and bowed. "I'm in."

As am I, thought Raka. He'd told Shukra about Yahvi. He was in.

Lavya wasn't at his usual post at the desk, performing electronic sentry duty with Baby's help. Neither was Ash pacing the chamber with a medical volume in his hands. Figured that the only time Karna needed his friends, neither would be available.

He'd left *her* at the lagoon, alone and cackling like the devious witch she was.

A filthy expletive erupted from Karna's soul and spewed out of his mouth. He stalked to the wooden console lining one wall of Ash's den. The glass-topped buffet was laden with silver trays heavy with heavenly and earthly spirits. He picked up the jug of *soma* juice, poured a dollop into a silver goblet. His larynx felt raw after the severe workout he'd put it through, so he added four fingers worth of Bagpiper to it and drained the concoction in three gulps. Grimacing, he waited for the inferno blazing through his gullet to bank, then repeated the procedure. If he couldn't bite Lavya's head off then he was going to get insensible with Ash's favorite whiskey.

*Is your pride worth more than our souls?*

"Fug doom it all to hell!" he thundered and flung the goblet across the room. It nicked the ivy-vined wallpaper and fell with a *ting* on the floor.

He inhaled, held his breath, exhaled slowly. Inhaled, held, exhaled. She'd asked that ugly question, leaving him thunderstruck, and then she'd dropped to her knees in front of him and laughed. And cried.

*Inhale. Hold. Exhale.*

The door creaked open and Lavya strode in, phone in hand. "I have come to the conclusion that instant messaging is not the modern day equivalent of telepathy, however much the gods of technology might want it to be." He stopped short, did a double take at the goblet he'd nearly tripped over and whipped his head up to scrutinize Karna. "She told you," he said, nodding in deep satisfaction.

Karna's hackles rose. Had she beguiled Lavya too? "She told you and you didn't tell me?" He wanted to restructure something and Lavya's extra-smooth, pale mug would do nicely.

Lavya raised two fingers in the global peace sign. "No, I guessed an hour ago. Lotus-petal eyes. They all have them—the Six and her." He tipped his head up at the ceiling, mumbled something incoherent and looked at Karna again. "Ridiculous how we missed that for this long, but we do have a lot going on. I've been texting and calling you for the last hour and now I know why you haven't checked your messages."

"Phone's dead. It melted along with my clothes this afternoon." Karna picked up the bottle of Bagpiper and took a swig straight from it. He wondered if smashing the bottle to the ground would make him feel better. He wondered if a frozen heart could smash into a million pieces of jagged ice.

*"Ask my five husbands."* What in hell did that mean? That she was still married? Of course she was. She had freaking children with them. But she had a daughter with him too. *Fug!*

"Right," said Lavya, brusquely. "I'll set you up with a new one as soon as we take care of this."

"I don't need your help dealing with her," Karna growled.

"I didn't mean Draupadi. There are several other situations that need your attention right now."

Karna took another gulp of the whiskey and put the bottle down. Things were looking up already. *"Asuras* spotted?" he asked. A killing spree was just what the hole in his heart needed.

"Alas, no, not even one. Well, one spotted but...never mind, you'll see soon enough. Ved forgot his gun at the island. It's his police issue and he needs it immediately. He has to clock it in or out or something at the police station. I told him I'd find it and get it to him. And Lord Yama wanted an audience, pronto. So he's in there." Lavya jerked his head at the common wall separating Ash's office and private parlor. "Ash is keeping him company. I was on my way to Asht Dveep when I heard you in here."

"It has been busy around here." Mercifully, his mind began racing off in several different directions, and not one of those involved *her.*

"You have no idea," Lavya said with feeling. "How the hell do you deal with Yama? The God is nuts. You won't believe the kind of crap he texts and spouts."

Karna smiled thinly. "Maybe I should let you handle him from now on."

A blast of energy, suffused with perfume and smoke, brought *her* into the den, cutting off Lavya's pithy reply.

"How dare you disappear in the middle of our discussion?" she yelled.

Karna's smile turned into a snarl. Ignoring her, he strode across the honeycomb tiles, his boots marking his fury. She shoved him hard between his shoulder blades just as he reached the door.

He swung around, irate. "I am warning you, I don't hit women unless in battle, but with you I will make an exception."

"Do it." She got in his face. "Do it and be done with it. Yell at me. Hurt me, damn you. But ask them for help. It's the only way left." Her voice broke and her tear-stained face crumbled. "I beg of you, Karna. Don't let your pride destroy us."

Lavya's eyes bounced between Qalli and him in puzzlement. Then he slipped out the door and closed it, giving them privacy to sort things out. Karna exhaled sharply. There was nothing to sort out. He wasn't going to beg his half brothers for help. He didn't need help. He was the Soul Warrior. He knew better than anyone how to deal with *asuras*. He yanked the door open and cursed under his breath.

Five of the Six stood outside the den, hampering his escape. Iksa was absent. Karna shook his head at his *shishyas*, praying they would leave it alone. He didn't want to hear their apologies or explanations. He didn't want to think about the lies they'd told him too. Yahvi looked miserable.

Qalli's scent preceded her into the hallway. Fug! Not Qalli—Draupadi.

"Are you all right?" Ziva walked straight to her and hugged her.

"I think so, darling. I feel buoyant. Like I've lost several kilos of fat with my confessions."

Karna snorted. Yeah right. *Confessions.*

"Speaking the whole truth does make one feel weightless. Hence, the 'weight off one's chest' metaphor," said Satya.

Karna wished someone would take a knife and stab him in his chest. At least then the aches and pains he felt would be real.

"I am so proud of you, Moo-Moo. But..." Amara paused to gape at Qalli—*damn it*—Draupadi's garments. "What the heck are you wearing? Are you impersonating someone else now? If you are then tell me who because I just don't get it."

Draupadi cracked a smile, slanting her evil eyes at him. "Amara is the last soul in the Cosmos to care about fashion, so for her to comment on my attire reaffirms the outfit's hideousness. I should go change." She didn't move.

She was wrong. It wasn't her clothes that made him mad for her. He tore his eyes away from her face when Lavya cleared his throat.

"There's about two hours of daylight left. I should go. Everyone, I'm making a quick trip to Asht Dveep. If anyone wants anything from there, let me know now," Lavya said.

The offer triggered an avalanche of requests from the females. Amara had misplaced her pearl-hilt dagger and was sure she'd dropped it somewhere on the island. Ziva wanted her crystal chest to use on her patients. Lavya began to look harried at the outpouring of demands and ordered that one of them go with him to fetch all of the stuff back as he had no clue in hell what eyelash dye looked like. After a lively debate as to who'd go with him, it was decided that Amara, Lusha and Yahvi would have the pleasure as they had the most things to fetch.

"Where's Iksa?" Karna asked.

"She's resting," answered Satya, making Qalli—*fugdoomal*—Draupadi frown. "It's fine, Matri. She has a headache and is sleeping it off."

Lavya vanished with his entourage after Karna warned Lusha, Amara and Yahvi to be careful, and stick together, and not get into mischief.

Satya and Ziva stayed by their mother's side like guardian angels. They probably thought he was angry with her because of her deception. Little did they know it was her other demand that had pissed him off. Ask the sons of Kunti for help so they could lord it over him again? No chance in Hell.

"We need to talk," Qalli said.

He tried to tune her out. He had everything under control. Then the doors of Ash's parlor swung open and chaos spilled out.

# CHAPTER NINETEEN
## KATHA: TALL TALES AND INSANITY PLEAS

The parlor's double doors were crafted from thick oak and sinuously carved with illustrations of divine woodlands, complete with naked *apsaras*, *yakshas*, *naga* and a whole host of otherworldly creatures. As if he'd taken form straight from one of the panels, a rock star-type apparition strode out.

"*Bho!* Hallo!" he boomed at their group gathered in the hallway. "Thought I heard voices, though Ashwathama insists his parlor is soundproof."

Another apparition—a leather-clad half man, half bat, handcuffed and leg-shackled in chains of silver and iron—flew out behind the rock star with a musical jingle-jangle. Ash made up the rear end, fitting in well with the parade of masqueraders in his fluid robes and intimidating height. His dark eyes, when they met Karna's, expressed his thorough exasperation and reluctant amusement at being stuck with entertaining the God of Death.

In all that confusion, Karna still noticed Draupadi gasp in horror at the three newcomers. She wobbled on her feet and would've fallen had Satya not caught her in time. What the hell was the matter with her now? Was she shocked by Yama's getup? Baital? Or no. Karna smirked in grim satisfaction. She looked as if she'd come face-to-face with Dev-Il himself because of Ash. She hadn't known his full name.

She expected him to make nice with his slayer? Well, tit for tat, lady. Karna slashed a hand across his neck, warning her to kill the drama.

"My lord, if you'd be so kind and explain this diabolic development, please?" Karna quirked an eyebrow at Yama and waved a hand in Baital's general direction.

*Diabolic* was the word of the day. The term fit her perfectly. Diabolic. Devious. She'd had her husbands waiting in the wings all along to charge in and slay him again. She should brand the letter *D* over her heart.

"He's here on Kalika's behalf. He shall dwell with you until all the *raakh* is found, collected and returned to its owner," sang Yama, the rock star.

Even that announcement didn't shock Karna as much as the devious woman's ultimatum had. "You want the *pisacha* to roam free on the Human Realm? How insane, my lord."

"I'll tell you what's insane, my Lord Karna—me rigged up as the poster boy for BDSM." Baital's pained face hovered in front of Karna's. "Have you any idea how uncomfortable leather is?" He twisted away from the females to adjust his junk discreetly under the zipper. "I wouldn't wish such torture on an enemy. Believe me, I wouldn't have chosen to come today either. I'm missing the party of the year, my lord."

"Oh! You must see this." With a flourish, Yama extracted a minitablet out of thin air and held it aloft so everyone could have a look-see at the live video feed.

Hell was in carnival. Gone were the airport-like counters and conveyor belts and long, winding soul queues. In their place stood confection stands, a large dance floor and a five-soul band belting out *raagaas*. The disco lights remained intact and most souls were pulsing inside incarnated bodies, boogying on and off the dance floor.

"Is it any wonder that the Hell Realm is so crowded? Who wants to ditch a perpetual party-zone?" Karna commented.

Lord Yama took that as a compliment and grinned. "Ah! There's Doota. I thought up his costume. Wave, my children, wave!"

Doota, disguised as a baboon, slurped on a color-changing milkshake with gusto. A hooting, whistling train of merrymakers meandered through the Great Lobby behind him, throwing candy, stardust and live snakes into the air.

"I'm truly amazed at such gargantuan willpower and strict adherence to death duties that you've managed to pry yourself away from the party of the year," remarked Karna.

"Are you mocking me, Soul Warrior?" Hurt squashed the rock star's rouged-up face for a heartbeat, but on his next breath his mouth puffed into a delighted, incisor-sharp smile. He held his arms wide for Satya. "Granddaughter, I see you're flourishing on the realm. Ah! Draupadi, I haven't seen you in ages. You're visiting your children, I see." Yama jabbed Karna in the solar plexus with an elbow. "Told you Draupadi is a very hands-on mother."

Qal—Draupadi, her face still leeched of color, bowed and touched Yama's feet. "How are you, my lord? And how is Mother Yami? Give her my regards."

"I most certainly will. Why are you dressed like that? Wait, wait don't tell me. Let me guess. You're impersonating a deflated Hulk? A depressed factory worker? An undercover cop?"

Baital clapped his hands and chortled in midair. "It's going to be awesome, just awesome. I love family reunions."

Karna pressed his thumbs against his temple and groaned. Lavya was right. Wasn't he always? Dealing with Yama was like performing a three-ring circus act—while it was fun in the doing, the stunt always brought on massive amounts of pain in the end.

"My lord, what's going on? Why is Baital here?" Karna asked as his body temperature tried to compete with Venus's.

Baital snapped to attention three feet above ground and gave a crisp salute, chains and all. "Am on a mission to save the humans, sir lord."

"Well, I must get going," rumbled Yama instead of explaining that absurd statement. "Here's the key to the shackles. Don't remove them, and always keep the key on you. It binds the *pisacha* to you. Here, sign this." Yama drew out a touchscreen stylus and pulled up an I-have-a-demon-in-my-possession form on the screen. "Baital will explain the rest."

"I wish you'd explain it yourself," said Karna through clenched teeth. The fine print read if he lost the red soul, he'd be flogged for a year. Un-*freaking*-believable!

"Can't. Have important duties pending. Don't worry, children, all will work out with hardly anyone dead, or so my Death Due-Date calendar reveals. *Toodleedoo!*" Yama waved and vanished.

Karna closed his eyes and counted to twenty. He rolled his shoulders and rotated his head, took a deep breath and opened his eyes. Nope, Baital still hovered in front of his face. "I need a drink. Come with me, *pisacha*. And keep the explanations honest, short and clean, please."

He stalked into Ash's parlor ahead of the others. The females took their seats on a black velvet sofa. Ziva sat close to her ashed-faced mother, alternately rubbing her back and hands. Karna nearly rolled his eyes at the drama. Satya too sat by her mother but kept her focus on Baital. Fascinated by evil, was she? He'd have a talk with her about that and about keeping diabolical secrets, but later. Ash parked himself by the doors, back against the wall.

"Begin, Baital," said Karna once he'd knocked back another drink.

The *pisacha* levitated in lotus position above the coffee table in the middle of the chamber. "It's the prophecy, my lord: He, O Kalika, who in the graveyard, naked and with disheveled hair...yada yada yada. Vala fulfilled the prophecy. His skull chanted Goddess Kalika's mantra for ages without stopping, or so it's whispered in the Demon Realm. Eventually his prayers reached her ears. So Goddess Kalika had to appear before him and grant him a boon."

"Explain this boon to me." He was going to force the Council to reconsider the business of giving boons.

"It grants Vala the status of Lord of Earth, my lord Karna. Goddess Kalika's ashes hold some badass mojo, and she had to gift them to her best devotee for his soulful—skullful?—prayers. So now the Stone Demon, is on his way back to the Human Realm, and once he consumes Kalika's bone dust will gain the strength of a million demons in one gulp."

If an avalanche of boulders had rolled down the Sagarmatha Peak and hit him face first, Karna wouldn't have felt so staggered. The *raakh* had the potency of one million *asuras*? No wonder Vala wanted to eat them.

Karna's mind began whirring with possibilities and improbabilities. Vala would need a body to consume the ashes. Well, Karna would destroy him before his skull found one. Besides, he had one fourth of the ashes. That was one fourth less invincibility.

"That's it? That's the prophecy?" he asked.

Baital nodded his oddly aristocratic blue head. *Pisachas* were as well known for their beauty as their sadistic cruelty. And Karna had just been ordered to nest this viper.

"You better not be lying by omission, Baital. Liars bore me." Karna briefly glanced at the beautiful liar sitting on the sofa. She looked as stricken as he felt.

"This is hardly my fault," said Baital indignantly, ditching his lotus pose. "I'm here to clean up the mess Goddess Kalika and you two created." Baital's black-rimmed red irises zipped between Draupadi and him a few times.

Karna's gut hollowed. He was talking about creating Yahvi, the human harbinger. "I created the mess. And I will clean it up."

"Every action has an equal and opposite reaction," Baital droned in a non sequitur.

"Stop talking in riddles, *pisacha*. I'm in no mood for entertainment."

"How about scientific dogma, my lord?"

"Baital," Karna growled, feeling the urge to strangle someone again.

"You're no fun at all, my lord. You had your chance with Vala. I have no idea why you couldn't, wouldn't or didn't vanquish him, but when you let him go, you spared his fate. And now he's back with the boon of invincibility tucked into his skull."

"Fine. I let him go. I had no choice then. I won't this time."

Baital looked skeptical. "The minute he consumes the *raakh*, he's indestructible. Even more so than before when he was merely made of stone."

"I have part of the *raakh*, the ashes of her head." That had to account for something.

"And that's super-fortunate, but it isn't enough." Baital waited several beats before adding, "There's another way to vanquish the demon. It has to do with your daughter, my lord Karna. I'm surprised the child hasn't told you about her agreement with Goddess Kalika."

Yahvi retrieved the old-fashioned journal that was stuffed inside her rolled bedding in the attic room and straightened. They'd left Asht Dveep in such a hurry last time that she hadn't thought to retrieve it. Then again, she hadn't written in it in a while. She'd realized it was missing when she'd looked to write in it after the Draas fiasco. She made it a point to write down important events, feelings, and moments she wished to remember.

She skipped down the stairs to the hallway bathroom on the first floor. She used it, awkwardly aware of how small and dingy it felt compared to her new bathroom (that she didn't have to share even) in her grand chambers in Har-ki-doon. She hoped Iksa's vision came true and they all lived happily ever after there. Although, Yahvi was convinced Iksa had made that vision up. She did that sometimes, to cheer people up.

Yahvi critiqued her reflection in the vanity mirror while she washed her hands, and ran her towel-dried fingers through her unruly hair in lieu of a comb or brush within reach. It needed a cut. She'd have to get Ziva or Mama to style it before her birthday. A nervous giggle escaped her lips. Well, no reason to die ugly, was there?

She picked up her journal and walked out of the bathroom. The doorbell rang as she made her way down the stairs. Amara yelled that she'd get the door. Amara, Lusha and she had been putting a suitcase together in the kitchen with the things they had to take back. Lavya was taking one last look outside for Ved's gun.

The lights suddenly flickered out and immediately came on. Yahvi blinked, startled out of her thoughts.

"You're early, dumbwit. We still haven't found your clutch-piece. Are you sure you lost it here?" Amara's voice drifted up the stairs. A very un-Amara-like quiet followed. Had Ved taken objection to *dumbwit* and stomped off in affront? Not many souls appreciated Amara's wit.

The lights flickered again as Yahvi jumped down the last three steps to the foyer. But she hardly noticed, as her jaw dropped open, taking in the sight of Amara and Ved in a lip-lock at the door.

Yahvi giggled as shock gave way to amusement. "So, you guys are the reason for the flickering lights, hmm?"

Amara was really doing it. She'd promised Yahvi a Tokarev TT-30 pistol for her birthday and Ved, they'd decided, would know exactly where to buy such a gun and possibly get it for them. Amara was obviously trying hard to persuade him to procure one.

Then Ved's awful condition registered on Yahvi. His jeans were ripped in odd places and were filthy. Were those bloodstains? He had no shirt on, which was odd. Odder yet were the bruises on his muscular, hairy back. Oddest of all, he wore thick, boxy sunglasses that Yahvi understood blind people wore. He slanted his face toward her, still smooching Amara.

One glimpse at his face and the last trace of Yahvi's amusement evaporated. He was a mass of bumps and bruises even the dirty grey salve smeared on him couldn't hide.

"Are you okay? Were you in a fight, Ved?" Yahvi rushed to the door, surprised that Ved kept kissing Amara even as she reached them. She yelped when Amara simply slid to the floor at her feet, eyes wide open and utterly blank.

The shock hadn't even settled, much less worn off, when Ved grabbed her neck tightly and shoved her through the door, outside. The porch light flickered.

"Have you lost your mind?" Yahvi struggled to break free of his painful grip, wondering what the hell was going on with the lights?

Ved didn't answer. He merely reached up and removed the sunglasses. Ghastly red eyes glowed out of his swollen, ash-smeared face.

Yahvi's heart banged against her ribcage. She scrambled to get back inside the abode, but a great, hulking presence blocked her way. The dark, hairless monster stopped her struggle and her screams by wrapping his thick arms around her and clamping a paw over her mouth. The appendage smelled as nasty as an unflushed toilet, and she gagged. The demon's mother sure hadn't taught him hygiene, she thought hysterically. Then an ice-cold chill froze her bowels as her predicament registered in her mind.

"That's right. Be scared, human. I want to smell your fear. Taste it," the *raaksasa* purred into her ear. He sniffed at her neck and slowly licked a path from ear to collarbone as if she were a lollipop.

She strained against her captor, her eyes darting toward Amara, who lay stiff as a corpse in the foyer. Was she breathing? Yahvi couldn't tell. Where was Lavya? She tried to scream when Lusha ran into the foyer. Yahvi willed her sister to vanish. *Save yourself. Get help. Get my father.*

"Come outside. Or we kill her," Ved demanded. No, this wasn't Ved. His voice had changed. It sounded odd—guttural and clipped. And his accent was odd, formal, with the lilt of Old Sanskrit. "Don't try to be clever. Do as I say. Now."

*Don't, Lusha,* Yahvi screamed silently. *Don't leave the protection of the abode.*

A *danu* demon stepped on to the porch. He wore sunglasses too, and his naked body was partially hidden by his stinky, filthy dread-locks. The rest was covered in colorful scars coated in *raakh*. He raised a serpent-shaped knife the size of her forearm, used by Naga mages, and held it against her breast, right over her heart. Though the *danu* looked like a human and was more her size, he was revolting and scary.

Stupidly, Lusha strode through the door, and instantly, dozens of *asuras* burst out of their holes in the mangroves and surrounded her. Chunks of sand and roots and leaves rained down on her as more and more *asuras* jumped out of the ground. Yahvi lost eye contact with Lusha. She couldn't see past the wall of *asuras*, wearing jeans and thick iron breastplates, each one drenched in demon-sized armaments. They disappeared into the mangroves, dragging Lusha with them. Her captor shifted, turning Yahvi to face the abode.

"Hold out her arm, Raka," said Ved.

"As you wish, *agrata* Mhat." Raka, her *raaksasa* captor, pressed his paw over her mouth harder. She'd bite him, she vowed, as soon as she got a chance—hygeinic or not. *Agrata* Mhat—leader Mhat, she thought with a start. Raka had addressed Ved as if he were leader Mhat.

Ved had been possessed by a demon called Mhat. No wonder he hadn't dared enter the abode. He'd been standing just over the threshold while kissing Amara. Cosmic custard! Amara. Yahvi tried to turn her head to see her sister.

"You know what to do, Dund." Mhat/Ved nodded at the *danu* and gave him room to step up to the doorway. The *danu* gripped Yahvi's forearm tightly and thrust her whole arm over the threshold, raising the long, serpent-shaped knife aloft. The forked tip gleamed against the ceiling lights. She struggled to yank her arm free. But they were so much stronger than her.

"She's resisting." The *danu* with the knife smiled savagely. He flicked her hair off her face with the forked tip and brought his ugly, scarred face close to hers. He inhaled her scent and shivered. "It's been too long since I've taken one. She seems untouched. Auspicious."

Yahvi fantasized about head-butting the *danu* demon. She'd follow that with a spinning roundhouse kick at the *raaksasa* holding her and knee him in the groin. Then they'd see who remained auspiciously untouched, Yahvi snarled against the *raaksasa's* paw.

It was possible the *danu* mage had the power to read minds. She hoped it was so. She wanted to piss him off. If she died tonight, she would do so spectacularly. *Spinning satellites!* But she couldn't die tonight. Everything hinged on her not dying before Vala fulfilled the prophecy. They could both die after—only after.

The *danu* demon's eyes glowed like red fireballs as he began to chant, his voice pitch-perfect and hauntingly beautiful. In the middle of the second verse, he tightened his grip on her hand and slashed the blade across her palm. Tears sprang up and ran down her face as she tried to fight the pain. He squeezed her hand until blood dripped from the cut freely. It burned so badly that she bit her cheek, drawing blood there too. The floor rushed up to her face and her vision blurred. The demon song sounded like buzzing. Was she going to faint? She couldn't faint. Amara would never let her live it down. Yahvi took a deep breath and focused on her sister. She was alive. She had to be. So did Lusha.

The tone of the chants changed. Became more intense. At a signal from the *danu*, the *raaksasa*, Raka, lifted her high. Mhat/Ved took her bloody hand and slapped it against the lintel. A sonic boom blasted through the abode. An alarm began to screech. The demons staggered. The ones on the boardwalk fell to the ground screaming. But her captor held fast.

Yahvi grappled to understand what was happening. They were trying to nullify Asht Dveep's protection charms? They repeated the procedure twice before the abode was rendered defenseless. It was the blood, she realized. Her blood. Her father's blood ran through her veins.

Yahvi bobbled in Raka's arms as they lumbered inside. They were the first to breach the abode. *Where was Lavya?*

"What are you doing?" Mhat/Ved kicked an *asura* who'd fallen to his knees near Amara. He had Amara's wrist raised to his mouth.

"Eating, *agrata*," the demon said with a lascivious moan.

Mhat/Ved kicked him again. "Get up! We're not here to slake your hunger."

The thick-skinned, thick-skulled *raaksasa* clearly wasn't pleased.

"Get up and take your post right now! We are under a time constraint."

Enraged, Mhat/Ved led the procession through the abode. He knew exactly where to go, which meant at least part of Ved's brain was still Ved? Yahvi was frog-marched up one floor, then across the gym and to the armory. *You are a warrior. You are fearless. You are not meant to die today.* Any hope of rescue rested on her shoulders. She had to stop crying. Stop whimpering. Stop getting pushed around. But what could she do? What was she to do? She felt as useless as two thumbs on one hand.

The chanting began again, and the weapons room crashed open in no time. Yahvi gawped at the empty shelves. Had her father had anticipated this breach? Just not in daylight. Or had Lavya emptied the armory? Either way, she had to break free now.

She kicked the *raaksasa* holding her with the back of her boot. He didn't even flinch, simply tightened the arm wrapped around her midriff and squeezed. She couldn't breathe.

Mhat/Ved performed the blood-smearing procedure on the vault safe. He cut her hand deeper to draw more blood. The sting was unbearable this time. He squeezed her palm as Lusha would a lemon and dribbled blood over the safe's handle. Raw pain spiked up her arm but she didn't scream. She puffed out breaths in short bursts. *Steady,* she commanded herself. *Steady now. The pain will fade.*

With a shout of triumph, Mhat/Ved pried the safe open, and the moment he did, another sonic boom fractured the noisome atmosphere, triggering a secondary blast inside the vault. He let out a hair-raising screech as energy brighter than the sun shot out of the safe and flooded the space. The explosion of light knocked him back ten feet into the iron wall. Mhat/Ved slid to the iron floor and didn't rise again.

All around her, *asuras* howled and stumbled, trying to flee the armory, the gym, even the abode. Some had shut their eyes, while others hid their faces completely. *Asuras* became blind in sunlight.

Yahvi kicked and thrashed, and suddenly the demon holding her relaxed his grip. She whirled away from him, assessing her options. Jump out the windows in the gym. She had to get to Amara. Lusha. Lavya. But the door between the armory and gym was jammed with *asuras*.

Another blast took off half the wall of the armory along with a dozen demons. Her heart rocketed into her throat. Then suddenly, Lavya was there, running through the fiery hole. With a hoarse cry, he pulled her into his arms and hugged her so tightly the wound on her palm throbbed. But she didn't care. She hugged him back just as fiercely.

"No," she said, shaking her head frantically when she felt his body tense up, getting ready to vanish with her. "Not without my sisters."

"I'll come back for them."

"There's no time. Amara's unconscious by the door and Lusha has been dragged into the mangroves. We need weapons." She fell to the ground and groped for the serpent-knife. It had to be there. She'd seen it drop right here.

Lavya cursed above her head. Raka and Dund stood against the blaze of light with the thick, boxy sunglasses protecting their eyes. Swallowing curses of her own, Yahvi frantically looked about for the knife.

"What we seek was not in the vault," said Dund to no one in particular. "Where is the *raakh*?"

"Maybe it got blown up," Lavya replied.

"Seize her," Dund said. "We're not finished with her."

Raka grabbed for her arm. Yahvi scrambled backward just as her fingers closed over the blade of the serpent-knife. *Careful. Don't cut yourself.*

"Fuck you." Lavya stepped between her and the demons, aiming the fire blaster he'd used to blow out the armory wall at them.

Yahvi pushed to her feet, gripping the hilt of the knife behind her back.

"*Tcha, tcha, tcha.* Such language from a *noble* soul. What *has* the human world come to? Don't forget your place, lowly Nishada. Only the highborn get to be heroes." Dund raised his hand toward the fire blaster in defence. "You can't win against my powers."

Lavya had grown steelier and steelier. "We'll see about that."

Yahvi had had enough. She refused to be a puppet dangling between the strings of good and evil. "I'll come with you of my own free will if you swear to let everyone else go."

Lavya's cursed most foully—at her now.

Dund looked at her in gravely. "You show good judgment, human, unlike the Nishada. We will, of course, barter you and your sisters when the Soul Warrior brings us the *raakh*. We don't wish to harm you."

Raka reached for her, thinking it was settled. It was far from settled as far as she was concerned. Clumsily, Yahvi slashed him across his arm with the serpent-knife. But Raka was huge, his *raaksasa* hide was tough and the knife hadn't been in her dominant hand. She managed only to anger Raka with the scratch. He yanked her left arm and twisted it hard, snapping it. The knife dropped as it snapped. Red-hot pain radiated out from her bones, robbing her of breath. She couldn't even scream. She wouldn't faint. She pressed her lips together and hissed out air.

Bellowing in rage, Lavya launched himself at the demons. The three rolled and crashed and spun in a symphony of punches, kicks and bites. Dund hadn't been kidding about his supernatural talents. He landed on Lavya's chest, choking him. The knife and blaster lay close, but neither Lavya nor the demon seemed to need them.

Yahvi's orange-ish world went topsy-turvy as Raka flung her over his shoulder and ran out of the room. She clutched her broken arm to her chest, absorbing the shards of pain shooting through her body. She was terrified. She didn't want to die like this. Without purpose. Without saying goodbye.

Twice Raka slowed and tried to vanish, she thought in surprise. But he couldn't. Was it the light? Was it a charm? They ran past Amara, no longer prostrate in the foyer. Yahvi stopped struggling to stare at her sister, who was gesturing crazily with her eyes. Amu wanted her to flick…? Oh!

Yahvi wrapped her legs around Raka's chest for leverage and heaved up, knocking his sunglasses off his face with a slap. Raka howled as the still bright light hurt his eyes. He slammed into the doorjamb and dropped her. Yahvi hit the ground and rolled out of the way.

By then, Amara was up in a fighting stance, her Joysticks in her hands. She rushed at Raka, slashing a blade across his face, ripping off half of it. He roared like a speared boar, but in spite of it charged Amara, face bathed in blood. Amara jumped up high to bring the sword down on his head. She miscalculated. He feinted one way, pivoted at the last second and, with a boulder-sized backhand, knocked Amara to the ground. Her blades skittered across the floor. He kicked her hard in the stomach before she could even think of getting up. He kicked her again and again and again, roaring with every strike.

Yahvi leaped onto the *raaksasa*'s back, bit into the fleshy part of his frond-like ear and ripped a chunk of it off. Screaming, he flung her away. She lay on the floor gasping. Through a haze of pain and fear, she saw Amara trying to reach a Joystick. It lay far away in a corner. Far away from Amu, but if Yahvi crawled a few feet she'd reach it.

Gathering every ounce of strength left in her, Yahvi crawled, her body screaming at the abuse she was putting it through. She picked up the blade, hand shaking like crazy. If she hit the mark, the shock of impact would hurt like a lance through her arm. If she missed…

Missing was not an option. Raka stood over them, snarling, bleeding, his eyes narrowed to slits. The incantation welled up from her soul, one of two she'd memorized that afternoon:

*"May potent Agni who destroys the* asuras *bless and shelter me from greedy fiends who rise in troops at nighttime when the moon is dark.*

*Varuna's benison hath blessed the lead and Agni strengthens it; Indra hath given me the lead; this verily repels the fiends.*

*This overcomes Vishkandha; this drives the voracious fiends away; by means of this will I overthrow the* asura *brood.*

*If thou destroy a cow of ours, a human being or a steed, I pierce thee with this piece of lead so that thou mayst not slay our men again."*

Yahvi lunged upright into a warrior's stance and plunged the knife to its hilt in Raka's thigh, severing, she hoped, several important blood vessels. The *raaksasa* staggered back, almost out of the door, but did not fall. With a howl that must've surely shattered the windows of the abode, he vanished from sight.

Her burst of adrenaline depleted, Yahvi collapsed next to Amu and watched the rest of the ragtag bunch of *asuras* race off into the night as if their tails were on fire. The *danu* demon, Dund, included. She caught sight of a blood-soaked Lavya leaping down the stairs. And from the corner of her eye, she saw Lusha stomping out of the mangroves, breathing like an over-worked racehorse.

Only then, Yahvi gave herself permission to faint.

# CHAPTER TWENTY

## GATI: LIFE GOES ON

Should one embrace fate or fight it?

Should one forgive a foe or annihilate him? Embrace or fight, forgive or annihilate, what did it matter? The truth was one couldn't escape one's fate or one's foe or the past.

Draupadi wanted to flee. As soon as Lord Yama had addressed Ash as Ashwathama, she'd wanted to run away with her daughters…after spitting on the fiend's face. But Satya and Ziva had sandwiched her between them on the sofa, effectively blocking any escape.

The chamber reeked of sandalwood like the fiend. Her daughters had obviously known who he was as none of them had appeared horrified by his full name. It was outrageous that they seemed perfectly okay associating with the fiend who'd hacked them to pieces in another life.

But she wasn't okay with it. She'd danced with him last night. She'd allowed him to give her a neck rub. She refused to acknowledge him now. If his fiendish eyes smiled at her or offered her a beverage like he'd done a few minutes ago, she would scratch his eyes out.

She couldn't deal with this right now. She didn't want to deal with it ever. She fixed her eyes on Karna. Him, she could deal with. Even the fact that he was furious with her for mentioning her husbands didn't faze her. Flat, cold eyes, lips thinned in anger, the tick in his jaw, the veins in his temple throbbing in time with her pulse, not a thing about his demeanor bothered her. Besides, she was right. He needed all the help he could get if he was going to defy the Gods.

"Leave my daughter out of it, Baital," Karna said.

"That's not possible, my lord," the *pisacha* answered, looking regretful.

"Relax, Matri," Satya whispered when Draupadi tensed. "Everything will be fine."

Draupadi closed her eyes and wondered how things would ever be fine again. Fine would be when her daughters stopped this madness and came back to Alaka, away from *asuras*, away from fate and men and Gods.

"Your daughter was born at the very moment Goddess Kalika granted Vala his boon, my lord, creating a fortunate bond between the two events and the two souls."

Karna's accusing stare didn't faze Draupadi either. He couldn't possibly make her feel any worse than she already did. Fine, he wanted to blame her for Yahvi's fate? So be it.

"Their destinies were linked eighteen years ago, my lord. That makes your daughter the key to Vala's destruction."

"The Gods made it sound as if Yahvi was three hundred years old, like her sisters." Karna whipped his head around to glare at her. "She's only eighteen? She was created in Devlok?"

Draupadi nodded, unable to speak at all. The secret identities they'd used since Yahvi's birth had them all listed at three hundred years old.

"Only I am three hundred years old, Uncle Karna. Yahvi will turn eighteen the day after tomorrow, on the first of November," Satya clarified further.

Draupadi waited for him to make the connection. Yahvi's birthday was Karna's death day. Whose death would this year bring—Karna's or Yahvi's? All of theirs? She was numb. Numb from shock, from terror, from helplessness.

"I see," he said gruffly. Yes, he'd made the connection.

"An ancient prophecy came into play at the moment of the child's birth, my lord."

"Came into play or was made to come into play?"

"I wouldn't know the Goddess's game, my lord. I'm a pawn, just as you are. And I did try to warn you. Thrice did I give you the opportunity to avail yourself of my stories and thrice you refused me."

"What in hell are you talking about?" said Karna, narrowing his eyes on the *pisacha*.

"In Hell is exactly what I'm talking about. I asked you thrice if you wished to hear the story of Lord Tvastar and you snubbed me every time."

"If you wanted to say something to me then you should've just said it, *pisacha*," Karna exploded. "You don't wrap up information in riddles and jests and expect to be taken seriously."

Baital drew himself upright, arms crossed at chest level. "Opportunities are everywhere, my lord. Is it my fault you failed to recognize and seize yours thrice?"

"Okay, relax, everyone," said the fiend. "Stick to your tale, *pisacha*."

Baital sniffed haughtily. "The prophecy is as such: *On Tuesday at midnight, when Heaven and Earth conjoin and Desire mounts an Elephant while Love spills as freely as the fragrance of a Pushkara, shall a Slayer of Souls be born.*" Baital hovered from Karna to her. "You see, Lord Karna is Earth and the elephant and desire. You, my Lady Draupadi, are Earth and love, and I believe your symbol is the divine blue lotus, the *pushkara*."

"Lady who?" Behind her, the fiend let out a horror-struck shout.

"Ash, Qalli's Draupadi," Karna said tersely and turned back to Baital. "Slayer of souls? Yahvi is the slayer of souls?"

Draupadi was shocked to hear Baital recite the Tvastar prophecy. So much so, that she forgot to take exception to the fiend or the way Karna had introduced them. She'd heard the Tvastar prophecy a long, long time ago, as a maiden in her father's abode. The day after her fire-birth, her father, King Drupad, had invited the Seven Seers of Aryavarta to chart her twin brother, Dhri, and her destinies. Baital had left out the final sentence, which mentioned the sun and the fire. She couldn't recall what the exact line had been.

Before they could delve further into the new prophecy, Eklavya brought her daughters back from Asht Dveep, and things went from wrong to awful in a heartbeat.

The main healing room in Har-ki-doon's hospice wing was a large, airy space, with half-a-dozen beds and two thick-walled stone baths built into the floor. The floors and walls were inlaid with parallel lines of inch-thick calcite crystals that enhanced, amongst other things, the powers of other healing stones. Two heavy-duty steel carts were parked in the center and loaded with surgical instruments, medicinal compounds and an assortment of curative substances of the edible and nonedible varieties.

The Siamese Twins lay on two beds, battered and broken. Ved was hurt too, and was being attended to by Ash's acolytes—under guard in another room. He would be treated as a hostile until he told them what the hell had happened. He'd been possessed, that much they knew. They also knew why. How and where the *asuras* had taken him, only Ved could answer when he woke—if he woke as himself.

Lavya and Lusha had given them brief, bare facts of what had transpired. Lavya had been ambushed while making a final inspection of Asht Dveep for any lingering damage from the previous attack, and drugged when a *danu* demon had failed to possess or enslave him. By the time he'd woken up, it had been too late.

Lusha, luckily, had nothing more than a couple of scratches and minor bruises on her arms from her skirmish, and Satya had patched her up with salve and bandages. She'd been more than a match for the thirty-odd *asuras* with no magic and normal battle skills who'd taken her captive. Lavya needed to be looked at—he'd been choked, stabbed and bitten twice—but he refused any fuss until the females were taken care of.

The most troubling detail of all was that Baby hadn't picked up any red souls. She'd not sounded the alarm. Not at Asht Dveep, nor at Har-ki-doon.

Karna needed to learn the details of the attack and Lavya needed to figure out Baby's issue soon. Then there was the whole new Tvastar prophecy. Karna didn't know what was going on. Was Yahvi the harbinger of doom or was she the slayer of souls? Should they believe in Vishnu's vision or the Tvastar prophecy?

He refrained from demanding answers for the moment. Plus, there was no need to encourage full-blown hysteria in Draupadi by discussing Yahvi's fate in front of her—Satya's judgment, not his. From his point of view, Draupadi didn't appear the least bit hysterical—shell-shocked, maybe, but not hysterical.

After a brief consultation, Ash and Ziva split up to take one patient each. Yahvi's left arm was fractured in two places and needed to be set, and her right palm needed suturing. Most of Amara's wounds were internal. Ash rolled a surgical cart closer to Yahvi's bed and made preparation for...what? Surgery?

"She needs surgery?" Karna wouldn't give in to the dread hammering at his nerves. He needed to keep his wits strong.

"No. Her ulna needs to be set." Ash carefully picked up Yahvi's right hand and turned it over. Her palm was caked with dried blood. She moaned softly, rolling her head from side to side, and quieted when she lost consciousness again.

"Don't touch her."

Karna whipped around and glowered at Draupadi. She was staring at Ash with unmitigated revulsion.

"Don't touch her," she said again, her expression violent, mad.

Ash froze. He gently set Yahvi's hand down on the bed and stepped back.

"Are you nuts, woman?" Karna shouted.

"Matri, what are you doing?" Satya touched her mother's back.

"I won't have him touch her. I won't have him touch any of you. I won't stand for that. I'm taking them back to Devlok. Dhanvantari will take care of them."

Iksa sank to the floor at her mother's feet and buried her face in her hands, weeping.

"Ma, look at me," said Ziva without taking her hands off Amara's abdomen. Her hands glowed like the crystals she'd arranged around Amara's body. "Ash is as good a physician as the Celestial Healer, trust me. And we mustn't move them again. They need to be treated immediately, Ma. They are both very badly hurt."

Ash went to his knees before Draupadi, shocking them all. "I have wronged you, my lady. I have wronged you greatly. But please, let me help your daughter. Then I'll do whatever you wish."

Karna looked away from the raw shame that glittered in Ash's eyes. Two fat tears rolled down Draupadi's cheeks and on a heart-wrenching sob, she turned and ran out of the room. Fugdoomal, Karna cursed. *Fugdoomal.* If only the Triad had told him—warned him of even some of these things, so much could've been avoided. Why hadn't they told him? What game were they playing?

"Do your thing, Ash. She'll get over it," Ziva said briskly.

Satya had begun to follow her mother out of the chamber, but suddenly she stopped and looked at him. "Uncle K, please go talk to her. You're the only one she'll listen to right now."

And say freaking what? Karna shook his head.

"Go to her. Sort it out, once and for all," said Lavya in an awful tone. He hadn't taken his eyes off Yahvi for a second.

He thought he had sorted it out. Maybe this was as smooth as it could get between him and Draupadi. Karna heaved a sigh and tried for smoother.

He found her on the terrace of her own chambers, in the same clothes he'd dressed her in. She wept noiselessly, as if bawling would be an acknowledgement of weakness. He raked his fingers through his hair and walked up to stand beside her by the stone balustrade. She stiffened at once.

"He's paying for it," he said.

"It's not enough. He should burn in Hell," she said harshly.

"By karma, Qalli...*fugdoomal*...Draupadi. What the hell do you think his existence is? A pleasure-fest? He's covered from scalp to soles in lesions and sores. His entire body, inside and out, is a mass of intense physical pain—continuous, bone-shriveling pain. And all that is beside the raging guilt that constantly consumes his soul."

"It's not enough." She hugged herself, rocking back and forth. "For a mother, it is not enough."

"Revenge will only hurt you, you know," he said, trying to reason with her.

"You bloody hypocrite." She whirled about to face him, her voice and expression incendiary. "You live for revenge. Your whole existence is based on getting even. I lied to you about who I was, so you lied to me about knowing who I was. That is my great crime in your eyes, isn't it? That I had the temerity to make a fool out of you? And you have the bloody cheek to sneer at my anger when your friend did so much worse to me and mine. Are only men allowed to hold grudges? Are only men allowed to feel insulted and outraged and seek vengeance for slights endured?"

She slapped both her hands on the balustrade, shocking him with the vehemence in both her actions and words. "You men are all alike. Every decision is just and righteous and noble when it is personal. And the same action is declared unjust and unrighteous and ignoble for the enemy. I want to know, why such bias?"

Karna opened his mouth to respond, but what could he say?

"Besides bruising your silly pride a couple of times, what have I done that's so heinous? Let's for a minute consider that I rejected you at my *swayamvara*—which I didn't, not to my recollection—and married your brothers. So what? Shouldn't I have had any say in which man I was to marry? It was my *swayamvara* and I was entitled to my choice of husband." She took a deep shuddering breath and glared at him with her diamond-black eyes. "For that one rejection, you have rejected me over and over."

"Over and over?" When he continued to look blank, she enlightened him.

"One: during our affair at my *swayamvara*."

"I told you why I had to end it," he interrupted her. "Vishnu's vision."

"Now I know that." Her eyes flashed when she looked at him. "I've lived my entire mortal life and half my Celestial one thinking you took your revenge and walked away. I hated you for that, Karna. I hated you even as I loved you."

A warm rush of emotions flowed over his heart. Draupadi moved his soul. She was his soul. But he couldn't tell her that. It wouldn't be fair.

"Next you rejected me when Mother Kunti offered you the throne of Hastinapura."

Karna started at the mention of his birth mother. He had to dig deep for the memory, but once he brought it to mind, he recalled it in brutal clarity.

At first he'd thought she was joking about the throne, but eventually he'd believed Lady Kunti. She'd left him no choice but to believe her.

Her revelations that day had crushed even the illusion that maybe, just maybe, his birth mother hadn't abandoned him, that he'd been snatched away from loving parents by force or cunning.

A naïve, foolish curiosity had led the young princess Kunti to recite the mantra Sage Durvasa had taught her, a mantra she was meant to use only after marriage. The incantation had summoned an aroused Sun God to her bedchamber. He'd impregnated her in spite of her protests and she'd been forced to give birth to his son. She'd had to abandon the child to his fate. She had to preserve her family's good name, you see.

After that heartwarming tale, Lady Kunti had offered Karna the Crown of the Kurus as if it had been hers to give away. As if it would miraculously wash away all ill feeling. *"As my eldest son, it is your right,"* she'd said to him.

He'd refused it, of course. Not one to admit defeat easily, Lady Kunti had pointed out just what he was refusing. *"The kingdom comes with a queen."* In truth, he'd been most mightily tempted then. The only reason worth losing his honor over, he'd thought. But honor and friendship and Vishnu's fear had won. Bearing in mind he'd have to share the queen with five other princes had also helped his decision.

"What the hell do you mean, you didn't reject me at your *swayamvara?*" asked Karna, coming back to her outlandish claim. "You said you'd never marry a lowborn chariot driver's son."

"My brother said that, not I." Tears fell from her eyes unabated. "I didn't know who you were, you moron. I only asked your name because I didn't know it. I didn't know who any of the contestants were. I was only asking for a formal introduction. I wasn't insulting your caste or your pedigree."

"Bullshit!" He frowned down at her distraught face.

"Your head is full of shit," she cried out. "I was sixteen, Karna, petrified about leaving my home, my family, alarmed that I'd be married to a stranger by the end of the day. Then you came bounding up the podium. What were you, a dozen years or more older than me? You were so confident, so arrogant and worldly, and I was scared. I was so scared of what you were making me feel."

Whoa! Her version of the event didn't compute with his at all.

"You didn't look scared," he said. She'd looked beautiful...sweet. And that night in the royal gardens, she'd been gloriously daring.

"You didn't either." She shuddered out a sigh. "But you were scared, weren't you?"

He'd been scared shitless even before his chat with Vishnu. "You want to know why?"

"You thought you'd fudge the contest." She meant it seriously, but he suddenly wanted to roar with laughter.

He flicked her earlobe, setting her dangly pearl earring swinging. "No. My skill as an archer was the only thing I was confident about back then. I was there to compete on Duryodhan's behalf. But once I saw you, I wanted you for myself and was going crazy wondering how I'd convince him that you'd suit me better."

"What!" She wiped her face with both hands, blinking in shock. "You mean if you'd competed and won, I would've ended up marrying the creep?"

"Possibly, yeah."

"Then it was fortunate that I insulted you," she said.

Karna narrowed his eyes. "I thought you didn't insult me."

"Same difference."

They both fell silent then, devouring each other with their eyes, hiding nothing. Pride and prejudice, he thought with a shake of his head. His pride and prejudice had twisted an innocent question into a savage animosity. But whatever their surface stories, fate had played an even meaner game with them. So which one had come true: Tvastar's prophecy or Vishnu's vision?

Qalli—Draupadi shivered, and he became aware of the chill in the air. Yet they stood under the starlit sky, staring at each other and trying to see past the shadows of mistrust.

Who was she? he wondered. The princess who'd rejected him, the queen who'd hated him, his long-lost love, or was she simply a mother afraid for her offspring?

"What about Ash?" Confused, he focused on the one thing he was sure of: Yahvi's care.

"I'll stay out of his way," she said, her eyes bleak. The mother had won. "What will you do, Karna?"

He blew out a breath. They stood at the crossroads of a fault-ridden past and a merciless fate. Time and his options were running out, but not yet. Not yet. "I'll figure something out."

Baital wanted to barf.

It was all so emotional and dramatic on the Human Realm. What was it about the non-red souls and their need for martyrdom? It made them into such gullible nincompoops that Goddesses and *asuras* took advantage of them—all the time.

Baital air-surfed high above the martyrs, the vaulted ceiling allowing him uninterrupted movement. Through the strands of his long thick hair, he observed the outrageously beautiful medic and the robed Ash work on the injured.

Karna's daughter was a pathetic little thing. She looked as if a soundless fart might kill her. Was she going to die from her ailments? Eek! He started sending her get-well-soon vibes from the ceiling. Once she woke up, he would stick to her like leprosy on a leper. She was the key to his freedom, and he wasn't going to let her mess it up by dying at the wrong moment, or at the wrong hands.

He hadn't told the Soul Warrior the whole story. To counterbalance her blooper with Vala, Goddess Kalika had made sure Tvastar's prophecy also came true. A prophecy all the Gods in all the realms had dreaded since time immemorial. Secretly, they'd contrived to keep the son of the Sun God and the daughter of the Fire God apart because such a union would bring forth the Slayer of Souls, who would have the god-power to extinguish an immortal soul. Hence, making him or her the most powerful being in the Cosmos.

So, natch the Gods were all whiny and wanted the creature dead. Goddess Kalika wanted Yahvi dead too, but only after she vaporized Vala's soul. Such a big to-do in the Cosmos, really.

Baital did a flyby over martyr number two. Miss Boo-Hoo Iksa was curled up on the floor, her head resting in Satya's lap. She blew her nose and moaned every now and then, to Baital's immense irritation. He'd gag her, but that would make the Celestials mad.

Ash, martyr number three wasn't crying even if he was garbed in a whole lot of regret. See? *Pisachas* didn't do regret. No red soul worth his salt regretted anything. Regrets were for fools. Fools who in a fit of passion did things they wouldn't normally do. A *pisacha* did not execute an action without thinking through it first and, once it was performed, never second-guessed. That was the difference between the truly wise and the wicked. Wait! He was truly wise and he was wicked. It was the difference between the wisely wicked and the pathetic—that is, the difference between the *pisachas* of the Cosmos and the martyrs.

And there was martyr number four: Eklavya, the Thumbless One-Duh, standing at the foot of Karna's daughter's bed, bogged down by guilt and Dev-Il knew what else, second-guessing his actions of the night.

Weary from the martyr-energy overdose, Baital curled himself into a ball, much like Iksa, in one corner of the ceiling. He tried to bring happier times to mind, like the time he'd terrorized Meenakshi's village. Meenakshi wasn't a martyr. Before a nostalgic moan oozed out of his mouth, Lord Karna and the teary-eyed Lady Draupadi walked back into the room.

"Amara's healing beautifully. I've given her a sleeping draft so she sleeps through the night. She'll be her boisterous, bouncy self by morning," Ziva informed the parent. She jumped down from the stool and groaned, presenting her back to Lusha. "Massage, please. My neck and shoulders are killing me." Her slurp-worthy skin had become as dull as month-old yogurt.

"Yahvi?" asked martyr number five. Sorry, Lord Karna.

Ash was applying a thick white paste around the child's bandaged arm. "Almost done. I managed to heal the cuts without stitches. The arm will need watching. She has several hairline fractures and one clean break, but she'll be fine."

Oh goody! Yahvi would be fine. Now all Baital had to do was make sure she stayed on the martyrdom path.

Finally Ash stood up and washed his hands in the sink in the corner. He made a beeline for the door. "I'll check on Ved. You might want to see to the guests. They'll be wondering why none of us are at the festival."

"Guests? Festival? You've been keeping the fun stuff from me." Baital unfurled himself, his depression vanishing at the thought of merrymaking.

"Simmer down, *pisacha*. You're not in Hell anymore. You must stay out of sight," said Lord Karna.

"But why? Just tell the humans that I'm an out-of-work actor still in costume. Trust me, it works. I've tried it. My Lord? Wait!" Baital flew behind the male martyrs. "Warrior-lords are so strict," he said, making a couple of the females giggle.

In the adjoining chamber, they gathered around the bed of a mummified human. Ash checked the man from eyeballs to privates and finalized a treatment plan with another healer.

"Is his soul tainted?" asked Lavya.

Well, well, the human was tainted? The man appeared half dead to Baital, not half evil at all.

"Still green," said Karna. "But we'll keep watch."

Morose again, Baital watched the human being watched by the warriors.

"Mere cleansing won't work this time," said Karna abruptly. He did not look happy. "We'll have to burn it down and build a new dwelling. We'll salvage what we can. The rest must be destroyed."

Cleansing? Dwelling? How was he supposed to understand anything with everyone talking in code? And they accused him of talking in riddles.

"I'm sorry for that, my lord," said Lavya stiffly. "I'm sorry I failed you."

*Drama, drama, drama! That was the Realm of the Martyrs.*

# CHAPTER TWENTY-ONE
## ADBHOOTA: HISTORY'S MYSTERIES

*Sometime between midnight and dawn…*

The Earth quaked, waking her.

"What?" Draupadi asked, struggling to sit up in bed. "Is it Yahvi? Amara? Are we being attacked?"

*"No. Nothing of the sort,"* a disembodied voice whispered gruffly in her ear.

She flopped back down.

*"I'm confused why you waited so long to use your last boon for Yahvi?"*

"What boon? Yahvi is a blessing," Draupadi mumbled and pulled the quilt over her head, letting sleep claim her.

*Sometime later…*

*"Blessings and boons aren't the same thing?"* The whisper and the shakes were back.

"No, you twerp." She rolled onto her stomach and pulled the pillow over her head. Tension, she thought foggily. It was tension. Nightmares, dreams, voices in her head, migraines and ulcers, all were side effects of tension. The pillow lifted off her head.

*"Didn't Ma Aditi bestow boons on you to beget the children?"*

*"Hmm? Yes. Just not for Yahvi."*

*"Oh?"*

*Some more time later...*

*"What do you mean not for Yahvi?"*

The whisper from Insomnia Hell was back. This time accompanied by a relentless shoulder shake that rivaled the tremors brought on by an epileptic fit. Draupadi blinked several times, allowing her groggy eyes to adjust to the candlelight illuminating the healing room. Karna stood by her bed, hair exploding all over his face. He looked about as pleasant as an electrocuted lion.

"What is it? What's happened?" she asked, alarmed by his appearance.

"Would you two lovebirds please take your domestic disturbance elsewhere?" Amara grumbled from her sick bed across the room. "Vee and I need our beauty sleep. Don't we, Doctor Ziva?" Ziva and Yahvi giggled from their beds on either side of her.

With a dignity she wasn't quite feeling, Draupadi slid out of bed, grabbed Karna's T-shirt—it was soaking wet, stinking of sweat and pizza and something else, something heavenly—and pulled him out of the room. She found an empty chamber four doors down and dragged him inside, shutting the door in their wake.

The room was cold with dark. Karna flipped on the lights while she waved her hand over the fireplace, making it flame to life. She'd slept with a woolen robe pulled tight over her silk pajamas and thick, fuzzy leg warmers and was surprised by how inordinately cold she still was. She came from the lineage of the Fire God. She shouldn't be cold at all.

"What did you find out?" If he was in this great a hurry to share stories, it couldn't be good. "And why are you icky and sweaty but not bloody? Weren't you out exorcising the realm of evil again?"

"I can't exorcise *asuras* if I can't find them. Lavya and I have been moving stuff here from Asht Dveep," he said starkly, sliding his hands into his pockets.

"Oh," she said. No wonder he was upset. "I'm sorry for the loss of your home." It was hard to let go of things, of people and life. It was hardest to let go of anger.

Karna walked over to the fireplace and stared at the flames that were all but licking the top of the hearth. The room was small enough to be instantly suffused with heat. It had one bed, a single cabinet in one corner and a TV riveted into the wall above the hearth. The azure walls and floors were lined with crystal, like the ones in main healing room.

Would the stones help heal their hearts as it did the wounds?

"I asked five boons from Ma Aditi, five boons that would bring back my five sons whom Ash slaughtered." The memory brought a shudder of pain in her heart, but she set it aside to tell her story. "Satya I found first, three hundred years ago, then Lusha, two hundred years ago, then Ziva and Iksa within weeks of each other around a hundred seventy-five years back. Amara I found thirty-four years ago. She was sixteen Celestial days old when I met you in Devlok."

"Your sons? Your daughters are the reincarnations of your sons?" he asked incredulously. Did he think she was still lying?

"Yes. It was easy to locate them as I'd kept tabs on them through their various rebirths, to see how they fared. But it was hard to wait until they were between lives before approaching them with my plan. It was a condition Ma Aditi put on the boons, that the souls had to want me as their mother again. No coercion." Draupadi had convinced them, some more easily than others, that it would be the best thing for them all.

"And you chose to recreate them female for a reason?" he asked.

"It wasn't a choice. It just happened." She'd been glad she'd begotten girls this time around. But now, with all that was happening, she wasn't so sure.

"If you only had five boons...how was Yahvi...?"

"You got me pregnant," she said baldly. Karna's flabbergasted gaze dropped to her flat stomach. "Yes," she said to his unspoken question. "The traditional bun-in-the-oven pregnant."

"But that's impossible!"

"Saraswati calls Yahvi a miracle. She is a beautiful, delightful embodiment of both our soul-deep desires."

Slashes of red highlighted his cheekbones—in anger or embarrassment or from the heat of the fire, she couldn't guess. "Really? A desire so soul-deep you ran from it?" His eyes flashed gold, and one skeptical eyebrow arched high.

"You ran first," Draupadi said angrily. But anger wasn't going to help her. She sighed and sat down on the edge of the bed. "What did you want me to do? Our affair began on a lark, a fluke. I didn't plan any further than a couple of days of nymphing. You didn't know who I was, and as far as I was concerned, didn't ever need to. I was just... curious, I guess. I wanted to know if it had been real...what I'd felt before. I thought we could have a bit of fun and games and go our separate ways."

"But you left in the middle of the fun and games," he pointed out.

"Because...because...damn it!" She clasped her hands together and pressed them to her lap. "The minute you touched me I knew there would be no happy ending to it. No peaceful goodbye. I left before matters got worse, deeper for both of us. I left while I still could."

His Adam's apple bobbed against his throat, as if he found her words hard to swallow. "Why didn't you come to me when you found out you were pregnant? Or when Kalika told you of Yavhi's fate? Did you think I wouldn't believe you? Or wouldn't care about our child?"

"Honestly, I didn't trust you. Things were very complicated for me already. My husbands weren't ecstatic I'd brought back our sons. I was playing with karma, according to them. Don't even ask what Mother Kunti's opinion is about it all. Plus, I was desperately trying to keep my daughters—especially Amara—from messing up their karma by their overzealousness. To add you into the mix would've turned me into a raving lunatic."

"Like you aren't anyway," he muttered.

She allowed him one jibe. "You would've insisted on raising Yahvi here on this realm because she was your daughter. I couldn't risk that. Not after what Kalika told me."

"Again, you're making an ass out of you and me by assuming what I would've done."

"Again, I know your type. You wouldn't have been able to help yourself."

Karna's nostrils flared. "And what type is that? One who owns up to his mistakes and atones for them? One who does not shirk his responsibilities and run away?"

She heaved up from the bed, furious and horribly hurt by his opinion of her. "How dare you judge me? You uptight...duty-bound...*warrior!* How typical to look down your nose at souls who do not abide by your rigid codes. For your information, I didn't run away from either you or my husbands. I moved on. There's a huge difference between the two actions."

Feeling hot and bothered all of a sudden, she smoothed her hair in her hands and in one deft twist knotted it up behind her head. "This is stupid. I don't know why I'm trying to make you understand. You never will. You cannot. It's beyond your comprehension."

She'd wished he was different, but he wasn't. Karna was just like them—like her lord husbands—and she did not gel with such men for long. She had to let him go or she'd be trapped in another toxic relationship where his rules, his desires, his life would consume hers.

"I'm sorry about some of it, Karna. I hope you believe that," she said. She waited a beat for a response, for him to say he believed her, and that they'd work it out somehow. But he didn't. He stood there frowning into the fire.

So this was it. She walked to the door and grabbed its handle. She'd survive this. She'd survived worse, and she had her daughters to think of first and foremost. It had been wishful thinking anyway, she thought hollowly. A lovely dream while it lasted. She pulled the door open.

"It wasn't a lark."

Draupadi froze with a hand on the doorknob. "What?" She turned around slowly, her nerves screaming.

"Didn't you hear Baital? Our getting together in Devlok...Kalika maneuvered it. So Yahvi would exist."

All souls were pawns of fate—be they green, blue or red.

Karna locked the chamber after Qalli—Draupadi—one or both of them—disappeared to wake the Six. He'd called a meeting ASAP and he wanted full attendance—no exceptions. He'd leave it to the healers to get Yahvi and Ved ready at least to listen, if not to participate in the discussions. They had less than two days till D day.

For one fleeting moment, he wondered if he should leave the females out of the equation, and let Qalli spirit them away against all odds. But he discarded the thought as soon as it formed. It wasn't his decision to make. It never had been.

Karna's stomach growled, demanding sustenance. The extra-large pizza pie he'd scarfed down a couple of hours ago hadn't been enough for what he'd put his body through for the past eight. He drew out his phone and dialed Lavya.

"All set?" he asked.

Lavya was manning the security around Har-ki-doon. They had upped it even more, stationing extra hired warriors and mercenaries Karna had brought back from the *loks* and the ones Salabha had sent from Vitalas at the weakest fissures in the valley. Baby had been taken down for the time being and they'd be relying solely on instinct, trust and magic now.

"Yup," said Lavya. "No *asura* can get in. Or out," he finished, looking at Baital.

Karna had left the *pisacha* in Lavya's care so he could have his chat with Qalli in private. He doubted Baital would escape, though. One did not displease Kalika without consequences.

"And when they try, we'll know of it instantly," added Lavya.

"Do me a favor. Arrange for food at the meeting, tons of it. I'm starving." He'd keep stuffing his face till D day. He'd been locked in battle with Vala for three full days the last time. He wanted to be prepared.

"Check. I could use a bite too. See you in fifteen in Ved's room. Ash said he can't be moved," Lavya said and clicked off.

Karna would make sure the females stuffed themselves too, packed in the energy between training sessions, as there was little else to do until Vala actually breached the Human Realm and showed his hand. It would be an event that lit up the dark sky, his source had said. They definitely wouldn't miss it.

He toed off his shoes and socks, and went into the attached bathroom. He stripped off his clothes, used the toilet before stepping into the shower. Turning the lever all the way to scalding hot, he splayed his hands against the peach tiles and let the pulse-jet shower pound down on his head, shoulders and back. The strain, the problems puddled beneath his feet like sweat and grime and drained away. They would be back soon enough. But for the moment, he stood there drained of all thought.

He turned the shower off and, grabbing a fluffy peach towel, dried himself vigorously. He needed a shave, he saw, swiping the fog off the vanity mirror with a hand.

It always boiled down to duty and desire. He ran the electric shaver over his jaw. Throughout his life, he'd been torn between the two. Duty had him striving to fulfill the obligations of a son, to follow in Adiratha's footsteps and become a royal charioteer, while desire had drawn him to the war arena. Duty had him bowing to the wishes of his father and bloodline as the Soul Warrior, even as he'd desired oblivion.

Duty would have him push Qalli away, while his heart—fug, what his heart wanted wasn't seemly. Their daughter's soul was at stake.

Karna closed his eyes. As always when his heart and soul waged war, he brought his mother's image to his mind. Her gentle face settled him. The memory of her touch on his head gave him strength. He opened his eyes, took a deep breath and blew it out. He put the shaver back on its charger and dealt with his hair next, simply brushing it off his face in a wet tangle.

His mother had been a great admirer of the young and intrepid queen of Indraprastha. Had she guessed Karna's feelings for her? Had his wives? They'd admired Draupadi too. *"Any woman who can juggle five husbands with that much grace and aplomb deserves our sympathy,"* they'd said when he spoke of her in derogatory terms. He hoped his wives hadn't known of his affair. His cheeks flamed, a lifetime too late.

Supriya, the younger and cheekier of the two, had even joked that though she and Vrishali had but one husband to handle, they were quite weary of his I-am-the-king-of-my-jungle attitude, and would he please curb it or she'd take a vow of silence and celibacy and then what would he do? And if he even thought of getting another wife, it would seriously piss her off as there wasn't enough room in their palace anyway with the three of them, their growing number of offspring, his parents and nearly half their village residing with them at any given moment.

Roots. His roots had dug deep and spread wide. Karna couldn't remember a day when his parents' abodes—the small, three-chambered brick hut in the city of Hastinapura or the thick-timbered dwelling on the banks of River Charmanwati—had not been filled with guests. The tradition hadn't changed when he was awarded vassal-ship of Anga. Kith and kin, villagers and princes, kings and peasants, merchants and priests, all had been welcome in his abode. He'd once coaxed Duryodhan and his brother, Dushasan, to share their larger guest chambers with a family of fisher-folk for the night. The princes had gone one step further and vacated the chambers completely, and had slept under the stars in the garden—Karna figured, to get away from the fishy smell. His wives had marveled at his inexplicable ability to get his way in every single thing, however inconceivable the idea might be at its conception.

Karna laughed at his clean-shaven reflection. Some memories weren't half bad, even if they brought on a bittersweet ache in his heart. He would suffer a thousand heartaches and a million headaches to relive those moments with his family.

He wondered what his mother and wives would think about his relationship with Draupadi and the child they'd created. He shook his head, his smile fading. He needn't wonder. He knew what they'd think, what they'd wish for him. They would want him to be happy. They'd always wanted him to be at peace with himself and with the world.

He'd been a warrior for the better part of seven thousand five hundred years. He didn't think peace had ever been an option for him.

Karna padded back into the healing chamber. The crackling fire dried the residual moisture from his body, heating his skin. He paused by the casement windows that framed the night. To an inexperienced eye, it was night. But he knew the ways of the Illuminators intimately. He was the son of Surya and brother of Usha, so he noticed the slight paling of the black, a precursor to dawn.

The built-in wardrobe in the corner offered a meager selection of clothes. He pulled out a sheet of cream silk and deftly wrapped it around his hips, knotting it tightly at his navel. He pleated one long end, tucking the pleats into the knot and sweeping the folds between his legs, then secured them in the back. He put on a knee-length tunic made of rough grey cotton wool and rolled the long sleeves to his elbows. He slipped on his tan loafers, more comfortable in his own shoes than borrowed ones.

Refreshed and somewhat clearheaded, Karna strode out of the chamber to address some hard choices they'd all have to make in the approaching light of day.

Duty and desire had just found a new battleground.

# CHAPTER TWENTY-TWO
## KAMANA: KERNELS OF DESIRE

Karna strode into the healing room where Ved convalesced as a small army of servants filed out, murmuring greetings to him. The chamber was pleasantly redolent of burning pine, medicinal herbs and food. To his surprise, Ved was awake, albeit prostrate on the bed, watching Ash replace the poultices on his chest. The lower half of Ved's face was fitted with an elastic brace, holding his smashed cheek and dislocated jaw together and at the same time providing flexibility of movement for eating and speaking.

With a plate piled high with food, Lavya lorded over an armchair right in the middle of the room. He'd showered and changed too, and wore a black polo-neck sweater over his shirt and jeans to hide the wounds and bandages he'd earned last night. And he didn't look as haunted.

"Where's Baital?" Karna grabbed a plate, filling it with several flatbreads and veggies.

Ash did a double take when he looked up, his dark eyes sweeping over Karna in amusement. "Lord Karna, you look regal."

"I do on occasion wear a *dhoti*," Karna said self-consciously, though he hadn't in a while. He wondered why. The garment was unbelievably roomy and shockingly more comfortable than a well-worn pair of jeans.

"Found it in one of the rooms down the hall, the only option of garment for men. There was a bigger and better selection for females. I wonder why."

"There should've been a whole selection for men too, jeans and shirts included. I'll see to restocking it," said Ash.

"I wouldn't. Life is infinitely simpler with fewer choices," Lavya murmured around a mouthful of papaya. He jerked his head toward the window. "Baital is hanging out in one of the trees. His battiness cannot be suppressed any longer. His words, not mine." The odd placement of the armchair made sense now. Lavya had a direct line of vision to the closest cluster of trees outside.

Karna peered out the window and immediately located the red soul not fifty feet away. He was fast asleep, dangling upside down on talons from a high, thick branch. He hadn't changed out of his leathers, although someone had unburdened him of his silver and iron arm accouterments.

"Why is he uncuffed?"

Lavya took a large swig from a bottle of soda. "Your daughter insisted. She made me remove the handcuffs, saying it was inhuman to bind any creature so. Plus, they've become Monopoly pals and the shackles kept disrupting the board when he rolled the die. I took off the ones around his forearms, and left the ones on his ankles—do bats have ankles? Anyway, the ones on his bat-legs are still on. And here's the key, back in your safe keeping."

With great reluctance, Karna took the key. Yahvi was obviously doing well if she was playing Monopoly and bossing his aide. Still, he asked Ash for an update and was reassured that all three patients were doing fine. Better than fine, as Ved's soul remained green despite the possession.

"Do you remember what happened?" he began the interrogation, then groaned, remembering the missing females. He jerked his head at Lavya. They really should get this show on the road. "Can you see what's holding them up?"

Lavya got to his feet and set his plate down on one of the food carts. "They wouldn't have thanked you for starting without them. Can't wait for more secrets, untruths, half truths or what have you to tumble out. And I'm recording everything," he shouted over his shoulder, marching out the door.

"Who rolled out of his chair and parked his ass on a pinecone?" Karna shook his head after his friend.

"He feels nasty about what happened," said Ash. "He wants to make sure nothing else is left to chance."

And because Karna knew intimately there was nothing to be done for guilt, misplaced or not, he sat down and wiped his plate clean. He'd just washed his hands and gargled when the door whispered open and the females filed in, fanning out across the chamber in deathly silence. They were in various stages of dress with Satya, an early riser like himself, ready for the day in jeans and sweater. Qalli was still in her nightgown. She wouldn't meet his eyes. The frailness of her posture was an illusion; nevertheless, it struck a chord somewhere inside him.

He'd been too blunt with her. But he wouldn't make promises he couldn't keep.

Lavya walked in last, carrying a bundled up Yahvi in his arms. The sight so distracted him that all he could do was gape. Lavya set Yahvi down in the armchair, fussing over her like a mother hen, arranging the woolen blanket and pillows about her. Then he stood on her right, implacable and unshakeable as a bodyguard on duty. Karna personally thought Lavya was taking his GQ—guilt quotient—to a ridiculous extreme and was about to make a sarcastic comment when Iksa startled him by snaking her arms around his waist and burying her face in his chest.

He kissed the top of her head and, smoothing the baby-soft curls off her face, he gently tipped it up. Her face was blotched and swollen. Her dimples flashed dully as she sniffed her tears back.

"Were you weeping all night, sweet child?" He swept his eyes over the solemn Six. Even Amara was humorless this morning, as if waiting for the proverbial shoe to drop. Yahvi's eyes were fixed on Baital, snoring on his tree. "What's the matter?" Frankly, they were scaring the crap out of him by their behavior.

"I can't do this anymore," said Iksa and stepped back from him.

The statement was like a sucker-punch right in the solar plexus. They didn't trust him. It'd been too much for them—the danger, the demons, the unstable realm. They wanted to quit and it should not have mattered. That they would be safe in the Higher Worlds, once he negociated their return, should have been all that mattered. He closed his eyes, trying not to show his disappointment. And damn his craving for roots and family. Would he never learn?

"No! Oh no!" Iksa gave him a quick hug again, looking horrified. "That didn't come out right. That's not what I meant, Uncle K. I've been having visions. I know I should keep them to myself, but I *have* to share them with you, regardless of the taboo. I mean, what's the point of me seeing glimpses of the future if we can't use it to our advantage?"

Iksa had told him repeatedly she read faces, not minds. Whether she'd read his face or his mind just then, she'd read him right. He didn't want them to leave. He didn't want them to be hapless targets either. If he had to cheat a little to keep them safe, then that's what he'd do.

A muffled snort followed by an obnoxious gagging sound had Karna turning his head to the windows. The blue-faced *pisacha* hovered right outside, the strands of his overlong, silky hair quivering in the nascent breeze.

"Sorry. Involuntary gag reflex in the company of martyrs." Baital bobbed up and down along the windowsill, pouting like an orphaned puppy-dog. "Carry on, carry on, just pretend I'm invisible. Of course, when the sun breaks over the summits, I'll actually have to make myself invisible or risk blindness. Do you have a specific dank, dark dungeon in mind where I can dawdle for the day, my lord?"

"You'll stay within my sights." Karna opened the windows wide to let him in. Baital nodded elegantly in thanks and claimed his corner on a shadowy part of the ceiling.

By then, Qalli had come out of her stupor and taken hold of Iksa by her forearms. "You can't, my darling. How I wish you'd been spared such torment. But it's the price you pay for your god-power. Just like your father paid before you and his father before him. You mustn't tell a soul what you foresee."

"It's too late, Ma. I've already told my sisters what might come for all of us."

Qalli gasped in shock. Hell, Karna would've gasped too had he not thought the whole taboo ridiculous to begin with. It was one of the idiotic Catch-22 situations that the Celestials loved to sprinkle over the Cosmos: divine clairvoyance at your disposal that couldn't be used because it would hamper free will. Why create such powers, then?

"But you can't!" Qalli began to shake her daughter. "What have you done? The Council will call it cheating, tampering with fate. You'll be punished, don't you understand?"

"So it's okay for you to thwart the rules but not us?" Iksa asked.

"I didn't thwart the rules. I took a calculated risk," Qalli said through clenched teeth.

Karna laughed outright at the patently ludicrous excuse for what she'd been doing for the past three hundred years, maybe even before that. He choked it off into a cough when she skewered him with flinty *pushkara*-petal eyes.

He winked at Iksa. "So, sweet *shishya* of mine, what is to come?" He too preferred proactive inclinations of will, so he could hardly condemn Iksa's actions. The Patriarchs had made him their guru, for better or worse, and as he'd never done the expected in his life, he wasn't about to start now.

"Oh, for Heaven's sake, this is not a joke!"

He wasn't taking any of this lightly. But he wouldn't have minded a peek into a fancy crystal ball. "Listen up blue, green and red souls, it's time for all revelations—past, present and future. So, who wants the floor first?" he asked, finally winning a grin of approval from Amara.

Through an act of inhuman will, Draupadi folded her arms across her chest so she wouldn't be tempted to do bodily harm to her own offspring. How awful a mother was she that she'd sown such unorthodox seeds in her orchard? Not only sown but also cultivated the rebellion into full bloom. Had she willfully chosen to overlook the signs, believing that childish obstinacy would just evaporate in the boiling cauldron of time?

Amara jostled Lusha and Ziva apart, eliciting a "Hey!" and a "Watch it, Amu!" and plunked herself down on the arm of Yahvi's chair. "Come on, Vee, don't panic now."

Yahvi did seem to be on the verge of an anxiety attack. She was biting the skin around her thumbnail, a nervous habit she didn't display often. Amara pulled her hand away and nodded in encouragement.

"About a year ago, Goddess Kalika came to me and told me the real reason I'd been born," Yahvi said, looking at Draupadi for a second and immediately shying away. "I wasn't born of love, but for sacrifice."

"That's not true," Draupadi cried out in dismay. She jolted when Karna's hand caressed her back, coming to rest about her waist.

"Let her finish," he said with nauseating calm.

Draupadi wanted to smack him, smack them all. Let her finish? Yahvi was talking of finishing herself. Why wasn't he upset? Why hadn't he burst into flames?

"I won't stand here and…"

"Let her speak, Qalli," he said, raising his voice. "We have to know everything before we can decide what to do."

Draupadi didn't want to know anything. She wanted to put a full and final stop to this lunacy.

"My birth wasn't a random occurrence, she said. I was born for a purpose." Yahvi tried to smile, failed. "I'm the only one who can vanquish the Stone Demon."

"And of course, as soon as Kalika cons you into believing her, you rush in like an overenthusiastic legendary warrior and enlist your soul as a sacrifice. Why didn't you tell me she'd come to you?" Draupadi shouted. "How dare she appear before you behind my back."

"Well, Matri, your current reaction justifies our keeping it quiet," said Satya.

"This is amusing to you?" Karna squeezed her waist in a gesture meant to soothe and Draupadi erupted. "What? You find this amusing too? A righteous duty worth dying for, right? Of course you think that. You bloody Kshatriya. Die while performing your sacred duties and reserve a spot in Heaven, isn't that right?" She whirled back to Yahvi. "Is that what Kalika promised you? Answer me!"

Yahvi slowly got to her feet, shrugging in answer. The quilt fell off her shoulders and exposed the plastered arm in the sling tied to her neck. Her right hand was thickly bandaged, leaving only her fingers and the thumb free. The sight of her daughter's injuries, both visible and hidden, of the danger Yahvi had been in yesterday, of the danger that she *planned* to put herself in tomorrow, pierced Draupadi's soul like a poisoned dart.

Exactly what was it that she was supposed to learn from the last few days? That everything was preordained and would come about no matter how much she fought against it? To pretend she was a piece of driftwood floating in the river of existence, and care for nothing—stones or weeds or fish or banks? That was Yudhishtir's way, not hers.

Draupadi shook Karna's arm off. "I told you how naïve they were. Do you believe me now? She thinks all it takes is that one deed and her soul will turn blue. Why don't you tell her how it really works since none of them will take my word for it?"

"Your mother's right. There are no guarantees, *vatse*. Not even Yama can promise your soul will transform. And..." he paused, sighed heavily. "The very moment you put a price tag on your actions, it negates their virtue. Deeds are to be done for their sake alone and not as a means to an end. Your actions have to be selfless in order to count, *vatse*."

Yahvi nodded vigorously. "I know that, Daddy. But these are special circumstances. And Iksa's visions confirm it." Her gold-brown eyes gleamed feverishly. "I was going to visit you after my eighteenth birthday. I'd always planned on coming here, introducing myself. I've wanted to meet you for so long."

Yes, Draupadi had known her daughter's heart, had dreaded it for years. She waited for Yahvi to blame her for holding her back, keeping her from her father. Hidden away, barricaded from everyone but her sisters and mother. But she didn't. Yahvi had never held it against her.

"Then time ran out and I had to come immediately or I'd never know you. And you'd never know about me. So we"—Yahvi broke off and smiled at her sisters before sending an apologetic glance toward Draupadi, and said in a rush—"we contacted Uncle Arjun to fetch us from Alaka."

Draupadi was beyond shocked. Arjun's visit to Alaka hadn't been an accident? Their daughters had summoned him? Sweet Heaven, why hadn't her daughters trusted her with this? Surely she didn't come across as such an ogre?

And what was Arjun's game in this? Her mind scrambled to latch onto some sort of foothold. But her thoughts kept slipping, sliding, fracturing in a million directions.

Iksa took over from Yahvi, describing her visions. Most of her dreams seemed banal, of movie theatres and car races and beach parties. She dreamed of Yahvi a lot. And *asuras*. The last vision was a strange one, she said. No sounds, no background, no color, like a charcoal sketch. In it, Yahvi's arm was painfully stretched out and her wrist gripped by another.

"You know it could've been a boyfriend holding Yahvi's hand," Amara jumped in with her opinion. "What? You said your visions have many interpretations."

With a withering glance at Amara, Iksa said, "Was I wrong? Didn't it happen just like I said? But I'm baffled that I'm still dreaming of it."

"Did you know beforehand what would happen at the island?" Karna asked softly.

"No," said Iksa, clearly shocked that he'd think so. "I'd never have let Yahvi go if I'd known. I'd have locked her up like Mama."

Draupadi didn't feel validated, not at all.

"I have no time frame for the visions, or any sense of where they'll happen. I try really hard to understand what I see, Uncle K. Whether it's an actual event or simply a metaphor for what might happen. It's not easy to decipher them, and I'm so afraid of reading them wrong."

"Don't second-guess. Trust your instincts. They won't fail you," Karna said. It was exactly the right advice to give Iksa, exactly what Draupadi would've said. "Why did you wait? If you knew this a year ago, why didn't you come to me then? Why drag Arjun into it?"

Because their mother was stubborn and scared and foolish, and she'd left her daughters no choice but to go against her. Draupadi closed her eyes altogether then. Her whole existence was unraveling like a rogue thread on fate's tapestry.

Satya took her hands in her own. When she opened her eyes, her brave daughters stood before her. "Matri, you know our fathers better than we do. Did you really think they didn't know about Yahvi?"

Sahadeva's sight was a thousand times more powerful than Iksa's. It'd been foolish of her to think that she'd fooled him. No, she'd never thought that. But she'd been confident he wouldn't tell another soul, so certain her secret would remain safe. Sahadeva never revealed his visions or confidences. Not even to save the world. He hadn't even tried to save their sons from being butchered the night after they'd won the Great War.

Draupadi shook her head. No one was behaving like they were supposed to.

"Okay, folks. Let's debunk the next mystery." Karna steered the conversation back to the salient point, giving her a moment to wipe her face.

"Might I comment, my lord?" Baital asked, hovering parallel to the ceiling in a sideways prone position with his head resting on his right arm. "I must say the young godlings are on their way to becoming cosmic-class con artists. I am quite impressed. Might they have some *pisacha* blood running through their veins?" All ignored the unnecessary addendum.

"What I'd like to know is how you came to the conclusion that you have to die," Eklavya asked Yahvi.

Draupadi should have been embarrassed that Eklavya and the fiend were listening in on the family drama, but she was too busy being distraught.

Yahvi looked taken aback by the question. "Well, Goddess Kalika appeared before me as I was bathing…or maybe she came to me in a dream in which I was bathing…whatever, the point is that I was bathing…"

"She tends to do that a lot." Baital nodded gravely. "She has no respect for personal space."

"You too?" Yahvi shot a quick grin at Baital. "Anyway, she said it would be great if I did vanquish the Stone Demon, but if I couldn't and I died, that would be acceptable too. Our souls are linked, apparently."

"She gave you a choice." Karna's remark made Draupadi's nerves thrum with excitement. There was a loophole.

"Not really. Everyone here knows I'm not going to defeat Vala. I have no god-powers. No strength," Yahvi said. "I know you think I'm doing it for selfish reasons, but I'm not, Daddy. I swear. You know Vala can't be let loose in the human world. He'll destroy it."

The bitter taste of frustration soured Draupadi's mouth. Yahvi was so gullible. Just because a Goddess had asked her to do something, she thought it was the right thing. Oh! She didn't know. She didn't know what kind of games Gods and Goddesses played to stay in power.

"Was it a verbal acceptance, *vatse*? Did she make you sign an agreement, a blood-oath?"

"If I may, Uncle K," Satya interrupted politely. "Yahvi agreed only to think about it. She hasn't said yes yet."

"But I've made up my mind now, Satya." Yahvi contradicted her sister with the air of a martyr.

Draupadi wanted to strangle her own child.

"Let's discuss your options, *vatse*. This has given us room to play around."

"Discuss?" Draupadi jumped in before she killed someone or had a stroke. "What's there to discuss? Tell her to un-make up her mind right now."

That did it. Pandemonium ensued. Her five oldest started arguing with her. Yahvi started crying. Karna grabbed her arm and literally chucked her out of the room. He followed her out and shut the doors with a loud smack.

"You're not helping. Antagonizing them at this point will only make matters worse. It'll make them dig in their heels. Let me handle it," he scolded her as if she were a child.

That infuriated her even more. "Let you handle it, Mr. Lord of Self-Sacrifice?" She poked a finger into his chest. "Don't think I don't know to what extent you stretch your sense of honor and obligation to all life-forms." She poked his chest again. "Who was it who gave his divine armor away as alms on the eve of the Great War?"

Lord Surya had gifted his warrior son with impenetrable armor, which had made Karna an indestructible force on a battlefield. Surya had warned Karna that Indra would ensure Arjun's victory in the Kuru War by any means possible. He'd implored Karna not to go to the riverbank for his prayers that day, further warning him that Indra would lie in wait, incognito as a poor sage begging for alms. Even knowing all that, Karna had gone, bound by oath, honor and ritual, and had returned home empty-handed. He'd gone into battle wearing ordinary armor—a joke of a shield against divine weapons. What kind of courage ran though Karna's veins? All five of his brothers together didn't have half his strength.

Draupadi looked into his beautiful stoic face. As always, he left her feeling completely confused and unbearably vulnerable. "You are unreservedly noble and see nobility in everyone. You demand it of everyone. Wasn't that why you were chosen to be the Soul Warrior? The world was never fair to you, but you are never unfair. You give souls a chance to be better than they are. You encourage them to redeem themselves, even *asuras*. Karna, I beg you, put aside your scruples for once and forbid Yahvi from taking the path she wants to take. Don't let her make such a foolish mistake."

Karna took her hands and pressed them to his chest when she would have wrenched them away. "I can't, Qalli." His heart thudded against her palms. "I can't forbid Yahvi to follow her heart, not when I've done no less." He smiled grimly, the gold in his eyes firing up with resolve. "But I will promise you that our child will not die tomorrow."

# CHAPTER TWENTY-THREE
## MAHAVRATTA: GREAT VOW

The effects of disasters should be thought of beforehand. It is not appropriate to begin digging a well when the house is on fire.

Calling one of Adiratha's favorite adages to mind, Karna ushered Qalli back into the room to resume the discussion only to find Ved asleep. Yahvi fared no better, though she was desperately trying to keep her eyes open by sipping on a pistachio-green smoothie. The rest were breaking their fasts, Lavya for the second time. With a large goblet of coffee in his hand, Karna told his tale of the Stone Demon, right up to his latest fruitless hunt the previous night. He'd thrown his senses out further than the moon but hadn't caught anything.

"I felt him but couldn't see his soul. He's wrapped up tight in *asura-maya* or something even more powerful."

"Imagine what'll happen once he consumes the *raakh*." Baital kept driving the point home, as if any of them could forget.

Karna flicked a glance at Qalli. There was nothing he could do to reassure her beyond performing his duties and contriving to keep his promise to her.

"Is this your wish? To battle Vala?" he asked his daughter.

"I don't think I have a choice. I'm the only one who can defeat him," she replied, as red-faced and wretched as her mother.

"And if you had a choice?"

Yahvi glanced at her sisters, then Baital. "I can do this, Daddy. I'm not afraid."

Karna finished his coffee in one long gulp. He set his mug down on the tray. "Come on, then. We have about thirty-six hours to cram what I know about Vala into you." He wasn't going to waste any more time, or energy, running after myths and prophecies and ways out.

She sprang up and hurried to the door, as did her sisters and Baital, while Karna barked out orders to the rest. "Keep me informed about the nibbles on our traps, Lavya. And unless it's the Apocalypse, I'm not leaving Yahvi's side. Deal with any zombie sightings and missing humans on your own. Ash, get every *pahadi* down to the citadel and arm as many as are willing for either attack or defense." Highlanders knew how to handle weapons. One didn't dwell around Har-ki-doon without knowing how. Plus, they'd be safest here.

Yahvi gave her mother a hug. "I'd like a huge, smashing birthday party, Mama. Will you organize one for me?"

"Oh, lovely idea," said Ziva, clapping her hands. "I'll help you, Ma."

Karna fully approved of the foolproof way Yahvi and Ziva had dealt with Qalli's hysterics, and strode out of the room and down the hallway with his daughter in tow.

"Uncle K?" Satya called out tentatively.

"Yes?" Karna jogged down a broad stone stairs with a hand-woven brown-and-blue carpet running down its middle. His *shishyas*—minus Ziva—kept pace with him. Yahvi no longer appeared sleepy. Good. She didn't have time to be timid, nor he gentle.

"I believe you met with Uncle Arjun today?"

"What of it?" He'd actually hoped Indra would help him hunt down the Stone Demon, but the War God was still on his cosmic goodwill tour, and the captain of the Storm-gods had come in his stead. Arjun had also lent Karna a few dozen of the elite Maruts, the defenders of the Higher Worlds, to stand guard over Har-ki-doon.

"My father says you've invited all our fathers for Yahvi's birthday," Satya said.

Karna stopped in his tracks at the bottom of the stairs. Yahvi and Satya, who'd been dogging his heels, careened into his back with exclamations and *oof*s.

"I have," he admitted reluctantly. "I don't know if they'll get here in time...what with all the travel-between-realms protocol. So don't tell your mother yet."

"That one was so not predictable, Humpty-Dumpty," Amara said, slapping his back.

He figured it would be like cauterizing a wound—a brief moment of sizzling pain followed by blessed numbness. In truth, meeting Arjun hadn't been nearly as awkward as he'd expected, though they'd barely conversed other than the necessary. All said and done, he'd put up with anything to keep Yahvi smiling and safe.

Draupadi made her way to the den in search of Karna after seeing to her daughters' afternoon meal. She wanted to catch him alone and... She stopped short, pressing herself into the triangle formed between the open door of the den and its wall, when she heard the odious fiend singing inside.

*"Who slew the Dragon, freed the Seven Rivers,*
*And drove the kine forth from Vala's Cave?*
*Begat the fire between two stones,*
*The spoiler in warriors' battle, He, O men, is Indra."*

Her heart began to pound when she saw Lavya, the fiend, Karna and Baital lazing inside the den. They were lazing! And singing!

*"Praised by the Angirases, he slaughtered Vala,*
*And burst apart the bulwarks of the mountain.*
*He tore away the deftly built defenses.*
*These things did Indra in Soma's rapture.*
*In Soma's ecstasy, Indra spread the firmament and realms of light,*
*When he cleft Vala limb from limb."*

Draupadi ignored the pull of the melody.

"There, on the bottom screen," Karna rumbled over the Vedic verse. "Right about there. Beneath that rubble should be Vala's Cave and the Naga portal."

Draupadi tried to peek through the slit between the hinges of the doorway. She couldn't see the LCD screen on the wall, but heard Baby purr like a pleased cat, regurgitating information. She really should cease lurking and just go in. She had one last confession to make. Karna could use her in the forthcoming battle.

"The portal's closed," Karna continued explaining. "The *asuras* will need to open it to come through to the Human Realm. I think this is why we haven't found them. They're buried beneath the rubble, waiting on the other side of the portal for D day."

Draupadi strained to hear him. Why wouldn't the fiend stop singing?

*"When He with fiery lightning cleft through the weapon of reviling Vala;*
*Consumed him as tongues eat what teeth have compassed:*
*He threw the prisons of the red cows open.*
*Lord of Thunder, thou didst burst Vala's Cave rich in cows.*
*The Gods came pressing to thy side and free from terror aided thee;*

*Mid shout, loud shout and roar with the Nav-gvas, the Seven Singers, hast thou rent the mountain;*

*Thou hast, with speeders, with Das-gvas, Indra, Shakra, with thunder rent obstructive Vala."*

"Ash, shut up," Karna growled in irritation. Finally!

"Aren't you pissed there's no mention of you in the *Rg* Veda and all the glory went to Indra?" The fiend's gloved finger marked the place where he'd stopped reading the tome.

*Rg* was the oldest Veda, containing hymns in praise of the divine, some of them tens of thousands of years old. They'd been passed down orally, even after the advent of parchment, until someone got the bright idea to write them all down lest they vanish from memory.

Karna snorted. "The poet of that particular Song of Praise was no eyewitness, and to compensate made good use of a vivid imagination and liberal sense of drama to eulogize the event. Garnish the verse with a divine melody and who cares if it is historically accurate or not? Anyway, I'd rather be kept out of any such glorified mentions."

The fiend shut the book and placed it back on the bookshelf. "I prefer the Canons of Kali Yuga for the same reasons. Still, it was an accomplishment, Karna."

"What accomplishment? The only reason I got my hands on the Stone Demon was because the Naga cornered him. You know the saying: between a rock and a hard place. Well, that's where it comes from. We managed to vanquish Vrtra and exile Vala, but can you call it a victory after losing that many human lives?"

Karna's bare feet peeked out from under his *dhoti* while he paced. After a heavy silence, he said, "Let's go over the details for tomorrow again. And let the past rest in peace, shall we?"

"You can't let her go on this suicide mission, Karna," said Lavya.

Draupadi sucked in a breath.

"Shout it from the mountaintop, why don't you? You know the females are coming to get me any minute for their afternoon session, and you ask such a trigger-happy question?"

Draupadi pressed a hand to her throat. Suicide mission. He'd promised Yahvi wouldn't die.

"You know it's already too late, Karna," said the odious fiend. "Her fate was sealed yesterday."

"What the fuck do you mean by that?" asked Lavya.

Draupadi pushed off the wall and stormed into the room. "You bastards." She didn't scream, didn't shout out loud. She screamed inside. She'd known. Didn't she know the ways of glory-seeking warriors?

Their heads whipped toward her, guilt clear on their faces. Disgusted, she spun on her heels and stalked back down the hallway. Karna called out to her, but she didn't stop. She'd fetch her daughters and whether they wanted to or not, they were coming with her.

Karna caught her upper arm, forced her to a stop. "Let me explain…"

"Do it," she cut him off, frigidly. "Explain how you can give up on your own child."

His face shone a pale gold—stark against the black bandana he'd tied around his head. "Yahvi's soul is turning, Qalli."

"Turning? Red? Because of Asht Dveep?" She felt faint.

"Yes," he said. He framed her face in his hands, forcing her to look at him. "I'll find a way to help her. I made you a promise, Qalli, and I mean to keep it."

Was she trembling or were they both?

"Don't tell her," Draupadi whispered. It would kill Yahvi to know that. Dear Heaven, she couldn't think. She couldn't think what to do.

"She knows. They all do. They have known it would come to this, don't you see?" he said, making her gut twist further.

The girls had known? Yes, of course they'd known. That's why they hadn't told her. "I'm taking her away. Kubera will shelter us. He holds no bias toward red souls."

Karna's fingers bit into her upper arms when she tried to draw back from him. He apologized and eased off when she flinched.

"Don't act in haste. Give her a chance…give *me* a chance to make this right."

"No, it's too risky. What is the need to delay? The longer she stays here, the more exposed she'll be. Her soul can't have turned fully red. Not in one day."

"It hasn't. That's not it."

"Then what, Karna? You can't still want her to carry out her crazy plan? If she dies now, she *will* transform into an *asura*." Then it hit her, the reason behind his caginess. He would actually use his own daughter to kill the Stone Demon. "Let me go," she said, trying to shake off his arms. She felt sick. "I want you to let me go. I'm taking my children with me. You can say your goodbyes now."

"I asked you to trust me. I'm begging you to believe in me like I believe in you…in spite of everything…like I trust you." He released her arms and cupped her face again.

She'd trusted her father, but vengeance had been dearer to him than his own children. She'd trusted her husbands and they'd abused her trust over and over. She'd stopped trusting in anyone but herself a long time ago. She wrapped her hands around his thick wrists and pulled. It would be foolish to trust another duty-bound warrior.

"Please, *manmohini*, let me make this right," he said, his liquid-gold gaze earnest.

"The only way you can make things right is by taking your hands off our wife!" Bheem's thunderous roar ricocheted off the walls of Har-ki-doon like cannon fire.

Draupadi stared at Karna in shock. He'd listened to her. He'd called his brothers.

# CHAPTER TWENTY-FOUR

## SHATRU: ENEMY

Raka was in outrageous trouble, but Draas hosed down all the admonishments bubbling on her tongue with saliva. She hocked up and spat a glob of spit on the ground instead of saying, "I told you this was madness," like she wished to. She remained silent, not because she was angry with him for using her as one of the rungs on his ambitious ladder—which she was, make no mistake—but because Raka was more than sensible to the stigma he'd put on their clan.

She watched him with no small amount of sympathy as he stood trial for his stupidity. He was in a terrible state, feverish, fearful. But Raka didn't let on. He gave Shukra no more ammunition than the mage already had in his arsenal. For that, too, Draas held her tongue. They'd bound him in chains. Iron and silver, so he couldn't vanish. They needn't have bothered. Raka wouldn't escape. He was too proud to turn chicken.

Only Raka's eyes exposed his shame. Periodically, rivulets of blood seeped from his eyes, running down his face, dripping from his chin to the charnel ground of the Cave of the Tomb. He'd been flogged. His ear dangled from its root, torn but clotting already. The wound on his thigh festered. From groin to knee, his leg was swollen and shiny with infection. If the *danus* didn't heal him soon, there wouldn't be a Raka for their sire to free.

"The wound is mortal and inflicted with Celestial magic," the *asura* Mara had informed her family when he'd come to fetch Char Mani from their dwelling on orders of Preceptor Shukra.

Raka had truly made a mess of things. The blame for two failed missions in the name of Lord Master Vala lay squarely on his shoulders. As punishment, Shukra refused to use Sanjeevani Vidya—the magic of life renewal and revival—on Raka, as Shukra should on any warrior under his command. Shukra would save Raka only when Char Mani paid heavily for his heir's life. If Raka died of such a wound, his soul would go to Hell and be lost forever.

Greed made Shukra demand that Char Mani beggar himself. No, it was Raka's stupidity that had put their blood-sire at a disadvantage. Char Mani had hoped for news of Raka's promotion. Not this. That's why Draas had accompanied him to Naga Lok for this meeting. She stood solidly to her brother's left on the edge of a great big abyss in the middle of the cave while Char Mani negotiated with Shukra. No matter their personal discord, Raka was kin.

Draas peered into the gaping abyss that had once been a portal between the realms of the Naga and the humans. The portal had been shut down a long time ago and the cave deemed an inauspicious zone— probably why the missions had failed. But Shukra needed a scapegoat, or he would deal with Dev-Il and Vala's wraths himself. Who was the bigger coward here? Draas wanted to know.

"Don't worry," said Draas out of the corner of her mouth as Shukra shouted insults at Char Mani, at Raka, at their clan. "You know Char Mani can negotiate the fur off a demon bear." Their blood-sire had the soul of a Pani demon, Draas sometimes thought. "And once we go home, you can help Char Mani rebuild his fortune." *As you should have done to begin with*, thought Draas, but she swallowed that admonishment as well.

They'd brought a chest full of rubies and sapphires and diamonds from the mines. Char Mani was promising Shukra more, a lot more, to heal Raka.

"It was your little human friend," Raka growled abruptly. "Yahvi."

"What?" Draas's head snapped toward Raka. She tightened her hold on the fist-sized rubies that worked as handles on the bountiful chest she held.

Raka told her of the mission, breaking a vital taboo. He shouldn't be revealing this story to her, as Draas wasn't a recruit. He spoke painfully, his words slurring, his face hard and cruel. He told her a fantastic story about how a little human female had wounded him. Draas's mind raced over the events of the last few moonrises. She hadn't believed Yahvi's accusations regarding the photographs. Yahvi had been right? Lobha had betrayed Draas. Lobha and Raka, not Yahvi.

Draas felt as if her guts were being ripped into two pieces. And Yahvi had done this to Raka? That puny little human had poisoned her mighty brother with a spell?

Raka had a strange expression in his bloodred eyes that Draas had never seen before. He was sad, she realized wildly. Raka was never sad.

"Blood is thicker than water, even when diluted," Raka said, raising his chained arms up to touch her face.

"What are you thinking?" asked Draas, shaking her head. Her heart began to pound like a sledgehammer. "What do you mean to do, Raka? Don't be foolish." She threw the chest to the ground and caught her brother's forearms in a death grip. She would hold him back from his death wish, from madness. "If you just come home, everything will be fine."

"Don't mourn me, baby sister," he said, confirming Draas's doubts. She began shouting, pulling on his arms with all of her weight. From the corner of her eye, she saw the *asuras* Mara and Dves run toward her, weapons drawn.

"Avenge me, Draas," Raka roared. Weak as he was, raging with fever and loss of blood, he still jostled her to the ground and, with an insouciant bow to Char Mani and Shukra, jumped into the abyss.

Draas screamed as a blast of fire belched up from the dead, cold portal. A terrible, terrible moaning followed.

*The little fraud…*

From Har-ki-doon's rooftop, Karna watched the group of Celestials picnicking on the banks of the stream in the middle of a picture-perfect meadow. The valley floor sparkled in the sun's radiance, and the waters burst into wondrous rainbows as they leaped and gamboled across the rocky waterbed. If Hallmark made videos instead of cards, the cutesy family montage would be the top hit of this century.

The Six were standing around a pair of chestnut-brown stallions, taking turns petting and nuzzling the equine beauties. The horses belonged to Ziva and Iksa, brought as presents by Nakul and Sahadeva, much to their daughters' delight and appreciation.

Bheem, after he'd indulged in his favorite pastime and gorged on food for three continuous hours, indulged in his second-favorite pastime and dozed under the benevolent shade of a handful of Himalayan birch. As Karna understood from Lusha, roaring his lungs out always sparked the giant's hunger, and eating voraciously tuckered him out.

Without a pinch of remorse, Karna spied on Qalli and her husbands. She seemed to be on extremely good terms with all of them. Except for Yudhishtir, they'd all hugged her after the customary greeting between spouses in which the lady wife reverently bowed before her lord husband. In fact, pretty-boy Nakul seemed to be having a hard time keeping his hands off her.

Karna knew the feeling on several levels. He found it hard to keep his hands off Qalli too. And right now, he was finding it very hard to keep from imagining his hands wrapped around Nakul's throat and squeezing the larynx out of it. It was the reason why Karna was on the rooftop and Nakul was not. Distance was the key to perspective.

Qalli was reading the riot act to Arjun, who—absurdly—stood with his head bowed, nodding and shrugging and answering questions with a docility that Karna had never seen the warrior exhibit. Definitely not a stance one would associate with the captain of the Storm-gods. He'd donned a leather bomber jacket and black leather pants for his earthly excursion. What hadn't been on display due to his war helmet last night had been his hair. Liquid silver, it fell thick and straight to midthigh. Like Amara, Arjun carried more *astras* than necessary round the clock.

The little fraud, he thought again, giving free rein to his humor. It shouldn't amuse him to see her surrounded by her husbands. It hadn't amused him to watch Yudhishtir lecture her as soon as he'd greeted her. Karna had nodded to the oldest of Kunti's sons and excused himself from the rest of the show.

He'd taken Yahvi to the lagoon. There he'd called Surya and Yama to his aid and accrued their permissions to set his plans in motion. Then he'd grilled Yahvi about the plans until she'd screamed in exhaustion. He'd taken a brisk swim while Yahvi rested, then grilled her again, then once again, before heading back to the abode. Not yet ready or willing to break his silence with the sons of Kunti, he'd beelined for the rooftop to soak up more sun. Unfortunately, he'd spotted the group immediately from his vantage point and had been spying on them since.

Karna's amusement evaporated when Arjun took Qalli into his arms. Fugdoomal. They were husband and wife. He had no business feeling jealous over a man hugging his woman. An innocent hug too, one more of comfort than anything amorous. Arjun simply held Qalli while she cried. *She is mine*, Karna wanted to roar from the rooftops.

He turned away before he actually said such an asinine thing out loud, and was startled to find himself face-to-face with Yudhishtir. Karna hadn't felt him manifest on the sun-bright rooftop, busy as he'd been eavesdropping on the Celestial's wife.

"My lord," said Yudhishtir with a shallow bow and a Namaste that noblemen made to one another. He came forward and bowed low to touch Karna's feet, as one did to an older relative. "My wholehearted greetings and respect, older brother," he added with formality.

Tall, lean and dark, Yudhishtir was a handsome man. If he loosened up a bit, he'd even be the ideal man. He had his mother's midnight-blue eyes, which he'd bequeathed to Satya, and was as darkly foreboding as his sire, Yama, though not blue-skinned. He wore a *dhoti* and tunic with a simple shawl thrown over one shoulder. The garments were made of hand-spun cotton and their white starkness made him appear gaunt, as if he'd been starving for days. It was weird. No one hailing from Devlok should have looked starved even if they hadn't eaten in ages. The sallow skin and skeleton-like body frame made his shoulders seem droopy. Yudhishtir's shoulders had always been droopy, as if he constantly carried the weight of the world.

"I bid you welcome to my abode. Too bad we're not meeting in more auspicious circumstances," said Karna with equal formality.

And that's all it took—a loaded look and a brief greeting—for a lifetime of enmity and quarrel to…maybe not end, but seem not as important anymore. They'd come together to protect their women, and they would each put aside their personal feelings to do just that. It was the way of the warrior. It was the duty of a man.

"Can you handle it?" Yudhishtir asked.

Karna's hands fisted. Handle what? That the woman he wanted for himself had five husbands already? That his daughter was devolving while he wasted time on a rooftop roiling in jealousy? That he was a bastard and would always be one? That he was cursed? That he brought nothing but bad luck to the people he loved?

"I will handle it," he said roughly. If that meant he'd burn for all eternity, so be it.

Yudhishtir nodded. "The biggest problem, older brother, is we can't trust our friends any more than our foes. The Gods cannot allow her to live if she doesn't vanquish the Stone Demon. And the *asuras* most certainly will not if she does."

Karna had already come to that conclusion. Down below, Iksa galloped across the grounds with Yahvi riding shotgun. Ziva raced against them, leaving a kaleidoscope of color in her wake. Satya shouted encouragement while Amara and Lusha looked on in boredom, as they weren't part of the action.

Karna started. Yudhishtir had said *we*, as if it was his problem too. Wasn't it? His daughter was involved too.

"Your offspring need not be involved," Karna said. Damn it. He couldn't afford another mistake. "None of you need to be. I can handle it."

Yudhishtir did smile then, a slow unfurling of wit that started with the curl of his lips and rose past the blue depths of his eyes. "And you think you can stop them?"

Karna glanced down at his family, the whole mishmash of it. The sons of Kunti were his brothers. They'd always been his brothers even when none of them had known the truth. But the truth was out and acknowledged by all across the Cosmos. He was Kunti's eldest son. And by that virtue, and the virtue of the oath the lady held her sons to of sharing all and sharing alike, he was Draupadi's husband too. Yahvi wouldn't be labeled a bastard.

It was clear the sons of Kunti and Qalli considered each other family. He was glad she would have them when he was gone. "Take care of her and Yahvi."

"I always have." Yudhishtir squeezed his shoulder. "When she lets me."

Karna heaved a sigh. "Not the ideal world you left behind, is it, Yudhishtir?" He'd meant it as an offhand remark against the frustrations of fate, but it made his two-fold kinsman stiffen as if insulted.

"In an ideal world, a mother does not abandon her child. In an ideal world, I would never have been king." As always, Yudhishtir was honest to the bone.

"Didn't any of you hear me knock?" Karna asked, indicating the locked doors with a hand gesture as he manifested inside Ash's office. He made straight for the side buffet and poured himself a tall glass of *soma* juice. It amazed him how calm and relaxed he felt after his chat with Yudhishtir.

"We did, but you didn't say who you were, so we didn't answer." Lavya sat at the desk, stroking Baby.

Ash reposed in his armchair, robed elbows resting on the armrests, gloved hands steepled, eyes closed. Baital flew by Karna, belched a "Boo!" and resumed singing "Happy Birthday" as tunelessly as he could.

"Why the hell not? They know about Baital. I told them." He flopped down on the first divan he came across. He was bloody tired. It seemed as if he hadn't slept in forever. "What a day," he said and closed his eyes, placing his joined hands over his stomach.

"Did you tell them about us?"

Karna opened one eye, looked at Lavya. "Who, us?"

"Me and Ash, us."

He opened both his eyes and raised both eyebrows. "Do I need to?"

"Don't you need to?"

"Well, I don't think you need to," cut in Ash, sitting up straight. "They can't still be holding grudges. And even if they are, we cannot just stay in here till kingdom come or till they leave. But this fool refuses to let me out. He even suggested we take a long vacation, somewhere abroad. I'm thinking Bora Bora."

Karna laughed at Ash's jest. Yeah, like either Lavya or Ash were going to abandon him. "You barricaded yourselves in here because you're scared of my brothers?"

Lavya placed a hand on his chest and gasped like a British Raj debutante facing her suitor for the first time. "Wow! In one afternoon you've gone from 'the pox-ridden sons of Kunti' to 'my brothers.' You, Nathuram Godse, you."

Karna flipped him twin birds.

"Children, children, grow up. Immediately. I insist." Ash stood up and walked to the door. "If there's nothing to worry about, I'm heading out. And no, not for Bora Bora, Baital. I have mountains of work pending on our own sweet piece of coconut right here."

Baital bobbed above the desk. "Can I leave this dungeon too?"

"Hold on a minute," said Karna and quickly filled the *pisacha*, the Celestial and Lavya in on everything. "Lok Vitalas is in place?"

"Vitalas is parked and prepared by the rubble of Vala's Cave," Lavya said. "Salabha awaits further instruction."

The forces had gathered. The boundaries were marked. The prize had been set.

Tomorrow would tell which prophecy came true first: Kalika's or Tvastar's.

# CHAPTER TWENTY-FIVE
## SIMOLLANGHAN: CROSSING BORDERS

In ancient India, the Feast of Simollanghan marked the last day of the harvest season. The males of a tribe would throw down their sickles and ploughs and pick up their spears and shields. They'd leave their homeland, their wives and children, and cross the border into enemy territory to raid and pillage and vanquish the competition.

Simollanghan spread dread through all families. Simollanghan was a point of pride amongst the warriors. Simollanghan was the beginning of the war season.

Yahvi stood on the dais of the Throne Hall surrounded by love and contemplated death.

Her personal Simollanghan was only ten minutes away. At midnight, in the span of a shallow inhalation, the second hand would cross over into the eighteenth year of her life. November first was the day of her birth. It was the day of her father's death. A day of sacrifice.

Yahvi tried to banish the fear, the despair and the resentment tainting her heart. Resentment directed at the god-like blue souls laughing and dancing around the twelve-pillared great room before her. That it was she who'd insisted on the full-scale birthday party was of no consequence at the moment. She'd demanded presents. She'd demanded a behemoth birthday cake baked by Lusha's magic hands. She'd demanded that everyone get dressed as if it was a queen's coronation, and she was about to be crowned queen on her father's gorgeous lapis lazuli and silver throne commanding a prime spot in the grand Throne Hall. She'd be the queen whose reign wouldn't last past a single day.

Such evil thoughts crammed inside her head, brought on by the evil spreading through her soul. And that added fuel to the already present resentment. It was totally unfair that Ved's soul was fine in spite of being possessed by a *danu* demon while her pathetic, puny female soul was infected because she'd swallowed *raaksasa* venom-blood when she'd bitten the *asura* Raka's ear. Ash and Ziva had theorized that Yahvi's stupidity was the cause of the turning. Yahvi wanted to see them bite an *asura* and not swallow reflexively.

Yahvi absolutely loathed Ash. Mama had been right about him. Ash was a monster. Ziva, under his tutelage, had become one too. The quacks had been pouring disgusting liquids down her throat every hour by the hour. Ghastly stuff, nasty stuff that made her want to puke her guts out. Next time they made her choke on the antivenom, she'd take careful aim and vomit on them.

"You okay?" Her father sprang up in front of her.

She hated the way candlelight bounced off his golden hair. It made her eyes throb and hurt. "Why? Has my soul turned redder?"

A massive scalloped skylight was cut into the ceiling of the Throne Hall. The vast blackness beyond it soothed her eyes. Yahvi wished someone would douse the firelit torches in the chamber so that the moon's light would reach her. Why was everything so bright and glowy?

Why was her father talking to his slayer? All of a sudden the whole gaggle of blue souls had become BFFs with each other? What happened to the ages and ages of mutual hatred?

"*Vatse*, what's wrong?" The golden creature peered into her eyes with his golden eyes.

"Are my eyes changing? They feel as if they're bleeding." He didn't answer. She didn't need him to. She could feel it. The need to destroy, the desire to annihilate simmered within her belly.

A Celestial hurried up the steps of the dais, festooned in a gossamer white sari and golden blouse. She took one look at Yahvi's face and seared the Soul Warrior with her fierce eyes.

*Celestial? Soul Warrior?*

Spinning satellites! For a second, Yahvi had felt absolutely no connection with her own mother and father. She took a deep, deep breath and whooshed it out. *I am a good soul. I am a good soul. I am a good soul.*

"Come on. Let's go for a walk. We can both benefit from some fresh air." Her father took her cast-free arm and led her off the dais.

She embarrassed him. Hadn't she known it? He didn't want the others to know about her. "Don't want to send panic flares through the party, do you? Don't want to call attention to your weak bloodline?"

His jaw tightened but he held his tongue.

"This is scaring me, Karna," Mama said tremulously. "I think we should reconsider this plan. Why can't we go to Alaka?"

Scary? She'd show Mama scary. Show her what it felt like to be locked in a palace fortress forever.

"She's fine. And we spoke about this. There's nowhere safe for her now."

Except the Demon Realm, thought Yahvi. Dev-Il would welcome her with how-many-ever open arms he currently sported.

"We cut the cake in ten minutes," said Mama, sighing in defeat, and Daddy nodded.

Oh yes, the big bad death-day cake that she'd stab at twelve sharp.

Ash was waiting for them outside the Throne Hall. "Drink this. All of it." He thrust a huge goblet in her hands.

Yahvi drank every single drop and immediately felt the pressure ease from her diaphragm. Every nasty, horrible thought vanished from her head. She felt like herself. She was just glad she could breathe again.

"Good?" Ash asked and she nodded. She didn't feel like throwing up. He patted her head and disappeared down the corridor, boots scrunching.

Of course, guilt and embarrassment quickly filled up the empty pockets of her soul that the darkness had left behind—guilt for obvious reasons and embarrassment because the stupid green thing inside her wasn't even defending its territory. It was letting the venom swirl right in and set up house.

A labyrinth of passageways surrounded the Throne Hall, connecting it to the various parts of the abode via pretty little gazebos. Daddy led her down a long, tree-shaded *shamiana* to the courtyard. They sat side by side on the old silver swing that had become her nightly haven. Yahvi loved watching Har-ki-doon at night. Everything glimmered and sparkled, even the sequins and pink faux stones on her outfit. The whole abode was alive and alit. Not a single room was dark. Not a single soul slept. They wouldn't leave her alone. Not tonight.

Daddy wore a suit to honor her last requests. It was black, stylishly cut and incredibly flattering to his fair coloring. He drew her to him, tucking her into the shelter of his arm.

"It's all right to be afraid, *vatse*," he said softly, rubbing her good arm. "And remember, no matter what happens or doesn't happen, I will move Heaven and Earth for you."

Tears stung her eyes and she blinked them back. She'd made them all promise not to cry, most especially Mama. She'd made them swear not to fight or bicker about stuff. Even Uncle Bheem had agreed and was restricting himself to nasty looks directed at Daddy rather than calling him out to fight a bloody duel over Mama.

Yahvi tried to shake off the gloom. She wanted this. She'd volunteered for it. She had no business feeling sorry for herself.

"I am so very proud of you, *vatse*. Here, open your hand."

Yahvi sat up, obeying her father. Then, in shock, she watched him call *Asi* to his open palm. He gave her the dagger, hilt first. It was twenty-two inches long from tip to base. Not heavy, but heavy enough. She tested its weight, flipping it in the air—so different from the serpent-knife or Amara's Joysticks. Longer, lighter, easier to handle.

"For me?" she glanced at her father quickly, then dropped her gaze back to the gleaming *Asi*. The sun motif was carved into either side of the iron-and-gold hilt. She ran her fingers down the adamantine blade. It was thick at the base and tapered evenly to the tip. "But it's yours to call. Grandsire Surya gave it to you on your first kill."

He smiled. "And I'm giving it to my daughter on hers. It is your heritage, Yahvi. *Asi* will obey you from now and not me."

Her heart expanded with love. He honored her by his faith. She wouldn't cry. She would not let him down. She would protect him. "Thank you."

"My pleasure, *vatse*," he replied. He caressed her hair, touched her face—her cheeks, nose, chin—as if he was reading her by Braille.

"I'll make you as proud of me as you were of your nine sons," she promised softly, not wanting this moment to end.

His body tightened as if she'd touched a nerve. She knew he hadn't kept track of his sons' souls even when he could have. Lord Yama wouldn't have denied the Soul Warrior that. But Yahvi guessed why he hadn't kept track. One shouldn't hold on to the past. But how could one help it when the past so often found its way into the present? It also had something to do with emotions and how one dealt with them. Some souls were far braver than others when it came to matters of the heart. Ziva said that most men would rather flounder around the Cosmos wallowing in self-imposed loneliness than actually work at achieving a blissful soul state. Whether Ziva meant men as in *male* or men as in *mankind* was anybody's guess. Well, her parents weren't going to suffer such a fate, not if she could help it.

"Daddy, will you promise me something?"

"No," he said, grinning at her. "I've made you enough promises tonight."

She pouted and his reaction was instantaneous. He kissed her forehead and said, "Shoot."

"Promise me you won't let Mama grieve for me. Not a lot, anyway. You won't let her go mental. You will always be by her side, no matter what, even if she angers you or yells at you or anything. Promise me you'll never let her be lonely ever again."

He went utterly still, staring at her for a long, long moment. "I promise you will not die, *vatse*. And that's all the promise I'm willing to give."

Midnight came and brought with it her birthday.

Everyone inundated her with wishes and blessings and gentle teasing as she blew out eighteen candles in one breath. Yahvi slid the bow-tied *Asi* into her cake. She drew the blade down and sliced the Tokarev TT-30 in half. Another wish had come true. She'd gotten a gun for her birthday—a smoking gun-shaped chocolate cake, a Lusha special. Her family came to her and fed her pieces of the cake. She fed them bits in return. She hugged them and told them how much she loved them. They all cried, just for a few seconds. Even Amara. Tough, tearless Amara had tears swimming in her flash-silver eyes. Yahvi held Amara's gaze and made sure her sister minded their blood-oath. Then one by one her sisters' arms came around her until they formed their awesome group of six.

"I love you so much. Thank you for coming with me," she said, overwhelmed by what they'd done for her—would do for her. This was her fight. It was her destiny. They hadn't let her face it alone. "You're right, Iksa. It's so much better with family all around you."

"Silly sister." Satya pulled Yahvi into a hug. "As if we'd let you have all the fun alone."

High above them, a single shooting star streaked red and yellow against the night sky. But Yahvi sought only the Soul Warrior's face, and wished her father a long and happy life.

Perfect timing, thought Karna, watching several meteorites burn through Earth's atmosphere. A single shooting star-like object raced ahead, its trajectory guided by fate. He cursed at it, instead of wishing on it.

Lavya and Arjun stared at the spectacle through the skylight and asked in unison, "It's Vala?"

"Who else?" He glanced at the Six huddled together in a familiar show of solidarity. "Ready?"

"As we'll ever be, O Captain, Our Captain." Amara's enthusiasm and utter refusal to court negativity amazed him.

Karna addressed the crowds filling the Throne Hall. "All right, everyone. It's time. Go change. Gather your gear. We rendezvous in five minutes."

The Six disappeared before he'd even finished talking. The hall emptied rapidly. Every soul in the room knew his or her duty. The warriors would join them in battle and rest would wait behind, preparing for the aftermath.

His brothers' would assist him as he'd asked, except Yudhishtir, an eternal pacifist. He would wait at Har-ki-doon. He'd laid down his sword after the Great Kuru War, swearing a blood-oath never to pick it up again. The other four seemed almost eager to do some damage. They were adults. They knew what they risked by choosing to act rather than remain karma-free in the Age of Kali.

He held his hand out to Qalli. She took it immediately, in full view of her husbands. They vanished to his—their—chambers. Their garments were laid out already, black against the silver-and-oak-wood valet. Every piece of clothing was treated with magic potions and protection mantras. He pulled on leather pants and a T-shirt, then strapped on the full-body Kevlar armor—a ridiculous suit Qalli insisted he wear.

"Karna," she whispered, raw pain in her voice. "I never thought...I never knew what my actions would bring about. I can't lose her. Lose any of them. But I...oh, cursed fate! I don't want to lose you, either. I'm sorry for dragging you into this. So sorry for everything."

"I'm not. I wouldn't change a thing." He kissed her. Rough, hot, a kiss that did not try to allay her fears but one that expressed his own—a kiss that said goodbye.

She pressed her cheek to his. "Why can't we change it...fate? Why can't we all just vanish from this place?"

"Hush, *manmohini*," he said and tapped her chin one final time. "There's no turning back."

# CHAPTER TWENTY-SIX
## SENA: FORCES OF GOOD AND EVIL

At twenty-five minutes past midnight on the first of November, legion leaders of the army of the Soul Warrior huddled around a makeshift conference table inside the Shrieking Sura, pouring over a map of the enemy terrain.

To call the crude, haphazard scribbles on the Doodle app "a map" was a joke. And to call the eighteen hundred motley soldiers making up the ranks "an army" was pushing it, but Karna couldn't think of another term to apply to the forces awaiting orders outside.

There were the half breeds and outcast Celestials from the *loks* that on occasion helped him out, and the Maruts led by Arjun. There were the *pahadis* of Har-ki-doon who'd freely volunteered their services because they felt that they owed Ash and him their lives. Then there were the denizens of Vitalas who were in it for the gold and nothing else. He just prayed that the human-*asura* hybrids or the shape-shifters under Salabha's command didn't flip over in the middle of the siege and join their kind inside Vala's Cave.

He'd once commanded an army of a million-plus warriors and had trusted every single one of them with his life. And even then he had lost the Kuru War. Arjun had commanded an army with half as many warriors and won it. Good fortune and good strategy won a war, and Arjun had both those in abundance. He always had.

"Since there is only one entry port into the cave, we'll attack in waves," Arjun said. "Celestials to the Earth-dwellers, strongest to the weakest, male to female."

"Pops!" Amara glared at her father.

"Quiet!" Arjun's reprimand cracked like thunder inside the roomy tent, his silver eyes and hair flashing steel at being interrupted. But his gaze softened as it met his offspring's pugnacious pout. "Even coming in last, Amara, you will see plenty of action. There will be more than enough *asuras* for you to vanquish."

Twenty thousand *asuras* lay in wait for them, and that was a conservative estimate. The Serpent King had finally chosen a side. He'd declared his allegiance in favor of Light even though Vala was one of his own. While the Naga would not actually fight against their own kinsmen, they'd given permission to Karna to invade Naga Lok and extract Vala out.

"What do you think, brother?" Arjun's inquiry was mired in apology. Karna nodded. "Sounds good."

"If I may point out that we are basing our strategy of the terrain on the hazy recollections of a heavily drugged and soundly beaten human, the desperate confessions of a couple of captured *asuras*...who most likely have passed on false information. If we go inside that bottomless tomb, we'll be at their mercy. I say we drop a tornado in and smoke the evil out, fight them on our turf," said one of the Storm-gods.

"That's one possibility," began Arjun. But before Karna could shake his head in a negative, he added, "The thing is, we don't want to smoke them out. We want them trapped inside their comfort zone. We want them to feel safe and superior and mighty. And we definitely don't want them crawling out into the Human Realm. Right, brother?"

All true. The battle must not go above ground or anywhere close to human turf. Luckily, craggy, sparsely forested hills and desert-like land were all anyone could see for miles. Human settlements were sparse around this inauspicious spot, but they were there, and these days even the sparse settlements ran into populations of thousands. Yeah, below ground was best.

Lok Vitalas was camped right on top of the ruins of Vala's Cave. Salabha had soon discovered a way in, not five kilometers downhill from where they stood. Early tonight, a couple of *asuras*—of the young and stupid variety—had predictably swaggered into Vitalas to make merry. The fools had been arrested, questioned and dispatched to Yama in Hell.

"Any visions that tell us whether this will work or not?" Karna asked the two resident *rsis*, seers.

"It will work," said Sahadeva unequivocally. In contrast, Iksa looked stricken.

Karna sighed. He'd known better than to ask, but he'd asked anyway and got the usual conflicting predictions. He glanced sideways at Arjun.

"It's your call. You're in charge. Cease this, Arjun," he growled when the war-god apologized again for usurping Karna's position. "It's your command, your decision. Do what you think is best."

An army cannot have two commanders just like a war cannot have two victors; it was as simple as that. An army needed a commander that would see it safely through to the end, not one who was setting himself up as bait.

Arjun stiffened at the reprimand and—*whoopee!*—barked out orders. It had been Karna's decision to have Arjun in charge of the operation. Yet envy clenched his gut when Arjun took command and addressed the assembled troops. Qalli squeezed his hand painfully, reminding him exactly why things had to be this way. She hadn't moved from his side, not since midnight. Not since he'd gifted his god-powers to his daughter on her birthday.

Here's the thing about portents: They were riddled with loopholes.

The moon curved like a serpent's head in the sky, predicting a win for the Naga. Did that mean the Soul Warrior's army held the upper hand as the Serpent People supported it or did it mean a victory for Vala, who was part Naga?

As a small number of warriors boasted the power of vanishment, they'd been called on to transport the legions to a predetermined location close to the entrance to Vala's Cave. The mouth was small and a scouting mission had revealed an endless tunnel snaking beyond it. The army would breach the enclosure in bursts. Karna would lead the last wave in, with the females.

He was keeping a close eye on Amara and Lusha, in case they disobeyed commands and ran off into the cave before they were meant to, when he caught sight of Bheem, dodging through the hordes toward him. He was clad in a short *dhoti* and nothing else—no shield, body armor or shoes. He held his *Gadda*, the club of destruction, over one shoulder. Glowering like a rogue elephant, he came to a halt before Qalli. He ignored Karna totally.

"I don't like this. You should be in Devlok, safe with Mother."

"Don't be silly." Qalli smiled at the menacing aspect without fear. "I might not be a war veteran, but I've been a peripheral part of enough battles to know how to take care of myself and our children. And I was our offspring's guru before their fathers took over."

"I don't like this," Bheem grunted again. He hadn't taken the news of Karna joining the ranks of the sons of Kunti at all well.

Karna braced himself for some lovely words of loathing from the petulant giant.

"Stop trying to make trouble where there is none." Qalli poked Bheem's bare chest, rough with hair, hard with muscle, damp with sweat. It was humid and hot even in the middle of the night, and as they would soon descend into a furnace-like atmosphere, the males had stripped down to their skivvies or loincloth-like garments.

Bheem flashed a deadly smile. "There's still hope, Wife. He'll be dead soon. Then all will return to normal again."

"Bheem!" Qalli cried in shock. "What is the matter with you? Apologize to Karna!"

Instead of an apology, Bheem shoved Karna out of his way and stalked off. The glancing blow almost knocked Karna on his butt. But Qalli and Nakul came to his rescue.

"Glad to see we're all getting along," said Nakul, laughing, while Qalli sputtered apologies for Bheem's behavior. He slapped Karna on the back in a gesture of manly camaraderie. "I've got your back, brother. You too, sweetling," he said, kissing Qalli on her check before he too strode off to take his place at the head of the troops.

One by one, the brothers came to wish Qalli and him luck. Paying their last respects, Karna thought dourly. How he'd survived an entire day of Bheem's infantile behavior, Nakul's incessant laughter, Sahadeva's all-knowing smiles, Arjun's apologetic arrogance and Yudhishtir's compassionate words without murdering one or all of them was anybody's guess. He rolled the shoulder Bheem had attacked, checking for muscle damage. Each one of the brothers was a head case. No wonder Qalli had run away from them.

"Here, let me massage that for you," she offered, digging her thumbs into his shoulder and neck muscles. It felt good and he groaned in appreciation.

While Qalli got rid of the kinks in his back, Karna took stock of his *shishyas* again. All accounted for, presently. Yahvi flitted from sister to sister, full of nervous energy. The doses of antivenom and *amrita* had arrested the evil virus, and the god-powers had completely healed her body. Her cast was off; the cuts and bruises had vanished. Her soul should be moss green too, but impossible to confirm until the powers reverted back to him come midnight.

"Menacing mercury! Did you get hurt, Daddy?" she cried when she spotted him getting a massage. "I told you this was a bad idea. I don't know why Grandsire Surya and Lord Yama agreed to this."

"Try and relax." He pulled on her ponytail when she ran up. She swatted his hand away.

"I can't. I feel as if an ocean full of *soma* juice is flowing through my veins," she said, bouncing on the balls of her feet. "There's this weird thing happening right here, in my solar plexus, as if I'm going to burst like a bomb."

Qalli ceased her magic massage. "Is that normal? What if something went wrong with the exchange?"

"It's normal," Karna assured them both. He missed his god-powers, missed the feeling of invincibility, the constant pressure of strength. Missed the colors swirling about him. Missed seeing souls, period.

"How does it feel to look into the depths of a soul, *vatse*?" he asked, just as a loud whistle pierced the night air, silencing them all. The exodus was complete.

Another long bleat signaled the beginning of the next phase. Arjun and Salabha would lead the first wave into Vala's Cave. Lavya and Ash would lead the second. The sense of urgency increased as the troops began to squeeze into the narrow opening in the hill. No vanishment would be used from this point on, to conserve energy and to keep them all together in one pack. It made no sense to manifest amongst the *asuras* blindly and in limited numbers.

"You have matching souls. Did you know that?" said his daughter, grinning at them both.

Qalli's soul was the deep blue of a *pushkara* in bloom, sprinkled with stardust. His was too? He'd never been able to see his own soul. He bent and planted a quick kiss on Qalli's lips before she even thought to get emotional.

"Daddy, what if I fail? What if…"

"You won't fail," he said firmly. He wouldn't let her fail. He would challenge the Stone Demon first. After all, it was Karna he wanted. "You are made of the sun and fire. Remember that. Just remember that." He wrapped his arms around his daughter and met Qalli's eyes over her head. He'd done the best he could under the circumstances. He'd given their child a chance to survive. He'd made her too powerful to kill.

Blasts of lightning burst out of the cave's mouth. Arjun was clearing a deadly path through the *asuras* to the mother lode. Soon the ground began to shake and roar beneath their feet and they had to fight to keep their balance. News channels would report a midsized earthquake in the news tomorrow, ideally with zero human casualties.

Amara and Lusha jumped up on a couple of massive rocks flanking the entrance, shouting encouragement to the marchers, urging the hordes to move faster. Lusha made grotesque faces, waving her can of mace in the air. Her combat strategy was to use pepper spray to blind the *asuras*, then rip them apart with her hands. Amara swished the Joysticks about and accompanied each move with asinine Bollywood blockbuster sound effects. *"Dishum-dishum-dishum! Pow-pow! Boom!"* Briefly, they'd distracted the non-soldiers from their panic.

Baital flew close, hooting madly. "Reporting for duty, my lord," he said, saluting with one blue hand. The other he slapped on his naked hips. Not naked—he wore a black loincloth, adroitly hiding whatever it was that resided between his bat-legs. "Come child, get on my shoulders and we'll be off." The flying *pisacha* would give Yahvi an added advantage in the danger zone. Karna lifted Yahvi and seated her on her ride.

"Keep her safe. And close to us," ordered Qalli.

When Qalli went to take his hand again, Karna shook his head. "This is it, my love. This is where we part. I need both my hands. So do you."

He drew an adamantine broadsword out of its scabbard, swishing it about in preparation. He wrapped his left hand around the handle of a *chabuk*—whip—hooked to his belt. Crafted with the aid of thunder and lightning, the divine *chabuk* belonged to Arjun. Karna had grudgingly accepted use of it for the battle, as his own *astras* would heed only Yahvi.

Qalli stripped off her T-shirt and tossed it to the ground, exposing a lean-muscled torso in a black tank top. She conjured a fiery gold ball, juggling it effortlessly from hand to hand. He drank the lady warrior in. She smelled so good and looked even better. He'd never seen this side of her and had to admit it was sexy as hell. Words leaped up from his soul onto his tongue. Scary words. Foolish words. Words he dared not say out loud.

She stared turbulently at Yahvi, pupils glittering like diamonds under the shorn hair that framed her pixie face.

"Try not to bomb the place down," he said, distracting her with some tongue in cheek.

She flicked him a glance as insouciant as Amara's. "Try and stop me. And don't make this into a bigger tragedy than it already is, either one of you. I'm fresh out of boons."

Then she whirled around and took off, her ass flashing like a perfect black heart above golden thigh-high leather boots for a second before the cave swallowed her up. By karma! She truly was the perfect mate to his soul.

Grinning from cheek to cheek, Karna howled in lieu of a conch shell that would've signaled his entry onto the battlefield. Then he too raced through the stone crevice to keep the unexpected promise of his blood alive.

# CHAPTER TWENTY-SEVEN
## DHARMA-YUDDHA: JUST WAR

A just war is a myth.

War by its very nature is unjust. It generates a wanton waste of life, thriving on hatred and enmity, forcing souls to perform the most heinous acts in the name of victory. Who in his right mind would call such a thing just?

The reasons for waging wars can be and often are noble. Wars are fought to uphold ideals, to restore birthrights, to preserve a way of life, to change a way of life. Wars are fought so virtue can prevail and vice be destroyed. But who decides what is virtue and what is vice? Surely it can't be the war itself. The war that indiscriminately claims all winners as virtuous. For that matter, who is to decide that the reason to wage war is righteous enough to justify the resulting atrocity?

Nearly twelve hours after breaching Vala's Cave, a bloody, grimy and grim-faced Karna slashed his way down another flight of stairs. No, not stairs. *Stairs* was too elegant a word for the treacherous footholds he clambered down. Whirling the *chabuk* over his head, he brought it down with all his waning might on the three *asuras* advancing on him, cutting all three in half. The halved bodies thrashed about on the steps until Karna kicked them over the edge of the stairs, plunging them down eleven levels in a vertical drop.

He was still stumped by how deep and wide the cave was. Ninety-nine levels of stairs spiraled in ever-widening circles to the bottom. The path had been cleared as per the plan. His wave of the legion hadn't come across a single Red until they'd descended to the sixty-sixth floor, where the battle raged across several flights of stairs.

He'd prepared for the unexpected. After all, he'd witnessed Vala's Cave being sucked into the ground and a mountain collapsing on top of it, so for it to be in use again meant that the *asuras* had begun to restructure parts of it. *Restructure* was an understatement; they'd excavated the bloody thing and then some.

It was a hive. Vala's Cave was like a monster beehive. Bell-shaped and peppered with honeycomb fissures through its innards, the tomb-like abodes of the *asuras* and a vertigo-boosting staircase carved into the wall from mouth to womb.

Karna took a much-needed breather, letting his heart playing a bongo in his chest calm down. There was no one five steps above or below him, so he quickly took stock. Their army had dwindled down to less than fifty percent, but so had Vala's.

Did the survival of one soul, his child, justify the hundreds—no, thousands, if he counted the *asuras*—of lives snuffed? Was he selfish? Were they wrong? Should he have let Yahvi succumb without a fight?

Lavya materialized, doing his whirligig impersonation. He seemed to be everywhere at once, bow and arrow at the ready. "Is that a good idea? You are vulnerable today, Karna."

It was hot as Hell and Karna, blood and sweat streaming down his body, had begun stripping off his body armor and T-shirt. "Fug vulnerability. I'm being boiled alive. If I don't let my skin breathe, I'll die of a heatstroke." He flung the suit away. "Much better." He heaved a sigh, rotating his arms, liking a lot that his range of motion had taken a turn for the better.

Lavya cleared his throat and pointed his arrowhead three flights down to Qalli, shooting them both very dirty looks while throwing firebombs at the Reds, making Karna grin.

His grin turned into a full-blown laugh when Lavya pithily said, "Pray you do die in battle or of a heatstroke. I wouldn't want to survive and face her wrath, I tell you."

"Ah! Gods! I'd needed that," said Karna. But they'd dallied long enough. "Stay whole, my friend. I'll see you at the bottom."

He snatched up his weapons, leaped down to the landing on level ten and bulled his way into a gang of screaming, writhing Reds as Bheem and Lusha treated them like Ping-Pong balls. Karna swung his sword up, cracked the whip down and dove right in.

"Careful, your father's the bait," Baital shouted as Yahvi taunted a couple of nasty, pointy-fanged blood drinkers with huge black wings. "You are the Trojan horse. Don't show the Catcher yet."

They shot upward as the enemy *pisachas* gave chase. Yahvi twisted around and shot two arrows through their hearts, two through their heads. Shifted aim to her left, took down a *daitya* advancing on a fallen ally. She was supposed to bide time and conserve her energy until the main event. Not happening! She was *not* going to sit in a corner and pray while their side got trampled all around her. Not that she had anything against praying. She sent up a quick prayer to the Matriarchs in apology.

The cave periodically went pitch-black when the chasm below choked like a faulty chimney and billowed noxious smoke through the space. It was thick with fumes now, but the smoke was dissipating, showing her clearly what should've been invisible to her. Baital's soul was a tiny red button that grew and shrank, grew and shrank at the base of his skull between her legs. That tiny button was Baital. Destroy his physical body and Baital would still exist in that tiny red button, as that tiny red button. Amazing!

A soul was immortal. Once created, it couldn't be destroyed. It could only transform.

Unless someone accidently (on purpose) created a slayer of souls.

"Daddy was a fool to trust me with his powers," Yahvi said. She fit another arrow to her bow, pulled, took aim at a red dot and shot it down. "But hey, who listens to puny little green souls who are about to turn evil?"

"Oh, stop moping. It's quite annoying," said Baital crankily. "Being red is not so bad."

Lightning flashed through the space as Uncle Arjun brandished his thunderbolt on the *asuras*. She heard his whistle, signaling yet another level conquered. The Soul Warrior's army was gaining ground, literally. Yahvi looked down, way down through the rising smog where the meat of the action was.

"Take me lower," she urged Baital with her words and her thighs.

Baital pinched her calves. "Stop that. I'm not a horse." But he flew lower and lower, carefully, always carefully, keeping her safe from the battling throngs.

Amazing! She hadn't even felt the pinch and it wasn't because of her bodysuit. It was the god-powers.

Yahvi discharged a steady stream of arrows the whole time. They passed nonnerdish Lavya. He sat on his haunches at the edge of a step, masterfully plying his bow. He'd fascinated her over the past two weeks, but since gaining the powers, she hadn't been able to stop gaping. He knew exactly why she stared and refused to meet her eyes. Lavya's soul could be classified as a dull brick red. She hadn't told anyone about Lavya being an *asura*, not even Amara. She wasn't sure why but she wanted to keep his secret. Just like Daddy was.

Baital flew lower. Lavya moved above sight range. They passed the next level and that's when Yahvi spotted Draas.

Ninety-six floors down, three more to go and the bottom of the damn hive was a jump away. Karna was tempted to leap. Just get it over with. But he didn't. Commander Arjun's orders were to stick together in enemy territory. So he'd stick together to the very end and into the very depths of the enemy territory.

"My lord! My lord!" Baital flew straight to Karna, red eyes frantic. He was shockingly pristine. No signs of battle smeared his blue-black body. No sign of Yahvi either.

"I told you not to set her down," Karna shouted, trying to spring free of the *asuras* advancing on him. Satya came to his aid, drawing the Reds to her, and Nakul rushed in to help her out by slashing their heads off. Freed temporarily, Karna zeroed in on Baital.

"She took her...she took the child," Baital moaned.

"Who took whose child, *pisacha*?" Qalli was by Karna's side in a flash.

Baital's eyes bugged out in disbelief. "My lady, how many children did you leave me with?"

Karna got between the Red and Blue. "Enough! There's no time for this. Speak, Baital."

"It was a *raaksasa*, my lord—a pretty one, at that. The child called her Draas and waved at her—it was abnormal. But the *asura* grabbed Yahvi's wrist in the normal nonfriendly manner. They grappled. They shouted at each other. The child toppled and they both poofed."

Karna swore viciously and gripped Qalli's hand. "Tell everyone, *pisacha*. Go!"

Baital didn't waste time. Qalli didn't either. Together they vanished to ground zero, near the abyss that had once been the portal between the Realm of the Naga and the realm of humans. It was charmed shut now, in compliance with the Treaty of Quarantine and because of Vala's destructive actions.

It was way, way hotter down there. The atmosphere was ugly and pungent as the odors of searing flesh and hair and bone bombarded them. The abyss hissed and spat fire and smoke. It obscured his view of what lay behind it, and what lay in front made his stomach turn. Half-mutilated bodies of humans, animals and *asuras* lay heaped, gilded monstrously by firelight. Most were alive, barely. Close to twenty humungous *daityas* waded through the bodies, picking them up at random and hurling them into the pit. This was Vala's doing. What surrounded him was not the carnage of battle but the manic actions of a soul gone mad.

"Vala!" Karna shouted wrathfully. He toed the rim of the fire pit, trying to look beyond the mounds of death. This would end now. He shouted out to Vala again and again until a hoarse chuckle wove itself into the broadcasting echoes. It grew louder, became a fanatical laugh. Soon it was the only sound bouncing off the walls all around them.

Dare he manifest on the other side and into an ambush, or should he fight his way through the *daityas*? No! He couldn't do that. He couldn't climb over the bodies as if they were already dead. He wouldn't do that even if they were dead.

Karna grabbed Qalli's hand and signaled for her to take them across the pit when sudden movements behind them made them both freeze. Qalli looked back but he didn't. He didn't dare take his eyes off the fire and what lay beyond it. She squeezed his hand hard a split second before he heard a voice in his head.

*Relax, brother. We've got your back. I shall be your eyes.*

*Sahadeva?* Karna thought incredulously.

*Yes, brother.*

*When did I give you permission to freakin' read my mind?* Outrage at his privacy being so invaded fueled the temper already simmering in him. All-knowing freaking bastard! Who wouldn't be all-knowing with the power of telepathy?

*Maybe we could deal with your unrealistic privacy issues at a more leisurely time?*

Karna clenched his jaw tight. *What's happening? Can you see over the fire and smoke?*

*No. But I can get into their heads.*

A series of facts implanted in Karna's mind all at once. The females stood behind him. Lavya and Bheem were to his back left; Sahadeva, Salabha and Ash were to his right; Arjun and Nakul guarded the stairs at the bottom with the remainder of their army, not letting any creature pass up or down. The *asuras* were deserting their ranks, melting away into the walls. They were vanishing to safe locations, or their cells were escape routes leading away from the cave. Satya now mind-controlled the pallbearer *daityas* and had bid them to freeze like ice sculptures.

*The ones on the other side are top-tier asuras. I can't read their minds at all. Can only sense them. Not that many. But they are powerful.*

*And Yahvi?*

*Don't worry. She's unharmed. A bit frightened. The* asura *Draas holds her captive. They are arguing like a pair of siblings. There seems to be a dispute over who should feel more betrayed between them. Amara is inching toward them.*

Karna exhaled, and the viselike grip on his gut loosened a bit. They hadn't failed.

"Vala!" he roared and charged forward. Satya's mind-fucking was working superbly. The *daityas* bent, and he leaped over them to the other side, landing on his feet, sword and *chabuk* in hand. His eyes quickly sought out and found Yahvi dangling from Draas's arms, captor and captive nose-to-nose and muttering at each other. She really was fine. No blood anywhere, nothing broken. Draas panted heavily, in fatigue or fury? Two *asuras* stood close to her.

*The massive one is called Mara and the armed one is Dves.*

Both *asuras'* eyes were fixed on the same focal point. Karna followed their gaze to a darker-than-dark space staining the anus of the cave. He wondered how in hell it remained pitch-black with the massive fire raging so close to it. Equidistant from the pit and the darkness, two *danu* demons sat cross-legged on the ground, cloaked in skin-tattoos and *raakh*. They were in the throes of a ritual, eyes shut, their bodies churning in continuous circles, their mouths moving in faultless incantation. Four jewel-cast goblets sat on a serving tray before the fire pit. Other ritual paraphernalia were strewn about, objects of oblation to be offered to the deity they sought to appease.

"Vala!" shouted Karna like a broken record.

"Lord Master Vala," growled the colossus Mara.

"Do I look like I fucking care about his title?" Karna snarled. He stepped toward the darkness. Dves raised a hand and a battlement of *asuras* filed in, blocking his path. "What?" Karna raised his eyebrows at the sentries. "He's hiding? Spinning around the Cosmos has turned you into a chicken, eh, Vala?"

Karna braced himself when Mara and Dves both raised their swords in clear threat. It was obvious Satya hadn't yet reached into their minds, or the *danus'*. The chanting went on unhindered around them. And Vala still didn't show himself.

*He seems confused, brother, like he doesn't understand you. Try another tongue.*

Karna mentally smacked his forehead. Vala had been exiled for five thousand years. Obviously he'd be conversant only in the Language of the Ancients, a language that predated even Vedic Sanskrit, a most rudimentary form of communication that had prevailed in the Realm of the Naga, Vala's home realm. Karna hadn't spoken it in a long time.

"Vala," he began again, trying to recall how one said "fucking bastard" in the obsolete tongue. Then he remembered that one couldn't. *Bastard* wasn't even a word in the Language of the Ancients, as marriages hadn't yet become formalized institutions. As for fucking, the propagation and survival of most life forms depended on fucking—in its infinite varieties—and therefore it was not an insult at all but a mandatory duty for any species. *Asuras* enjoyed fucking every bit as intensely as the next organic species.

The sinister laugh abated to a snigger. Something shifted within the depths of the darkness. It rumbled forward.

Karna remembered the sound of Vala, like rocks sliding down a mountain, the hair-raising sound of the Stone Demon's menacing stride. The sentries parted and Vala came into view. Gooseflesh broke across Karna's skin. Impossibly, the Stone Demon looked exactly as he had the day Karna had challenged him to a *dwanda-yuddha*—a duel.

A *dwanda-yuddha* was the highest and only form of just war. Two warriors, matched in size, strength and skill locked in personal combat until the loser surrendered his life and an indisputable winner emerged.

Karna would've liked today's duel to have the same odds. But it wasn't to be.

The last moments of his battle with Vala flashed through Karna's mind. The *Manav-astra*. The screams. The darkness. He'd been tired of duelling, terrified for his own soul, and had taken the most expedient route to get rid of the scourge. The spear had met its mark, but the spell of humanity hadn't touched Vala's soul at all.

Vala scraped to a stop a few feet in front of Karna. Metallic black stone rippled in the light of the fire. The demon was perfectly chiseled from the curling hair on his head to the rounded curves of his toenails, black as night except for the bloodred eyes.

"I see you bullied someone to carve you a new body," Karna said. The last time Karna had seen him, the Stone Demon had been missing his arms, one full leg and a good portion of his torso.

Vala's lips parted, showing bunches of sharp, cruel fangs. Karna glanced at Yahvi. She still argued with Draas. *Tell her to get ready,* he silently bade Sahadeva.

*She is ready, brother.* To confirm it, Yahvi ceased her argument and looked straight at Karna. She nodded imperceptibly. Draas froze, her frown darting from Yahvi to him. Behind them, Amara had moved into position. Bheem and Ash too.

"Give up, Vala. Surrender your soul or kiss defeat," Karna said. The demons needed to remain focused on him for the time being.

Vala's laugh grated out like stones being ground at a wheat mill. "I think not." He glided past the *danu* mage. "You have deprived me of my desire again, Soul Warrior. The Goddess's *raakh* is to be consumed in order—head, chest, womb and limbs. You have the head, I am told."

Karna didn't bother replying. He took stock of the surroundings.

"Here we are, once again at cross-purposes, as we were five thousand years past. I hold your blood-kin hostage again. Your human offspring, I believe?" Vala's laughter shook the very air inside the cave. "How quaint to beget a human daughter, Soul Warrior. But then, I know how much you love them."

Vala strode toward Draas and bid her to release Yahvi. Yahvi landed on her feet, standing straight as an arrow while Vala inspected her. He dismissed her within seconds. "Your daughter in exchange for the *raakh*."

*Brother, Yahvi says she can't see his soul.*

*Tell her to wade through the magic it's bound in. There has to be a soul.*

"No deal. The *raakh* is part of the Soul Warrior now," said Karna.

The hourly doses of Yahvi's medications had been mixed with spoonfuls of *raakh*. Thankfully, Yahvi wasn't allergic to ash like he was. So now Yahvi had the powers of the Soul Warrior and Goddess Kalika within her.

*She sees it now. It seems his soul is as metallic black as his body. It's not the red-gold of a demon.*

"No!" Vala shouted, half turning to Karna.

"Yes!" Karna hissed, his mind racing to understand what Yahvi was seeing. "Your plans are thwarted again. You'll never be invincible." A metallic black soul? He'd never come across a black soul, not literally. What the hell could it mean?

"I will kill your daughter." The roar shook the very foundations of the cave.

The threat put everything into perspective, at once.

"Has no one told you? My daughter is the harbinger of your death, demon. Kill her and you die. Instantly." That more than anything would keep Yahvi alive. Not safe, but alive.

"Did you think I didn't know Kalika would play her games with me? I know how the Heaven-dwellers work, warrior. I might have been in exile, but I know exactly how you all operate. I'll ruin your daughter. I will enslave her soul."

"You can try." Karna spread his arms out wide to indicate all the *asuras* standing around them. The demons shifted from foot to foot as awkwardly as puppets on a string, scratching their heads or grunting at one another. Satya was in complete control of most every *asura*—for now. "There's no one here to help you, Vala. Your insurrection is crushed."

Vala roared, gibberish pouring out of his mouth. He flung out his massive arms, hitting the *asuras* closest to him, knocking them to the ground. He kicked one, then another, shouting at them to get up.

Karna was sure some of the Reds weren't as mind-fucked as they were pretending to be and could move, but no one did. They knew they were outnumbered. "Surrender, Stone Demon."

"Never!" Vala rushed at Karna. Baited and hooked. "I challenge you, Soul Warrior. Let's finish what we started five thousand years ago."

"Okay," shouted Yahvi before she lost her nerve, making Draas gasp in shock.

"You're on," her father said at the same time. He did a double take at her, growling, "What in hell? Stay back!"

She sidestepped her father's grope on her arm. It was so easy to shrug him off with her god-powers. She giggled nervously. She was so strong. She felt unshakable. How could she let him get hurt? Had he really thought—had her mother, her uncles, Lavya, all of them—really believed that she'd simply usurp her father's powers and let him get beat up? Let him die?

She looked up and up at the walking, roaring mountain of stone as she strode closer to him. She stopped when she was a distance of ten feet from Vala and found it hilarious that her head was at height with his stony navel. There was no expression on his chiseled face, but she got the sense he was confused. The black dot of his soul pulsed like a heart beating inside his head.

Her father stalked up to her. "What in heck do you think you're doing?"

Everywhere she sensed confusion. Amara would hold Mama back. They'd planned it. But for now, she was holding Draas back. Yahvi looked up into the fiery darkness that glowed with souls and shouted, "Baital, now."

Immediately smoke billowed up and swirled around her and her father. She heard the flap of giant wings, and suddenly her father was lifted off his feet. He began roaring to no avail.

The Stone Demon glared at her through the smoke. "What do you want, human?"

"You challenged me. I am the Soul Warrior. And I accept your challenge," Yahvi said, trying to stop her knees from quaking.

"What?" Vala said.

He seemed as if he was trying to frown. But stone couldn't really move that delicately. She repeated her sentence. Roaring—Vala really needed to develop a different form of communication—he took a step forward. Yahvi leaped back.

"If you think these games will stop me, think again," he bellowed, his flat red eyes searching the cave. "Such chicanery is beneath you, Soul Warrior."

"Excuse me?" She swept her arms overhead as though directing an airplane down a runway. "Didn't I just say I'm the Soul Warrior?" She raised a fist and thumped her chest twice where the Soul Catcher was pinned on as a shield over her heart, then pulled both fists up to block her face in a boxer's stance.

In two ground-shaking strides, Vala had her by the throat and lifted her clean off her feet, dangling her eight feet from the ground. "I shall tear you apart and drink the *raakh* straight from your veins," Vala roared.

She grabbed on to his arm and twisted free of his grip. "You can try, demon."

And the battle was on.

Karna scrambled to his feet as Baital dropped him on his butt next to Qalli and flew away. "I'll kill you for this, *pisacha*. Just you wait!"

Qalli turned to him, frantic. "Do something," she hissed. "This was not the plan."

"I can't. He issued the challenge. She accepted. Now it can only be between them," he said, watching his daughter swing herself up and over Vala's arm and use that momentum to deliver a kick to his face.

He took heart that Yahvi had started off strong even though she'd changed the game without warning. This would work. It bloody well had to work.

Vala got hold of Yahvi, raised her high above his head and flung her across the cave. He leaped into the air and would've landed on top of her had she not rolled away.

Qalli clutched at Karna's arm in a death-grip. For what seemed like an interminable age, they watched Yahvi and Vala roll around on the floor, in the air, over the fire, through the fire. The combatants were evenly matched in strength, if not in size or skill or experience. Karna had drilled a thousand pointers in Yahvi's head over the last day and a half. He'd told her to keep chipping off pieces of Vala until he was forced to assume a new form—an organic form.

Karna winced when Yahvi bounced off the wall and landed flat on her back for the twentieth time. Being invincible didn't mean you didn't feel pain. You did. Acutely.

*Brother, we have a problem.* Sahadeva reappeared inside Karna's head.

*No. No problems. I don't want any problems, Sahadeva.*

*No one does, but such is life. Observe the* danus.

Karna observed the *danu* demons. With Yahvi and Vala's battle cries filling the air, he hadn't even noticed the chanting had all but fizzled out. The *danus* were on their feet. One was enthralled by the *dwanda-yuddha* going on and the other stared into the chasm. Their lips still moved, but it seemed the focus of their chants had shifted. Shit!

*Satya's control frays, brother. She can't hold them back for much longer.*

*Tell her to cease, then. Tell everyone to prepare for battle.*

He raised his sword and readjusted his grip on the *chabuk*. "Keep her in your sights at all times," he said, scanning the cave minutely before his gaze came to rest on Qalli. "Don't interfere in the duel even if things seem bad. Swear to me, Qalli. She must do this on her own now." He had thought to give her an advantage. He hoped her bravado hadn't been false.

"Oh, go away. Go kill some *asuras* and gloat." Qalli's eyes were glued on their child.

Karna launched himself onto the first midnight-hued asshole he came across. Simultaneously, thunder, wind and lightning cracked though the cave as the symphony of their battle resumed. They went at it for hours. Both sides relentless in their goals, neither showing the least sign of tiring.

Karna was not at his best. His attention was divided between his own fights and that of Yahvi's. She was holding up well, as well as a recently promoted chieftain could. And Vala, praise karma, was as rusty as a five-thousand-year-old relic. Yahvi had managed to blow off his arms, one at the shoulder and one at the elbow. Still he went after her like a battering ram. A little thing like missing arms wasn't going to stop the Stone Demon, but it had slowed him down.

Then Vala did something Karna hadn't expected. The Stone Demon's powers had evolved. Of course they had. Powers, like souls, evolved or devolved through karma.

Vala threw back his boulder-sized head, opened his mouth and drew in a huge breath. His stony chest, his rocky belly grew three times bigger. He vibrated like a mountain about to collapse and, like a geyser, spewed black metallic goo straight up into the air. The goo splattered across everything within its range, including Yahvi. She screamed as if she was being burned alive and fell to the ground, thrashing like an eel. Qalli was by her side instantly, metallic black goo raining down on both of them.

Desperate, Karna fought off the *asuras* he was locked in combat with. *Stupid. Stupid. Stupid.* He should have insisted Vala fight him first. He should have tested Vala's powers out first. He had to get to them. The battlefield suddenly seemed as vast as the Cosmos, impossible to traverse. He hacked an *asura* through his heart, brought down his sword on another's head. It lodged in the skull. He didn't wait to free his weapon. He saw an opening and charged through.

"You're mine now," Vala gurgled when he stopped vomiting. He staggered through the goo, triumph lighting his bloodred eyes with every sticky step.

Karna ploughed forward, but he was still too far away. Vala would reach them first. *Sahadeva! Help them!*

Karna knew Vala's intent. He was going to chuck Yahvi and himself into the fire—self-immolation, the ultimate oblation to please a deity, be it a God or Dev-Il. The portal was closed. But if enough souls were sacrificed in its fires, it would open.

Why wouldn't Qalli vanish with Yahvi? How could she lose focus like that?

"Vanish!" Karna bellowed. He ran flat-out, uncaring of the obstacles. "Damn you, vanish now!" She couldn't hear him through the roaring in the cave. He changed tack, ran straight for Vala. He leaped into the air, launching himself at the Stone Demon. The next second, he landed on his butt in the middle of a goo puddle and a cloud of toxic black fumes. He flipped around, coughing hard, looking to and fro with frantic eyes. No Vala. He'd disappeared. What the fug? Scrambling up, he ran to the females and fell to his knees beside them before Vala reappeared. He wrapped his arms around them both, his mind so jumbled, so relieved, that it took him a few seconds to realize Qalli was sobbing and screaming.

"She's not breathing. She's not breathing."

He went cold. He stared down at Yahvi, black from head to toe, as Qalli shook her and shook her to no avail. She lay dead in their arms. Was that why Vala had vanished? Had he been vanquished by Yahvi's death?

Ziva dropped to her knees beside them and forcibly took Yahvi from their arms. "She's alive," she informed them at once, her fingers pressed against Yahvi's pulse under her jaw.

Karna shuddered out the breath he'd been holding. She was alive. He wrapped his arms around Qalli and finally let his emotions go. When they'd both calmed down, he got to his feet. Vala's Cave was empty save his battle-worn and bloody tribe. Baital hovered close with a tray of goblets in his hands. Other than Baital, he couldn't spot a single *asura* in the cave.

"All gone?" He looked about for Lavya to confirm that the Reds were indeed gone. Cleanup would be a bitch. But how in hell had Vala vanished?

"Yup! As soon as Braveheart Lavya leaped into the abyss with Stone Face, the rest of the evil pebbles rolled away too," said Amara, grinning like a maniac.

Karna froze. "What?" Lavya had vanished with Vala? He mulled over it in silent shock.

They'd done it. They'd thwarted Kalika's prophecy.

# IT'S ALL KARMA

Karma is action and consequence.

No soul can know beforehand what the consequences of his actions will be. A soul can stipulate, sometimes even with a reasonable amount of certainty, what the results of his actions might be. But it is a far cry from what might happen to what actually happens.

Karna stood at the foot of Yahvi's bed in the healing room and took heart as his daughter breathed. She hadn't gained consciousness since the demonic goo had dowsed her. They'd managed to take it off, with difficulty at Vala's Cave, and more thoroughly at Har-ki-doon. Her skin was discolored in patches, and Heaven knew if it was due to the remnants of the goo or bruising from the beating she'd taken. The healers assured him that Yahvi hadn't been damaged internally from her ordeal. His god-powers still flowed in her, healing her. Yahvi would be okay and, fate willing, live a long, long life.

All thanks to Eklavya.

Six hours ago, Lavya had vanished. He hadn't come back to the cave. Karna had waited for him for two hours. Lavya hadn't come back to the abodes either. Was he still locked in combat with the Stone Demon wherever they'd landed? Yama had confirmed Lavya wasn't in Hell. Neither was Vala. That meant wherever they were, they were both alive.

Love for a child, desire for a family, had cost Karna a good man—many good men. Would Goddess Kalika be satisfied by what they'd done? Would Vishnu? Karna grimaced, knowing the answer. They wouldn't. They'd need—demand—a more finite solution to Vala's threat.

Though he hadn't made a sound to wake her, Qalli rose from the bed across the room. She slipped on a pink robe and fuzzy slippers and came to him. She bent to kiss Yahvi's forehead, then slid her arms about his waist. "Stop brooding. We'll find him."

He brushed his lips over her tousled hair.

The door to the chamber opened and his *shishyas* poured in, disheveled and chatty and not at all sleepy-eyed.

"Told you they'd be in here, watching Goo Girl with laser-beam eyes." Amara held out a hand to Satya. "Pay up." With a slight tightening of her mouth, Satya took a slip of paper out of her pajama pocket and slapped it on Amara's palm.

Karna watched the transaction narrowly. "I *will* break you of this vice," he swore and Qalli laughed against him. It lightened his heart, the normality of his largely female household. Once Yahvi woke and Lavya was back, he'd consider himself the most fortunate of beings.

"Is it time?" asked Lusha when Ziva touched Yahvi's forehead and placed her palm over her heart.

"Twenty seconds," replied Satya.

"Ugh! I think I want to throw up," said Amara, clutching her belly.

"Told you not to stuff yourself at dinner. Why don't you ever listen? You shouldn't eat when stressed," Ziva scolded Amara.

"Ten seconds...nine...eight..."

"Fighting makes me hungry..."

"...five...four...three...two...midnight!"

Power rolled into him as gentle and intimate as the blood flowing through his veins. Color brightened his eyes. Heat flashed through his body. Ice froze his soul. Karna stared at Yahvi, his heart bellowing in denial.

Qalli drew back to first frown at him, then at their daughter. "Is it still red?"

He shook his head. No, it wasn't still red.

Yahvi's soul was metallic black.

# ABOUT THE AUTHOR

**Falguni Kothari** is a hybrid author of all sorts of fiction. Her stories pluck at the colorful and cultural threads of her South Asian heritage and expat experiences. She is traditionally published in contemporary romance, and launches her mythic fantasy series, The Age of Kali, with Soul Warrior.

Learn more about her writing at *www.falgunikothari.com*
Follow her on Twitter: *@F2Tweet*
Like her Facebook page: *www.facebook.com/falgunikothari.author*

Also By Falguni Kothari

*It's Your Move, Wordfreak!*
*Bootie and the Beast*